# *Unconditionally*

Sarah Sahyoun

truelove gift

"For God so loved the world that he gave his only Son, so that everyone who believes in him may not perish but may have eternal life." – John 3:16

For my mum, who sacrificed her life so I may have mine.

# Table of Contents

# Chapter 1

On a serene summer's day, it began. The sun's glorious rays brightened the land of Estleton. A gentle and calming breeze lightly swept through the open fields, over the rounded hills, and between the multitudes of trees until it made its way to the wondrous walls and garden of Mallow Hall Estate. For a moment, all was well and quiet. But this serenity was broken by the brisk trot of horses' hooves. The grey road began to vibrate and gravel burst out from underneath the billowing dust as the horses made their way to the entrance of the estate.

Inside the estate's kitchen, the servants gathered in preparation for the arrival of their visitor. One of the servants rushed towards the window. "He has arrived!" she called.

Only one of the older servants, Molly, paid her any mind. "The wealthy gentleman? From Kingston Manor?"

"I'm sure that's him," she confirmed.

Molly headed to the window and looked out into the front courtyard. There she spotted a set of dark-brown horses attached to a black carriage that was travelling quickly yet steadily along the path towards the entrance. "Oh my! Poor Nora. She doesn't know what's to become of her." Molly held onto her apron tightly, thinking of the tragic event that was to come to fruition sooner than expected.

The kitchen door swung open, and Eleanora, the youngest servant girl, entered and asked with wondering eyes, "What is all the commotion, Molly? Who has arrived?"

"My dear child," Molly said. "Come here." She gestured for Eleanora to come to the window. The servant girl followed her bidding, her eyes shifting with confusion. Molly pointed to the carriage that loomed ever closer as the road dust circulated around the horses' tall, strong legs.

"I didn't know we were expecting a visitor," Eleanora said. "I wonder who it might be?" She turned swiftly to face the older woman. "Molly, who is this visitor?"

Molly was about to answer, but the other servant beat her to it. "The gentleman who lives in Kingston Manor, Sir James Christian Kingston."

"Why should he come here?" the girl questioned further.

"Eleanora, my dear," Molly started. Whenever she called the young servant girl by her full name, she noticed Eleanora's demeanour grow uneasy. "He is here to make a deal with your aunt Dusilla…" Molly paused, not knowing what else she could tell Eleanora about the man's business there. She didn't have the courage to explain, so she dismissed the entire conversation. "It is best if you don't ask questions. You must accept whatever happens because it is out of your hands and mine."

"Oh, Molly, you're frightening me! Please tell me what's going on." Eleanora's eyes fixed onto the servant woman, begging for answers.

"Look! Do you see him?" The other servant in the room rushed over to the window again and pointed to a tall, well-dressed man who had hopped from his carriage and was greeting the mistress of the estate.

The other servants looked out at the mysterious man who had come. However, they couldn't quite make out the man's features in the distance, and he disappeared from view as he entered the house.

Moments later, the kitchen door opened abruptly with a loud bang by the hand of a young lady dressed in a lavender-purple silk gown with slightly puffed sleeves that hung down to her wrists.

"You had better be ready with all the preparations because our guest has finally arrived," she said in a commanding tone. She stepped inside the kitchen with her hands clasped together in front of her dress. With that quick mouth of hers, she began barking orders. "Molly, make sure everything is up to a high standard." She paused. "Eleanora, you will serve the tea and biscuits to our guest."

A smirk appeared on her coloured lips. Her fierce, russet-brown eyes scanned the other servant woman who stood nearby. "And you, you will need to start making the tea." She took a deep breath, trying to retain her tight posture and concluded, "If I were all of you, I would start getting ready."

She spun around gracefully and left at once.

"That girl turned out to be one bossy lady," Molly noted as she headed towards the bench. "I still cannot believe she has any relation to you, Eleanora. She is nothing like you. Ever since you were little, you have always been the good one."

"Yes, well, she will never get anywhere in life with that sort of character," Eleanora said, joining Molly in her distaste. "I better put my apron on so I can serve the tea as soon as it's ready."

Eleonora tied a white apron around her waist, covering her dress that had become off-white from overwearing. She took the silver-plated tray from the other servant woman when the tea was prepared and headed into the drawing room, where the guest was first being situated.

*

The drawing room was rather spacious. The high cream-coloured ceiling complemented the pale-green-painted walls and pure-white tiles. The room held all the necessary furniture and had been purposefully arranged to create an air of sophistication. Olive-green vintage sofas were at the centre of the room, surrounding a short chestnut-brown table that held a crystal-glass bowl as its centrepiece. In the far-left corner was the old family piano that had been passed down through many generations, still intact. In the other corner was the drawing table with a few accompaniments: a bookshelf and a cream-pink high-top lamp. The fireplace stood against the wall on the right side behind one of the sofas, and though not lit with fire, it created a warm, earthy atmosphere that spread across the entire room.

"I do hope the estate is to your liking, Sir Kingston." The mistress of the estate smiled as she gazed at her guest, hoping his thoughts were approving.

"It is a lovely place," he acknowledged flatly. "The atmosphere is certainly different – fresher and more alive, I would say," he then added.

"That is pleasant to hear."

"This is your daughter, I presume?" the man asked as he shot a glance at the young woman sitting next to the hostess.

"Yes, this is Mandy, my only child. She is nineteen years."

The mother, feeling a surge of pride and hope, threw an artful look at the man. He now gazed directly at the daughter as she sat confidently on the double sofa. Her posture was graceful as she sat up straight, her spine never bending. She took the fawn-brown braid that was nestled between her breasts and flipped it over her shoulder. She then gave a hard smile as she showcased her pearly white teeth. The man returned a simple smirk and focused his eyes back on the hostess.

"Ah, if you don't mind me asking, Sir Kingston, what of your age?"

"I turned twenty-nine last month."

"My, such a young man you still are!" She then turned her eyes back to her daughter and smiled enthusiastically before again facing her guest.

"I don't suppose you have a wife back home?"

The man sighed as he realised where their conversation was going.

"I have never married."

"Well, you ought to soon! A handsome and wealthy man with many connections such as yourself should be thinking about these things, especially at your age, don't you agree?"

"Madam, I think I will worry about that for myself." His eyes glared in irritation at this interrogation that had nothing to do with why he was there.

Madam Dusilla closed her mouth at once and looked grim as she was forbidden to broach the subject completely.

"Now, I have come here to claim my deal, if you please. I am a very busy man, you see," he immediately went on, not wanting to waste any more time.

"Of course, of course. But first, you must have some tea." Madam Dusilla was now becoming agitated in her seat. She called the butler to ask the whereabouts of the tea. He went over and opened the two doors to seek out the servant girl, who then appeared, arriving just in time. Eleanora walked through while carefully holding the tray with all the tea components placed on top. She looked puzzled as all eyes were on her, and she felt that if the scrutiny continued, her movements were going to be unsteady and would cause her to drop everything and cause an embarrassing scene. Thankfully, she had enough self-control to safely place the tray onto the chestnut-brown table. As she rose to stand up straight, she glanced at the face of the strange visitor sitting not far from where she stood. She didn't manage to get a good look at his appearance, apart from his expression. His face was very still, and his glaring eyes made him seem awfully strict and quite singular. Her eyes widened in fright at his look, but she continued to cast a curious gaze over him.

"You may leave now," said Madam Dusilla and signalled for her to leave.

Eleanora left at once; she was quite flustered, and the image of the stranger continued to inhabit her mind.

"Now, Sir Kingston, what do you take in your tea?" Madam Dusilla offered.

"Two small drops of milk will do," he responded.

"Sugar?" she then suggested.

"No sugar. And do not over-stir, please. Once will do," he told her in a very particular manner.

She did as he pleased. "Darling Mandy, would you give this to the gentleman along with some biscuits." She held the teacup out in front of her and waited.

Mandy rose from her seat and took the elegant teacup, which was patterned with little daisy flowers around the rim. She handed it to the man, and he took it at once with a mumbled, "Thank you, miss." She curtseyed to him with a jolly smile and returned to her seat, as light on her feet as could be. He took a slight sip after blowing on the tea and placed the cup back down, seeming ready to continue with what he was there to do.

"Now, I believe you have the servant boy I asked for as I have the sum of money in the form of a cheque. I would like to have a look at him before finalising the deal."

Madam Dusilla looked over to her daughter with anxious eyes. She then turned back and chuckled a little before saying hesitantly, "I'm sorry, but there must be some mistake. The servant I am offering to you is, in fact..." She paused, hoping he wouldn't react badly. "A girl."

His eyes shot up to her, and with a confounded expression on his face, he exclaimed, "I specifically have asked for a boy servant in my advertisement, and I expect my distributor to deliver me what I have asked for!"

"Yes, I realise that, but I am telling you the servant girl I have is really much like a boy." She laughed while saying this. "She is wild and can do many heavy tasks that require strength. She will obey you as she has me, I can assure you."

"I refuse to continue with this." The gentleman looked rigid with anger at the waste of his time.

"Please, she is no longer needed here at my estate. I am happy to sell her to you. Please reconsider," Madam Dusilla said, trying to remain calm.

Sir Kingston looked to his tea and sighed. "I wanted a boy servant, not a girl," he muttered vehemently in between his teeth. He looked away for a moment in grave silence.

Both ladies waited impatiently for his answer. Madam Dusilla bit her plumped bottom lip hard, hoping he would take the girl despite her not being the gender he had requested.

12

After some time, he gave them an answer. "I will only agree to this if the money I owe you is reduced by thirty per-cent."

"Thirty per-cent!" exclaimed Madam Dusilla as if she were going to have a heart attack.

"Yes, because I didn't get what I asked for, and you instead offered me a girl," he explained. "Take it or leave it, Madam Dusilla, but I know for a fact that you are still receiving more money than you should from me just for a servant."

Madam Dusilla looked once again at her daughter, who hurriedly nodded her head in desperation. "Very well then. I accept," she agreed, making her decision.

"Excellent. Now then…" He took another sip of his tea. "I would like to see the servant girl before I go ahead with this."

"You already have," Madam Dusilla confirmed to him.

His eyes narrowed in puzzlement. He then frowned and placed the teacup back into its exact resting spot as realisation showed on his face. "Do you mean the girl who brought over the tea earlier on?"

Madam Dusilla nodded her head with a grin glued to her wrinkled face. "Yes, she is the one I am selling to you." Madam Dusilla noticed how his eyes lowered to the floor as he seemed to be contemplating the situation.

He raised them towards her again and accepted her offer. "You have a deal!" He stood hastily from his seat while the others followed suit. "There is no need for me to see her again. She may arrive at my manor in the morning, and she will be in my possession from then on."

"I will have her ready on a carriage first thing tomorrow," Madam Dusilla said with a smile, thrilled with how all had played out.

"Here is the cheque." The man handed over the printed form. "Now I must take my leave. Thank you for tea," he said while making his way out.

Madam Dusilla followed after him as he eagled away in a rush. The daughter, Mandy, followed too, without a question, to see him off.

# Chapter 2

The horses took off at once and left by the entrance gate. Both mother and daughter waved their farewells until the carriage disappeared beneath a pile of road dust swirling in the air. Madam Dusilla inhaled a great breath, and when breathing back out again, stretched her lips into a wide grin, expressing her wickedness.

Miss Mandy turned to face her mother. "We just lost thirty per-cent of our sum," she said, wanting to make this clear. She then paused before asking, "Aren't you displeased?"

Madam Dusilla didn't move a single muscle except for her lips as she expressed a sneering laugh. "Displeased? Ha! How can I be displeased when we are finally getting rid of that foolish, worthless servant girl?" She now turned around to face her daughter and continued, "That Eleanora will never be a blood relation, or a niece, or your cousin. After she leaves tomorrow morning, she will forever be forgotten and cast off into this poor, sorrowful world."

Miss Mandy was glad of this as she believed her cousin was a nuisance to the family.

Madam Dusilla commanded, "Mandy, I want you to bring Eleanora to me in the drawing room. I will tell her about her departure tomorrow. This is something she will not be expecting." A conniving grin formed on her face once again.

Miss Mandy obeyed her mother's instructions at once. She felt a desperate excitement herself and longed to see the reaction of her poor cousin to the situation. She immediately headed back into the kitchen room, where the servants were tidying up. Once again, Miss Mandy noticed their startlement at her unwelcome presence. She walked further in and started by announcing, "Sir Kingston has accepted the deal!"

Molly was left looking speechless with her mouth parted open; she seemed appalled by all this. She instantly looked over to Eleanora, who was still looking confused and completely unaware of the state of affairs.

Mandy smiled and continued her way to Eleanora, who was wiping the benches. "Eleanora, do you have any idea who that gentleman was that visited just moments ago?"

"Just his name," the girl replied innocently to her cousin.

"Did you know that he lives in Kingston Manor? Well, it was owned by his late father. It is well-known to have its…secrets," she said with a chuckle, wanting to create an air of suspense.

"Why are you telling me this? And what do you mean by *secrets*?" Eleanora left the damp cloth sitting on the bench.

"Ah, so now you are interested!" Mandy paused and then continued, "Well, first of all, the manor itself has its many mysteries hidden within its very walls. People say that it possesses something dark and sinister within, which is why no one would dare to ever set foot inside the manor. Sir Kingston, they believe, is a horrifying man who cares for nothing but himself and all the wealth he gathers. No wonder he isn't even married, because no one would dare marry a man such as him, for he believes he is much more worthy than any other human alive."

She told this story to ignite an unsettled feeling in the pit of Eleanora's stomach. "Did you ever notice anything unusual about his face, Eleanora, while you served the tea?" she then asked, eyeing Eleanora's worried expression. Eleanora shook her head in mute reply. "I wish you did. But I guess I will just let you know that on the left side of his face is a long scar. Nobody knows exactly how he got it in the first place, but there have been many rumours around about it, too scary to even tell."

"That is enough, Miss Mandy! You are telling these stories that aren't even true. Shame on you!" Molly admonished her and heaved uneasily about it all.

"Do not tell me what I can and can't say. Know your place, servant!" Mandy challenged the old woman. "Besides, I wouldn't be speaking if I were you since you haven't mentioned anything to Eleanora yet. And I thought you were her friend," Mandy said provocatively, eager to cause further trouble.

"What did you not mention to me, Molly?" Eleanora waited for her response as she faced her friend. Molly looked down in embarrassment. But as she lifted her eyes back up, looking to confess, Mandy had beat her to the punch.

"The deal was for my mother to sell you to Sir Kingston. You will no longer live here. You will become the property of Sir Kingston instead. You will serve him from now on."

Eleanora froze on the spot. Her eyes became as clear as glass at what seemed to be the betrayal of a friend. She looked into Molly's eyes as her expression begged for reassurance that all this wasn't true and just a silly joke. But when her friend couldn't even face her, Eleanora lowered her head in dismay. It seemed as if suddenly a fiery spirit rushed through her veins and burst out as she held herself up and said, "So, I have been kept in the dark about all this? Never have you once told me that I would be leaving this place not of my own will!" Eleanora turned herself away, ashamed of Molly. She now looked helpless and alone, without anyone in the world to help her.

"I am so sorry, Eleanora. I wanted to tell you so many times, but they forced me not to. I feel so ashamed of myself. Please forgive me." Molly's eyes became watery as she delivered her defence.

"I don't think I ever want to speak to anyone within this household again." Eleanora's voice broke midway through delivering this statement.

"My mother wants to speak to you about the arrangements. She is in the drawing room right now, waiting," Mandy stated, not wanting to waste any more time.

"Tell your mother, who is supposed to be an aunt to me, that I never want to speak to her or you again! And I will not leave this place to serve some man who will ruin the rest of my life forever! I would rather die than serve someone like him!" Eleanora pushed past Mandy, putting her off balance as she shrieked out in horror and fright as if her life had been threatened in just that blink of a moment.

*

Madam Dusilla impatiently turned around as Miss Mandy entered through the double doors. She asked in frustration, "Where is that Eleanora?"

"She didn't take it too well and said some nasty things," Mandy explained briefly yet cruelly.

Madam Dusilla cried out furiously, "When I get my hands on that girl, she will regret ever disobeying my words." As she was about to take a step to leave the room, she then said with an exasperated growl, "I was supposed to tell her of the news, not you!"

"I just couldn't help myself," began Mandy. "She was so scared by the words I used to describe Sir Kingston; they even made me a little scared, if I say so myself."

"Well, I see you have accomplished that. I guess that leaves it to me to break her now for good." Madam Dusilla's brown eyes darkened and narrowed with determination to do exactly that.

*

Eleanora heard someone stomping up the stairs with fury. As that someone made it into Eleanora's room, Eleanora was picked up off the bed by the arm and forced to stand and look ahead.

"Wipe those tears away, you stupid girl!" Madam Dusilla began harshly. "Mandy told you how you were supposed to come and see me, and instead, you disobeyed me completely!" She paused to take a breath. "You will be leaving tomorrow morning very early to Kingston Manor, and you will never return to this place again. Do you hear, girl?"

"I am not going anywhere!" Eleanora said defiantly. "I will not serve some man whom I know nothing about. Your daughter has told me all about him, and just thinking about it makes me utterly sick!" Her courageous tone reflected her determination to stand her ground.

"You will serve him as your master, for goodness' sake! And you will go whether you want to or not. Don't forget you belong to me and live under my rules and authority." Madam Dusilla cleared her voice and stated to her, "You will pack your things, not that you have many, and you will go to bed without any supper tonight. This will be your last sleep here, and if you say another word, I will show you the consequences!"

As her aunt turned around to make her leave, Eleanora could no longer bite her outwitted tongue and yelled back in spite, almost in tears, "How could you? I have done everything you ever asked me to do, and this is the way I have been treated! I have served you well, and all my life, I have done nothing to wrong you."

Madam Dusilla now turned, facing her with a snarl on her devious-looking face.

"You have never taken good care of me ever, and your silly, spoilt-rotten daughter will become just like you in the future: the most snobbish, ungrateful, and selfish woman to have ever lived!"

"You bad-mouthed, worthless servant girl!" As she exclaimed her displeasure, Madam Dusilla's brown eyes widened and grew darker by the second until they seemed almost black; her face heated, with an intense red colour spreading across her whole wrinkled face. She finally erupted like a heaving volcano. "This will teach you to talk back to me that way!" She held out her big hand in the air and, hard as a rock and forceful with speed, slapped Eleanora across the face.

Eleanora fell instantly to the floor, her hair all messed up and in her face. She began to cry and wail in agony from the hard blow her aunt had given her. Madam Dusilla stayed a moment to inspect her while she was on the floor. A grin was upon her, and Eleanora felt her leave without any remorse or regret.

The poor young Eleanora lay as if she were lifeless on the cold wooden floor. New tears trickled down her wet-stained face, but her tears fell silently as the pain was too extreme for her to even weep. She felt her life and dignity were shattered into a million pieces, never able to be put back together again. She felt helpless and weak, almost unworthy to live anymore.

# Chapter 3

Many times, Molly tried to enter Eleanora's bedroom to provide her with some nourishment as she hadn't eaten a single crumb or taken a sip of water the rest of that afternoon, even till nightfall. She begged for Eleanora's forgiveness and to make up and be friends once again. But the betrayed Eleanora ignored every knock and plea and shut herself off from the world outside her walls. She had not the energy to endure anymore pain than that which had already come upon her.

The morrow morning, which Eleanora dreaded with every bit of her mind and body, had come. However, after what was displayed yesterday, she thought any place would be better than where she was. At the crack of dawn, hurried knocks scrambled at her door. Although these intrusive taps infuriated her, she had not the willpower to strangle whoever was on the other side of that door.

"Eleanora, do wake up! Open this door now!" one of the servants whispered loudly.

The lids of Eleanora's eyes lifted slowly, heavy from the lack of sleep and nourishment. The salts of her tears remained pinned to her eyelashes.

She finally managed to rise from her bed and take a glance outside to see the time of day. As she looked out her window, the first sunlight appeared, wakening all with its brilliance. However, the sky was a little gloomy at this time, as many clouds overlapped each other just as the hills were seen to overlap one another out into the distance.

"Eleanora!" the old servant growled under his breath, trying not to be loud. "Madam Dusilla has asked for your presence downstairs this instant, out the front courtyard. Bring all your things with you. You are to leave now, do you hear?"

Eleanora took a deep breath in and knew that fate was not on her side and never would be, for she was just a servant girl with the least amount of hopes and dreams.

Before the old man could knock any further, Eleanora opened the door. "There you are!" he said, seeming annoyed and impatient. She looked down at the floor, feeling defeated as she always was. "Look, Eleanora, you are a good lass. And I don't think I will be seeing you anymore, but take care of yourself, okay?" Seeing the way she looked this early morning made him react with a sort of pity that twinkled in his eyes.

"Yes, you too," was all she could respond. She picked up her little brown satchel that leaned onto the side of her leg and walked across to the washroom, where she wiped all the distraught and unhappy tears away. She rushed down the stairs while the servant followed. Before exiting the building, she examined the whole place inside. Everything looked clean and just right. Another breath was taken before she continued on her way.

The horse carriage awaited Eleanora at the front.

"Finally, you are here!" Madam Dusilla said in a glad tone.

Her cousin stood by her mother in just the same way and with a similar facial expression. Madam Dusilla looked the happiest creature to be alive, with her eyebrows raised high and an enormous grin that stretched her wrinkled cheeks. Miss Mandy looked glad herself, but something in her eyes showed a spark of consideration towards Eleanora.

Eleanora walked over and stood before them.

"Your carriage awaits," her aunt spoke and then turned her face. Eleanora gazed at Mandy, whose lips remained sealed and face looked down to the ground as if she had no power to rule over her, for she was no longer her problem.

Eleanora walked past them both and placed her bag inside the carriage. A sudden feeling rose within her that made her turn back swiftly and speak her thoughts. "I am glad that you have finally sent me away from here. This used to be my favourite place in the world when I was only a child. But now, I have turned against it because of you." Her eyes were full of angry passion. She continued, "You think I am miserable because you are turning me away. Well, you are wrong! I am indeed the happiest I can be because now I am free, free from all the pain I have suffered all these long, dreadful years of serving both you and your daughter. I will never consider either of you a relation of mine for the way you have treated me."

"Treated you?" Madam Dusilla exclaimed; her eyes beamed with shock from all the words that were being flung at her.

Eleanora ignored this and continued, "I will finally be free, feeling liberty at last even if it means spending the rest of my days with a man I have never met or come to know of." Eleanora spoke these words with the emotion of everything she had been through over the course of her life.

She stood her ground when her aunt rushed in and said in her furious way of speaking, "You will live an unhappy life with your new master. Just as Mandy said, he is someone you should be afraid of, and, oh, you will be. Mark my words, Eleanora. You will never see another happy day for the rest of your life, however long that may be."

Eleanora tried to hold in her frightened tears as her courage was slowly draining away. She bit her bottom lip nervously and took her last look at the hateful faces of those who had been nothing but evil towards her. Madam Dusilla's brown eyes darkened like thunderous clouds, leaving Eleanora to hope it would be the last time she saw them.

Without any more delay, she hopped into the carriage, and the coachman signalled for his horses to start moving along the path. As the carriage approached the front entrance gate, Eleanora took one last gaze over Mallow Hall Estate, the place where she had grown up and lived. All her memories, both fond and detestable, would stay within the estate, never to leave with her, for she wanted nothing to do with them. An escape, Eleanora was hoping for, but unfortunately, she didn't think there would be one.

The sun was now glowing from high up in the sky, and the light beamed onto the path that the horse carriage was taking to continue the journey ahead. The horses paced along the road between the many fields. Feeling the fatigue of remaining in the one seating position, Eleanora felt herself slowly become drowsy and drift into sleep.

A sudden bump awakened Eleanora from her sound sleep as the carriage jumped onto a rougher road that was rather unpleasant to ride on. She rubbed her eyes while exhaling a soft yawn, and as she finished the act, something incredible caught her eye. Far ahead was a large, tall building, one the size of a mansion. It stood firmly and proudly in a solitary state, and surrounding it were low pastures of a gentle green colour that spread uniformly across the land. Eleanora distinguished the differences between this place and the estate she had left. This place looked to have a rather quieter atmosphere with an eerie feeling to it all whereas the estate was indeed livelier.

The carriage took a turn to a curve heading towards the manor as the horses trotted uphill. Eleanora began to feel nauseated as she was getting closer and closer to the place that she thought would haunt her forever. She pondered all the tales her cousin had spoken about the manor and the owner himself.

The road was now smooth, and the carriage was moments away from passing through the entrance gate. Eleanora popped her head out the window of the carriage and glanced at where they were headed.

Soon the carriage stopped and the coachman hopped off to speak to a man who stood just inside the gate. Shortly after, the coachman arrived back at his station where he waited for the man as he opened the entrance gates from both sides. The gates themselves were tall and made of a black metal that was stained with rust along most of the edges. Various vines had strangled themselves through parts of the gate, and the way they were all tangled produced a creepy feeling. There was a screech upon the opening of the gates, which signalled for the carriage to be on its way, and the horses paced slowly through, entering the grounds. Eleanora spotted a sign while passing by that was plastered onto the front. The gold sign was engraved with a black text that read "*Kingston Manor*". Eleanora fell into her seat and took a deep breath knowing that now there was no turning back.

*

It took a few minutes before the horse carriage rolled around a wide, circular fountain that was in the middle of the front courtyard. The centrepiece monument was a tall stand with a large bowl made of stone that pooled with water. As it overflowed, a stream of fresh, clean water gushed down onto a kneeling stone angel whose arms were outstretched before it and hands were placed together in a cupped shape as it received the falling water, which continued making its way down until it flowed with the rest of the water.

The carriage shortly after halted on stone pavement. The coachman opened the side door of the carriage and waited patiently as Eleanora stepped reluctantly onto the firm ground. Her satchel was tightly embraced at her chest, and her body trembled at the aura she felt emanating from the mighty walls. She heard the horses neigh from behind before they took off, leaving her all alone, feeling small in front of this awe-inspiring place. However, the sound of water trickling from the fountain soon soothed her worries.

Eleanora looked behind her to see if anyone else was out in the courtyard. That there was no sign of a single soul unsettled her the most. She turned back around and lifted her eyes to take in the manor itself. It was built from solid stone of a brown-reddish colour that gave the manor a distinguished beauty. Seeing it from this close really allowed her to appreciate how grand the building was. To her left was a block of the building that stood forward from the rest of the manor and featured a rectangular balcony. Double glass doors that were framed by tawny-brown wood stood behind this balcony. The railing was a rustic marble. High above the space of the balcony was the roof, with a thick stone chimney planted on top. Other windows spread across the right face of the block in three rows, depicting the number of floors that there were altogether. Continuing on from this was the middle section of the building, where the dark-brown roof held other small chimneys on top. The other side of the building featured the same style of windows, two of them in each row this time. Between these were bundles of dark-green shrubs filtering out carelessly and vines gripping the edges and corners of each of the window frames.

Eleanora finally looked over at the three stone steps that formed the entrance of the pathway. A marbled archway, with the same rustic appeal as the balcony railing, led to the front door, which was also in the shape of an arch. On either side of the doorway were a couple of long, thin frosted glass windows that too formed an arch at the top.

Observing every fine detail and every fascinating feature of the manor gave Eleanora a new outlook. The place still brought an anxious whirl to her stomach, yet it was the enigmatic nature of what she saw that engaged her curiosity.

She took a hesitant step forward. Then, taking a deep breath, she took another step, and another, as her courageous heart willed her to continue forth. But before she could even reach the door, a rusty old voice sounded to prevent her next movement.

"Do not go any further!"

Eleanora froze on the spot, her eyes widening at the sound of a stranger's voice. She heard the man approach her from behind. She turned around to see whether this stranger would be a friend or foe. She spotted an old man who was clothed in farmer's apparel, which included a loose and stained caramel-brown shirt that hung over the side of his trousers. He wore a round brown hat that was tipped to the side and seemed to express an easy-going nature that was nothing to fear.

"Wh…who are you?" Eleanora stumbled over her words as she held her bag tighter to her chest.

"I should be asking you the same," the man replied, almost reaching her. He stood a few feet before her when he continued, "But I already know who you are." He took a look at Eleanora, and a smile formed upon his dried lips. "You are the new servant that will be staying here. I was the one who opened the front entrance gate when the carriage arrived."

"You know who I am?" Eleanora gazed at the man as she tried to judge his intentions.

"Well, not your name, if that is what you mean. Just that you are a servant that was to arrive this early morning. My master told us of this yesterday and said we were to prepare for your arrival." He paused, placing his hands down into his pockets. "So, do you have a name?"

"Oh yes…" She cleared her throat and made known, "I'm Eleanora. But you can call me Nora for short."

"Nora will do then!" His smile turned into a grin. He took his right hand from his pocket and put it out in front of her as he said, "Pester is the name. Tennent Pester."

They shook hands, which eased Eleanora's mind and made her think favourably of the man.

"So, you are the gatekeeper, I suspect?" she asked, wanting to learn more about his occupation there.

"You could say that. I am the farmer, and I usually take care of the difficult tasks around here. I may be getting older, but I will always have the spine of a young fella."

Eleanora chuckled at this.

"You are mocking me?" he teased.

"Oh, I was just…" she began to explain.

"I'm just cracking with you. I am said to be the funny one around here, you know." He gave her a wink.

"Well, I can see that." A smile gleamed on her face.

"I guess I should take you in now. The master would want to see you, and I don't want to get you in trouble for being late on your first day here," he notified her.

"Yes, I guess I should go in. Thank you, Mr Pester," she responded.

"Please, Nora, no need to be formal. Tennent will do." He started to lead her up the steps.

Meeting Mr Tennent Pester allowed Eleanora's fears to be washed away, and she brightened with new hope. He led her until they reached the arch door, where he brought out a large, rusted, bronze key from his back pocket and unlocked it. He pushed the black ring of the knob, which opened the door.

Eleanora entered through; her eyes were immediately intrigued by the interior design of the manor. She stood at the beginning of the corridor before walking further in and entering the main hall room, which she guessed was the largest room of the manor.

Tennent slipped off his hat and held it beside him. He turned around and flattened his messy fawn-coloured hair with the palm of his hand. He stood close to Eleanora, his light-brown eyes focused on her. He then nodded his head once, and instructed, "Wait here, while I go see where the master is situated."

Eleanora was once again left alone, and she took the time to examine the area as a whole. The floor was spotlessly clean, and its brown marble tiles shone. The walls were of a cream shade and were filled with various paintings, mostly of natural landscapes. The skirt borders at both the top and bottom flowed along the edges and to every corner. The high ceiling held down a grand vintage chandelier with a stand made of majestic gold. Golden chains branched out and carried a large marbled glass bowl as the centrepiece, which was surrounded by identical but smaller bowls. Stemming from the root of the chandelier on the ceiling were golden floral patterns that completed this enchanting sight.

The chandelier indeed had its beauty, but the staircase was the showstopper. The steps, covered in a maroon carpet with a diamond pattern to it, flowed down into a wide, rounded shape at the bottom. The railing that accompanied the staircase was thick and of a lighter brown colour. At the bottom of the railing was a short, thick stand with a sphere shape at the top to mark the end of the staircase. To the right was a set of wide doors that were left unopened.

The large room itself held pieces of furniture that included a vintage cabinet topped by a large arch-framed mirror that rested up against the wall. Next to where Eleanora stood was a simple table that carried a lamp with an emerald-green head. Eleanora was fixed on every part of the room as it was completely different to what she was used to back at the estate. Both residences had similar grand features, but it was this manor that had a character that made it rather singular.

After admiring the elegant lamp before her, Eleanora switched her eyes to a large painting that was placed up beside it on the wall. The frame was of a shiny silver that ran around the portrait of a man who Eleanora guessed to be in his early forties. Everything about the image seemed mysterious, from the dark monochrome background to the small, crooked smile displayed by the man himself. While Eleanora continued to gaze curiously at the painting before her, she felt a presence approach her, and she asked, "Tennent, who is that man in the picture?"

"That is Master Kingston's late father."

"Oh, really!" she said and further examined the features of his face.

"Nora, the master is situated in the drawing room and would like to see you now. I will show you the way, and then I shall be off."

Eleanora was suddenly terrified as the eerie feeling returned within an instant and spread all over her body, causing her to shiver. All her negative thoughts of Sir Kingston arose within her mind, making her feel like her scared poor old self. "Tennent?" she called softly.

"Yes, Nora?" He waited, looking oddly at her.

"What is Sir Kingston like? I mean, is he a good master?" She was hesitant to ask this but felt the need to know before she met him.

He gave out a chuckle and replied, "You're not scared, are you?"

"A little," she admitted, and her eyes confirmed the truth of this.

"Don't be afraid, Nora." He paused. "I will tell you this, however…" he started off again. "He is different."

Eleanora was perplexed, not understanding what he meant.

He further explained, "Everyone has a different impression of him when they first get to meet him. He has this mysterious aura about him that not even I can ever understand. I'm not saying you should be fearful of him, but instead, you should come to know him. I will leave the rest up to you and let you judge for yourself what he is truly like."

Eleanora was left speechless.

"Come on. Stand tall and do not worry. It is time." Tennent led Eleanora across the room, past the right side of the staircase. A single door stood slightly ajar, and Tennent soon opened it.

A voice echoed from inside as it ordered, "Let her enter, Tennent, and then shut the door behind."

Tennent faced her and signalled for her to go through, expressing a soft smile as she walked past with a fast-beating heart.

# Chapter 4

Eleanora entered the drawing room, breathing quietly to herself and stepping as lightly on her feet as possible, not wanting to make a hint of sound to break the suspenseful silence. The room seemed spacious enough, but it was hard to distinguish the features and appearance of the room as all the closed curtains blocked the sunlight from entering. A cosy and rustic marbled fireplace sparked with flames of fire, which should have made the room feel warmer at the very least, for this new place was, for some reason, drastically cooler than elsewhere. But, instead, it made the room feel intimidating as each spark crackled from beneath the logs of wood and each flame continued to grow higher.

Eleanora had not gone any further as she couldn't see where the man of the manor was. Her heart began to beat frantically, and her worried eyes scanned the room a couple of times, hoping to see that she was not alone in this dimmed room. Eleanora was not sure now if Tennent was just trying to lighten the mood for her sake or if he was truly sincere in his views of the master.

"You may come forward," the voice came again, causing Eleanora to shiver. She took another breath, trying to calm herself as she continued on her way. An armchair facing her was empty so she knew the next one was where the man must sit, waiting for her to appear in front of him. She walked around the armchair and turned around slowly.

After she made her turn, she stood completely still, not moving a single muscle except her eyes, which studied the man wholly, the way he did her. The image of his face reappeared to her, but now, she had a longer and clearer look at him that filled in all the missing details about his appearance. The only feature

Eleanora recognised from previously were the gentleman's eyes, and she remembered the way they pierced through hers that day she served tea during his visit. The light sparking from the fireplace gleamed onto the man's right side, allowing it to be seen more easily than his other half. The man sat imperiously on the grand chair, both of his arms resting on an armrest. His shoulders were perfectly postured, and after a moment of examining Eleanora, he sighed, causing them to fall slightly before he brought them back into position again.

"So, this is the servant girl Madam Dusilla has sold to me," he stated, his tone implying he was interested in his newly bought possession.

Eleanora held her hands together, placing them in front of her, as her fingers rubbed against themselves to calm the nerves that kept building up. This nervous action of hers caused the man to smirk.

"You seem nervous," he commented in a teasing way.

Eleanora's eyes fell to the floor as she didn't want to respond to this truthful statement.

"What is your name?" he then asked.

"My name is Eleanora, sir," she replied softly.

"Just Eleanora?" he questioned. "Do you not have a second name...your last name?"

She answered, "Birch. Eleanora Birch is my name." She paused and then spoke again, "But you may call me Nora for short if you prefer."

"Hmm...Nora," he muttered. "Very well," he accepted, placing his hands together on his lap now.

This gave her a sense of relief, but she still felt on edge, especially when his eyes, which she perceived as dark at first, focused on her. She looked straight to the floor again, noticing the way he gazed at her as if he were studying an unusual artefact of some kind.

"Do you not speak?" he then said.

Her eyes brought themselves back up to his again when he uttered this. But she remained silent.

"Cat got your tongue?" Another smirk formed on his lips.

Eleanora didn't want to feel like she was small and that her feelings were being disregarded in the way they always had been in her entire miserable life. She built up courage and spoke her mind, passionately and as she pleased. "It is not that I do not speak, sir, but the fact that I am here against my own will. I have been sold to you, a strange man I have never met and wish I didn't have to meet." Her irritation ignited inside of her, and she spoke more harshly than she intended. She realised that she had spoken out of turn when the man's expression changed.

"You wish not to be here?"

"*Precisely!* I wish not to be here or to return to the estate," she replied.

The mood in the room seemed to have changed.

"Well, you have definitely stunned me, Nora," he said in a charming, sleek tone of voice that confused her deeply. "Unfortunately for you, however, I cannot go against my deal. And fortunately for me, as your master, I will have another servant to serve me."

He paused, taking a glimpse at the fire. He turned back to her and began, "Do you know who I am?"

"You are Sir Kingston," she answered. "I had never heard of you before yesterday, when I only learned of your name and that you would be my new master," she told.

"Yes, well, the name is Sir James Christian Kingston," he proudly stated. "Of course, you do not have to call me by that name every time. 'Sir Kingston' or 'master' will do," he allowed.

Silence had crept in again, and this time, it was Eleanora who was gazing over at Sir Kingston and, particularly, the left side of his face.

"Is something the matter with my face?"

Eleanora was caught off guard and noticed the way his dark eyebrows shadowed his eyes. She shook her head quickly, shocked that he had caught her staring at him in wonder.

"It is the scar on my face that you stare at, isn't it?" he growled.

"I didn't mean to." Eleanora's voice trembled, and she shrunk back, scared of what he may do.

He shot right up from his seat when Eleanora took a step back. He took a few steps towards her and could now see the way she trembled and how her panicked eyes darted about. He watched them widen with fear yet the colour of her eyes, an azure blue, sparkled before him. He saw the way her eyelashes fluttered, as gently as a butterfly's wings, and how her lips were formed like delicate rose petals but were dry and stiff; perhaps she had been left without any nourishment. Her nose was neither large nor petite but of a perfect size, and her face was shaped like a soft heart. Her skin was youthful looking – fair and smooth it was indeed.

But during Sir Kingston's examination of the girl, he located a red mark that stained her left cheek. He took his hand out as if he almost wanted to touch it. But realising what he was doing, he moved it away and placed it back down at his side. Instead, he muttered softly in a tone full of compassion, "Where did you get that red mark from?"

Eleanora's eyes shifted as she hesitated. "It is just a rash...nothing serious."

"Hmm..." he grumbled to himself. He knew for a fact that it was no rash and that someone had struck her. But he left this topic and didn't continue to further question her about the evidence of her mistreatment.

Eleanora couldn't turn her eyes away from his intense gaze. Sir Kingston had the eyes of a hawk, and now that she was this close to him, she could see that they gleamed an emerald green. His hair, which was raven black, was pushed neatly to the side. His nose was straight and long, and his lips were thin and pale. She then had the courage to look more closely at his scar, for she didn't

34

want to miss the opportunity. The scar ran from near his left eye and straight down his cheek, where it ended almost touching the edge of his mouth. It stood out vividly from his clear skin.

So, the rumours were true. He did have a scar that singled him out. But Eleanora was more curious than ever to know how it came about.

Sir Kingston sighed and took a step away from her. He then spoke, "You must be wondering how I got this scar? Everyone has always wondered how I got it. But the only ones who know are those I trust."

This caused Eleanora to be enthralled by the mystery of such a secret…whether it was a dangerous one or not, she wanted to find out the truth, somehow.

Sir Kingston made his way over to the other end of the room, where he drew one of the curtains, allowing some sunlight to brighten the room. Eleanora could better see where she was being held. Before her were two large pale-red armchairs that faced each other. A long caramel-brown sofa was placed against the wall opposite the fireplace, which was just next to another door. Once again, many paintings were displayed within this room, and they seemed to give the olive-green coloured walls their purpose. In the middle of the ceiling was a candle chandelier that would allow the room to not only be illuminated but would infuse it with the warm atmosphere that comes from lighted candles.

He came back over and began circling Eleanora very slowly. His hands were clasped behind his back, and his eyes travelled up and down her. He continued to do this until he completed one full circle around her.

She thought this strange and commented, "Do you inspect all your servants this way or just me?"

He chuckled as he made a last turn before he faced her again. "No, it is just you, for you are special," he said in a sarcastic tone and smirked. "You know, you don't seem like a *wild boy* to me at all," he observed.

Eleanora furrowed her eyebrows in disbelief at the term he used. "What do you mean by *a wild boy*?" She couldn't believe he could utter such an improper statement.

"Do not let out your anger on me, for it was Madam Dusilla who made you out to be one."

"She called me a wild boy?" Eleanora questioned. "She has called me worse things than that," she then muttered. "But why?"

"It is because, originally, I advertised for a servant boy, and, instead, she wanted to compensate me with a servant girl. It looks like she had no need for you, and she tried everything she could to make me accept. I did, but I reduced the sum of money by thirty per cent for her cheating."

"How could she do this? How could she do this to me?" Eleanora felt hopeless. "I was never meant to come here, after all. She lied, and she sold me to you!" Eleanora then thought for a moment. "But why did you say she tried everything? You were not going to accept, but then you did because here I am."

"She thought she had me when I accepted, but I didn't really accept because of her. It was you...I somehow pitied you for the way she made you out to be. I thought it would be better for you to work for me rather than her. I could have rejected her offer within a blink and bought any other servant that was more precisely what I advertised for, but I felt a pull towards you for some reason that is unknown to me."

Eleanora was looking quite confused at all that was said.

"I feel as if there is more to this story. How long have you been serving Madam Dusilla?" Sir Kingston then asked.

"Since I was four years old," Eleanora answered, feeling upset as she remembered her unhappy childhood days.

"You must be no more than eighteen years, for you look very young."

"I'm nineteen years old," she corrected him.

"Oh." He looked down at his shoes and then turned back to her. "How did you become a servant? Didn't you have parents? Or were they, too, servants?"

He asked many questions all at once, and Eleanora decided to give him a basic introduction to her life even though it was unsettling for her to speak about.

"My mother died a month after she gave birth to me. I know nothing about her or what she looked like. My father died three months after I turned four years. He was riding one day when he had a tumble from a heart attack he suffered. I know little of him, but I try so hard to make sure my memories of him are secured in my mind. Though it is hard."

She continued, "My parents weren't servants, but I am unsure of who or what they were. My father is Madam Dusilla's brother-in-law as she is the sister of my mother. She, unfortunately, is my aunt, and her daughter is my first cousin. We have never gotten along, and ever since my father died, I have been working as a servant to my aunt. In his will, it was stated that she would look after me and be my guardian while I would work for her. But instead, she degraded me my entire life and left me thinking all these years that I was nothing. She has never loved or cared for me, and her daughter followed in her footsteps."

"A pitiful life you have lived," were the simple words that escaped Sir Kingston's lips. He turned away from her and stared down at the fire as it continued blazing. He took a deep breath in and then mumbled, "A pitiful life I have lived." He sighed and turned back around again.

Eleanora heard these words and wondered what he meant by them exactly. Sir Kingston was indeed a mysterious man who seemed to enjoy keeping all his secrets to himself.

"Now then…" he said more brightly, changing the mood of regret and sadness. "Let us begin with what your obligations are while you are under my authority."

He walked to the other side of the room and opened the door as he called out in his loud, hard voice, "Dana! Dana, come down here!"

A faint voice replied, "Coming, master."

After a moment, a middle-aged woman who wore a simple white dress, a uniform fit for a servant, came rushing from the door and stood midway across the room. The woman, with glasses placed conveniently above her nose, ran her eyes over Eleanora in examination.

Eleanora stood quiet and still as she waited for further instructions.

"Dana, this is Eleanora, the new servant girl who will be living here from now on," Sir Kingston said by way of introduction. He then began to pace slowly in front of Eleanora as he instructed, "Work begins at 5 am sharp and usually concludes at 8 pm. When you wake up, you will complete all your morning duties, and Dana will assist you and be your guide." He stopped and faced Eleanora as a little smirk appeared on his face. "For she is the head of the servants." He continued pacing while he notified her, "Your job here will be to help out with the cooking and the cleaning, both indoors and out. You will also work in the garden and farmhouse and will attend to me whenever I will need you." He paused again and faced Eleanora, this time with a bigger smirk plastered onto his face. "And, yes, I will need you very often, Nora." He spoke pointedly, calling her by the shortened form of her name.

He then went up to her and looked down at the dress she wore. "Your dress has a tear at the bottom, I can see."

Eleanora looked down and noticed the ripped hole.

"It is unpleasant for you to wear something as terrible as that. Dana will provide you with the proper uniform." He paused, seeming to try to think if there was anything he had forgotten. "You will start your duties tomorrow. For today, I want Dana to show you around the manor so you can see how things work around here. I think that is all for now." He paused and then mentioned, "Dana, make sure you serve breakfast to Eleanora, for it seems she hasn't been properly nourished. But before you do, make sure she is settled in her chamber."

Eleanora was surprised to hear this kindness.

He took another step closer to her and warned, "I hope you will show me that you are a trustworthy and loyal servant, Nora."

"Yes, master," she replied softly.

"Excellent! Enjoy your stay here at the manor."

He looked to the servant woman and nodded his head.

"Come with me, child," she instructed, and Eleanora obeyed after one last glance at Sir Kingston, who they now left in peace.

# Chapter 5

The head servant led the way out of the room, and Eleanora found herself back in the main hall. Seeing it from a different standpoint, she was once again amazed at the magnificent beauty this room possessed. The woman turned right and walked up the grand stairs, with Eleanora following closely behind.

They glided up the steps until they reached the second floor. Another set of stairs appeared as they continued their path onto the third and then fourth floors. They took a left turn and walked through the corridor, passing by different chambers until they reached the very last. The woman stopped before a door and took out a key. Once she opened the door, they entered, and the head servant made known, "This will be your room from now on. All the servants sleep on this floor while the second one that we passed is for the master and guests and the third holds other rooms, which I will be showing to you later."

Eleanora felt a sense of safety and security within this room. It was much more well-appointed than the room she had back at the estate. This room was a perfect size and contained the perfect-sized bed. The soft cream colour of the walls brought a soothing appearance to the room, and the candlelight created a comfortable and cosy atmosphere. It was not luxurious as this was a room for a servant, but to Eleanora, it was better than luxury as it produced a relaxing feeling where she could be herself without anyone intruding on her. Against the window at the back was a sky-blue sofa that would be used as a reading seat while feeling the breeze waving through delightfully.

"Is it to your liking?" the woman then asked.

Eleanora turned around, a gleeful smile on her face that emanated from her pure heart. "It is more than I could ever ask for. Just lovely!" she added.

"That's wonderful, my child." The woman's light-brown eyes lit up with a spark of yellow. "As you have heard from the master, my name is Dana, and I am the head servant of the manor."

"It is nice to meet you, Dana," Eleanora began. "My name is…"

"Eleanora. Yes, I know," Dana said instead. "And such an appropriate name it is. A name can say much about a person's character, you know."

"It can? Well, what do you think it says about me?"

Dana smiled and said without hesitation, "I think you are humble and kind. The name Eleanora expresses beauty both within the heart and soul. I know I only just met you…" She chuckled before continuing. "But I feel a caring and spirited aura around you. And I hope to see it be true."

Eleanora smiled sweetly at her kind words. "You are too kind. But you may call me Nora for short. It is just easier, and to be honest, I think the name Eleanora is too good for me. I am just a servant and to have such a name seems impossible for someone like me. So, please, call me Nora."

"All right, dear, but I would have to disagree with you on that." Dana paused and started again, "Now I will let you freshen up and unpack your bag while I prepare breakfast for you. I won't be long bringing it up. And then after, I will be more than happy to give you a tour of the manor. I will tell you now, you won't be left unimpressed." She gave a little laugh and began her way out of the room.

"Thank you, Dana."

"You're welcome, my child." Dana then shut the door quietly and was gone.

Eleanora placed her satchel down on the bed. She walked towards the window and opened it to allow some fresh air into her

41

room. Upon doing this, Eleanora gazed outside at the expansive view. Scattered just below a hill were tall trees with winged branches that spread out with abundant jade-green leaves. She took this moment to be lost in her thoughts.

She sat down on the sofa and thought about how this place could redeem her, that perhaps she could have a better, more comfortable lifestyle. She now knew that there was nothing to worry about and that her anxiety about coming here was unnecessary. She then thought about how her cousin was cruel to say such things about Sir Kingston and how they didn't match her observations. Yes, he was a strange man with perhaps peculiar ideas, but he wasn't the dangerous or scary man she made him out to be. He had a certain air of finesse and character about him.

Soon, her thoughts shifted more deeply to Sir Kingston as his face reappeared in her mind, this time in much detail. The scar on the left side of his face was no doubt the feature that stood out. But it was his eyes that made her question him. Those strident emerald-green eyes made her want to look away but also deep within them at the same time.

Eleanora was awoken from her reverie by a voice.

"Wonderful view it is out there, isn't it?"

Eleanora swiftly turned her head and saw Dana holding a tray of breakfast.

"Oh yes," she said, a little startled. She cleared her throat. "It's very beautiful."

Dana placed the tray onto a small table and brought it over to where Eleanora sat. As she did so, Eleanora asked, "Tell me, does Sir Kingston own all this land, even the small forest over there?"

Dana smiled and, rising up from her bent position, answered, "Why, yes, he does. He owns this huge piece of land. The hills at the back, this small yet beautiful forest that you can see from here, the garden at the front – everything here belongs to him. Well, his late father passed it on to his son."

"He is very wealthy, I dare say?"

42

"Yes, very! He is one of the wealthiest men around," Dana replied, happily confirming his lofty status. "I should advise you to eat now so I can show you around. I have some work of my own that I must complete later on."

Eleanora nodded and began eating the toasted bread with butter and jam. She took a sip of her tea, which she dipped her biscuit into.

"My, Nora, you are hungry, aren't you!" Dana watched as Eleanora smiled with her mouth full. "I should leave you to finish your breakfast in peace then." She was about to head off when she said, "You know how to come back down to the main hall?"

Eleanora gulped down her bite. "Yes, I remember."

"Good. Well, when you are done, just come down, and onto your right from the stairs there is a door that goes through to the kitchen. I will see you down there."

Eleanora nodded. "Yes, all right."

Dana took one more look at her before she left.

*

Inside the kitchen, Dana was preparing the *mise en place* for dinner time. While she was chopping up some root vegetables, one of the servants, named Jill, asked, "What is the new servant like? I can't wait to meet her!"

"Yes, when is she coming down?" another, named Marie, then questioned.

"Hold your horses, ladies! She will be here in a moment. Let the child be free for a while and relax. She only just arrived, you know." Dana continued on with her work.

"Yes, well, she won't be relaxing after today. Wait till she sees all the work she has to do around here," Marie went on.

"Well, I'm sure she is used to it from her previous work," Dana retorted.

"What was her name again?" Jill then asked.

Dana looked up and replied, "Her name is Eleanora, but she likes to be called Nora for short."

"Such a pretty name!" Jill commented happily. "Don't you think so, Marie?"

"Yes, it is, I have to say. I have never heard a name such as Eleanora before. It sounds beautiful, how it just rings."

Dana smiled and went over to help Jill prepare the dough that would be made into buns while Marie was doing the stacking and sorting of things.

While they were all up and about, doing their kitchen duties, the door opened and Eleanora arrived with the tray in her hands.

"Thank you for breakfast, Dana. The food was delicious!" She smiled and then stopped, gazing at the other servants in the room.

"I'm glad you enjoyed it, dear," Dana said. She had already finished what she was doing and so walked up to Eleanora. "Nora, these are the other two servants in this manor who you will be working with from time to time." Dana then pointed out, "This is Jill."

Jill curtseyed in a jolly way, her brown eyes beaming with friendliness.

"And this is Marie," Dana announced as Marie, too, gave a curtsey.

Eleanora greeted them, smiling also. "It is very nice to meet you both, Jill and Marie."

"It is also nice to meet you, Nora," Jill replied for the both of them.

"I told Jill and Marie to call you Nora. They already know your full name is Eleanora," Dana mentioned. "Here..." Dana opened her hands in front of her. "Let me give the tray to Marie to clean up." Eleanora passed the tray to Dana, who brought it over to Marie. "Now, shall we start with the tour? Since you know this is the kitchen already, we shall exit from where you entered."

Eleanora stepped out back into the main hall, and Dana followed behind.

*

Dana began the tour of the manor. "Now, as you know, this is the main hall room, which is formally known as the *Grand Hall*," she said reverentially. "Sometimes we have parties held here since it is the grandest and most magnificent area of the entire manor."

"I definitely agree with you there. When I first stepped into this place, I was completely amazed."

"Everyone does have that sort of reaction when they are new here." Dana paused. "I won't show you the drawing room since you have been there also. But I will show you this," she said eagerly. She hurried across the room and folded open a series of doors before turning back to Eleanora. "Isn't it wonderful!" she exclaimed. "This room extends from the Grand Hall, which is very useful for the parties that I mentioned earlier."

Eleanora stepped inside this next room. It was very open and nearly empty. All that was in the room itself was a grand marbled piano that announced itself from all the way across the room. The walls were of a champagne gold and featured patterns where they met the ceiling. The ceiling, this time, held up a large crystal chandelier in the centre that shimmered with tiny crystals that hung down perfectly. Eleanora was left parting her mouth in awe.

"This is usually where the dancing takes place during the parties and events."

Dana then went to the other side of the room and opened up another set of doors; this time, they were glass doors with the same champagne-gold frames that also folded in against the sides to extend the space to the outdoors. The platformed floor was tiled in marble. At the end of this was a ledge railing made of the same marble and design as the balcony ledge at the front of the manor.

Eleanora held onto this railing and took a breath of the air.

"This is the side courtyard. You can see some of those trees you saw earlier planted here also."

"Oh! Imagine a party being held here! I would love to see one."

"You really would love it." Dana smiled at Eleanora's tone. "Hopefully, there will be one soon. Now, let me show you the dining room."

The dining room was on the left side of the grand staircase, opposite the drawing room. "This is the dining room hall, as you can see," Dana announced. The room was long and perfectly sized for a dining table made of dark and glossy timber. The chairs were of the same material, each tall at the back and cushioned on the seat. A candle chandelier was suspended from the ceiling, and paintings hung all over the walls, allowing the eater to not only enjoy their meal but also the art that was placed before them.

"Let us go upstairs," Dana now directed.

On the second floor, Eleanora continued to follow Dana through the corridor, passing by many rooms.

"These rooms along here are the guest rooms for when people come over and decide to stay, usually for business, or pleasure if Sir Kingston brings along some of his friends."

"He must have many from all the parties you mention," Eleanora wondered aloud.

"He does indeed! Too many to count," Dana summed up simply. "Now, across all these guest rooms, just by the stairs, is Sir Kingston's chamber, which we, of course, won't go in. You are only allowed if he summons you to his room for whatever reason. Or if you are on bedroom cleaning, you change the sheets and clean up the place, but that is usually my job. You won't need to go in there much, I don't think."

She then walked over to the next door, which led to a large area. "This is a room for entertainment purposes or for his guests to relax in when they are over."

This room was similar to the drawing room downstairs. It had a similar fireplace mantel, this time made of stone, and it had the same candlelight chandelier. There were more vintage sofas of different kinds and colours, and a large, round table was over at the far-right side with chairs surrounding it.

Eleanora spotted the balcony area, and she walked straight across and opened the glass doors. She looked out and remembered how yesterday she was, just below, staring in awe at the incredible manor that stood before her. Now, having a different view, Eleanora looked out into the front garden and further ahead, where she could see the front entrance gate through which she had arrived.

After this room, the next floor up was to be investigated. Inside the library were the tallest bookshelves Eleanora had ever seen, with multitudes of books all distinguishing themselves in different colours and sizes. A ladder was built in for the simple purpose of reaching the books that were too high. "I have never seen this many books in my entire life!" Eleanora's mouth opened wider by the second.

Another grand fireplace was built here with a stand above that was decorated with some white marble statues of various Grecian-looking heads. To the right side of the room, was a long caramel sofa, similar to the one in the drawing room. The windows, which were placed on either side of this, were also very long, and the olive-green curtains draped to the floor.

After another moment of Eleanora examining the place, Dana directed, "Let us continue on, shall we?" Eleanora jumped by her side, and Dana smiled. "My, you are very excited, Nora."

"This is all so new to me, and I have never in my days seen anything as brilliant as this. The estate back where I come from is grand…but nothing compared to what my eyes have now seen."

Dana showed the other rooms, which consisted of storerooms and some other smaller ones that were quite empty and not very often used.

Next, they headed to the fourth and final floor. The rooms there were where all the servants slept in their bedroom chambers. The only other room on this floor was the common room, mostly used by the servants, as explained by Dana.

However, there was still one more door to be looked upon. "Up here is the staircase that leads you to the roof of the manor. I've only been a few times myself. I think this will take your breath away more than the others." Dana opened the final door to reveal a set of small, old stairs that led to the rooftop.

Once Eleanora made it to the roof, the wind danced with her dress and breezed through her long, tawny-brown hair that was tied into a simple, loose braid

"It is very windy up here," Eleanora mentioned.

"That's because we are so far up. You can see everything from up here and miles away." Dana then pointed her finger. "Look."

Eleanora observed the great beauty that was before her. She could see the horizon that stretched along a large hill. She held onto the bricks and bent her head below, seeing how far the ground was from where she stood. She laughed into the fresh air and closed her eyes, taking this all in – the freshness, the tranquillity, and the beauty. Reopening her eyes, she saw how close the sun seemed, shining ever so brightly at this time of day, with only a few small clouds to accompany it. Eleanora rushed to the other side, where she could obtain a different view, and saw all the way to the trees and, beyond them, more hills and dozens of fields of various shades of green with some single trees scattered here and there. She then returned to where Dana waited.

"Which would you say is the place that captured your attention the most?" Dana asked.

"Definitely the rooftop. It makes me speechless to see the land from a different perspective. All the nature I can see below. Oh, it is very beautiful!"

"I knew it! It is very serene up here."

"May I come up here whenever I feel I need some peace?"

"Only when your duties are finished or when you have a break, but, yes, then you may. But you must notify me or someone else. We don't want an accident to occur heaven forbid or not have a clue of your whereabouts."

"Of course, Dana."

"Good! Let us now head all the way back down. The tour has ended."

\*

Once they arrived back into the Grand Hall, a man dressed in uniform, a black suit and white shirt, came passing by. "Eleanora, have you met Mr Smite yet?" Dana said, stopping in front of him.

"No, I haven't," she answered, wondering who he was.

"Mr Smite is the butler of the manor and tends to certain affairs with Sir Kingston."

The old man smiled, and Eleanora noticed his eyes were inspecting her. "How do you do, Eleanora," he said and bowed slightly.

"I'm well, thank you, Mr Smite," she greeted him with a little curtsey.

"Please, you may call me by my first name, Dashier. Everyone around here does anyway."

"All right then...It does sound very dashing. And only if you call me Nora for short."

"Deal!" he said with a chuckle.

"Dashier, is the master still here in the manor?" Dana now asked.

"No, he is not. He went out but will arrive in time for dinner."

Dana nodded her head. She then mentioned, "We better head off now."

"Yes, I have some matters to attend to myself," responded Mr Smite before moving off.

"Now, Eleanora, you have officially met everyone at the manor. I am going to help get dinner prepared for when the master arrives."

"Oh, then let me help?" Eleanora offered willingly, wanting to be polite.

"Oh, bless you, Nora!" Dana said and chuckled. "Thank you, but it is best you rest for today because, from tomorrow, you will be non-stop on your feet."

Eleanora gave a soft smile.

"How about you go stroll around the front garden? I'm sure having a smell of all those lovely flowers will really freshen you up and make you feel quite at home. If you need to rest after in your room, then you may. Do not forget you live here now, so this is your home."

"I will take your advice. Thank you, Dana."

"You're welcome, dear. I will see you later then."

# Chapter 6

Taking a stroll in the front garden made Eleanora feel calm and at peace. She walked along the pebbled footpath and could smell all the luscious aroma emanating from the bulbs and nectar of flowers. Each flower had its distinct smell that infused the air, creating a serene atmosphere to linger in. Eleanora stopped and bent over a bunch of lilies. The petals were bursting with colours of indigo, ocean blue, bright yellow, and sunset orange. She brought her nose down and sniffed delicately, breathing in the satisfying smell they provided. Beside these multicoloured ones, some pure-white lilies that spurted out red nectar were growing. These too smelt heavenly, and Eleanora bent down to these ones next.

She then rose and continued her walk. Seeing some daffodils in the left corner caught her eye. The bright yellow colour reminded her of butter, which she could almost taste when sniffing the petals themselves. Tulips were also grown on the far back, and not far from them were some pale-pink primroses that bunched up together.

There were other flowers along the way, and she took the time to enjoy their comforting smells also. After making a turn to her right, a bush filled with gardenias that were pure white caught her attention. Eleanora rushed to these and touched them delicately, feeling the soft texture beneath her fingertips. Not far from this was another bush, this time filled with red roses. Their vivid colour attracted Eleanora, who admired the way they contrasted with the green leaves. Eleanora took a sniff of the roses, smiling softly to herself. As she did, she heard a voice from behind, which startled her.

"Didn't expect to see you here."

She turned around and saw Mr Pester coming her way. "Tennent?"

"Sniffing all the roses, aye, Nora?" he asked with a grin.

"Uh, yes!" She blushed as she stepped back.

He came forth to her; his shirt was dirty, and he was carrying a tool in his hand. "Do you have a favourite?" he then asked.

"No, I don't. They are all nice in their own individual way."

He smiled as he looked down at himself, and then fixed his shirt.

It was silent for a moment. He then went on to another subject. "So, what did you think of Sir Kingston?"

"Not what I was expecting, actually. There isn't any word to describe him exactly. But he is mysterious." She paused, thinking if she should ask him something. She decided she would and said, "Do you know how he got that scar of his?"

Tennent's eyes widened a little as if he were trying to think of what to say. "It was a long time ago. I don't know exactly what happened. But it is not my place to tell anyway."

"Oh, right. I'm sorry for asking."

"You're curious about it, aren't you?"

"Just a little," she admitted as she bit her lip.

"Well, it's best that you don't know. It will keep you out of danger if you don't know the truth."

Eleanora thought about how Tennent described it as a danger. She wondered greatly how it had affected Sir Kingston himself and what had transpired. But since she would probably get no further answers from anyone, she decided to just let it go, at least for the time being.

"So, how did you like my wife?" Tennent said and smiled, his eyes narrowing from the sunlight.

"You are married?"

"Yes, of course. To Mrs Pester. Dana is her name," he confirmed.

"You are married to Dana?"

He nodded in response.

"She is a lovely woman. She showed me around by giving me a tour of the entire manor."

"I hope she doesn't give you too much work on your first day tomorrow." Tennent chuckled, and Eleanora joined in.

"Do you have any children?" she then asked.

"No, not yet. It is a little hard for her because we got married in our later years, and we're not getting any younger. We were only married two years ago, but we are trying."

"I hope you will be blessed with a miracle soon," Eleanora spoke, sincerely hoping he would.

"Thank you, Nora." He looked down to the ground for a moment and then said, "Well, I better be getting back to work out in the fields. I will perhaps see you later. Goodbye now." He tipped his hat.

"Goodbye," she returned.

*

Late afternoon came, and Eleanora was resting up in her chamber and taking some time to be alone. She lay quietly on her bed after waking from a little nap.

Not long after, a knock was heard at her door. She rose quickly, wondering who it could be. She wiped her dress down, trying to remove all the creases, while heading for the door. She opened it quickly, and there stood Mr Smite, the butler. "Mr Smite...I mean, Dashier. How are you?"

"Very well. And yourself?" His light-blue eyes shimmered with friendliness.

"I'm doing well too after relaxing here for a while."

"I've heard relaxing by the garden really freshens up the mind and the soul."

"I went to the garden at the front a while ago."

"Splendid then!" He smiled. "Nora, I have come to give you a message, and something else."

Eleanora thought of what this could be as she gazed at him with those curious eyes of hers.

Mr Smite continued on with his message. "Sir Kingston would like to invite you to accompany him for dinner tonight. He wants you down at the dining-room hall at six o'clock sharp."

"He wants me to dine with him?" Eleanora was puzzled by this invitation.

Mr Smite nodded his head, affirming this.

"But I thought the servants never dine with their masters, or anyone else for that matter."

"I found it rather strange myself, if I must admit it. It is very unlike someone of his status to give such an invitation. You must have caught his interest in some way."

Eleanora murmured, lost in thought.

"Well, he explicitly stated that you should join him. And Mrs Dana Pester has ordered me to give you this dress to wear. It is simple, but she noticed that you had no other suitable dress to wear, which you especially need if you are to dine with the master."

Eleanora took the neatly folded dress that was being handed to her. "Thank you, Dashier. I will see to it." She smiled at him and closed the door as the butler left her. She opened up the dress and spread it across the bed in front of her. The long, caramel-brown dress was plain and simple and looked as if it had never been worn. Eleanora was grateful to be given this even though it wouldn't be worn much. She thought of the dinner invitation, which she had not expected. She was rather nervous as she paced about the room knowing that she would perhaps have to converse with Sir Kingston, who caused her to feel mute so often.

She looked over at the clock and saw it was only half an hour before six. She took this time to get herself ready, determined not to be late and displease the master. She took off her old servant gown and slipped into the brown one she had been offered for the evening dinner. She washed her face and fixed up her hair in front of the mirror in the common bathroom that the servants used. Her tawny-brown hair was tied up in a low bun that sat comfortably on the back of her neck. She looked at the time again and realised she had ten minutes to spare before she had to head down.

*

Eleanora waited by the open doorway. She saw the way Sir Kingston sat comfortably in his chair, the one closest to the door. She noticed his eyes were fixed on the clock ahead of him as it struck six, upon which, he gave a sigh. Eleanora spotted too the way he tapped his finger onto the hard table before him in a rhythmic tune as if tapping the same piano key repeatedly. Sir Kingston seemed an efficient man, Eleanora thought, one who never liked to be kept waiting.

The butler turned to Eleanora and announced her name before entering. "Miss Eleanora, Sir Kingston."

Sir Kingston waited in his chair as she entered.

Eleanora saw that he had changed his attire and looked brighter than his previously dark self.

"Eleanora." As he said her name, he expressed a small smile.

"Sir Kingston," she responded, also smiling in a polite manner.

Mr Smite showed Eleanora to her seat, which was on the right side of Sir Kingston, facing towards the doorway. After she took her place at the table, she felt very awkward as the room returned to silence once the butler had left them alone. But not long after, Sir Kingston broke this silent tension within the room.

"I hope the manor is to your liking, Nora," he said, going back to calling her by her shortened name.

"Yes, I like it very much surprisingly. I really didn't know what to expect when arriving here."

"And your chamber is to your satisfaction?" he asked further.

"Very much so," she said and smiled.

"I'm glad."

Eleanora was suddenly mesmerised by the way Sir Kingston's emerald-green eyes gleamed in the light from all the candles of the chandelier that illuminated the room brightly. His hands were placed together out in front of him, and he now looked down at them.

"There is something I would like to ask you, however, sir," Eleanora began.

"And what might that be?" he responded with a rather lavish tone, seeming to take interest in Eleanora's sudden inquiry.

"Why have you invited me here to join you for dinner when it is expected that no servant should be in the same room with anyone of higher class to them? Isn't it rather unconventional?"

His reaction puzzled Eleanora greatly as he chuckled, leaving off with a smirk afterwards.

"Why do you laugh at my question?" she asked hesitantly.

He chuckled once more before caring to explain. "I realise that is to be expected. However, you fascinated me earlier today, and I have found a sudden interest in getting to know you better."

Eleanora looked down at the table as Sir Kingston said this.

He then said, "There is nothing wrong with wanting to get to know you better, is there?"

Eleanora shook her head in response. "I guess not," she spoke shyly.

"And also, you are looking very thin. You must eat, for I do not want any of my guests to go to bed hungry."

Eleanora felt confused when he performed all these kind gestures. She continued to be surprised by the interest he was showing in her though they had just met.

"Your guest?" Eleanora questioned.

"Only for today, that is," he said with a smirk. "From tomorrow, you shall be just a servant girl."

"Yes," she muttered to herself as he made this statement to her, making her realise that this was just once-in-a-lifetime special treatment. She lowered her eyes to where her hands were clasped together underneath the table.

He called her name again. "Nora?"

"Hmm?" She swiftly lifted her eyes back up to him.

"Shall we eat?"

She nodded her head again in response.

Sir Kingston turned around and called for the butler. He ordered that their meals be brought to the table.

Momentarily, the meals arrived and were placed in front of them. Eleanora watched as each dish was brought forward. She could feel her mouth watering with temptation as she had never eaten quite a feast such as this.

The butler opened the lid of one of the main dishes and said, "Bon appetite!"

"Thank you, Dashier," Eleanora quickly and politely responded.

Mr Smite smiled at her innocence while Sir Kingston gazed strangely at her.

"All this food looks positively delicious!" Eleanora made known, eager as she was.

"Have you ever had anything like this?"

"Not like this, no. All I ate back at the estate was porridge for breakfast, and some soup or leftover chicken and bread for lunch. And I was allowed supper only some of the time."

"Why were you not allowed supper all the time?"

"Whenever my aunt was angry with me, she would send me to bed without supper."

"You must have upset her to not have supper?"

"The only reason why she ever got upset or angry with me was because I always proved to her that I was right. I would rather not talk about it anyway." She began cutting through her roast lamb that was already carved for her to pick at and enjoy. She poured some gravy over her meat and ate it with the roasted root vegetables.

"Nora…"

She looked his way, and his piercing eyes gazed into Eleanora's azure-blue ones. "Earlier today, you said that you wished you hadn't met me or come to this place. Do you still feel that way now?"

Eleanora placed her cutlery down onto her plate when she heard this simple yet profound question. She thought about it for a moment and then replied, "I was upset before because I was sent away against my own will. But now, I realise that it must have been meant for me to come here, so I wouldn't have to live the rest of my life being cruelly dictated to. I believe this will be a good change of atmosphere, which should brighten my spirits."

He sat still, and his eyes now gazed somewhere else.

"I realise you have had a hard time. I didn't think your aunt would be that kind of woman, even if I don't know everything that has happened."

He paused before saying, "I want you to know that you are safe here and are under my protection. No one can touch you, so you don't need to ever feel frightened."

"Thank you, sir. I appreciate all that you have done," Eleanora said and continued eating.

After some time, another subject was spoken about.

"I believe, Sir Kingston, that I do not know much about you," Eleanora said, trying to focus the conversation on him instead of her. He gave her an unusual look that gave Eleanora the impression that he didn't want to be the subject of their discussion. She lowered her head again like a poor, innocent kitten and mumbled, "I'm sorry. I didn't mean to pry."

Sir Kingston cleared his throat and asked, "What is it that you would like to know?" He took a sip from his glass, which was filled with red wine.

Eleanora looked up again and felt persuaded to continue by the friendliness of his tone. "Well, I want to know what you do for your occupation."

"I am a businessman. I own a furniture factory as well as two hotels in town."

"That is pleasing to hear. Do you help make the furniture?"

He laughed. "No, I don't have the skill or craft to make the furniture. I just own the business, and the employees must make what is required. I usually go down there to check the progress. The majority of the furniture in here was made at my factory."

"It all does look very well designed," she complimented.

"Of course! It is the very best. No other factory makes furniture the way we do. I only hire the best workers since I have the money to do so," he said, and Eleanora could see that he was proud of his wealth and reputation.

Eleanora took a sip of her water before she continued to another subject. "You seem to be fond of paintings since you have so many hung up on every wall of the manor."

"Yes, well, they elevate the rooms, brighten them, provide a sense of creativity."

"They are very nice. But there is one I noticed that is of your father. The large one in the Grand Hall." She observed the way Sir Kingston swallowed hard.

He looked elsewhere, and when he returned his gaze to her, his smile looked forced.

"That is my late father, yes."

"I hope you don't mind me asking, but what happened to him?"

Sir Kingston's expression was very strange at that moment. His eyes were fixed on Eleanora, but his mind seemed to be elsewhere. He then exhaled before speaking. "What happened to my father was a tragic accident. It is something I do not like to speak about...especially while eating."

Eleanora looked away quickly from his frightening gaze that continued to grow in intensity. "Forgive me," she mumbled while lowering her head, regretting ever thinking she could just ask something like that so directly.

Sir Kingston then sighed and continued, "My mother, however, died two years after I was born. She fell ill with some sort of fever. I do not remember her, much the way you do not remember your mother."

Eleanora faced him, reflecting on how they shared the misfortune of losing a mother at an early stage. This made Eleanora see a vulnerable side to Sir Kingston although he would not open up to her completely.

*

The food served had been eaten. It was now time for Sir Kingston to retire and continue with any other work he had to finish before the night was over.

Eleanora situated herself in the drawing room, where Dana served tea and biscuits to her before she was to go off to bed. "How did you find the dinner with Sir Kingston, Nora?"

"It was interesting, I would say. The food was pleasant, thanks to you, and the conversation allowed me to learn more about the man I will be serving during my time here." She then went on, "By the way, thank you for lending me this dress to wear for tonight." Eleanora held up her tea and began to blow gently, making sure it wouldn't be too hot for her tongue when she took a sip.

"That dress is for you to keep. I know you will mostly be wearing the uniform by tomorrow, but it can be for the evenings, when you have finished your work. I'm sure you wouldn't want to wear the uniform all the time."

"Yes, that is true."

Dana then acknowledged, "However, while it was sent up to you by my order, it was Sir Kingston's idea to get you that dress.

He saw the way the other one was torn, so he wanted to provide you with one to wear when needed."

"He bought me this dress?" Eleanora was surprised to hear this. She thought how kind he was to do such a thing for her. "I should thank him then."

*

Tea was over after an hour of talking with Mrs Pester. It was time to retire to the bedroom and ensure a good night's sleep so she would be ready to wake up early for the day to come.

When Eleanora reached the second floor, she saw that Sir Kingston was coming her way.

"Sir Kingston," she called as he looked up to her.

"Yes, Nora?"

"I just wanted to thank you for the dress you bought me to wear. You really didn't have to, however."

"Nonsense. I couldn't allow you to stay in that other dress you wore."

"Well, thank you," she said and blushed.

"You're welcome. Good night then." He made his way down the stairs.

"Good night, sir," she wished him in return before heading up the stairs in the opposite direction.

# Chapter 7

I t was raining the next day. The sound of trickling drops of
water continued as the rain poured down from the great
cloudy sky above. A tapping noise came from the window,
which awoke Eleanora from her dreamy sleep. She rose from bed,
stretching her arms out to start waking up her muscles. She went
over to the window, noticing the tapping sound had come from the
rain as each bead of water drizzled down the glass. She opened the
window slightly to sniff in that cool, fresh, earthy aroma that comes
with a downpour. Eleanora knew she wasn't going to be hearing
the sound of birds chirping early this morning due to the rain; they
usually would sound their high-pitched whistles just after the crack
of dawn as they too awoke. They must be nested over by the
forest, sheltering amongst the thick-leaved trees, she thought as she
looked over that way. She decided to shut the window before any
of the rain got in.

Another tap was heard suddenly, this time at the door.
Eleanora rushed to it, keen to see who it could be. When she
opened the door, the butler stood holding the uniform neatly
folded on the palm of his hand, while the other hand held onto a
pair of boots.

"Good morning, Nora! Did you have a pleasant sleep on
your first night here in the manor?"

"Yes, I did. Thank you," she said with a smile. "I can't
believe it is raining this morning."

"That only means there won't be much to do for outdoor
chores today, I think. But it should clear up perhaps by the early
afternoon." He looked down at what he was holding in his hand.
He then gave it to Eleanora saying, "This is your uniform, Nora. I
was sent to give it to you so you may get dressed before you go

down to the kitchen, where Dana and the others are waiting for you."

"Of course. Thank you, Dashier. Have a good day."

"You too, Nora."

Eleanora shut the door after this. She went over and undressed from her nightgown before trying on the uniform she had to wear. The colour was ocean blue and of sturdy cotton material. It came with a long white apron that was to be tied around her waist. She put it on, and it reached down to her ankles, where the dress also ended. She put on the brown boots and tied them. She visited the mirror in the common bathroom, where she gave her face a wash. She tied her hair up in a simple bun and got ready to go downstairs.

*

Eleanora made her way down to the kitchen, and all the servants wished her a good morning as she entered.

"My, don't you look just like us!" Jill commented while she stroked her arm. "You fit right in. We are going to have some fun while working together," she continued.

"All right, Jill. Leave the poor girl alone, would ya?" Marie interjected.

"How was your sleep, Nora, dear?" Dana then asked.

"It was the most pleasant sleep I have had in such a long time."

"You didn't get scared, now, did you?" Marie asked and laughed.

"Why would I get scared?"

"Because it can get pretty scary, especially during the night."

"Leave her alone, Marie," Jill said and went back to her place.

"I'm just letting her know. This whole manor is mysterious and can be eerie."

"All right. That is enough, Marie. Do not scare her any more than you already have."

"I'm not scared, Dana. There's no worries there." Eleanora tried to be brave about it, when, really, she'd only just realised how scary it could be.

"All right then. Let us get to work. We have breakfast to make before the master awakes. He has a busy day today, so he will need his meal before he leaves." Dana began to instruct the servants on their tasks. Jill and Marie would start preparations for breakfast while Eleanora would help Dana collect the eggs from the farmhouse.

They opened the door to where the rain fell continuously onto the muddy ground. They hastily exited the kitchen from the side, making their way into the farmhouse that was just down the path. "This is the farmhouse that I forgot to show you yesterday. Nevertheless, we are here now, and I want you to take notice of the animals here. The chicken coop is over there, and the cows are closed in behind that gate on your left. The horses are shut up in their places. Your job will mainly be to collect the eggs while I fetch a bucket of milk." She handed over a basket and led her to the chicken coop. "You must have done this before, am I right?"

"It was part of my daily routine, but I didn't milk cows."

"That you won't have to worry about."

Dana gave Eleanora a sack of food for the chickens. She then went over to start milking the cows while Eleanora opened the chicken coop. She sprinkled the food on the ground, and the chickens ran out all at once. She poured out some more to keep them busy. As they scattered about, Eleanora took the opportunity to start gathering as many eggs as she could. She reached out for some that were easily seen while she had to dig into the hay to search for others. Once she collected all that she could find, she went out while some of the chickens made their way back in.

"Were there enough eggs laid?" Dana asked as she came around with a heavy bucket filled with creamy milk.

"Yes, about two dozen."

"That would be enough to last a week or two," she said, looking down at the eggs that filled the basket. "All right, hurry along. Back into the kitchen."

When they returned to the kitchen, Dana continued her instructions.

"Now, Eleanora, you can start boiling some of those eggs for the master's breakfast. Just three will do."

Eleanora did exactly that, and while she did so, Dana was on to the milk, separating it to use both now and later.

"Jill, dear, would you start making the dough with Marie?" Jill nodded her head and did so.

While they were all at work, the side door opened, and Mr Pester entered from outside. "Dana, honey, I need those carrots to feed the horses before I give them a wash down."

"The carrots are sitting just over there on the bench by Eleanora."

Tennent went over and joked, "She's working you hard already, aye, Nora?" He gave her a quick wink. He then faced his wife with a smirk lurking on his face.

"I'm used to it anyway. This is nothing compared to what I did back at the estate."

"Well, there will be more to do when it stops raining." He picked up the carrots and left, shutting the door behind him.

"Dana, your husband is a very nice man. You are very lucky."

"Did Tennent tell you that we are married?"

"Yes, yesterday."

"Tennent can sometimes be mean," Marie then blurted.

"How so?" Jill interjected.

"He always teases me, and it's not ever funny."

"He never teases me. He only compliments me," Jill remarked with a smile.

"Do not forget who is the wife around here," Dana butted in.

"Oh, Dana, you know we are only joking with you," Jill responded, rolling out the dough.

"Of course, I know. I am not a jealous woman, you know."

"Yeah, right!" Marie replied with a laugh. "But I can tell he is fond of Nora just because she is new and all."

Eleanora smiled while checking on the eggs.

"What else needs to be done, Dana?" Eleanora offered as she went over to her.

"This bread from yesterday needs to be toasted to go with the master's butter and eggs."

Eleanora took the bread from her and got to it.

"We have fifteen minutes. The master will come down here at six demanding his breakfast," Dana announced.

While they all continued with their duties, Marie asked, "By the way, how old are you, Nora?"

"I'm nineteen."

"Nineteen! That is young. Well, I expected you to be that sort of age."

"And what about all of you?" Eleanora asked in return.

"I'm thirty, and Jill over here is twenty-eight. Dana is, of course, the oldest, being forty-five."

"Well, you look and sound as young as can be," said Eleanora, complimenting Dana.

"Why, thank you, Nora. See, you two can learn to be more like Nora here. Especially you, Marie."

"What did I do?" Marie protested.

"You are always making jokes about my age."

Jill giggled from behind.

"Oh, I can see you too, Jill."

"Is Dana the only one with a husband?" Eleanora then asked.

"As is seen," Marie answered. "Who has time for men anyway," she concluded.

"Well, that is not the case for me," Jill chimed in. "How about you, Nora? Is there anyone you have ever liked?"

"Well, no. I have never really met anyone to like them in that sort of way," she stated.

"What do you mean?" Jill asked.

"Back at the estate, I was never allowed to go into the village, or town for that matter. I have stayed within the gates of Mallow Hall ever since I was a child."

"Really?" Marie parted her mouth, and her eyes widened.

Eleanora nodded her head, feeling quite dismayed.

"Poor child," Dana commented.

"So, we are the only other people you have met, besides the ones you worked with back home?" Marie questioned.

Eleanora nodded.

"Why weren't you allowed?" Marie further questioned.

"I just wasn't. I lived with my Aunt Dusilla and her daughter, Mandy, who is my cousin. They never treated me right. They never gave me any independence, and all freedom was taken away from me. How I longed for some sort of liberty," she added with a melancholy sigh.

"Well, I am most glad Sir Kingston hired you when he could," Dana said with a soft smile.

"He didn't hire me," Eleanora muttered reluctantly.

"Didn't hire you?" Dana repeated, seeming puzzled.

"I was sold by my cruel aunt to Sir Kingston," Eleanora finally admitted, feeling ashamed and downcast.

"Sold!" Dana widened her eyes while Marie and Jill gasped.

"Yes, I was sold," she repeated firmly.

"How awful!" Dana went up to Eleanora. "Oh, Nora, I am truly sorry to hear that of you. Sir Kingston informed us that we would be having a girl servant rather than a boy, but he never mentioned anything about buying you off." Dana held onto Eleanora's wrist.

"How could that be?" Marie came forward.

"My aunt was my guardian, but she never took care of me the way she was supposed to. I despise her for all she has done to me. And now, she is the gladdest she could ever be for getting rid of me. But I am glad to be getting rid of her."

"I'm so sorry," Dana said again, her eyes expressing sorrow and pity.

"I guess that was my life, and to be sold to someone I knew nothing about really tore my heart. I thought it would be the end of me. I thought I would be a slave to someone much worse from the way they described him to me."

"They? What do you mean?" Dana asked.

But Eleanora couldn't explain any further as the kitchen door was opened from the Grand Hall. Mr Smite had entered and was making himself known. "The master is seated at the dining table and has ordered for his breakfast."

"We will be there in just a moment," Dana replied. Mr Smite nodded his head and returned to the master to deliver the message. "Nora, would you give the master his breakfast while I go to serve him tea? Just place all the food onto the tray," Dana directed.

Eleanora filled the tray, and they headed to the dining room.

\*

Eleanora observed Sir Kingston sitting on the same chair with the same upright posture. His face was impassive and expressionless. She then watched as Dana poured the master some milk into his tea and stirred it only once. Eleanora stepped forward and placed each dish in front of him while holding the tray. His eyes fixed on the breakfast meal before he slowly turned his head and gazed at Eleanora as she was doing her duty. Her eyes were lowered, and her lips were pressed tightly together.

"How are you this morning, Nora?"

"Just fine, master," she answered, addressing him as "master" for the first time.

He chuckled. "You may leave now, Dana," he said and turned to bid her off. Dana left at once. Eleanora was also about to leave, but Sir Kingston called her before she could.

"Is something the matter with your breakfast, master?"

"No, nothing is wrong. It's just you seem troubled this morning. Why?"

"I do not feel troubled," she replied softly, even though the conversation she'd just had with the servants had made her think about her life again and how carelessly she was always treated.

"Are you sure?" he further questioned.

She placed a smile on her face. "Yes, of course."

"All right then. You may go," he said in dismissal.

Eleanora went back with the empty tray in her hands. She helped clean up with the other servants until it was time to bring back all the empty plates from the dining table, which she did with Jill to help. When she returned to the dining room, the master had already left to do his business for the day.

"Looks like the master enjoyed his breakfast. Every plate has been all cleaned up," Jill remarked.

"Yes, less work for us to do," Eleanora commented.

Jill chuckled in agreement.

They went back and finished cleaning the dishes.

After all that was done, they had some breakfast for themselves, eating together at the table near the window.

"Why doesn't your husband come and eat with us, Dana?" Jill wanted to know.

"You know how he is, wanting to finish all his morning work before taking time to eat."

"What is there to do next?" Eleanora then asked.

"Well, it seems it is still raining for now. So, the indoor chores must be done. I usually do the washing while Marie takes care of the sweeping, and Jill sometimes does the dusting unless she is working with me in the kitchen. But since there will be no washing today, Jill will help with preparations for lunch and dinner. Eleanora, you can do the dusting. Just start on the first floor and work your way up. We usually do each floor on different days, but since it is raining, there's not much to do. Just do whatever you can, dear, except the second floor and the bedrooms. They do not need to be dusted."

After breakfast, they went straight to their work. Eleanora was given a duster to start dusting around the furniture and paintings in each room. She went from top to bottom, cleaning out every edge and corner clustered with dirt. The dusting took the full two hours to complete, and she made sure everything was perfectly cleaned without a speck of dust in sight. Eleanora had just finished the library, which, with all the books there were, took the longest of all.

After everything was complete, lunch was served. The rain had eventually stopped pouring over the land, but the soil was too muddy to do much of the work. For the rest of the afternoon, Eleanora rested in her chamber and was called down when it was time to help serve the dinner to the master.

Later that night, she decided to retire early to her chamber, wanting to be alone for the remainder of that day.

# Chapter 8

The following day arrived, and the morning duties were as expected for the preparation of Sir Kingston's breakfast. It was the same routine that was set for each and every morning. After this, Eleanora began her work outside in the fields alongside Tennent and Jill.

The fields were wide and open. The rain from yesterday had moistened the soil, which was beneficial for starting the planting of new seeds for the crops. Tennent began razing the grass to make more rows where the new vegetables would be grown, while Eleanora and Jill each held a basket of their own, harvesting what was already there.

Eleanora started off by digging out the carrots from underneath. She held onto the tops and gently pulled them away from the soil. Then she continued on to the tomatoes. She visited each plant and twisted the tomatoes that were ripe and a vibrant red off the stems.

"Your basket is almost full, Nora. Let me get you another one," Jill offered. She handed her another, and Eleanora continued to pick tomatoes.

"There are so many of them," she finally commented.

"There is an abundance," Jill said and chuckled in agreement. She bent down and got the last cabbage flower and placed it in her basket, which was already full of them.

"Do you know what these vegetables will be used for?"

"Dana usually makes some sort of salad out of them or just roasts them to accompany the meat. But with the extra tomatoes, she will use them for tomato soup, I reckon." Jill wiped her forehead with her apron. "It is hot out here, isn't it, compared to yesterday?"

Eleanora looked up to the sky where the sun scorched its rays down onto them. "Yes, it is," she agreed. Eleanora went back to her own thoughts for a moment. She then asked, "Jill, do you usually associate with the master?"

Jill looked up at her. "No, not really. I just do my duty, and that is it. Dana is the one who usually attends to him when he is in need of something. She is the head servant."

Eleanora nodded and continued her work.

"Ah! I think we're all done here," Jill finally said as she rose, stretching her back with her hands placed on her hips. "Ready, Nora?"

Eleanora stood up and nodded. "We should let Tennent know."

Jill waved to Tennent as she called his name. "Tennent! We are all done over here!"

"All right. You may go!" he yelled back. He started to sow the soil.

"Come on, Nora. I'll race you back to the kitchen!" Jill exclaimed enthusiastically. She picked up her basket and was off in a rush.

"That's not fair. I wasn't ready!" Eleanora responded loudly.

Jill looked back. "Hurry up then!"

Eleanora picked up the two baskets filled with carrots and tomatoes, holding one in each hand, and started to chase after her. "I'm coming!"

Eleanora raced up the hill, finding it difficult to hold onto both baskets. She felt like she was carrying bricks instead. She hurried herself as best she could, running towards the back of the manor. She could almost see herself catching up to Jill. She passed the side porch and turned to the right, where she watched as Jill made it inside the manor before she could. One of the tomatoes dropped from Eleanora's overloaded basket, so she quickly put her basket down to retrieve it. She picked the basket up again and hastily made her way toward the front door.

While her feet were quickening over the ground, she made her last right turn to the front porch and bumped into Sir

Kingston, who was pacing in the opposite direction, causing one of the baskets, the one with all the tomatoes, to tumble over. Her body had accidentally pressed onto his, which almost made her fall back.

"Oh my!" she exclaimed. "I'm terribly sorry, master."

Sir Kingston looked at her with wide eyes.

She began to pick up all the rolling tomatoes that surrounded her on the ground.

He then uttered, a little harsh in his tone of voice, "I hope you are going to wash those properly before they are used."

She picked up the last one and placed it back into the basket before standing up. "Of course," she replied, feeling embarrassed about what had occurred.

Sir Kingston remained still, and Eleanora saw the way his eyes scanned her. She realised her hair, which was always placed into a simple bun, had now fallen out loosely into a ponytail. She felt how her cheeks grew warm. They must have brightened, she thought, with heat from the running and the stare Sir Kingston gave. Eleanora lowered her eyes from him timidly.

A voice came from behind, "Nora, what is going on?" Jill then appeared behind Sir Kingston.

"What were you doing, by the way?" Sir Kingston's arms crossed over his chest, and his tone was demanding.

"We were just picking some crops from the field…"

As Jill was about to continue, he stopped her and said, "I know what you have been doing, Jill. I can see for myself. But why were you running?" He then turned to Eleanora.

"We were just racing, to see who could get to the kitchen first," she answered honestly.

"Yes, well, your little race caused you to bump into me. Now, you must be careful next time, for I do not want my food to be touching the ground before I have to eat it." He seemed furious yet calm at the same time.

"It was my fault, master. I told Nora that we should race. It was pretty childish to do so. I should have known that the baskets were too heavy to carry while running."

"Yes, you should have known better, Jill. Doesn't matter now. No one was hurt, were they?" He gazed over back to Eleanora.

She nodded her head quickly and looked straight behind him to Jill.

"I will be on my way now," Sir Kingston muttered, leaving them as he passed Eleanora's side.

Jill went up to Eleanora and suddenly they both began to laugh. "You should have seen your scared little face, Nora...It was priceless!" She helped Eleanora carry the other basket back into the kitchen.

"Yes, well, you should have seen Sir Kingston's stern-looking face."

"You bumped into him?"

"Yes, and it all happened so quickly. I think I hit him quite hard, especially his chest."

Jill burst into laughter once again. "Oh my! I wish I could have seen that. But I hope you're okay, Nora?"

"I'm fine. I was just unsure of what he might have done to me."

"Well, as the master said, no one got hurt, except for those poor tomatoes," Jill said and gave another laugh. Eleanora did the same, joining her in her good humour.

They returned to the kitchen, where they placed their baskets onto the bench near the other one, which was filled with bright-green cabbages. Not long after, Dana arrived, followed by Marie.

"Oh, these look very good!" Dana went over and inspected the vegetables. "They have grown nice and big."

"It did take a lot of work getting them in, especially with that sun out there." Jill gave a wink to Eleanora. "Nora's face was all red. Especially when she bumped into Sir Kingston," she finished off with a laugh.

"You bumped into the master?" Dana directed her eyes to Eleanora.

"It was nothing," Eleanora said, trying to brush off the embarrassing situation.

"She accidentally bumped into him when we were racing back inside. And I, of course, won!" Jill held her head up high.

"You should know better than that, Jill. You're not a child anymore, you know," Dana complained.

"I just wanted to have some fun and show Nora that we can have some while working."

"How did the master react? Did you get in trouble?" Marie interjected while she was washing the carrots and tomatoes.

Eleanora responded, "No, I didn't get in trouble. He just told us to be careful next time." Eleanora then faced Jill. "And he told Jill that she should know better than that."

"At least he didn't say anything too harsh," Dana said with a sigh. "But I don't see why you didn't go through the side door to enter the kitchen, especially with those muddy shoes of yours!"

"Oh, Dana, relax a little." Jill rolled her eyes. "There was no harm done."

"Was he hurt?" Marie continued.

"Well, I did hit him pretty hard, especially the way I bumped into his chest. But he seemed fine about it, I guess," Eleanora explained.

"All right, ladies. Let's not talk about this anymore," Dana puffed.

"At least something interesting happened today," Marie mumbled.

"What is that supposed to mean?" Dana instantly demanded.

"Nothing interesting ever happens around here," Marie began to complain. "And finally, we get some action, and we shouldn't even talk about it anymore."

"I didn't mean it in that way. Of course, we should talk about things, but sometimes there is a limit at which we should stop." Dana took a breath. "Now, let us all get to work preparing these beautiful, fresh vegetables," she instructed as she picked up one of the baskets. Dana directed the servants to their duties; Marie was to work on washing and peeling the carrots while Jill helped Eleanora with the shredding of the cabbages and Dana with the tomatoes, cutting some and leaving the rest for soup, just as Jill guessed.

*

It was almost time to serve dinner to the master, and Eleanora prepared the tray of food. When everything was complete, Eleanora departed from the kitchen, making her way to the dining room. She placed each plate of food down in front of him, and while doing so, she noticed the way his mouth was straight and held no expression. He looked to be thinking about something that was bothering him; his eyebrows were furrowed, and his eyes seemed a darker shade of green.

Once she was done, she stood there and called softly, "Master?"

He turned to her, his eyebrow raised. "Hmm?" he mumbled as if he couldn't speak.

"I was thinking that I would like to put a vase of flowers on the table. It is too empty and bare, and I think some flowers will help to lighten your mood. The ones out in the front garden are marvellous, don't you think?"

He didn't say anything at first. Eleanora thought he looked rather surprised to even hear this idea come from her mouth. He turned, his eyes gazing over to the table in front of him. He then gazed back at Eleanora as she waited patiently to see what he would think of this suggestion. She watched the way he moved his pale lips as he asked indifferently, "You want to put flowers here?

What makes you think I would enjoy the company of flowers here on the table?"

"It would be something different. I thought the flowers could have a purpose. They would bring a sweet and fresh aroma to the table."

"I never really thought about that before." He paused. "But if you think flowers would be best, then, yes, I will allow it," he decided.

"I will go out and pick some for you right now," she said, hurrying her words in her excitement.

She walked with haste back into the kitchen and asked for a vase.

"A vase?" Dana questioned. Eleanora explained her reasons for needing one. "That's very kind of you to do, Nora. Are you sure the master agreed to this?"

Eleanora nodded her head.

"I never thought of doing that myself."

"That's because she's frightened by the master," Marie teased, laughing about it as she was cleaning the plates.

Dana went over and found a shiny maroon vase that was the perfect size. "I will get this cleaned up while you go pick out the flowers that you want," advised Dana.

Eleanora nodded and rushed outside to the front garden. With a pair of scissors, she began to cut the bottom of the stems of some daffodils that blushed soft, beautiful colours of yellow, orange, pink, and white, which she believed would please Sir Kingston, especially in the gloomy mood he was in that evening.

Once she picked out enough, the best she could find, she went back to the kitchen, where she began neatly filling the vase.

"Those daffodils are pretty, Nora," Jill said.

Eleanora then stated, "I even have enough for another vase to put on the table when we have our meals together."

"Good idea, Nora!" Dana exclaimed. "I'll go get another vase for those."

Eleanora took the maroon vase and returned to the dining room. She placed the vase on the table and gave the flowers a good sniff.

"Don't they smell wonderful?" she pointed out as she faced Sir Kingston. Eleanora could feel the way his eyes fixed strangely on her.

He smiled and said with a laugh, "Yes, they do." He paused. "Eleanora?" he then called.

She stood back into place and answered, "Yes, master?"

He smiled again, saying, "I think this will be the first time I really get to enjoy my meal, thanks to you."

"Well, I'm glad!" She felt pleased that she could bring such a smile to his face. She had not seen him look that happy before.

\*

Mr Smite witnessed this rare moment from outside the room. His eyes widened, and he quickly went over to tell the others. Tennent was also in the room when Dashier began to describe this unusual event.

"I have not seen the master smile that way for such a long time. I'd forgotten how he looks when he does so."

"The master does need some happy things in his life after all he has been through," Dana mentioned.

"And it was Nora who brought him to smile," Dashier added.

Shortly after, Eleanora returned to the kitchen. "The master is pleased with his meal, Dana. He says it is very delicious and compliments us on all our work."

"The master's in a good mood all of a sudden," Marie said and chuckled.

"And we are all glad," Dana then said.

\*

It was the evening when Sir Kingston seated himself at his desk in the drawing room, completing some important work of business. He had ordered Eleanora to serve him some tea.

"How has the workload been so far?" he asked as he was writing something with his feathered ink pen onto a single piece of paper.

"I have gotten used to it very quickly. I was a servant back at the estate, you know," she replied.

He stopped his writing, looked her way, and smiled. He then continued with what he was doing. "That will be all for tonight, Nora. You may go and rest," he said, dismissing her. He then watched as she left him to his own thoughts.

# Chapter 9

The rest of that week flew by relatively quickly. It was not long before Eleanora really started to feel at home; she was at peace with herself and could finally feel free from the fear that had haunted her for so many years. The manor was a place of resurrection for her as she was determined to start afresh, to live a life where, by living a good and simple life, she would rise above those who had offended her in the worst possible way.

A month passed since the day of her arrival. She completed her duties as expected each day and also attended to Sir Kingston whenever he ordered her to do something. Some days, he was rather demanding. On others, he was mute, and not a word was spoken by him. This confused Eleanora as she was concerned for him, not ever knowing what happened in his daily life besides business, as she would not dare ask. Nevertheless, she continued to decorate the dining table with a vase of flowers. She would change the flowers at the end of each week and refresh the water every second day. It seemed to please him so, even on his worst days.

\*

It was Tuesday, in the late afternoon; the sun was still high but the light being cast over the land was not particularly bright. All the servants were down at the fields doing some hay work. Tennent was chopping up some wood that would be used in the fireplace while the women sorted and stacked the hay into bundles that were to be used for various things.

"Will this hay ever end?" complained Marie after stacking three bundles.

"The faster we get to it, the quicker we can go back inside and take a break," Dana replied, also fatigued.

"Well, I'm just going to take a quick break now," Marie said and sat on the grass.

"That's not fair!" Jill began to protest at her laziness. "How come she gets to take a break while the rest of us have not yet taken one? And we've done more than you!"

"Listen here, I've done most of my part. A little break right now won't hurt anyone," Marie argued back, her eyes bulging from her sockets.

"Ladies, ladies, what is all the commotion about?" Tennent came forth. Neither of them answered. "You are lucky you are sorting out the hay. What I have to do is more than what you girls do put together."

"Are you saying you do more work around here than us?" Marie demanded.

"Yeah!" Jill followed. "Are you saying you've done more just because you are a man?"

"I never said that. I've been working here longer than you two, so you better not complain. The number of things I've had to do over the years!"

They both kept their mouths shut. Marie got back on her feet and continued where she left off.

"You never see Nora complaining the way you two do," Tennent added before heading back to his axe. They all looked at Eleanora.

She avoided their stares and went forth with her work. She then mentioned, "I always forget to ask this question, but how long have you all been working here for Sir Kingston?"

"I've been here for five years, and God, does it feel like a lifetime," Marie answered first.

Jill then answered, "It's been three years for me."

Eleanora looked over to Dana as she responded, "I have been working here since Sir Kingston was just a little boy. I was fifteen years old when I helped nurse him, especially as his mother had died not too long after he was born."

"What about Dashier? Do you know?"

"He's been working here for a very long time. He started earlier than me even. He knows more about Sir Kingston's late father than any of us."

"And you, Tennent, how long have you been working here?" Eleanora continued.

"Not as long as Dana, I would have to say. For about nine years. After my seventh year here, is when I was finally married to my beautiful Dana."

"Yes, I remember how happy we were and still are." Dana's eyes gleamed with happiness.

"You two are wonderful together," Eleanora commented as she watched the way they looked into each other's eyes.

"Enough of this lovey-dovey moment. We have hay to stack," Marie interrupted, ending their loving gaze.

"You were the one who wanted a break in the first place," Tennent argued.

She narrowed her eyes at him and got back to work, with everyone else following suit.

When the job was almost done, Mr Smite came pacing from afar. He came down to the fields and hastily spoke, "Dana, I have some news for you all."

Eleanora looked up to see what was the matter.

"What is it, Dashier?" Dana rushed her words.

"Sir Kingston has just notified me that he will arrive shortly at the manor with Mr Rupert Nables, alongside his daughter, Miss Pearl Nables. They are to be his guests at the manor, but he didn't say how long they will be staying. All I was told, however, is to prepare the guest rooms."

"That does not give us much time, does it, then?" Dana looked away for a moment. She then thanked him for the message. He left at once as he, too, had some affairs to take care of.

"Mr Nables is arriving with his daughter," Dana announced clearly to everyone. "We must quickly prepare their guest rooms before they arrive. We better hurry." Dana looked over to Marie and instructed, "Marie, come with me inside. The

82

rest of you quickly finish out here and clean yourselves up. We want to look presentable when they arrive."

Dana and Marie rushed out of the fields.

"Who are the guests they speak of?" Eleanora asked, curious about the way everyone was acting.

Tennent came forth and explained, "Mr Nables is a wealthy man, not as much as Sir Kingston, however. He was the guardian of him when his father died, for he had no one else to look after him."

"So, Sir Kingston's father was friends with this man?"

"Yes, he was," Tennent affirmed.

"And his daughter?" Eleanora pressed.

"Miss Pearl Nables is a young woman in her mid-twenties. She and her father have stayed at the manor many times before. It's been a while, though, and I guess they have now returned to visit Sir Kingston again."

"I never liked that Pearl Nables," Jill let slip.

"Why? What is she like?" Eleanora asked with a tone of some urgency now.

"There's something about her that isn't very nice. You will see when you meet her."

"Enough about that. Let's carry these stacks into the farmhouse so we can wash up," Tennent advised them.

Eleanora became very curious to learn more about the two guests that would be arriving soon. She didn't know what to expect or how things would be different when they were staying at the manor. She thought over what Jill had said of the lady named Pearl Nables, having a particular interest in what her character might be like. Whether Jill was right or not, she wouldn't let that influence Eleanora's immediate impressions of the woman. She would judge her for herself. Only time would tell, she thought.

*

Eleanora had fixed her uniform and redone her hair to make sure she looked presentable in front of company. The carriage was arriving, and the servants waited patiently in a line in front of the manor. The horses came prancing around the fountain and stopped at the pathway that led to the front entrance of the door.

"Let's not look overly excited," Marie commented, which put a smile on Eleanora's face.

Eleanora tried to see the faces inside the carriage but had no luck. The horses neighed, and Dashier went over to open the door. First to come out was Sir Kingston, dressed in a black cloak that covered his olive-green formal vest. He held his black top hat to his side as he waited for his guests to come out. The first one to appear had to be Mr Nables, Eleanora thought. He was a tall man about the same height as Sir Kingston himself, and he had a similar stance to him when he stood. His hair was grey and came down in long waves to his shoulders. His attire consisted of a formal dark-brown suit, a top hat, and a cane.

Next to follow was his daughter, who put out one foot onto the step of the carriage. Sir Kingston reached out his hand in a gentlemanly manner, and she clutched onto it with grace. She hopped off, her long navy-blue skirt passing her boots and almost touching the gravel. She wore a formal jacket of the same shade of blue over her white blouse. She topped it all off with a stylish rounded hat with a black feathery prop glued to the side. Underneath this was her chestnut hair, which was tightly tied into a braided bun, allowing her face to be more prominent. She had a fair complexion, and her cheekbones stood out slightly, while her nose was small yet pointy at the tip. Her brightly coloured lips parted into a smile, and Eleanora saw a flash of her pearly white teeth.

The woman's eyes scanned over the entire manor as she exclaimed in her high-pitched voice, "I forgot how surreal the manor is!" She then returned her gaze to Sir Kingston, who showered her with pretty smiles. Eleanora had never seen Sir Kingston smile the way he did now. It felt very strange because she had hardly seen him smile at all, but he continued to do so now. They stood together, the young woman's arm wrapped around his arm, and they looked to be the perfect couple.

Sir Kingston led the way, while announcing, "These are my servants, as you know."

The lady didn't care to put a smile on her face, not even the slightest grin and nor did her father.

"Welcome, Mr Nables and Miss Nables," Dana said and curtseyed on behalf of the rest of the servants. Eleanora stood still and ensured her posture was upright, just like the others beside her. Her hands were clasped together; she was nervous about meeting these people for the first time as she wasn't used to seeing new faces. She peeked at Sir Kingston and saw the way his emerald-green eyes remained alit. He glanced at her for a moment, and she quickly lowered her eyes to her feet, feeling a rush of heat shoot up her body and a blush rise in her cheeks.

"Kingston Manor hasn't changed much since last you were here," he then said, his eyes looking up at the manor. "Shall we go in?"

He looked at Mr Nables, who then replied, "Please."

Sir Kingston took them in through the doorway. Dashier followed to attend to them while Tennent went over to pick up their bags; it seemed they would be staying for quite some time judging by the amount of luggage there was.

Dana looked over to the others and said, "We should go and prepare tea. The master will be seated in the drawing room with his guests and expecting it to be served at once."

The young servants followed Dana back inside and into the kitchen to prepare the biscuits and freshly brew the tea.

*

That evening, after tea was served, Sir Kingston remained in the drawing room with his friends for nearly two hours until night slowly came upon them.

"How long do you think they will stay?" Eleanora asked as she watched them follow Dashier up the stairs, heading for the second floor.

"I'm not sure," Marie replied. "Probably won't be more than a few days, I hope."

Eleanora released her breath, hoping the same.

# Chapter 10

It was Wednesday morning. Eleanora hastily made her way down to the kitchen; she knew much work would need to be done because of the guests who were staying. A big breakfast needed to be whipped up to cater for them all.

"Nora, would you mind getting some more eggs? We're starting to run out," Dana said after counting the ones that were left.

Eleanora rushed outside to the farmhouse and collected the remaining eggs, finding there were, thankfully, just enough. She hurried back inside and began cracking them for the special omelettes that they were to make. While Eleanora was busy in the kitchen with the others, Dana and Dashier arrived back from having served the meals to the guests.

Dana puffed and said, "My, that was a lot for one breakfast meal, I'll tell you that. But we're used to it anyway; it's just been a while."

"What are they doing besides eating?" Jill wanted to know.

"Well, conversing, of course," Dana said as she came around and started to clean up the dishes.

"Yes, but what were they talking about?" Marie restated the question.

"I'm not really sure. I came in halfway through when they were giggling and laughing. What does it matter to you anyway?"

No one answered, and instead, each continued with their work.

Dana then began to say, "I'll tell you this, though, Miss Pearl really knows how to maintain her appearance. She looks very bright and pretty even though she just woke up. I wonder how she can look like that."

"Looks are not everything. And who cares? I think she is just full of herself," Jill opined.

"Agreed! And her nose is so pointy and turned upwards. She looks like a posh pig!" Marie scoffed.

Jill burst into a peal of high-pitched laughter.

Dana glared at them both, seeming disappointed, which made them stop at once. "Shame on you both for talking about her that way when she is just in the other room."

"But it's true!" Jill exclaimed. "And you think she's pretty."

"What do you think, Nora?" Marie then asked.

Eleanora looked up. "I don't really know what to think at this stage. I haven't seen enough of her to judge her character."

"Well, do you think she is pretty?" Marie continued.

They all looked at her, waiting to hear her response. "I think she is, from what I've seen so far, but only because of the way she dresses. But I haven't seen enough of her to say exactly."

"Well, you will," Marie said, and the discussion ended on that note.

They finished up with the rest of the cleaning and had some breakfast of their own.

*

In the afternoon, Eleanora went out to harvest some vegetables for the stew Dana was to make the guests for dinner that evening. She set out with a basket and headed down to the fields where the crops were grown. Eleanora looked up when she suddenly felt a drop of rain. It started to sprinkle not long after as the clouds gathered upon the grey sky. She hurried with her picking before the rain could get any heavier. When she made it back safe and sound, the downpour began. She brought the vegetables over to Dana and helped her with the cutting.

After a while, Tennent entered through the side door, and when he stepped inside, his boots squeaked. Dana turned around and exclaimed, "Look at you!" She went over to her husband. "What were you doing?"

Eleanora also turned around and was shocked that Tennent had stained his clothes with mud and was dripping with rainwater down to his trousers.

"I was cleaning the barn, and when I was coming out, I slipped and fell."

"Are you all right?" Eleanora gasped, placing the knife down.

"I'll be all right." He shuffled over by the window. "Didn't expect it to rain that much," he added and tapped the window glass with his finger.

"Oh, poor Tennent!" Dana rushed and held onto him. "You better get yourself cleaned up. You don't want to allow the guests, or the master especially, to see you like this."

"I should head up then," he muttered and was on his way.

"And could you get Jill and Marie down here? We need them to help prepare the dinner."

"Will your husband be all right, Dana? He didn't look too good," Eleanora asked with concern.

"He will be fine. He should be more careful next time, though."

They continued to cut the vegetables until Jill and Marie were down to help them.

*

Sir Kingston galloped his way down the main stairs, heading for the dining room. Mr Smite opened the door for him, and he entered through, meeting with his friends, who were already seated at their places.

"Sorry for keeping you both waiting." He went over to shake hands with Mr Nables and then went around to kiss Miss Pearl on the hand. "Don't you two look splendid this evening," he added before sitting down.

"You are looking very well yourself, James," Pearl replied and winked at him.

He gave out a chuckle. "Are we ready to eat?"

"Please," Mr Nables responded in delight.

"Dashier!" Sir Kingston called, and the butler came in immediately. "Bring the dinner to be served."

Dashier nodded his head. "Yes, sir," he said and went at once to deliver the message. He returned shortly and went about the room, pouring some red wine into each of the empty glasses. He went back out the door and stood by his place again. Then Eleanora and Marie entered the dining room, each holding a tray. They placed the dishes down in the middle of the table and left.

"The meal is delicious, James," Pearl began after taking a bite of the food. "What is this, some sort of stew?" She looked up at him.

"I believe it is beef and vegetable stew." Sir Kingston then took a spoonful, enjoying the way the succulent beef melted in his mouth while the juices ran down his tongue. "How are you enjoying it, Rupert?" he asked, turning to Mr Nables.

"It is very nourishing," Mr Nables said and took another mouthful. "James?" he then called. "How is business going so far down at the furniture factory? Any updates?"

"My employees are all doing their jobs perfectly," Sir Kingston informed him.

"How many orders have you had in the past month?"

"We've had thirty or so orders. We have been mostly selling tables and sofas. Some of the employees are making new designs." Sir Kingston then paused. "But this month has also been down."

"What do you mean?" Mr Nables looked anxious.

"The hotels…I found out that one of the employees has been stealing from some of the guests' rooms. We have caught the man committing the act, I assure you of that. But I'd be lying if I said it hasn't been stressful."

"Why didn't you contact me to help you handle it?" Mr Nables glared at Sir Kingston.

"I didn't need your help, really. I took care of everything, and now the hotels are under full surveillance to ensure this theft won't happen again. Also, anyone wishing to work in the hotel must be approved by me and judged to be fit for the job."

"Thank heavens everything is under control now." Mr Nables took a sip of his wine.

"I'm sorry to have heard that, James," Pearl spoke. "But let's talk about something more positive at the table, shall we?"

"All right then. What have you been up to?" he asked her.

Pearl looked down at her food. "Everything is about the same back in Windleton. Sometimes I get lonely over there," she said and pouted her lips.

"Well, you won't be lonely over here, now, will you?"

"Of course I won't when I have you to keep me company," she agreed and looked brightly at him.

"You are how old now, James? Twenty-nine?" said Mr Nables, encouraging the direction the conversation was now moving in.

"Yes, Rupert," Sir Kingston agreed and placed his spoon down.

"Almost thirty! That moved extremely fast, I have to say. How quickly the years of you growing up ran by! And darling Pearl too." He then gave a hopeful sigh before stating, "There are things you must start thinking about, you know, such as...a *wife*." The word "wife" was emphasised heavily.

Sir Kingston chuckled, fully aware of his friend's intentions. "I will think about that when the time comes."

"Well, the time is now!" Mr Nables exclaimed with a laugh.

"Father, you know James is sensitive about the topic," Pearl stated and then reached for his hand. Sir Kingston felt her touch as her fingers wrapped around his.

"I think, however, James, you are too focused on all your business and wealth. You should really start making a commitment to someone before it is too late," Mr Nables then reminded him.

Sir Kingston looked down at Pearl's hand and had many thoughts about what was being said.

"However, I don't believe there is anyone out there who understands you the way I do, James. I'm sure no one in the world can make you any happier," Pearl said, making it clear that she was available.

"Wasn't there a gentleman you said attracted you? You seemed very fond of him, I remember. You met him at one of the town's parties, I believe you told me."

"James, that was a long time ago. And after spending some time with him, I realised he wasn't right for me."

Sir Kingston slowly removed his hand from Pearl's now, wanting to eat the rest of his stew. Mr Smite came back in after a while and refilled the empty glasses. He saw that they had finished eating and went out to notify the servants.

Pearl embarked on another topic. "So, James, I see you have a new servant girl, for I don't think I ever remember seeing her. Why is that? Because you don't seem to have needed another one of those." She played with her wine, swishing it around her glass.

He laughed and replied, "You're right. I didn't really need one. But the more, the better to get the work done. Besides, it was not supposed to be a girl that I put on but a servant boy."

"Then why a change of mind?" she probed.

"I had a deal with the girl's aunt," he began explaining. "She wanted to get rid of her so desperately. She answered my advertisement for a boy servant saying that she had one, but when I visited her, she told me it would be a girl instead. I accepted the offer still, reducing the price by thirty per cent."

"I would not have bought her if I were you," Mr Nables stated. "The woman cheated you."

"Yes, but she paid for it by losing a sum of money. I wasn't going to go through with it, but I thought about it and decided to accept. Besides, it does me good having her around here."

"She was sold!?" Pearl exclaimed with a slight chuckle.

Sir Kingston nodded his head.

Pearl took a sip of her wine again. "What is her name?"

"Eleanora," Sir Kingston made known.

"That name doesn't seem to suit a servant girl," she observed with a chuckle. "And how long have you had her for?"

"A month now," he answered, to which she reacted with a "humph".

"Is she obedient?" Mr Nables enquired.

"Oh yes, she is," Sir Kingston quickly affirmed.

"But she's only been here for a month? She's probably just trying to get in your good graces, for now."

Sir Kingston recognised Mr Nables was trying to make an accusation. "What do you mean?"

"Because I've heard about many servants like her who play along and obey their masters until they feel all warm and cosy under their roof, which is when they start making trouble."

"Oh, but Eleanora is not that way," Sir Kingston said defensively.

"How would you know? You've only had her for a month. You do not know what really lies within her." He paused to take a breath. He then faced Sir Kingston again, saying, "I'm just warning you, James, keeping you on your guard, just in case. If the woman who sold her to you cheated, then who is to say that this servant will not do the same? She was desperate to get rid of her because she must have been no good and troublesome for the lady."

Sir Kingston remembered what Eleanora had told him about how she was mistreated under her aunt's authority. However, Mr Nables' word of warning did linger bitterly in his mind as he suddenly wondered if he could trust her as he thought he could. But time would tell, and he would come to know, he concluded.

After some time, Sir Kingston ordered Dashier to bring him his case of cigars. He returned with a bronze-coloured case the size of a large book in his hands. He stood by Sir Kingston's side and opened it. There were six long and rounded cigars displayed in the case and a large brown pipe. Sir Kingston handed the brown cigars to both Mr Nables and Pearl, who lit them up and began to smoke. Sir Kingston lit his pipe also. Dashier closed the case with the golden locks and dismissed himself right after.

*

Marie had taken her share of the trays and empty bowls back to the kitchen while Eleanora continued to collect all the other plates from the dining room.

Pearl began to say, "How dreadful it must be to live a life as a servant. They are all the same." Eleanora looked over while she was stacking the dishes. "Especially those who have been sold and bought. Tragic, isn't it, that they have no real home, no family, nothing but themselves?"

Eleanora paused in her work as she continued to glare at Pearl, who was speaking or, worse yet, mocking her in such a condescending way.

"All servants are good for is to order around," Pearl laughed, almost choking from all the poisonous smoke that clustered around her.

"Well, they should obey if they want to continue to live under a roof," her father said, now joining in the mocking tone of the conversation.

"I'll tell you, though…" Pearl puffed once on her cigar and then took it away from her lips. "They are useless. Don't you agree, James?" she asked with a laugh.

Eleanora switched her gaze to Sir Kingston as he reacted with a laugh while holding onto the pipe with the side of his mouth. "Yes, some are."

"But especially the ones that have been sold. They are good for nothing." Pearl then gulped her wine to the very last drop, and another laugh burst from her.

It was as if they were all blind, completely disregarding Eleanora's presence in the room. But Pearl knew exactly what she was doing, Eleanora could tell, and didn't have a care for her feelings.

"I'll tell you, James…" Mr Nables began, introducing a story. "We had this one servant whom we bought, and after two weeks, we had sold her again. She was a conniving little thing who never did what she was told. A stupid girl, she was. We didn't care what happened to her after that."

Pearl laughed and added, "You should have seen her face when we kicked her out, begging to stay, saying she didn't want to go where she was to be sold again. Like I said, James, they are good for nothing, those who are sold."

"Perhaps," Sir Kingston allowed and chuckled.

Eleanora had heard all that was said; their words were toxic just like the cigars they smoked and breathed in without a care. She lowered her head, her eyes filling up with unwanted tears, and went away as quickly as she possibly could.

She rushed to the kitchen and placed the plates down on the bench. She then went out before anyone could notice and hurried off to the front to exit the manor. She closed the door behind her and stood just before the first step, underneath the shelter. The rain continued to pour down, and Eleanora watched the way the water dripped off the edge before her. She began to think about all that was said as she knew they were directing their comments to her. She couldn't help the way she was feeling, and a sense of hopelessness overcame her, causing her to feel worthless. She remembered the way Sir Kingston was there, agreeing and laughing with his friends. The way he didn't defend her in any way was shameful, to say the very least.

Eleanora suddenly couldn't control her breathing any longer, as tears swelled her eyes in the same way that clouds fill with rain. She covered her mouth with her hand and leaned back hard against the wall. Then she wept as the rain accompanied her in the background. All that she had done to serve and please the master was repaid by him degrading her further and not defending her name. How cruel this was! How selfish he had turned out to be! It tortured her mind and her entire being.

She had never really had an opinion on society, for she had not seen or been accustomed to society. But they...they were the role models of society, and such a society it was. To think society could be nothing but this: a snobbish, judgemental group. A group of individuals standing at the top of the world and held up to be higher than anyone else. They were to please no one and praise nothing but the accompaniments of their fellow companions, seeming superior and all mighty against all inferiors who have no light cast upon their shadow of despair. What a world! What a society! What a wasteful shame and lack of good purpose, their actions done for no reason but to humiliate those below them.

Eleanora finally understood that her master cared nothing for her as he was one of them. This brought her spirits to their lowest point. She thought she was welcomed here. She thought she would have a changed life. But how could she when she was being referred to as "good for nothing" simply because she was a servant who had been sold? Tears streamed down her face as she thought of all this. She clutched her aching chest that heaved every time she tried to take a breath. Eleanora no longer felt the need to carry on, to live a life, always being treated poorly, without salvation at the end of it.

*

Sir Kingston left the dining room and his friends temporarily to go over to the kitchen. He opened the door and saw the servants resting. They all immediately shot up from their places. He went in and praised them. "I have come myself to congratulate you all on a splendid meal. The dessert was wonderful also. You have well pleased Mr Nables and Miss Pearl. I thank you."

He was about to exit when Dana asked, "Pardon me, master, but have you seen Nora, by any chance? The last I saw her was about fifteen minutes ago, and no one seems to know where she went."

He saw the anxious expression on her face. "I will go and have a look," he replied and then left instantly. He was about to go in search for her, when he detected the front door was slightly ajar. He went forth to shut it and heard soft cries that whispered against the rain. He opened the door and stepped outside. He immediately spotted Eleanora, who straightened herself up once Sir Kingston's presence was known to her.

He had heard the faint cries of Eleanora and now saw the wet stains on her cheeks. He observed the way her azure-blue eyes had filled with water, like the way the sea rises above the horizon. The palms of her hands flattened against the wall behind her as her fingertips sank into the small gaps between the stones. He saw the way she looked frightened, like a helpless lamb, by his presence. Eleanora was frozen on the spot; tears no longer escaped her eyes. Sir Kingston took a step closer towards her with his eyes fixed on her, examining how distraught she looked. His mouth moved as words of pity were expressed through his deep, lowered tone. "Why are you here all alone crying?" He started moving towards her slowly. He took another step forward, and her eyes watched as he did so. She didn't seem to want to respond to his question of pity.

"Nora, tell me what is going on?" he said, trying again to get her to speak.

"Why should I tell you? Why should you care?" she challenged him.

His eyes widened at the way she raised her voice at him. "Because I am your master, and so you must tell me this instant."

"I shouldn't have to explain it to you. You should know why I am like this, for you are at fault here."

"At fault?" he questioned with a puzzled look.

"Yes, you are at fault!" she confirmed loudly, trying to raise her voice over the rain. "You and those wealthy friends of yours. Did you forget that I was in the room when they started to mock me and degrade me for my rank?" She paused, glaring at him. "Did you forget the way they teased me? And the way you allowed them to continue on without defending me in any way? And you say you are a caring master to your servants. I do not believe you one bit."

Sir Kingston looked to the ground. He felt remorseful for the way they treated her and the way he did nothing to stop it. "I am sorry. I didn't realise it," he said in apology as his eyes rose to hers again.

"I do not need your apology! Nor your sympathy! They have already shamed me in the worst way possible! And with you joining them and agreeing with them…!"

"I did not agree with them!" he protested.

"Have you all no shame or consideration of my dignity, or that of any other servant, for that matter?"

Sir Kingston could hear her breathing begin to quicken with the rain. "Do you know how it feels to live a life where everyone looks down on you simply because you are a servant?" Her voice trembled as she tried her best to keep her tears hidden and her voice from breaking. "I didn't get to choose what rank I would be for the rest of my life! None of us do! And you think you are better than us, better than me, because you are wealthier and were born in a much higher class!" She paused for a short moment. "You will never know what it's like. To wish that you were never born is the most unthinkable thing you could imagine, but when all hope is lost, you realise you have nothing to live for."

Sir Kingston had indeed felt exactly that way as her words touched his past. He then felt his heart and soul fill with shame and guilt, for he hadn't realised how much their words had affected Eleanora. He watched how her tears came upon her once again, the way they dripped down her face and onto her clean, pure skin. He saw how vulnerable she looked after the courageous argument she had mounted. "Nora, I honestly can't tell you how ashamed I feel right now. Believe me, I did not intend to hurt you the way I have. It was wrong of me. I apologise on behalf of my friends as well, for they too have wronged you."

"I do not need you to apologise on behalf of them. They can speak for themselves if they want to. But I know they will not, for they are too insensitive."

"Please, Nora, come inside," he pleaded.

"I want to be alone," she muttered, looking out into the rain.

"It is cold out here; we will continue this later inside."

He went even closer to her, and she quickly stepped away, warning him, "Do not come near me. I want nothing to do with you."

"Nora!" he said, raising his voice. "Come inside! That is an order!"

He was about to take another step towards her when she cried, "I said *leave me alone*!" And then, she was off.

"Eleanora!" He cried out her full name this time.

She ran down the steps and into the rain.

Sir Kingston dashed after her. "Eleanora!" he screamed into the rain.

She turned around while she continued to run. "Leave me alone!" she cried once more, and when she turned back around, her foot slipped in the soaking dirt that had turned into mud at the top of the hill, and she began to tumble all the way down.

Sir Kingston saw this and rushed to the edge as he screamed her name in fright. He hastily skidded down the hill after her, trying to avoid the slippery mud and rocks. He reached for her where she lay, almost motionless, at the bottom of the hill. He came to her side and turned her over, first seeing a scratch that dripped with blood just above her right eyebrow.

"Oh, Eleanora!" he exclaimed in alarm. "Why would you run away from me?" he said, looking as if he were in pain himself.

Rain continued to fall onto her pale face. He stood up and removed his black cloak and placed it quickly around her shoulders. He picked her up from the wet grass and held her, one arm underneath her legs and the other holding her from the side. She wrapped her arm around his neck, securing herself to him, and rested her head on his wet chest as she tried to ease her breathing.

Sir Kingston carried Eleanora up the hill and back inside the manor. He brought her inside the kitchen. As he entered, all the servants shot up onto their feet.

"Quickly bring a chair around!" he ordered at once.

Marie brought hers, and he placed Eleanora down on it.

"Dana, go bring a dry towel and some dry clothes. Quickly now."

She headed straight out to do as she was told.

"Someone hand me a clean, damp cloth, will you?"

Jill quickly went to get one.

Tennent looked down at Eleanora and asked, "What happened?"

"She took a tumble down the hill. It is my fault she's hurt."

"Your fault?" Tennent looked over at the master.

"I will explain everything later." Sir Kingston continued to tend to Eleanora as her eyes kept shutting and opening again. Jill handed the master the damp cloth, and he instantly took it from her. He gently patted Eleanora's forehead where the scratch had tainted her fragile skin. He cleaned the wound, wiping all the blood that oozed out.

Tennent went forth to get a cup of water and placed it in her hand. "Here, drink this, Nora." She pressed the cup to her lips and drank some water before handing the cup back to Tennent.

"How are you feeling, Nora?" Sir Kingston asked.

"I am fine," was her simple reply.

Dana returned with the towel and a dress for her to change into.

"Make sure she changes into this. Look after her. I shall return soon," Sir Kingston instructed before taking his leave.

# Chapter 11

Later that night, Eleanora was situated in the drawing room, wearing her caramel-brown dress. She sat perfectly still on the sofa that was opposite the fireplace. She remained on her own, taking advantage of this silent solitude to recollect the events of that evening. Her hands were placed firmly together as she reminisced about all that had happened. She still couldn't believe the way Sir Kingston had chased after her and carried her back into the manor after her disastrous fall. The way she could almost feel the strong hold of his hands again as they wrapped around her body brought shivers down to her very knees. Even though he had done her wrong, she still felt protected when she was in his arms, and this caused her great confusion. However, she remained calm as her thoughts continued to wander in the way they always did.

Not long after, Eleanora heard the door open. She felt a presence standing there by the doorway that she knew was Sir Kingston. He didn't come right over straight away, and Eleanora could sense he was gazing at her. Eleanora decided, though, to keep her head lowered and her gaze dropped to the floor. She then heard him shut the door very quietly and step towards her, though she still hadn't the energy to even acknowledge his presence. She now felt him stand before her and heard him begin with the words, "How are you feeling, Nora?"

She remained completely still as if she were frozen into a stone statue that had been cast by Medusa herself. She then slowly raised her eyes to him and simply replied, "I am fine."

For some reason, this answer didn't seem to satisfy Sir Kingston at all. He took a step forward and kneeled down in front of her feet, which shocked her completely, for no one would ever kneel down in front of a servant.

He began saying, "I know that you are not fine. You are still very angry with me, furious even. And you have the right to be, in every way, displeased with the entire situation. But I can only tell you how truly sorry I am for not defending you the way I should have." He paused, still gazing at her.

After a pause, Eleanora stated calmly, "You didn't defend me because you have a reputation to maintain, friends to please. You simply chose them over me, which is fine because I am used to it anyway." She lowered her eyes to her hands. She was then stunned when she saw Sir Kingston suddenly place his hands on top of hers for the very first time. Eleanora's hands trembled at his touch as his fingers wrapped warmly around hers.

"I made a mistake, and I know I cannot return to the past...If only I could," he muttered softly to her. She looked up to him again as he continued, this time speaking louder. "But, by God, if I could, I would, and I would change everything that was not right about that situation."

His emerald eyes were filled with sorrow and repentance. Eleanora knew she couldn't hold onto this grudge any longer, for she wasn't the sort to do so. She knew how remorseful he was and how deeply affected he was by her sorrow. The way he had helped her after that awful tumble down the hill elevated Eleanora's opinion of him, and she was led to consider him as a caring master, after all. She took a steady breath and spoke softly, "I forgive you."

His eyes brightened, and a small smile lit his face. He gave a little chuckle. "You forgive me?" He wanted to make sure he had heard correctly.

She nodded her head and smiled at how worried he looked.

"Thank you, Eleanora." He looked down at his hands, which still held onto hers.

Eleanora felt the way her soft and fragile hands were comforted underneath his solid touch; she was beginning to delight in this moment.

Eventually, however, Sir Kingston slipped one of his hands away from hers and caressed gently the scratch that had formed on her forehead with his thumb. "Does it hurt?" he uttered.

"No, it doesn't." She paused before thanking him. "Sir, I…I want to thank you for coming after me and helping me after my fall."

"You should have seen the way you tumbled. It was very like you, being clumsy as you are," he said with a laugh.

"You are calling me clumsy?" she said in a lighter tone.

"Very much so. I still remember the way you bumped into me earlier this month. A clumsy young girl you are," he teased her with a grin.

"So, you remember that?" She still felt awkward about that small incident.

"Yes, I do," he affirmed.

In this second, Sir Kingston's eyes locked with Eleanora's, which caused a smile to erupt on her face. She felt shy yet comforted by this intense moment. She then mentioned to him, "And I should apologise to you for calling you an uncaring master, and for the way I yelled at you. It was wrong of me."

"Yes, Nora. You were way out of line when you did so." He then curled his mouth into a smile. "But I, too, was out of line."

After a long pause, he stood up from his place. "It is getting late. I suppose you want to get some sleep?"

Eleanora also rose when he said this. "Yes, I should head to my chamber now."

"Good night then, Nora." His smile seemed to fill the room.

"And good night to you, master," she returned with a smile. She made her way out of the drawing room and headed directly to her room.

*

The next morning, an hour after breakfast, Eleanora and the other servants were summoned to the Grand Hall. Upon entering, she found Mr Nables and Miss Pearl waiting in the hall and realised that they too had been called. The other servants were already there waiting on the sidelines. Eleanora felt herself become uneasy, remembering how much his two close friends had disregarded her in every way. She looked down anxiously as she could sense their eyes were fixed on her walk as she cautiously drew closer to them. She held her hands tightly together in front of her, as she always did whenever she felt overwhelmed by nerves. As Eleanora stood near the other servants, she met the eyes of Sir Kingston, who gave her the hint of a smile to ease her discomfort.

He then turned around, facing the servants first and then Mr Nables and his daughter. He began, "I have called you all down here for a very important reason. It has come to my attention that the conversation that took place at last night's dinner was unacceptable." He paused as he paced a little. "All the hurtful and prejudiced remarks that you have made against one of my servants have affected her greatly…" He then turned to his guests once again and stated, "And me." He took a breath. "I cannot allow any of my servants to be mistreated this way in any circumstances. So, I would kindly ask if you would apologise to Eleanora for all the cruel things that have shamefully come out of your mouths."

Eleanora was stunned by this, and speechless, to say the least. She had no idea that this was coming or what was to happen next. She glanced over to Mr Nables, who appeared confused and dumbfounded also. But when she eyed Pearl, on the other hand, she saw an expression of feigned innocence as Pearl pretended she had no clue what Sir Kingston was talking about.

Mr Nables stepped forward. "What is all this about, James?"

"This might be very unexpected, Rupert, but your daughter has spoken disgracefully against one of my servants. I cannot tolerate this, Rupert. I won't."

"I didn't say anything that was hurtful, James. You know I never would." It was obvious to Eleanora that Pearl was trying to play the victim.

"Pearl, you may have said those things without thinking. But you still owe an apology," said Sir Kingston firmly.

"How could you do this, and in front of all your servants, James? Pearl just lets anything slip from her tongue. She didn't mean it," protested Mr Nables, speaking on his daughter's behalf.

"Then next time, she should learn to control her tongue!" Sir Kingston's voice echoed throughout the room. "And you yourself, Rupert, should know better than this, for you had some part in it too." He paused. "My servants deserve to know what is happening since they were all besmirched."

"If that is what you want, James, then I shall apologise." Pearl went up and stood in front of Eleanora, who lifted her eyes and saw how Pearl's chestnut-brown eyes had darkened to almost black and her nose pointed in a superior manner. "I am sorry for the remarks I made yesterday that offended you. It shall never happen again."

Eleanora nodded her head, her mouth too tightly closed to even inhale.

Pearl flicked her body to the side, holding onto the edge of her gown, and walked back to her father's side. Mr Nables then apologised from where he was standing.

"I hope this will never happen again, to any of my servants," Sir Kingston finished. "You may all continue with what you were doing," he then concluded and was away at a fast pace.

The servants looked amongst themselves and then at Eleanora, who remained quiet and still. Then they all headed back to their posts, and Eleanora followed behind them.

\*

Mr Nables and Miss Pearl stayed behind. Pearl was frustrated, and she could see her father was most shocked and embarrassed by what had just occurred.

"How could you humiliate us like that? Do you know what you have done? You have created a negative impression in James' head. How do you think you are going to have any chance of marrying him if you keep behaving this way?"

"It is not my fault that stupid servant girl blabbed everything to him. I meant every word of what I said last night, and if her feelings were affected by this, then too bad," Pearl said vehemently, her eyes afire.

"But it was her feelings Sir Kingston cared about, not yours," her father stated. "How could you be so careless!" he muttered. "I'm telling you one last time, Pearl," he warned. "Do not lose your chances of being with James. Not for any servant and especially not for that worthless girl!"

"I hear you, Father, and I will do everything in my power to make James mine," Pearl reassured him, determined to make that happen and let no one stand in her way.

"Excellent," he said, and a wide grin formed on his wrinkled face. "Do what you must. Woo him and make him chase after you."

Pearl smiled, thinking of all the ways she could do exactly that.

*

All the servants were seen gathered together in the common room as Eleanora walked in. The women rushed to her, asking many questions regarding what had just occurred.

"Nora, can you believe what just happened?" Jill jumped to her first.

"No, I cannot." Eleanora was still baffled by it all.

"It was right of the master to do what he did. And in front of everyone; even Dashier was there to see all." Dana then mentioned, "The master told us all last night what had happened."

"He told you?" Eleanora gasped.

"I don't think he told us everything. Just that Miss Pearl was saying some nasty things. Shameful is the right word to describe it, just as Sir Kingston did. He always cares for us – a real master he truly is."

"Yes, he is indeed," Eleanora muttered to herself.

"You should have seen the look on that Pearl's face, though. I wanted to burst into laughter the way her eyes narrowed like a scheming witch," Marie spoke wildly.

"So did I," Jill agreed with a laugh.

"What about the way her father reacted; his jaw dropped right to the very floor," Tennent now interjected. He then walked up to Eleanora and said, "But I'm glad they apologised for the way they hurt you, Nora."

She smiled at him.

"But was it genuine?" Marie remarked, looking at the others. "I know Pearl, and she is not an easy woman. She is very spoilt by her father, and all she's ever done is speak poorly of others lower than herself. I still cannot comprehend why the master would keep them around here. Why is he friends with people like them?"

Dana then answered, "I am not saying I disagree with you, Marie, but Mr Nables was the legal guardian of the master ever since he was a little boy and his father died. Sir Kingston must think that he owes him his life for all those years he took care of him."

"Well, that Mr Nables gives me the creeps," Marie pointed out.

"Let us not talk in that way about them anymore. The master would make us apologise to them if they were to ever hear us talk in such a way. And that would be embarrassing."

Everyone took heed of Dana and were off to complete their tasks for that morning.

*

Eleanora sat by the fountain at the front, waving her hand gracefully underneath the cool, clear water. She hummed to herself quietly as she continued to allow her fingers to run through the pond of water. She heard the sprinkling of the water filtered out from the monument at the centre of the fountain. After some time being alone there, she heard some footsteps approaching. She turned around, her hand still dipped in the refreshing water. It was the master who was coming her way.

"Good afternoon, master." She squinted her eyes in the bright sunlight.

He came by her and replied the same. He then asked, "What are you doing here?"

"I wanted to have a feel of this water." She looked down as she continued to wave her hand around. "It feels so nice and calming as it washes in between my fingers." She then looked back up at him and noticed that he was looking at her strangely. A small smile formed on his lips.

"By the way, I wanted to thank you for what you did earlier. But you didn't need to force them to apologise."

He took a seat by her on the stone bricks that formed the circular wall of the fountain. "You deserved an apology; was I wrong about that?" he questioned her. His eyes were narrower than usual, making it harder to see his emerald eyes.

She took her hand away from the pond and dried it on her apron while saying, "No, you weren't wrong. It's just, if they were really sincere about it, they would have had the heart to admit their wrongdoings. If they had a conscience, they would have known that an instant apology was in order. But I guess they didn't feel guilty about it at all." She gazed at him, watching how his eyes looked into hers. She spoke again, "I do not wish to mention any

more about this. But know that I am grateful for what you did."
She swiftly rose and added, "I must go now." She left him there
and went back to the manor. She turned around for a moment and
saw that he had put his hand into the water of the fountain.

# Chapter 12

A week passed, and Mr Nables and Miss Pearl were still lodging in Kingston Manor. All was well, for now. It wasn't known how long they would be staying with Sir Kingston or if they were to leave at all. Eleanora noticed the way Miss Pearl had been spending most of her time around him, trying to make up for what she had done by being on her best behaviour. Eleanora thought it was all part of her scheme, the way she followed him everywhere like a lap dog. He, too, began to act in a different way around her – making jokes with her, laughing and accompanying her wherever she needed to be.

Friday morning arrived. While completing her early chores, Eleanora noticed the manor was in a quiet state. There was a deathly silence; no one spoke, no sound was heard, and everything appeared flat. She headed to the kitchen with a bucket filled with clean water that she had drawn from the well. Dana had her head down and was focusing on her work in a sombre manner. Eleanora knew this was not like Dana at all. She went around the bench and asked, "Is everything all right, Dana?"

Dana popped her head up, and her spectacles fell to her chest, saved by the attachment of strings. "Oh yes, everything is fine," she quickly responded, placing the glasses back onto the bridge of her nose.

Eleanora didn't believe her and wondered what had kept her quiet and so focused all of a sudden. She then asked something else, "Why wasn't the master at breakfast this morning? Did he have other plans?"

Dana looked up at Eleanora and brought a small smile to her face. She then replied, "The master wants to be left alone for today and have no one disturb him."

This sounded very strange to Eleanora. She further asked, "Why does he want to be alone?"

"It's just…it's not a good day today."

Eleanora knew Dana was hiding something from her. "Do you not trust me, Dana?"

Dana stopped what she was doing, placed her kitchen tools down, and said, "Of course I trust you, dear."

"Then tell me, why does the manor have some sort of strange mood today? The whole atmosphere feels like it has changed all of a sudden, ever since I woke up."

Dana pursed her lips together for a moment. She took a calm breath before explaining. "Nora, the master wants to be alone today because…" She paused for a second, looking pale. "Because today is the anniversary of his father's death. It's been twenty-two years since. The master still has a hard time dealing with it all."

Eleanora could sense that Dana was still keeping some secrets from the way her light-brown eyes twinkled when she looked at Eleanora. But she didn't further question it, for she thought it wouldn't be right to put her nose into business she was not supposed to know.

Dana then added, "That is why things around here are a little duller than usual. Everyone is just doing their work for today. But Mr Nables and his daughter left soon after breakfast."

"They're gone?" Eleanora asked hopefully.

"Oh no, dear," Dana said with a chuckle. "Only to go into town. They will be back in the evening, no doubt."

"Oh," Eleanora said with a sigh. "Well, is there anything we can do for the master to cheer him up?"

"No, there is nothing. It's best that we leave him alone unless something urgent needs to be brought to his attention."

"Very well then. I guess I should get back to work."

"Take a break soon, Nora," Dana suggested.

Eleanora nodded her head and left.

*

111

Just before noon struck, Eleanora took a break after all the cleaning she had just finished. Being fatigued, she decided to get some fresh air and climbed the stairs that led onto the rooftop. When she was there, she walked towards one side to take a glance at that breathtaking view that always seemed to calm her spirits. Upon doing so, a puff of smoke drifted past her nose, and the smell of tobacco tainted the fresh air. She turned to see where it was coming from and spotted Sir Kingston, who was looking out thoughtfully into the distance at the land surrounding the estate.

"Master?" Eleanora called softly, and he turned around as if frightened.

"Eleanora?" He tried to calm his breathing as he put his hand to his chest. "You startled me."

"I'm sorry. I didn't mean to." She stepped closer to him.

Eleanora watched as Sir Kingston placed his pipe back into his mouth and returned his gaze to the land. She decided to take a few more steps and stood by his side, still leaving a gap between them. "I hope everything is well with you?" she then asked, breaking the silence.

"I assume you were informed what today marks?"

"Yes. I was told it is the anniversary of your father's death."

He didn't say anything at first, but when he did, he faced her and said in his deep tone of voice, "So you came up here to pity me!"

She saw the way his eyes were like stained glass, delicate and complex. She had never seen him this way before and never thought she ever would. "I came because I wanted to rest up here after I finished my cleaning duties. I didn't know you would also be here."

He glanced at her once more before returning his focus to the distance.

Eleanora didn't know what to do and thought perhaps he wanted to be left alone. "I should leave you on your own," she muttered into the cool air and was about to go when he stopped her.

"Don't go," he told her.

She waited, and he urged, "Please, stay."

She noticed the way his eyes pleaded with hers, almost begging for some company on this miserable day. Eleanora bit her bottom lip nervously and resumed her place. "Tell me about your father. What was he like?"

Sir Kingston took a deep breath, his shoulders rising and then slowly falling again. He began to explain, "My father was a good man...more than I, believe it or not. He was a successful businessman who worked hard for everything I now own. Without him...I would not be as wealthy as I am today." He took another breath and then exhaled hard. "But I don't deserve it..." He then faced Eleanora. "Any of it." He seemed furious with himself.

Eleanora was aware that something was bothering him...and perhaps had been upsetting him for all of these years. She wondered if it had anything to do with that scar that tainted the side of his face.

"There is something that happened years ago on this very day," he said, lowering his voice.

Eleanora perceived that he was about to reveal a past secret, one that seemed to be eating him alive. She gazed at him with warmth and open ears, hoping to give him the confidence to continue revealing the tragic story.

"Eleanora," he puffed, "there is something you do not know about me, about my sinful past."

The way he spoke caused Eleanora's body to shiver all over. She didn't know what he had done in the past, but she felt very apprehensive about what it might be.

She saw the way Sir Kingston struggled to take a breath before releasing it back into the air around him. He then began telling his story. "Twenty-two years ago, when I was just a little lad, seven years of age, I did something that I will have to live with for the rest of my life, until the day I take it to my grave. I regret the very damn day," he cursed.

He looked down at himself and cleared his throat. "Mr Nables had visited the manor for some reason I do not know. On that afternoon, it was pouring with rain. A thunderclap or two rang out across the land as a storm approached. I was sitting in the drawing room waiting for my father, who, at the time, was speaking to him about some matter, perhaps business. Mr Nables found me afterwards and gave me something that caught my interest. It was a pistol. I don't know what kind it was, but the handle was short, and the barrel was longer than my finger. He gave it to me just like that; he must've forgotten that the bullets remained inside. He thought he could trust me since I begged that I was old enough to handle a gun. I was fascinated by it, especially the charcoal-black colour of it. He went away, leaving the gun in my hands. Shortly after, my father entered the room coming from another room that was connected to the drawing room. I knew not to pull the trigger, not wanting to accidentally shoot something. I was swinging the weapon around, however, trying to learn some new tricks. As I was doing so, while my father was placing some paperwork onto the table by the window, I..."

Eleanora observed he couldn't speak the words; his eyes were unfocused and he seemed frozen in time as he reflected on the incident. She then realised that Sir Kingston was now looking at her, and her eyes grew large and her mouth was ready to open in shock as she trembled, for she felt terrified.

"Eleanora, I...I heard a gunshot even with the rain roaring wildly outside. The gunshot still echoed and continues to echo to this very day, ringing inside my ears, and it will haunt me for the rest of my life. There was my father, shot in the back, with a bullet that had gone straight through to his chest, by my own doing."

She automatically covered her mouth with her hand, so shocked that she couldn't think or even say a word. Sir Kingston went on, and he appeared to be taken back to the very year the tragedy occurred. "I still remember the very expression he made when he turned around. His eyes grew with the realisation that he was shot; his mouth was opened as if to speak, but instead, blood poured down bitterly to the floor; his body was still, and his hands were shaking incredibly. The last image he saw, his final memory, was of me and my terrified expression upon seeing this."

He took a moment to try to control his breathing. However, it didn't seem to work. He then placed his hand on his forehead and squeezed hard. His voice shook as he relived the moment. "I thought at the time that I didn't pull the trigger. I thought for sure it couldn't have been me, for I didn't feel anything pull away from my gun. But I was a child; what would I know? I pulled the trigger by accident and shot my own father. I murdered him. I murdered him and sent him to his grave. I was the one to blame for this. It was I who committed the deadly sin, the murderous act, with horrifying consequences no child should ever have to face. I…am a sinner!" Beads of sweat formed on his forehead and leaked down his pale face.

Eleanora saw how broken he was, the way he struggled to breathe and keep himself in control.

Eleanora took a couple of steps back, her heart racing, her instincts urging her to run away from this man who confessed to being a murderer. She didn't know what he might do if he weren't in the right state of mind.

"Are you afraid of me now?" he asked, noticing the way she stepped away from him. "You are not petrified of me now, are you, Nora?"

Eleanora swallowed hard, still feeling afraid. But for some reason, when she focused on his eyes, she only found a scared little boy trapped within his own dreadful past. She stepped towards him, coming closer this time; his eyes were bewildered by her move and softened as she came to him. "I do not believe you could have murdered your father. I won't believe that." Even she was stunned by her words, but she only spoke earnestly from the heart.

"It doesn't matter what you believe because I know I am the one who pulled that trigger. It was me."

115

"How did you get that scar?" she then asked, examining it more closely.

He sighed and looked down. "Mr Nables came rushing into the drawing room, where he found me there holding the gun in shock. He saw my father on the ground with a bullet hole that went through his back and to his chest and the blood oozing and forming a puddle. He was also in the greatest of shock. After the doctor was called and everything was cleaned up, Mr Nables came to me and scorned me. It was the worst day of my life. To teach me a lesson, he took out his pocket knife, and he held the sharp end of the blade near my left eye and dug the point all the way down to the end of my mouth. He used the knife to cut my skin, which has now formed this scar on my face. He told me that this scar would be a reminder of the act I had committed. That every time I look at this scar, it will remind me of the very day when I murdered my father." He took a breath. "This scar will forever torment me, taint not only my face but my very soul forever, which remains dark even now."

Eleanora almost felt a knife was digging into her heart as she learned the real truth of this cruel secret. She couldn't believe that Mr Nables had given this scar to him as a reminder of his father's death. She couldn't believe how cruel he was to do this to an innocent child who had accidentally made the worst mistake he ever could in his life. "I am so sorry." Her eyes swelled with tears. "Sir, I...I am truly sorry for what you had to go through. That is dreadful indeed."

"If you want to leave this place, leave me, I will understand. I will not prevent you from going."

"I won't leave you," she told him. "I promise I won't, and I never will."

Eleanora witnessed a small smile fill his saddened face after hearing those reassuring words come from her mouth. Eleanora looked out into the distance. She took a breath as she thought about the origin of his scar. She felt honoured that he had seen fit to trust her, especially with a secret as deep as this, but she also felt deep compassion for him. A tragedy it was…a terrible and complete accident. "What happened after that, if you do not mind me asking?"

He exhaled deeply. "Mr Nables told the doctor that my father had committed suicide by shooting himself in the chest, just so I wouldn't be taken away. It was hard to believe at first, but Rupert did everything he could to make them believe. See, the bullet entered from his back and went straight through to his chest, but he told them that the bullet was fired to the chest and plunged its way out of his back. The lawyer came and opened my father's will, which stated that I would receive all his wealth and possessions. Everything that he owned was to belong to me, his only son. I felt so guilty about all this. It also stated that Mr Nables would be my guardian until I was twenty-one years, and that he would take care of all the business affairs until then. He was also given a great sum of money by my father's will."

He paused and resumed after taking another breath. "Everyone else, including business partners and friends, was told that he died that way, a suicide. We didn't want anyone to suspect anything at all. Mr Nables covered it up in order to protect me, knowing I was the beloved son. He helped me in a way. But I have allowed my father's death to shame him while it should be me who is shamed and judged by others. No one would have expected him to have committed the act because he had everything in life going for him. So rumours began across the whole town and villages, saying that he was still depressed over his deceased wife, some saying it was because of me, and others were speculating it was work-related. The only people who know the truth are Dashier and Dana, for they were there at the time, and her husband, Tennent, as no secrets are kept amongst them. Of course, Mr Nables knows, but not Pearl. And now you." He looked carefully into her eyes.

"Your secret is safe with me," she muttered to him. "But I have this feeling that there is more to this story than what you describe. I am not saying you are hiding something from me, but for some reason, though this incident was accidental, I believe there is another involved, making it a crime. That you shouldn't have been the one held responsible. I will do whatever it takes to uncover the truth."

"No, Nora. Please. Do not investigate anything. They are not affairs you should associate yourself with. You must leave it. All is in the past, and nothing will change."

She sighed at his reaction. He, too, sighed and said, "I just don't want to see you put yourself in unnecessary danger. Understood?"

She nodded, her head obeying him. She then spoke her thoughts aloud, "I just don't understand why Mr Nables would leave his loaded gun in the hands of a child."

"If he knew the bullets were there in the first place. He probably thought he could trust me," Sir Kingston said. "But with the curious and easily tempted mind I had, I just couldn't help myself." He damned himself again, after which there was more silence.

After a short moment, Eleanora then changed the subject. "Do you smoke as a habit, for pleasure, or is it as a way of escaping…to calm yourself?"

Sir Kingston looked down at his pipe, which he held in between his two fingers. "I guess I do use it to calm myself down. It soothes me and helps me to control myself, especially at a time like this."

"Smoking shouldn't be the answer to that," she stated. His questioning expression caused her to continue. "You shouldn't need to smoke to chase all your worries and feelings away."

"I have been smoking for most of my life now," he made known.

"Yes, and you seem to use it as an escape."

"Are you trying to order me not to smoke?"

Eleanora saw the way he looked at her oddly with a little smirk lurking between his lips. "Not order, for I believe that is your job, master, but to persuade you perhaps that this is not the answer to your problems," she told him with concern.

He took another deep breath after listening to this.

"I should be on my way now." He paused. "Thank you for listening, and I hope this hasn't changed your judgement of me."

"It could never," she replied.

\*

Early that afternoon, Eleanora was passing by the master's chamber. As she was doing so, she decided she would go inside his bedroom for a reason even she didn't understand. When she stood before the tall door, she wondered if she should check up on him, for she hadn't heard a peep out of him let alone seen him since he revealed the dark story of his past to her. She knew she was supposed to leave the master alone for today, but something inside her was willing her to open that door. A strange feeling compelled her to do so. After a couple of moments of hesitation, she retraced her steps, about to leave and forget the idea. But when she observed that there were pools of liquid trailing along the floor and leading up to his door, which was left slightly open, she knew she had to investigate. Eleanora wondered what these spills were. She knew it wasn't blood, for it was much lighter in colour and a thinner consistency. She opened the door slightly with a little hesitation. But she knew that something must be wrong, so in wasting no time, she opened the door wider.

Empty. The bedroom was empty. His bed was all messed up, with maroon and white sheets all crinkled up. Some drawers were left open in a dresser by the window on the right. Eleanora entered and went down the two steps. She looked around anxiously as she tried to observe anything else that was out of the ordinary. While doing so, she scanned her eyes to the master's bathroom on her left. The door to the room was also left slightly ajar, which convinced her to take a look to see if anyone was in there. She stepped quietly, moving on her feet as lightly as she could. When she reached the door, she took a peek inside. She first spotted a clean, white bathtub with a golden pattern detailing around the edges.

Taking a closer look at the whole scene, she gasped, her hand covering her mouth when she saw something that frightened her stiff. She froze for a second before she hastily opened the door wide. She saw Sir Kingston's hand sticking out of the bathtub and barely holding onto an empty bottle that had '*brandy*' inscribed on it. She observed the way his arm was flung over the rim of the tub and the way his fingers curled loosely around the bottle, which appeared to be slipping. Eleanora gasped as greater shock overwhelmed her. "Master!"

She hurried to him and looked down into the bathtub, which was filled with water right up to the rim. The water looked like it had been sitting there for a while as the soap had almost disintegrated. When Eleanora realised his head was sinking into the water, she cried out, "Sir Kingston!" She swiftly removed the bottle from his frail grip and put her hands into the cool water. She reached for his shoulders and back, pulling him up above the surface. His head rose from the pool of water yet it was bent as his chin pressed down onto his upper chest. His raven-black hair was tousled and dripping with water that fell back down onto his bare skin. Eleanora realised he was completely naked. She tried to hold his body up, but she struggled under his weight. She placed each of his arms to rest over the rim of the tub while she quickly brought a towel over. She tried to pull his body up, but she only managed to retrieve his upper body with all the strength she had. She knew she wouldn't be able to pull him out alone, so she desperately tried calling out for anybody to come and help her.

"IS ANYBODY THERE?! PLEASE, THE MASTER NEEDS HELP!" she yelled as loud as she could, but there was no hope. She knew she had no time, so with all her might, she pulled his body out of the tub and slipped him to the floor. She covered the lower part of his naked self with the towel, wrapping it around him frantically. She quickly ran to the door and yelled out again. "DANA?! DASHIER?! ANYONE?! I NEED HELP!"

No one responded; the manor seemed forsaken. She rushed back to the master, falling down to her knees while panting excessively from the strain of carrying him and all the stress she was under. She began to rock his body from side to side to try to wake him, but it was no use. She then noticed that his body reeked of alcohol. Eleanora was beginning to panic, not entirely sure what she should do, for she had never had to confront this kind of situation before. "Please, sir, wake up!" she cried as beads of sweat ran down the sides of her face and neck. She ran back to the door, trying to find help one last time, but no one was in sight. She dashed straight to Sir Kingston, knowing she must save him while she still could. The idea that she might lose him was now placed in her mind, and it scared her completely.

Without any more delay, she did the next thing that came into her mind as a kind of instinctive act. She brought her mouth onto his and pressed her lips down while feeling how cold they were. She exhaled her air by breathing into his mouth, hoping this would awaken him.

She released herself from him, wondering if what she had done was the right move. "Come on, sir!" she mumbled desperately. "Oh God, please wake up!" she cried.

After giving all she had, his mouth opened and gurgles of water that he had swallowed came shooting out. He then gasped loudly as he began taking large gulps of air. Her heart beat quickly with exhilaration

"Oh my goodness," she whispered as a tear slithered down her puffed-out cheek. She left him there and searched for help until she spotted someone outside the Grand Hall. She yelled in desperation, "COME QUICKLY! IT'S THE MASTER!" She then saw that person was Dana, who rushed up the stairs while holding onto her dress. "HURRY!"

Eleanora led her into the master's room at once, and there, lying on the cold, hard floor, was Sir Kingston, wet and naked apart from the towel wrapped around him.

"OH MY WORD!" Dana screamed. "MASTER!" She rushed to him in alarm.

"Sir King…ston was not a…awake while in the bathtub," Eleanora began to explain, stumbling over her words.

Dana checked on the master.

"I called for help, but no one came to my aid. I realised there was no time to lose, so I…I helped him, and now he is awake again."

"You saved his life!" Dana stated as she faced Eleanora. Eleanora kept quiet.

"Quickly, Nora, go and tell Dashier at once to fetch the physician. And send Marie up here now," Dana urgently instructed.

Eleanora rushed out of the room, and her feet tumbled so chaotically down the stairs she almost fell. She came across Dashier, who had just entered by the front door. She briefly explained what happened and told him that a doctor was needed at once. She then ran outside to find Marie. She saw her by the well and told her she was needed upstairs immediately.

Eleanora made her way over to the fountain in the front courtyard. She almost fell, catching the edge for support as she tried to calm her breathing. She clutched onto her chest and looked up to the sky before washing her face with the water from the fountain to cool her down after all the anxiety and pressure she had to endure alone.

*

Eleanora waited by the fountain until the physician arrived. He was a tall gentleman who sped past in his haste to get to Sir Kingston. Eleanora was still feeling distressed and only hoped that the master would recover after the horrifying event that had taken place. She didn't know exactly how this had all come about, but the presence of the brandy led her to think that he had drowned himself while drunk. She never expected the master to be a drinker, but she believed this was a form of escape from his wicked past, just like the smoking. And considering what today marked for him, the memories of the past could possibly have been the cause of his near-death incident.

After a while of frantically waiting by the fountain, Eleanora was finally visited by Dana. She felt relieved to see a relaxed look on Dana's face.

"Eleanora, dear," said Dana, calling her by her full name this time.

Eleanora quickly asked, "How is the master? What did the doctor say?"

"The master will be well in good time, thanks to you."

Eleanora took a deep and steady breath.

"The doctor said he just needs to rest in bed for the rest of the day, especially after he was somewhat unconscious for quite a while and hardly breathing. He must regain his energy before he is up and about."

"Oh, thank heavens! That's wonderful news!" Eleanora exclaimed, elated to hear this. Her frayed nerves and pounding heart soon settled.

"Nora, I would like to ask, however, what happened exactly? How did you save the master? I must report back about it to the doctor, for he needs to know the full story to understand how this came about."

Eleanora recounted everything from the time she found Sir Kingston in his bathtub to the time he took his first breath again.

Dana was shocked. Her eyes widened, and she also expressed her apology to Eleanora for her having to save the master on her own without any help. "I am dreadfully sorry no other person was there to help. The one time when we are not inside, this occurs." She heaved a heavy sigh. "The main thing, however, is that he is awake. Nora, thank you again. You did all that you had to do, and you did it under a huge amount of pressure. No wonder you looked so stressed when I finally came.

But I must admit you handled yourself and the situation pretty well for a young girl like you."

"Thank you, Dana," Eleanora said with a heartened smile.

"Now, I must head back over to the master's chamber and tell the doctor all about what happened…in detail this time."

Eleanora watched as Dana headed off as quickly as her feet could take her.

Some moments time passed, and Eleanora returned inside. As she did, she found Dashier making his way down the stairs. He announced, "The doctor wishes to see you, Nora."

"Me?" Eleanora questioned, not expecting this.

Dashier nodded his head, "Yes, in Sir Kingston's chamber, if you please."

She went right up the stairs and took a left turn into the corridor. She made herself present in the open doorway of his bedroom.

"Come in, Nora," Dana said with a smile.

Eleanora stepped forth and made her way to just below the second step. Her eyes focused on Sir Kingston, who lay in a semi-upright position on his enormous bed with his shoulders and back comfortably relaxing against the pillow that was placed up against the bed frame. White and maroon bedsheets covered him up to his ribs. She noticed his gaze now fell upon her. She couldn't seem to move her eyes away, however, until she was spoken to.

The doctor spoke first. "You must be Eleanora! I'm Dr Marton."

"Nice to meet you, Dr Marton," she answered softly. Her eyes now paid attention to the tall figure before her. He was dressed formally as any other physician should be, and his brown hair was streaked with grey and combed neatly to the side. Eleanora noticed the way he inspected her with those small brown eyes of his behind the rounded glasses he wore.

"Well, Eleanora, I've heard you did a brave thing earlier today. And you are so young and inexperienced." The doctor then gazed at Sir Kingston as he stated, "You have a loyal servant, I must say. You are very lucky." He returned his gaze to Eleanora. "You, my dear, have saved this man's life!" he proclaimed. "For if it weren't for you, your master would not have lasted, I dare say."

"I did what any other servant would do for their master," was her reply.

He smiled at her. He then focused back on Sir Kingston. "You are very lucky to be alive, James. Please be cautious, especially when in the possession of alcohol." He then turned to Dana and advised, "Make sure he doesn't move from this bed until tomorrow. Let him rest and have a good meal before he sleeps tonight." Dana nodded. "I shall be back in the morning to make sure all is well." He walked over to Eleanora. "Well, thank you, Eleanora." She responded with a little curtsey. He then turned around to Sir Kingston. "Have a good afternoon and please rest easy." He held onto his brown briefcase, which was the same shade as his eyes, and gave a little nod to Eleanora in farewell before leaving the room.

All was silent. Sir Kingston managed to speak in his usual tone, "You may leave now, Dana." She lowered her head to him and was heading off when he then added, "Eleanora, you will stay." Eleanora was now left alone in the room with Sir Kingston.

"Come closer, Eleanora," he directed.

She took a few steps forward.

"Come right by my bedside."

She went over to him, the front of her dress slightly touching the side of his bed. As she was closer now, she was able to observe how bloodshot his eyes were. His face was still pale, but it was much improved from the shade it was before. His scar shone, glistening against his left side. Her eyes scanned down to his chest, which was exposed, and she saw the sweat on his fine hairs. Eleanora had never seen a man's naked body before today and this situation that had left her with no choice but to. However, it wasn't until now that she really looked at the way he was sculptured; he had a well-built body that caused her to examine him for longer than she should.

Realising the way she was staring at him, she quickly looked back into his eyes, seeing if he had noticed that her gaze was elsewhere. And when she did look back at him, a smirk formed on his face, which made her shy away and blush like never before. She found herself deep in embarrassing misery due to this.

"I'm guessing you have never seen a man's flesh before, let alone a naked body?"

She shook her head slowly, her eyes desperately wanting to free themselves from his intense gaze.

"Well, that's because you haven't lived here long enough," he said with a chuckle. "You are only young, after all," he reiterated.

She brought her eyes down to the floor, feeling ashamed of herself.

He gave a sigh and changed the subject. "There is something I told you the very first time you came to Kingston Manor. Do you remember?"

Her eyes looked up to his once more as she replied, "And what could that be?"

A smile formed on his lips as he looked down to his sheets. "I told you that you must prove your loyalty to me in some way, so that I may trust you." He lifted his eyes back to her, the emerald green lighting up. "You have proven to me just exactly that," he said slowly before returning to his normal speaking pace. "That I can trust you in every way possible. That I should always have faith in you. And I know that you will never displease me. I trusted you before when I revealed my secret to you, but now you have confirmed my judgement."

To Eleanora's astonishment, Sir Kingston then took her by the hand without taking his eyes off her. His eyes glowed in gratitude as he thanked and beheld his rescuer. When Eleanora felt the sudden touch of her master's hand placed on hers, her heart beat within her like a drum. She stared into his eyes, and seeing the gratification expressed through them touched her heart. When she felt his fingers curl around hers as if they were perfectly made to link, she looked down at his hand. Eleanora felt exhilarated yet terrified all at the same time.

"I want to thank you from the bottom of my heart for saving me. You came, and then you rescued. And that is something I will never forget for as long as I live."

After a moment's silence, Eleanora replied, "I am just glad that you are well now. For I couldn't bear it if you were to leave this world. You are the only master I can ever trust in. I would be heartbroken if you were to leave me now."

"I promise that I never will," was his promise to her.

Eleanora witnessed the certain way Sir Kingston gazed at her in special delight. It made her cheeks burn with incredible heat. She bit down on her bottom lip, a nervous habit of hers. She then said, "I shall go and open up the windows to freshen the room." She slipped her hand away from his and went over to do just that. She came back to his side and said, "It's best I leave you to get some rest now."

His eyes shot up to her. "Would you stay a little while? I am not tired now, and I don't want to be left bored and alone."

"Of course," was her reply. She then said, "I have a question to ask you, sir."

"Is it about what happened to me?"

"Yes, but please tell me, what were you thinking to drink so much in the first place? Does this have something to do with your father's death and the great impact it has had on you?" she asked, looking worried.

Sir Kingston sighed. "Yes, well, every year on this day, I grieve over my father's death this way. Do not ask me why. I just do. I feel weak and helpless when this day comes."

Eleanora didn't allow his secret and the way he behaved to alter her perception of him. She understood why he did this, but she only wished he wouldn't act in such a reckless way. For he could have been hurt today, or worse.

"I just wish you would look after yourself a little more. I was afraid, seeing you the way you were."

He sighed again. "I understand what I put you through was torture. Please forgive me. I will try not to indulge in that sort of behaviour again."

Eleanora was relieved by this.

He then looked at her with a smile.

"You must have been really strong to have pulled my body out of that bathtub, I shall say."

"It was rather difficult," she said earnestly. She then explained, "But determination brought strength to me and willed me to do what I had to do."

Now, a grin formed on his lips as he said, "So, I heard that you had to give me mouth-to-mouth in order to get oxygen inside me." She hastily lowered her eyelids down to her hands. "It's nothing to be ashamed of, Nora." He then said, "How did you feel when you pressed your mouth onto mine?"

Eleanora knew that he was provoking her with this question. "How did I feel?" She did not know how to answer.

He sat up a little more with the use of his elbows. "Yes. How did you feel?"

"I…err…"

"Well, did you enjoy it?"

"Enjoy it?" was her timid reply as she tried to avoid answering his silly questions.

"When you touched my lips with yours, it was almost as if you were kissing me."

"It happened all too quickly. There was nothing else I could do but put my mouth on yours," Eleanora said at last in answer to this awkward question.

He laughed for a long time.

Eleanora was beginning to feel uncomfortable with the way he continued to tease her so.

"Nora, I am just teasing you, you know that?"

She looked at him oddly, and he explained, "I understand that was the last option you had. And if it was to save my life, then you shouldn't feel shy about it but proud instead."

"I guess you're right," she muttered. She then looked over to his mouth, seeing his lips, thin and pale as they always were. She looked away, removing her gaze from him. "I should leave you to yourself now. I mustn't keep you entertained any longer, especially in your condition." She waited for a response, but he didn't give her one. "Is there anything you need me to do before I go?"

He shook his head.

"Goodbye, then, sir, and rest well."

He nodded his head once again to signal to her that she could go.

Eleanora left the room in an uneasy state. She stopped not far from the door and leaned on her arm against the wall. She held onto her neck, wrapping her hand around it as if she were choking herself. A tear ran down her cheek for a reason she did not understand. Her heart pounded heavily as she remembered the way he looked while she was saving him. Her vision then shifted to how he looked at her, especially when the touch of his hand caused her to tremble beneath his touch. She didn't know what was happening to her or why she felt the need to cry some more. A few more tears ran down her face before she swiftly wiped them away and headed back downstairs.

*

Later that evening, Eleanora found Sir Kingston up and about as he glided down the main stairs. She caught up to him and stated in a concerned manner, "Master, you know you are supposed to be resting."

He continued to walk while Eleanora followed by his side. "I don't need to rest anymore; I am feeling much better. You know they always say that walking it off is the best medicine."

Eleanora tried to walk at his pace as he was making his way quickly to the front door.

"Yes, but the doctor said…"

And before she could persuade him any further, he stopped and turned around to face her before saying, "Don't worry about what the doctor said, Nora."

Eleanora thought that he was being very stubborn.

He then stated firmly, "I do not want Mr Nables or Miss Pearl to know what happened earlier. Their trip into town has banished them from ever learning of the incident that occurred. So, please, speak no more of this."

"Yes, master." She lowered her head down, obeying him at once.

"Good." He turned around as Dashier opened the front door.

Eleanora sighed and remained in the doorway.

"Oh, James! Look at all the things we bought today!" Pearl exclaimed.

Sir Kingston walked to the carriage. "That is an awful lot," he said and began helping her carry the ones she could not.

"How are you, James?" Mr Nables asked.

"I am doing well surprisingly. Why don't you two come in, and you can show me all the things you've bought."

They went into the Grand Hall, where the bags and packages were placed on the floor. Dana as well as Jill and Marie, alongside Eleanora, watched from the background as Pearl eagerly opened all she had bought to dazzle Sir Kingston.

"Look at this pretty dress I bought from one of the gown stores." She held it up in the air as the dress rolled down, and then waved it around, showcasing its style and brilliance. "Do you like it, James?"

"Very much," he said and smiled, touching the dress from the bottom hem. The sparkly peach-coloured dress ran down naturally to the waist, where it then spread out across, making it wider at the sides as it came flowing down. When she turned it around, the back of the dress showed a big bow that was displayed prominently as the centre of attention. This came along with smaller-sized bows that were stitched at the top of each sleeve.

"Ugh! That's the ugliest dress I have ever seen," Jill muttered to the others.

Marie spoke next. "I agree...all the bows and everything. It's just too much. She is so spoiled, that girl," she then added.

Pearl pulled out a wrapped box. "This one I picked out for you. I hope you like it, James." She handed him a boxed present tied in a ribbon bow.

"I hope it is not a dress," he said, and they all chuckled at his joke. He untied the ribbon and tossed it to the floor carelessly. He unwrapped the paper and opened the lid of the box. He took the object out and held it in front of him.

"Oh, do you like it, James? I picked the best one for you!"

"A handheld telescope! It is incredible indeed!" He then laughed and said, "Thank you, Pearl, but it isn't my birthday, you know!"

"I can still give you a gift whether it is your birthday or not, James." Her eyes lit up, and she seemed very satisfied with herself.

"That would have been very expensive," Dana whispered to Eleanora and the others. They nodded in agreement.

Sir Kingston looked into the telescope with one eye closed.

"I'm glad you like it, James. I think it suits you," she commented.

He took his eyes off the telescope and looked at her. "I can hardly wait to use it," he said. "To look out into the far-off distance."

Pearl let out a peal of laughter. "I even bought my father a genuine pocket watch to keep with him wherever he goes." She showed him the golden shine of the cover. She then opened it and showed off what her money could buy.

"That is very impressive," he said. He then looked around. "Dashier!" he exclaimed as his eyes found him. "Would you come over here and take all these boxes to our rooms."

"Of course, master," he replied, bowing his head a little. He went over and carried them up the stairs.

"Well, I am very tired after a long day walking around town," Pearl began saying. "I do not feel like dinner tonight, but some tea would be nice. I will have it up in my room and rest."

"Of course, Pearl. The tea will be up as soon as it is ready for you and your father."

"No tea for me, please. I will just go take a nap right away," Mr Nables said.

"Very well then," Sir Kingston accepted. He caught sight of Dana. "Dana, would you prepare the tea and serve it to Miss Pearl in her room."

"Yes, sir, right away," she quickly said.

He nodded his head once, took a breath, and glanced over to Eleanora before he left. She noticed the way his eyes quickly shifted to hers for a split second, but she didn't think much of it.

# Chapter 13

It was Sunday morning, and breakfast was being served. Eleanora was in the dining room setting up the table. As she was doing so, both Mr Nables and Miss Pearl arrived, entering through the doorway, their heads held high. Once Pearl made her way in and was about to sit at her place, she screeched, "That smell!" She looked over at the centre of the table. "Primroses! What are primroses doing over here?" She backed away dramatically.

"I always change the flowers for the table," Eleanora told her, puzzled about her behaviour.

"I am allergic to primroses!" she said and sneezed. "Get those wretched weeds out of here this instant!" she demanded wildly.

"Primroses are pretty in their vivid colours; they are not some sort of dead weed," Eleanora objected.

"Girl! Get rid of those now. If you don't, you will cause my daughter to be dreadfully ill," her father demanded.

Sir Kingston now entered the scene. "What is the problem here?" he inquired immediately.

"Your servant girl…" Pearl immediately pointed her finger to Eleanora. "She placed those primroses over there. James, remember that I am allergic to primroses and just the smell of them circulating my nose is making me sneeze incredibly." She blew three more sneezes and blinked her eyes.

"I didn't know you were allergic to them," Eleanora protested. "They weren't put there to bother you on purpose."

Sir Kingston turned, shifting his gaze to Eleanora, and said, "We cannot have primroses here, Nora. Pearl will be in poor health if she even gets close to one. Any other flower but primroses will do."

"Yes, master," Eleanora said and took the vase away from the table.

"James, I never knew you were the kind to put a vase full of flowers on your dining table…ever." Mr Nables sounded curious about this new habit of his.

"It was Eleanora's idea to do so. She thought it would lift my spirits and brighten the room. She changes the flowers every week," Sir Kingston explained.

Eleanora smiled softly upon hearing this.

"My, he has changed! You have never liked pretty things before such as flowers, James," Pearl made known. She then looked over to Eleanora with a shifty, jealous look.

"I am still myself, I assure you," Sir Kingston said with a chuckle. He paid his attention to Eleanora now as he spoke. "Nora, how would you like to accompany Pearl and me this afternoon for a stroll? There is an open meadow just full of pretty little flowers that you can pick and fill the vase with. I think you will like it very much," he suggested.

Eleanora looked over to Pearl, who had an uninviting look on her wicked face; her sharp eyes seemed to demand that she refuse the invitation. Eleanora then returned her attention to her master and replied, "I would love to!" She felt grateful that he had thought of her.

"Splendid!" he remarked.

*

The afternoon came, and Eleanora was preparing herself to leave with the master and Miss Pearl. There was never much to do on a Sunday in regards to chores, so it was a rest day for the servants apart from having to still do their usual duties of serving meals and a few other minor jobs.

Eleanora changed into her caramel-brown dress and fixed up her hair to look presentable, especially in front of the master; Miss Pearl, on the other hand, she had no care for. She ran downstairs and made her way outside, excited to have a chance to go out into the fresh air and relax with a simple walk through nature. She met up with Dana, who had just fetched a bucket of water from the well.

"Dana, do you have a basket I could use to collect the flowers in?" she asked.

"I will go grab one for you. I'll just be a moment."

Tennent came walking Eleanora's way soon after. "Now, where are you off to, missy?" he enquired with a smile.

"We're going to the meadow with the master. And, unfortunately, Miss Pearl is going as well."

"You do not like Miss Pearl, do you, Nora?"

"Is it wrong to say I don't?"

"Of course not! Especially after what she's said about you, all those awful things. But I don't want to remind you of that and spoil your outing." Tennent looked over to Dana, who was coming their way with a basket in her hand.

"There you go, dear. This should be spacious enough, just in case you find many flowers you like."

"Thank you, Dana." Eleanora took the basket from her. "Why don't you two come along, and Jill and Marie?"

"Oh, Nora, we have better things to do around here. Besides, you haven't seen the place. It's very beautiful, I must say. You're going to enjoy it, I'll tell you."

"Oh, I can't wait!"

"And don't let Pearl be too much of a trouble to you," added Tennent. "Just ignore whatever comes out of that yappin' mouth of hers."

Eleanora giggled. "Yes, Tennent."

"Here comes the master and Pearl now," Dana said quietly before going on her way.

"You look like you're ready to go, Nora," Sir Kingston first said as Pearl followed behind.

"Yes, I am...and excited," she added enthusiastically.

A smile formed on Sir Kingston's face.

135

"Shall we go now?" Pearl asked hastily.

He glanced Pearl's way. "Uh, yes, of course."

He led the way, going down the hill and then into the small forest. Pearl walked beside him with Eleanora not too far behind.

After passing by many trees, they found themselves at a small river. It was a narrow river with clear running water that streamed down between the banks. The sound of the water was refreshing to hear, especially when they grew closer to it. The only way to get across was to walk onto the stepping stones.

"I don't want to get the bottom of my dress wet," complained Pearl, whining like a baby.

Sir Kingston chuckled. "Just hold up your dress."

"The things I have to do," she muttered, gathering her dress up above her ankles.

Sir Kingston went first like the leading soldier.

"Oh, wait for me!" Pearl seemed to be struggling despite only being on the first step.

"It's not difficult," Sir Kingston said, putting out his hand to her. She grabbed it while her other hand held her dress up at the side. She took two more steady steps and reached the other side.

Eleanora was there, waiting for them to get across. Once they did so safely, Sir Kingston asked, "Do you need help across, Nora?"

"What kind of girl do you think I am?" she asked with a raised eyebrow.

He smiled but seemed speechless.

Eleanora stepped onto the first stone, and with a quick motion, she balanced her hops all the way across the fast-running water. She looked over at Pearl, who rolled her eyes and crossed her arms.

"You are one courageous girl, Nora," Sir Kingston said admiringly.

"Unlike others," she remarked. She glanced at Pearl, who stared at her with a devious look, and Sir Kingston chuckled.

The trees thinned as they headed further out of the forest, and they passed the last few as they reached the top of a hill. They looked down below at the meadow. And what a meadow it truly was! Eleanora was amazed, her breath taken away by the incredible view. She gazed down at the vivid colours of the various flowers that grew from the grass, which was the greenest that grass could ever be.

Dana was right; it was a beautiful sight. But it was much more than that, Eleanora thought. The meadow seemed to be one full of wonders, a place that induced a feeling of freedom and dignity. It allowed for happiness to flourish and be lived out, for precious moments in harmony with nature to be experienced. It allowed for a great adventure, one that would be everlasting. Eleanora closed her eyes lightly, feeling the soft breeze on her face. She felt calm and at peace. She reopened her eyes, taking another long look at what lay before her. Out into the distance was where another forest grew, thicker and denser this time. To her left was where the meadow extended to the sky, with the sun shining ever so brightly high above.

"This is marvellous!" Pearl exclaimed.

"It is something, isn't it?" Sir Kingston responded before turning to face Nora. "What about you, Nora? Is it to your liking?"

"To my liking?" She paused. "It is the most magnificent place I have ever seen. It's so natural and tranquil."

He smiled.

"Do you own all this land, Sir Kingston?" she then asked.

"No, I don't actually. I only own the land up to the stream we just passed. Once you cross, it is not part of what I own. Anyone can come here if they like, but no one does, for they do not know about it," he explained. "No one comes this way." He took a breath. "Let us continue our walk down to the meadow and rest there."

"Oh, I simply cannot wait!" Eleanora exclaimed in pure ecstasy. She picked up her basket and ran her way down the hill as hastily as she could.

*

Pearl eyed Eleanora severely. She hoped to herself that the servant girl would take a fall and tumble down the hill and make a fool out of herself in front of Sir Kingston. She then remarked sternly, "If you ask me, she's more like a wild child than a mature woman."

Sir Kingston then replied, "I think it's adorable."

Pearl noticed a smile plastered onto his face as he watched the servant run down the hill. "Adorable?" Pearl looked at him in surprise and gave a single mocking laugh. "I've never heard that one come out from you before, James. She seems more silly than adorable to me."

He didn't answer and made his way down the hill, his hands placed in his pockets.

Pearl followed after him.

*

Eleanora scurried over to the beginnings of the meadow. There were hundreds of flowers growing from the rich and fertile soil. Eleanora couldn't decide which ones to pick, for she wanted them all to herself.

"I bet you want the whole lot, don't you?" Sir Kingston's voice was heard from behind.

She turned instantly. "They are all too pretty. How can I choose from them all?"

He laughed as she pouted her lips. He then bent down and picked off a flower, a white calla lily. "How about you start off with this one? It is so pure in its white colour. It seems so innocent...like you."

Eleanora smiled as he placed it into the basket. She saw the way his eyes were bright as they looked into hers, and her spirits lifted even further. She smiled and began wandering around the meadow, picking the flowers she thought would be best.

The meadow was filled with the aroma of flowers, and Eleanora enjoyed the delightful sensation of breathing in the floral scents. She took light steps, trying not to damage the delicacy of the flowers. She picked an abundant bunch consisting of various types and colours such as cyclamen, carnations, pansies, violets, hyacinths, gladioli, buttercups, and many others that caught her eye. After spending time picking all sorts of flowers, she placed her basket down and rested, laying herself amongst them all. She let her eyes wander up to the sky and watched the different shapes and forms the clouds made. She then closed her eyelids and placed her hands together with her fingers intertwined just below her bosom. She felt as if she were in a dream, an enchanting one where nothing could harm her anymore.

*

Sir Kingston and Pearl had followed more slowly behind.

"I'm going to go rest," Sir Kingston notified Pearl.

"All right. I just want to see some of the flowers over this side."

He nodded and left her to it. He went over and found Eleanora where she lay. He decided to rest by her. As he stood by her side, he noticed her eyes were shut. He looked down at her, seeing how calmly she lay there, like a beautiful sleeping angel. He quietly sat down next to her. He saw the way she breathed gently as her bosom rose a little and fell back down again. He simply could not take his eyes off her.

He looked away a little to see the whereabouts of Pearl, which was quite a distance away. He then turned his attention back to Eleanora, who still didn't seem to feel another presence near her. He looked down admiringly at her youthful skin that was clear, smooth, and untouched, and he had the urge to feel it against his fingertips. Her eyelids were like the delicate wings of a butterfly when they fluttered open and shut. He lowered his eyes to her lips, looking at their soft contours. He couldn't help but examine her from this proximity. He had always felt a curiosity about her. He then decided to reach out his hand and move it to where hers rested. He gently stroked it, not knowing exactly what he was doing but unable to stop himself.

Eleanora swiftly opened her eyes, and Sir Kingston quickly removed his hand from hers.

She lifted herself with her elbows and sat up, saying, "I didn't know you were here?"

"I'm sorry. I wasn't here long. I just wanted to wake you," he lied.

"I was just absorbing all this serenity around me," she told him. "I thought it would be best to do so with my eyes closed."

"It is peaceful out here," he affirmed, looking around him and feeling quite embarrassed.

A silence fell between the two, and they watched a couple of bees that were flying around and gathering the nectar from the flowers.

"Nora," Sir Kingston called.

She turned to him. "Yes, sir?"

He chuckled. "There is a small white butterfly caught in your hair." He reached out to grab it from her. "Must have thought you were a flower," he remarked while smiling. He held the butterfly on the tip of his finger and showed it to her.

"It's so pretty." She smiled as she looked down at it.

"Here, hold it," he offered.

"Oh, I don't know."

"Trust me," he said with a smile.

She brought her finger to the side of his, and they lightly connected. He turned his finger a little so that the butterfly was now attached to her finger. She brought it back close to her. A smile formed on her lips. Sir Kingston watched with satisfaction, enjoying this blissful moment.

Eventually, the butterfly fluttered its wings and flew off, hovering over the flowers as it moved away.

"I've never held a butterfly before," she stated.

"Me neither," he replied.

She looked back down to the flowers that were in front of her.

"Nora, tell me what it was like living at Mallow Hall Estate. I remember you saying it wasn't pleasant."

"It indeed wasn't," she affirmed. "It was like being trapped in a lion's den, where even the slightest movement could awaken the beast into fury." She took a breath as he watched her. "The estate was once my home. But when my father died, it became hell. Not because of the place itself but because of the people who lived in it."

"Your aunt?"

She nodded her head. "And my cousin. Aunt Dusilla was the worst."

"Tell me what she did. How did she treat you poorly?"

"You want to know?"

"If you don't mind."

"I guess it would be good to talk about it." She paused, inhaling more deeply this time. "She always told me that I was born to be a servant. That my mother was very poor and my father wasn't far from that either. Aunt Dusilla, being the sister to my mother, also shared that same low status of coming from a very poor family. But the difference was, as she said, that she married a well-off man, my uncle, who died a long time ago, which is why the estate belongs to her now. She lives in riches and has forgotten her past. So, I had to endure the suffering of my parents' poverty. My aunt never treated me like I was her niece. She never even treated me as anything more than a piece of dust, for the servants were treated slightly better than me. I lived all my days doing as she pleased. And her daughter was spoiled rotten. But it wasn't entirely her fault as she had a mother who taught her all the wrong things. I was never allowed out of the gates of the estate. I had never seen people besides the other servants who worked there and a few visitors who called, just like you did."

Sir Kingston was grave as he listened to all this.

141

"I guess that was my life, until you came and bought me."
She looked away.

"You do still like living at the manor, don't you?"

"Oh yes, I do. Any place is better than back at the estate; that's for sure. But if I had to choose any place in the world, I would much rather stay wherever you are, for I have nowhere else to go and no one I can trust. I will live to serve you for the rest of my life."

"Really?" He was stunned by this.

She nodded. "You know, even though I was sold to you, I now think of it differently. That fate brought me to you…to save me from all my pain and suffering. To live a much better life here instead. You saved me even though you didn't know you did, nor did I, for that matter…until now."

"Hmm…" he mumbled, thinking of her words. The way she put things had touched his heart and inflamed his spirit. He wanted to broach a quite sensitive topic but was still contemplating whether he should or not. "Nora, did your aunt ever…abuse you?"

Sir Kingston watched the way her expression saddened. He continued, "I can never forget that day when we first met officially, and I noticed your face was stained with a red mark on the side. It looked to be bruised. And I know for a fact it was no rash the way you tried to pretend it was."

She looked away for a brief moment.

"I'm sorry," he said, lowering his voice.

Eleanora returned her gaze to him before saying, "She abused me a few times. But that was the second time she struck me on the face. The reason for that was that I pleaded not to be sold and have to serve some strange man. I was really afraid at the time, not knowing how my life would turn out or if I would be abused more with you than with her."

He moved forward a little and said in a deep yet gentle voice, "I would never abuse you. Never in my life would I strike a lady."

"But I'm no lady…" She lowered her eyes. "I'm just a servant."

He placed his hand on her face and gently caressed her cheek. He continued to do so with his thumb getting to feel the precious warmth of her skin. "You are human," he uttered, seeing the way her eyes glistened before him. She bit down onto her bottom lip as she looked nervous about the way his fingertips stroked her skin as they pleased. This only caused Sir Kingston to struggle within himself for a reason he did not understand.

Eleanora looked like she wanted to say something. She then said, "It seems like you know Mr Nables and Miss Pearl very well."

His fingers stopped stroking her cheek, and he sighed.

"I know that Mr Nables was your guardian and a friend of your father," she began.

"Yes, he took care of me from a young age until I was twenty-one. My father and he were very close." He paused. "Pearl Nables was there almost all my childhood years because her father did look after me."

"Did you live at the manor at all during that time?"

"Sometimes, if he was away on business. I was living at Windleton for most of the time until I was allowed on my own, which is when I returned to my father's home, Kingston Manor."

"What happened to Dana and Dashier?"

"They maintained the manor, for they are trusted employees. And they looked after me whenever I was there for a short time."

"James!" called out Pearl, holding a small bunch of flowers she had also picked out. She began walking in his direction. He immediately rose and walked a few steps towards her. "I am finished with picking. Shall we continue our journey?"

"Yes, of course." He turned to Eleanora and signalled for her to follow.

\*

They continued their journey, exiting the meadow and travelling over the small hills. Ahead, they came across an arched bridge made of stone that was built over a lake.

Sir Kingston stood at the end of the bridge, where he pointed out over the lake, showing Pearl something. He then quickly took out his new telescope from inside his cloak. He pulled the bottom of it, extending the barrel, and put it to his left eye, searching for something he had spotted in the distance. He then gave the telescope to Pearl.

"They are simply precious, aren't they?" Pearl remarked, her eye squinting through the telescope.

Sir Kingston turned around to Eleanora, who had just arrived. He waved. "Nora, come and see the ducks."

Eleanora stood, her body pressed to the stone of the arch. Sir Kingston stood his ground behind her. He brought the telescope in front of her, and she held onto it. She put it close to her right eye.

"Do you see them?" he muttered into her ear, his body up close to hers, while his hand rested on her shoulder.

"Yes, I do! Look how the baby ducks follow their mother. It's adorable."

He smiled in agreement.

"Look!" Eleanora suddenly exclaimed. "There are two swans that have just arrived!" She handed the telescope back to Sir Kingston. He spotted the two swans swimming gracefully side by side. Their necks were long and curled like the end of umbrellas. One of the swans slowly moved in front of the other and rested its head against the other. The swans' heads connected in the shape of a heart as they floated in harmony across the lake.

"Well, you don't see that every day!" Sir Kingston remarked.

"They are beautiful, those swans," Eleanora then commented.

"They are very much in love," surmised Sir Kingston.

Eleanora turned and smiled at him. She then took another glance at the swans as they drifted further down the lake as the calming waters carried them away.

Sir Kingston put his telescope back into his cloak. He then started to stroll over the bridge, looking over to the other side of the lake. Eleanora was then approached by Pearl, who interrupted her thoughts by calling out impolitely, "You, Eleanora, girl" She said her name for the first time, which was strange for Eleanora herself to hear. "You know, I bet you can't even make your way across this arched bridge without falling."

"What do you mean?" Eleanora wondered where Pearl was taking this.

"I mean for you to climb onto the ledge and make your way across. I've done it before in front of James, and he was very impressed with my balancing skills."

Eleanora witnessed the way Pearl's eyes narrowed and fell to a darker shade. "I bet you can't even do that."

"How would you know?" Eleanora responded plainly.

"Because I don't think you have what it takes. I dare you to do it, but you look like someone who is afraid of heights."

"Says the one who is afraid of a simple stream of water," Eleanora teased her in return.

"That's so I wouldn't get my new dress wet; that is all."

"I'm not afraid, but I won't do it just because you dared me to. Besides, you have not been here before, so how can you say you've done it?" Eleanora questioned.

"I have been over this bridge, just not the meadow." Pearl paused. "Well, then, I guess someone like you doesn't have what it takes."

She was about to turn around when Eleanora, irritated by her bragging and the way she thought she was better than her simply because of her wealth and status, called out, "All right. I'll do it." Eleanora couldn't back down now. She was determined to prove her wrong, to show that she had just as much skill as someone high up like her. Eleanora placed the basket full of flowers down and climbed up onto the ledge of the stoned wall, putting one leg up and then the other. She carefully stood up tall with her arms outstretched to balance her weight. "How far do I have to go?" she asked.

"The whole way across. If I can do it, I'm sure you will have no problem at all," Pearl said with a chuckle.

Eleanora took her first step forward, placing one foot in front of the other. She took a few more steps and mumbled to herself, "This isn't too bad." She continued, balancing her way as she balanced on the rocky stones that were of a rough, uneven texture. She had to be extra careful this time as the arch was becoming steeper.

Just then, she heard Pearl's voice as she yelled out, "Yoo-hoo! James!"

Eleanora looked up when she heard Pearl's high-pitched voice trying to grab Sir Kingston's attention. For only a split second, she saw his eyes wide open, staring at her, when all of a sudden, her foot slipped from a crack between the stones, and she fell sideways, straight into the lake. "ELEANORA!" was the cry Eleanora heard last from Sir Kingston before she splashed into the water. She felt herself going deep under, and it was at that point she thought she would give in and allow the water to take her away while it had the chance.

But just when she believed there was no hope, someone grabbed her and persuaded her otherwise. Eleanora reached above the surface, trying to gasp for air. It was then she realised that Sir Kingston also floated on top and was the one who had saved her from her drowning.

"Eleanora," he panted while treading water and keeping hold of her.

"I don't need your help!" She was embarrassed as well as frustrated with how things had turned out. He let go of her, and she swam as best she could across the lake and to the safety of the shore. She pulled herself up and got back on her feet.

When Sir Kingston reached her, he paced in front of her to stop her from walking away. "What were you thinking, Nora?!" His tone was harsh yet his eyes expressed concern. She then noticed the way he examined her – the way her dress melted down onto her skin as if it were attached to her, the way her bosom heaved as she tried to catch her breath. She couldn't help but stare at him also – the way he dripped from all over, his clothes drenched as if he'd come in from a wild storm, the way water dripped down the sides of his face from his soaked hair.

She finally managed to speak. "I just wasn't!" She looked away for a moment, trying to control her breathing. She then turned back to him and said, "You didn't have to jump after me. I didn't need you to save me. I can take care of myself, you know." She walked around him, leaving him to himself.

The manor was quite far off. However, Eleanora insisted to herself that she should get back there alone. Once Eleanora had passed a copse of trees, she saw the manor and ran straight to it, not knowing nor caring about the whereabouts of Sir Kingston and Pearl or how far behind they were.

*

Eleanora rushed inside, where she had bumped into Tennent. He looked down at her, remarking in a surprised tone, "You went swimming, Nora?"

"Not now, Tennent," she replied, brushing him off as she continued her way up the stairs to the final floor. She went into the common room and took a few moments to relax her breathing. She decided she would take a bath and change into her usual uniform. She went into the bathroom, where she stripped down her dress. She then untied her hair, which still felt wet as it slithered down onto her naked body. Some time later, when she was all dry and herself again, she went downstairs to continue with her work before the evening's end.

Dana was in the kitchen and had already almost finished cooking dinner. "How was your little journey to the meadow, Nora?" she asked.

"The meadow was just like you said, Dana. I picked a bunch of flowers, all different kinds." Eleanora retrieved the basket that had been left sitting on the front porch. She brought it over to Dana to show her the flowers.

Dana bent down to sniff them all at once. "My, they do smell so sweet and fresh! You should start putting them in a vase and get some water into them."

Eleanora nodded and got right to it, admonishing herself for leaving them without water for so long.

"So, how were the master and Miss Pearl?" Dana asked.

Eleanora didn't say anything at first as she was too preoccupied thinking about what had occurred during their journey. She then replied, "Well, I haven't seen this side of the master before. He seemed really easy-going, enjoying the pleasures of nature. I have never seen him take such an interest."

"That's not much like him," Dana commented.

"And Pearl was her usual self," Eleanora added.

"What did she do now?" Dana stopped peeling potatoes as she looked up.

Eleanora explained what had occurred when she fell off the bridge. She cried out passionately, "She did it on purpose to embarrass me, to make me look like some sort of fool in front of the master!"

"You should know nothing good ever comes from a woman like Pearl. She is just too cocky about herself and will get whatever she demands." Dana paused. "But what about you, Nora? You haven't injured yourself by the looks of it?"

"No, luckily."

"Thank heavens for that!" Dana remarked. "And the master jumped in to save you?"

"Yes, he did. But I didn't want him to. I told him I didn't need him to save me and that I can look after myself. I know it was harsh of me, for he was only looking out for my welfare."

"And what happened after that?"

"I left without them and ran back to the manor."

Dana didn't respond to this for a moment. She then remarked, "Well, I guess it didn't go too well in the end with the master and Pearl, after all."

"What do you mean?" Eleanora looked up as she was placing the flowers in the vase one by one.

"Well, the reason they went out today was for the two of them to get closer to each other. Mr Nables suggested they should spend more time together. That's why he went back to his place at Windleton for a week or two, I'd say."

Eleanora was about to place a flower into the vase when she stopped herself. She placed it down delicately on the table instead. She then questioned, "Mr Nables returned home?"

"Yes, just before you left," Dana confirmed.

"And what do you mean when you say the expedition was so the master and Pearl can spend more time together? As friends?"

"I don't know if you have realised, Nora, but it is thought that they should get married to each other."

"Married?" Eleanora's voice rose and her eyes widened at the very idea.

"Why are you so shocked?" Dana gave a chuckle. "You know, both their fathers were very close and wanted their children to be together. Now that they have grown up, Mr Nables is doing everything he can to make that possible."

"They are to be married?" Eleanora's voice softened. She shuddered and felt as if her heart stopped beating for a moment.

"We do not know for sure that Sir Kingston even wants to make Pearl his wife. He is a very hard man to impress. He may indeed make a choice no one has foreseen. But the choice of Pearl is expected. We will only know in due time."

149

"Then I guess he should go where his heart leads," Eleanora muttered to herself.

"You don't sound too well, Nora. Are you sure you are feeling all right?"

"I'm just feeling tired right now. That's all. After the walking and all that has happened."

Dana then mentioned, "Sir Kingston isn't getting any younger, you know. He is twenty-nine, for god's sake. He ought to get married, and I think he knows it by now. But I myself don't think it should be Pearl."

After this was said, Marie and Jill entered.

"Is the dinner ready? Dashier said the master and Pearl are seated," said Marie.

"I'm nearly done, and then you can serve it to them. Eleanora is feeling tired after her journey to the meadow."

"How was it, by the way, Nora?" Jill asked.

"The meadow was spectacular. Here, I've put all the flowers that I picked in the vase. Would you mind putting it on the dining table?"

"Of course. These are lovely, by the way," Jill commented as she took it from her and made her way out, smelling the flowers as she went.

*

Dinner was served. The candles were luminous, and all was quite to Sir Kingston's satisfaction. He gazed at the flowers that were placed neatly in the vase. He thought about what happened that day, for he could not get Eleanora off his mind. A sigh escaped his mouth when he saw she wasn't the one to put the flowers in place on the table.

"Is something the matter, James?"

"No, nothing is the matter," he replied, feeling gloomy.

"Is it about what happened earlier on?"

Sir Kingston's eyes switched to Pearl in a blink. His mouth seemed thinner and longer than usual. "I just hope Eleanora is all right." He looked down to his plate with a downcast expression on his face.

Pearl then said, "I'm sure she is just fine. She was the one who wanted to act like a silly child. She obviously didn't understand the danger she was clumsily putting herself in. She should be more mature for her age."

He didn't respond, only listened. And even that he hardly could do. He then felt Pearl's hand squeezing his as she said, "It wasn't your fault, what happened. You were doing the right thing to save her from a potential drowning."

He couldn't help comparing the way Pearl's hand wrapped around his to the touch of Eleanora; Pearl's hand felt pampered and seemed to possess neither delicacy nor feeling, while Eleanora's touch felt like a blossoming flower, lightening his spirits and warming him from within.

Pearl continued to make her speech. "James, she should have appreciated what you were trying to do for her. And instead, she just dismisses you completely. You didn't deserve to be treated that way. Whereas I always have appreciated all you have done for me."

His eyes lifted to hers now. He tried to hide the emotions that seemed to escape onto his face. He smiled at her and nodded. "I'm just going to forget about it," he told her.

"And so you should." She smiled pleasantly, letting go of his hand and beginning to eat.

But as much as Sir Kingston tried with every part of him to forget, he simply couldn't stop thinking about the way Eleanora looked, the way she spoke, the way her eyes would light up in that beautiful azure blue that sparkled so heavenly like stars shining in the night sky.

"You know what you need, James?"

"And what might that be, Pearl?"

"You need to host another one of your famous parties. You haven't done so in a while, and I'm sure many of your friends are wishing to see you and hear about how you are doing. It would be good to take your mind off things and enjoy yourself." She paused. "Besides, I would love to go dancing again."

He thought about Pearl's idea for a short time and concluded that a party might do him some good. "Very well, then. I will agree to hosting a party right here in the manor."

"Oh, thank you, James! Oh, I cannot wait!" Pearl exclaimed with a grin. "What date will you set?"

"Some time soon, perhaps in a couple of weekends' time?" he suggested.

"Yes, perfect!" she said, jumping in her seat.

He smiled also and resumed eating while Pearl continued talking excitedly during the rest of dinner.

# Chapter 14

It was just after eight in the evening. Eleanora decided to head to the library, which she usually did during the day on a Sunday as there was not much work that needed to be done. But because of the walk and all that occurred, she hadn't the time nor the inclination to go in. However, in order to sleep that night and take her mind off things, she needed to consume herself with fantasies before heading to bed. She wanted to find escape in the books that were shelved there, ready to be picked out and read.

She twisted the knob and opened the door before her. While doing so, she spotted Sir Kingston across the room, staring at the books, his hands clasped behind his back. When she saw him, her immediate reaction was to step back quietly and return to the corridor before he noticed her. But as she was about to make her leave, his voice was heard, which had caused Eleanora to halt. Her feet seemed unable to move, and her eyes couldn't even blink.

"You don't have to leave, Nora, just because I am here."

She bit down on her lip, astounded that he guessed that it was her. She had no urge to turn around to face him, but she did, to show him respect. He then turned also and gazed at her face. "And what brings you here?" he asked, his eyes alight.

"I wanted to find something interesting to read before I went to bed. I sometimes come here to relax my mind," she said, taking a few steps towards him. "I hope you don't mind?"

"Not at all." He then looked down to his shoes.

"How did you know it was me?" Eleanora was curious to know.

After a short moment, he lifted his eyes back to her and said, "Because I sometimes see you making your way in here during the day, or someone notifies me that you are in here entertaining yourself with books if I ask for your whereabouts." He took a breath before he then said, "And since today you went on our little excursion, I thought you might come in during the night instead to make up for the loss." Eleanora kept quiet and placed her eyes elsewhere. "Well, go ahead. Don't let me disturb you. I was just finding something myself," he told her.

She inhaled sharply before walking by him. She noticed the way Sir Kingston looked to his side, his eyes on her as she walked past him. After a second more, she turned to him again and said, "I want to thank you for saving me today, when I fell. And I'm sorry for the way I treated you. It was wrong of me."

He turned his face around slowly, and his eyes immediately fixed on hers. "All is forgotten. I'm just glad you weren't seriously injured and that nothing happened to you."

"Because you rescued me, as it was you who gave me your helping hand."

"Well, then, I guess that's when they usually call it even. You rescued me, and I rescued you. However, I would never keep score, for I would rescue you every time you needed me."

His words warmed Eleanora's heart, leaving her mute with amazement.

He paused for a brief moment before saying, "You were brave, climbing up that stone arch bridge. But it was a silly thing to do, I must admit. I have never seen anyone take such a bold risk."

"Didn't you witness Pearl doing the same thing?" Eleanora asked in a puzzled tone.

"Pearl would never balance over that. She is much too afraid and wouldn't dare risk it the way you have."

Eleanora's suspicions were confirmed. Pearl had shown herself to be a selfish and dishonest person who was unkind and showed no true character whatsoever. Eleanora thought her intolerable. She looked down to the floor as she felt her forehead slightly crease.

"Is something the matter, Nora?" Sir Kingston asked.

She breathed out. "No, nothing is the matter." Though still feeling ashamed, she tried to smile.

She then turned herself around and went to search for the books. She began touching each binder of each book with her finger, trying to pick out what she should read this time.

"I cannot believe you own all these fascinating books!" she now exclaimed in delight. She went on, "My father used to read to me whenever he could. But I didn't learn how to read till I was eight, when Molly taught me." Eleanora suddenly remembered her once-good friend, which made her feel down. She had stopped giving the books her attention.

"Who is this Molly you speak about?" Sir Kingston then asked.

She looked over at him. "She was one of the servants back at the estate. She was also my friend until…until she betrayed me."

"Betrayed you?"

Eleanora explained, "She always told me everything. And she knew about your arrival and that you would make a deal with my so-called aunt. She knew I had a high chance of being sold, but she said not one word of it. I never wanted to speak to her again. And I didn't. You could say I left on bad terms." She returned her attention to the books, exploring those further down the shelves.

"Which ones are your favourites?"

"The classical ones." She glanced at him with a smile as he was now by her side. She picked one out and showed him the very one she loved the most. She touched the hard-covered binder of one as she stated, 'Charlotte Bronte's *Jane Eyre* is my favourite. I find it so interesting and fulfilling that I cherish it."

"Really?" He moved closer to her.

"Most of the books I have read were in secret at the estate. I was never really allowed to touch those books, but they were just getting caught up in dust and cobwebs. No one would ever read them, so I began to, in a secret hiding place. And now that I see you have them also, it makes me want to read them again." She paused, smiling. "But I may want to try something new since there seems to be a variety of books all stacked up here."

Sir Kingston then offered, "I think I have something you would like."

Eleanora watched as he went over to the portable ladder that leaned against the tall bookshelf. He climbed it, step by step, until he reached midway. He rolled it along and touched each book's binder with his finger as he rolled past. He then pulled one book out that caught his eye. He held onto it while heading back down again. Eleanora wondered about the book he had picked out for her. She was eager and ready to find out what it was. Then he was in front of her again with a smile on his face. He held the book in front of her, and Eleanora took it slowly from his hands. She looked up to him and felt a willingness to read every word that was inside.

"I've never had the chance to read poems."

"Then you can start now. I thought you might like to try reading some poems as they are rather good, and I do quite like them myself." He then took the book from Eleanora and opened it to its contents page. He explained while pointing with his finger, "Here, you can see the different genres. You can choose a style you think you might like." He returned the book to her hands.

"Thank you," she said with appreciation.

"You better start reading."

She nodded her head and took a seat on the sofa by the fireplace. She opened the book and her eyes started running through the contents page to see which titles would seize her attention.

*

A couple of hours later, Sir Kingston arrived back at the library to check on Eleanora and see how she was liking the book. Once he entered, he walked over to her and saw that the book was left open; however, her eyes weren't. He stood analysing the way she was sleeping, like a peaceful and pure angel. The way her eyelids were gently closed caused a small smile to brighten his face. She slept soundly, her chest rising up and down very softly. It was a cosy scene with the way the fire illuminated her face softly. It was warm, but she needed something else to ensure her comfort. He walked out of the room.

Shortly after, he returned – this time, with a woolly blanket in his hands. He went back over to her and gently removed the book that rested neatly on her lap. He placed it down beside her on the small rounded table. He then placed the blanket on top of her, making sure her entire body was well covered. She shifted herself a little, but she was still in that calm, serene sleep that had overtaken her. Sir Kingston did not know or understand why he was behaving so diligently towards Eleanora, almost being more than just simply compassionate towards her. He had never shown this side to anyone before, let alone a servant. Why was he so soft and tender towards her and her feelings? He thought this through for a moment but could not come to terms with it. He took one last look at her before he turned around and left quietly.

\*

The next morning, as Eleanora awoke, she looked around at her surroundings and realised where she had slept. The warm blanket that covered her body slipped down to the floor by her feet. She looked down wondering where it had come from and who placed it there. She then gasped, searching for the book that was supposed to be on her lap. She turned to the table and sighed in relief when she saw it placed neatly there. She placed it back in its spot on the shelf. She then folded the blanket to return it to whoever had offered it to her during her sleep. Before she left the library, she checked the time on the miniature grandfather clock that stood proudly on top of the fireplace mantelpiece. It was almost eight. She had slept in more than usual and was supposed to have served breakfast to the master.

She quickly rushed out of the library before she could get into any more trouble. She ran down the stairs, her feet slipping down each step in haste. She jumped from the second last step, and there, she met Dana. Eleanora ran up to her and stopped abruptly. "I know I'm extremely late, Dana. I don't know what got into me."

"This is the first time you have slept in, Nora. I will let you off the hook because I know you are not like that. But do try not to sleep in again."

"Yes, Dana, of course. I'm sorry." Only now did Eleanor start to regain her breath.

"Oh, there is no need to apologise," Dana said in a much lighter tone and laughed. "We missed you this morning, you know. I sent Jill up to your room to see if anything was wrong, but you weren't in there. Then the master told us you were still asleep in the library and to let you rest for the morning. I wonder what you were doing sleeping there?"

"Well, last night, I was reading a book before I was to head to my chamber to sleep. But instead, I fell asleep after a couple of hours of reading. I was very tired, I guess. And when I woke up, I found a blanket on top of me. But I didn't have it before I slept. Do you know who placed it on top of me?"

"I'm not sure, but it definitely wasn't me or Jill or Marie, for we didn't know where you were," Dana made known.

As she said this, the master came walking by and stopped to speak to them. "Ladies, what are you fussing about this morning?"

"Nora wanted to know who offered her a blanket during her sleep."

"Yes," Eleanora said and nodded softly. "But I think I already know who it may have been." She smiled at Sir Kingston.

"That would be me," Sir Kingston confessed with a chuckle.

"Dana, I need your help with the animals," Marie, who had just come in, interjected.

"Yes, of course," said Dana and made her way out.

"So, it was you, master."

He nodded his head in reply.

158

"Thank you for keeping me warm during the night. I should return this to you. Where would you like me to put it?"

"You may keep it, as a spare in your room," he offered.

"Well, all right. Thank you. I'm sorry I couldn't make it down to help serve breakfast this morning. It won't happen again."

"Do not worry, Nora. It has only happened the one time."

"I should be off now. Have a pleasant day, master." She left him to return upstairs and put the blanket into her bedroom chamber.

*

After lunchtime, the master called for everyone to meet in the Grand Hall for an announcement. The servants stood in a line all together; Dashier was on one side of Sir Kingston and Pearl on the other.

"I have an announcement to make." Sir Kingston spoke clearly with his hands behind his back, standing like a soldier. Eleanora was keen to know why he was so glad to tell his news. She only hoped, however, that it was not something that would catch her off guard.

"Pearl has persuaded me..." He glanced at her and then back at everyone else. "I will be hosting a party here at the manor. It has come to my attention that I haven't done so in a while and a party would be beneficial around here."

Dana caught Eleanora's eye and smiled.

"It will be held not this Saturday but the next one after. I will be inviting all my friends and business partners, who will be very important guests. I have called you all down here because I know you will help me make that possible. There are many preparations that must be completed for a successful party. I will give the list of things to be done to Dana as she will be the organiser. If anything is needed, please inform me. You may all leave and return to your posts," he concluded.

"I cannot believe we have to prepare for another party. This will be a lot of work for the next two weeks," Marie complained.

"I do love Sir Kingston's parties, but it means we have to do all the hard work," Jill agreed.

"Well, I cannot wait! I haven't seen a party in my life, and I have been waiting to see one since forever!" Eleanora spoke with enthusiasm.

Dana chuckled, "Yes, Eleanora has been wanting to see a party. Just imagine all the dancing and the graceful music as well as guests all dressed up."

Sir Kingston walked over to Dana and provided her with the list. He then turned back to Pearl, who gleamed with delight as he took her away. Eleanora observed this for a moment but then focused back on the list as Dana was reading it out to them all.

# Chapter 15

It was now Saturday, the week before the party would be held. Eleanora had many tasks and duties to fulfil in order to make this party a successful one, one she would always remember. She insisted to Dana that she was willing to take care of the preparations such as the decorations and many other important things. So Dana allowed Eleanora to be the head planner for the party. Dana was to take care of the banquet as always, Marie and Jill would maintain the cleanliness of the manor, Tennent would look after the outside jobs, and Dashier, who had created a guest list, was to deliver the invitations. Everything was running smoothly, according to Eleanora. She had been so busy that she hadn't seen much of Sir Kingston besides when serving the meals.

That morning, Eleanora had left with both Dana and Jill to go into town to buy some items and put in orders in preparation for the party. This was Eleanora's chance to step out and face the outside world. So today promised to be a thrilling day.

It was quite an experience for her; she had never seen so many people in her life. And yet, she could only imagine how the party would look when everyone arrived in their best attire. Dana went to order the food while Jill took Eleanora to show her around. They went into some shops and bought things for the party as well as putting in orders here and there. When they met back with Dana, they showed her the things they had bought before making their return to the manor by coach.

In the afternoon, Eleanora was up on the third floor when she heard some laughter drift in through the open window along with the wind. She went towards the window, and the fields at the back of the manor caught her eye. Sir Kingston was riding his horse alongside Pearl, who was galloping about on her horse. They seemed to be getting closer to each other than ever, which only affirmed the idea that they were most likely to be married. Eleanora saw the way Pearl continuously tried to impress him by showing off her skills with a horse. Eleanora despised Pearl, not because of this but due to the simple fact that she was not who she appeared to be. And with that, she was afraid that Sir Kingston would be making a mistake if he were to fall in love with her. Perhaps he was already in love? Eleanora scorned the idea and knew that it wasn't love. She felt that he only praised Pearl and gave her attention because she either begged for it or desperately threw herself in front of him.

She continued to stare down at them, hearing them laugh and make jokes. Eleanora shut the window tight, not wanting to hear another sound come out of Pearl's flirtatious mouth. But for some reason, she could not take her eyes off them. Hardly a sentence had been spoken between Sir Kingston and Eleanora all week. She missed their conversations. She missed serving him whenever he pleased and called for her. She missed being needed, and now, there were very few interactions, and this was for a very simple reason.

*

The week had flown by quite swiftly as preparations continued. Early on Saturday morning, Mr Nables arrived back to the manor and attended breakfast with Sir Kingston and Pearl. He had seen the way his daughter was looking brighter now, more cheerful than before. He was satisfied with his strategy of leaving them alone, and now that he had returned, he saw that she had everything under control.

After breakfast, Sir Kingston summoned Dana to the drawing room to provide an update for that night's party. She informed him, "It was Eleanora who took care of all the arrangements, master. I only managed the food, but she took everything upon herself. With our input, of course."

Sir Kingston was surprised to hear this. He thought to himself for a moment. "Eleanora planned the party? And you let her?"

"I trusted she could do it. I'm sorry, sir. I should have discussed it with you first. She is so very excited as this will be the first party she ever gets to witness, you see. But Eleanora did run everything by me before making any decisions."

"Hmm…" he mumbled as he contemplated this for a brief moment. "And what do you think of her decisions?"

"I think they are all well thought out with careful planning involved. The party will be a remarkable one, master, I assure you. Eleanora would never let you down."

He turned around now to face the window. He muttered to himself, "I know she won't." He then turned to Dana and said, "I will see how all turns out tonight. I cannot wait to be dazzled and surprised." With that, he smiled and took his leave.

# Chapter 16

The day soon turned into night. A wondrous night it was to be, with the accompaniment of the glimmering silver crescent moon and the twinkling stars that scattered all over the dark night sky. The manor was indeed a mysterious place, especially during the night; but tonight, it was to be the centre of attention. The entrance gate was opened wide, welcoming all the horse carriages that entered one after the other. Each and every one of them halted by the front after making their final turn around the great fountain that beamed with light from the monument. The coachman of each carriage would step down and open the door, and then each of the guests would appear. Every face beamed with delight as the gentlemen took their ladies by the arms and led the way into the manor.

The front door was managed by Dashier, and he welcomed all the guests in his best apparel. He was dressed in an all-black suit, receiving the coats that were given to him. Upon entering the Grand Hall, the waves of guests were met with the sight of the magnificent chandelier that brightened the entire room. The men were dressed in their fancy suits, and the ladies' gowns were popping with bursts of radiant colours. Flowers adorned the scene, and the room was infused with their aroma. The doors were folded together to create an extended room that held the dance floor and piano. An orchestra dressed in black suits played a smooth, welcoming tune to begin the night.

Eleanora was amazed by all this…and it was only the beginning. Though she knew she was not part of the party itself, she was still glad, for she would be overseeing the party, witnessing and cherishing every moment.

Eleanora made her way into the kitchen and helped the others to prepare the appetisers they would be serving on silver-plated trays to all the guests.

"The food looks exquisite, Dana!" Eleanora beamed with joy.

"My Dana is the best cook around," Tennent said with a smile, holding onto her.

"Yes, and now we are to serve these to the guests. Let us go and split up amongst the crowds," Dana instructed.

They all scurried off to serve the food to all while Dashier saw to the champagne.

Not long after, the first dance of the night was about to begin, and Eleanora quickly squeezed through the guests, wanting to capture a better view. As the music tempo sped up and a ripple of excitement went around the room, the couples began their quick dance around the floor, surrounded by a watchful crowd of people. Eleanora was in awe as she had never seen dancing such as this. She was amazed by the way they travelled like they were fairies, lightly dancing on their feet as the gentlemen swayed their partners around while the ladies' gowns twisted around and flowed through the air. Eleanora dreamed she could be one of the ladies dancing in that room that was so elegant, so charming in its own way. She dreamt she could but knew she couldn't, for she had a job to do, and that was making sure all the guests were satisfied.

During the party, Eleanora continued to serve the appetisers, prompting many comments about how spectacular and delicious the food was. She wandered around holding the tray with one hand by her side. Eleanora stood near the door to the drawing room, where she noticed she had caught the attention of a couple of young men who appeared to be around her age.

"What is a beautiful girl like you doing serving at a party like this?" one of them said, the one with shiny blond hair.

"I agree," chimed in the other, who had darker hair and was more handsome than the first. "You should be here serving only us instead."

They both laughed at their joke.

Eleanora ignored their remarks and was about to turn around when the blond one grabbed her arm and spun her around.

"Why don't we slip into this room right here?" He pointed to the drawing room with his head leaning to the side. "And you can entertain us privately." He winked at her, causing her to feel an uneasy sensation within her.

"I am not to associate with any guest, especially in the way you are suggesting," she said firmly. She tried to free herself, but they wouldn't let her past. She was becoming frustrated with them, and it clearly showed on her face, which only seemed to provoke them to continue unpleasantly teasing her. Before they could say or do anything else, however, Sir Kingston arrived in aid of Eleanora.

"What do you two think you are doing, cornering her that way?" He looked at them, all high and mighty, as he truly was. His tone of voice was deep and powerful.

"We were just…" The blond-haired one tried to speak, his smug expression now replaced by a look of terror. His eyes were raised as he looked fearfully at the powerful man who towered over him.

Sir Kingston didn't give him a chance to explain. "How would you like it if I explained this to your father now? Hmm?"

"We're sorry, Sir Kingston," they both hastily said.

He shook his head. "Your apology is not owed to me." He then nodded his head in the direction of Eleanora, who stood meekly behind them. They turned and said their apologies and were immediately off.

Sir Kingston stepped forward to Eleanora and said, "I'm sorry about those two. Lads these days have no respect for a lady." He sighed and then asked, "Are you all right?"

She nodded. "I'm fine, really."

He nodded, looking to the floor.

Eleanora could now properly examine how handsome Sir Kingston looked that night. He wore his black formal suit with a bow tie to match, which made him look very sophisticated compared to his usual dark and mysterious self. He stood tall, and with his great posture, he appeared more refined and sleek. His raven-black wavy locks were neatly combed to the side, and his eyes, the only feature of colour, sparkled a glowing emerald green. His scar didn't diminish his look, and never had, as it gave him a certain character, one of being fearless and courageous.

He looked up again, his thin lips forming a slight smile. "You have done an excellent job, Nora. The party is a huge success, and it is the best I think I have ever had. Thank you," he said, and his smile only grew.

"I'm glad," she replied.

They then both strolled further into the crowd. Eleanora then received a quick visit from Dana. "I will take the empty tray from your hands, Nora."

"Thanks, Dana," she called as Dana disappeared into the crowd.

A few of the men came over to Sir Kingston as one of them declared, "James, this party is just lovely! You have done a marvellous job organising the whole thing!"

"Oh, it wasn't I who organised it," he told them with a smirk. He then made known after a pause, "It was this lovely lady right here." He brought Eleanora over, closer to his side. She felt the grasp of his hand as he pulled her towards them.

"And who might this be?" the same man asked.

"This is my guest," Sir Kingston said instead of introducing her as a servant, much to Eleanora's surprise. "Miss Eleanora is her name."

"Then why is she dressed like this? She should be dressed in her finest gown and joining the party."

"James, you should allow her to join the party. What do you say?"

Sir Kingston looked over to Eleanora, who stood in her shy, modest way. He turned to his friend and agreed, "Yes, she will."

Eleanora was stunned by his sudden invitation to join the party as requested by his friend. She muttered quickly to him, "Sir, I do not have anything suitable to wear."

As Pearl was passing by, Sir Kingston called out to her. She came over in her peach-coloured gown, the one she had bought that day she went into town. "Yes, James?" she asked with a smile.

"Would you care to take Eleanora with you and allow her to borrow one of your gowns for tonight?" Smiling, he looked over at Eleanora. "She will be joining the party."

"But, James?" Her tone was one of protest.

"Go now, Pearl." He waved his hand and motioned for her to go. Eleanora was eyed by Pearl, making Eleanora feel uncomfortable with the idea.

Dana followed Eleanora and requested that she be permitted to come along with her.

*

Eleanora stood patiently waiting while Pearl rifled through her closet, which was filled with all sorts of gowns and dresses. Dana stood by her, also watching. Pearl seethed under her breath while her hands frantically searched. Eleanora could see that she was upset about wasting her precious time helping Eleanora when she should have been down at the party with Sir Kingston instead.

Pearl finally took a dress out and brought it over to Eleanora. She showed it to her, and Eleanora was displeased with her choice. The dress was a tarnished shade of blue, and it flowed straight down in its form. Springing from the dress were frills of a lighter-blue tulle material that hung from all over the dress including the sleeves. A bow was tied at the back, which was the last feature that added to Eleanora's distaste. Pearl smirked at her.

Eleanora glanced over at Dana, who also looked unimpressed by the choice of dress.

"I meant to throw this out long ago. You may keep the dress, though, since you have none, for I do not want it, especially after you have worn it. I think it suits you more than me anyway."

Pearl gave a quick laugh. "Now off you go, out of my room." She waved her hands to shoo them away.

As they went out of the chamber, Eleanora remarked, "She has no taste in fashion whatsoever."

"I agree," Dana said. "The dress is very ugly. This will not do," she concluded.

"Then what do I do? I can't go out to the party in this gown. It is not something I would wear." Eleanora sighed.

Dana smiled, and Eleanora witnessed her face lighting up. "I have just the thing, Nora!"

She took her upstairs into the common room, and Eleanora wondered what she had in mind. "Allow me to be your fairy godmother for tonight!" Dana exclaimed. She went and took out her sewing equipment.

"You are going to restyle the dress? Now?" Eleanora asked in shock.

"Yes, and you are going to help me. Now, we do not have much time if you want to spend most of the night at the party, so let's get to it."

Dana began cutting out all the unnecessary frills with the pair of scissors. She also removed the bow at the back, which Eleanora desperately wanted to get rid of. The dress itself had an undergarment made of silk material that was a cerulean-blue shade. Dana told Eleanora that it would suit her better than the original blue. With that, Dana began cutting off all the external material from the dress and creating the new one out of the internal silk piece. Dana was a natural at sewing and knew how to sew any material within minutes with her vintage sewing machine. She seemed confident in knowing exactly what needed to be done.

Not long after, the dress was finally complete and looked as if it were new.

"Thank you, Dana, for creating a complete turnaround of the dress!" Eleanora was astonished by Dana's fine skills.

"It wasn't much. Just some cutting and mending was needed, and, *voila*, a new dress was made!"

Eleanora chuckled. "It is a wonderful dress, and I appreciate the effort you have put in."

"Now, let me do your hair for you," Dana offered.

Once she had done up her hair, she concluded, "I will be downstairs now. Do not be long, for you have a party to attend." Eleanora then noticed the way Dana gazed at her before she made her departure. "You are very beautiful, Nora. You know that?"

Eleanora blushed and looked down to the floor.

"You must be very excited, for it is your first party."

"I am," Eleanora confirmed with a smile.

Dana came over, held onto her hands, and smiled. "See you soon, Nora." Then she slipped her hands away and was off.

Eleanora took one last look at the tall stand mirror. She sighed when she saw how different she looked when she wore this dress and not her simple servant uniform. It was a huge improvement on the one Pearl had given to her. Eleanora had never felt like this about herself before. This wasn't what she was used to. And now she would appear like this in front of everyone, including the master. What would he think of her? Probably that she looked like a servant who was fooling herself into believing she was living some sort of fairy tale.

After taking a couple of breaths, she managed to build up the courage to go down and join the party. She hoped not to draw any attention to herself, for that was the last thing she wanted – to be seen by everyone as a person she really wasn't.

Eleanora made her way downstairs to the second floor. She heard the multitudes of voices making themselves heard over the music that was being played so beautifully in the background. She took another easy breath, trying to remain calm and contain her excitement at attending her first party. She looked down from where she stood, holding onto the railing with her left hand. All the guests were too busy conversing with each other in their small groups, having a ball and laughing at the jokes they were making, to notice her. She knew this was the opportunity to seize, so Eleanora began making her way as gracefully as she could down the main stairs.

As she made her way down, she suddenly felt all eyes staring up at her. Strange faces all gazed upon Eleanora as they were surprised to see a lady they had never met before. But among these new faces was one that was very familiar to her.

*

Sir Kingston was standing in a circle with a few of his business acquaintances, laughing and sipping on their glasses of champagne. The gentleman who had recommended that Eleanora join the party was facing towards the stairs, and, pointing with the hand that held his glass, he exclaimed, "Ah! Here comes Miss Eleanora now!"

They all turned, and Sir Kingston was astonished by what he was seeing before his very eyes. His heart began to vibrate beneath his chest, his eyes were completely fixed on her, and his lips grew into a smile that never disappeared from the moment he saw her. He watched as she stepped down the flight of stairs in the most graceful but humble manner. Her skin glistened, and her hair was done up in a braided flower bun that framed her face perfectly. The dress she wore was unlike anything he had ever seen before, different in form yet elegant in a simple way. Her sleeves were off the shoulder, exposing her fine neckline and collarbone area. Hanging lightly from the sleeves was a tulle material that flowed in ribbons behind her. It was not like the gowns that the other ladies wore, as those were in umbrella shapes and full of layers. Instead, hers ran straight down and had a little flare at the bottom. The silkiness of the dress allowed for each and every curve of her body to be accentuated. Sir Kingston's spirit soared upon seeing this new appearance of Eleanora.

While he watched her entrance, her eyes fell onto his, and he tried to hold her gaze. He simply could not remove his eyes from hers. They were like precious gems that could not be overlooked. They required attention and a gaze of admiration. A small smile was then seen on her lips as she looked down nervously while taking the last couple of steps.

*

Amongst the crowd, Pearl steamed with frustration. She was shocked and annoyed that Eleanora had altered her gown. She crossed her arms as she saw the way Eleanora walked down those stairs as if she owned the place. She became envious as everyone gazed at the new arrival. She glanced over to Sir Kingston and saw the way his eyes brightened as he took in Eleanora's new look. She then looked at her father and stated in a frustrated manner, "I can't believe that servant girl! She had the nerve to ruin my dress that I helped pick out for her! How dare she!"

"What is she doing dressing like that? Who says she is allowed to join the party?" Mr Nables spoke in a harsh tone.

"James allowed her. He has changed and not for the better," Pearl stated.

She then noticed the way her father eyed Eleanora, his dark eyes shooting in her direction. "Well, we cannot do anything now, regrettably," he seethed to his daughter. He then went on, like a hissing snake, "Make sure you do everything you can to grab James' attention. I do not want him to be anywhere near that girl. Get rid of her if you must."

She nodded her head in obedience as a sly smirk formed on her pinched face.

*

Every step Eleanora made caused her heart to flutter in a way she had never felt before. However, she was a little uneasy about Sir Kingston's intense gaze as she didn't know what to make of it. It unsettled her but also made her wish for more. She could hardly breathe let alone contain her excitement with all this attention he bestowed upon her.

Sir Kingston walked up to Eleanora, and his friends followed behind. He went over and reached for her hand, taking her by surprise. Eleanora felt the touch of her master's hand, which caused a shiver to travel down the back of her spine. He held onto her fingers and brought them up to his mouth. "Eleanora," he spoke her name in a charming tone. He brought his lips down and placed a soft kiss on the top of her hand, causing passionate feelings to stir inside of her. She didn't understand the reason he acted this way, but she thought it must be to please his friends. She felt he was performing an act in front of all to show his well-mannered character. Her heart felt thrilled, but her mind told her it was all a façade. She decided to listen to her mind, and so she went along with this act for his sake.

"You are looking ravishing, Miss Eleanora," the gentleman who had suggested she be invited began.

"Yes, she does," the rest agreed from behind.

"Thank you," she replied modestly.

The same gentleman then remarked, "You know, your name Eleanora reminds me of someone. If I can just put my finger on it." After a brief pause, he made known, "Oh yes, you have the same name as the daughter of the late Sir Portina, who too sadly is deceased."

And before another word could be spoken on the subject, some other guests had made their appearance which swayed the conversation elsewhere.

As the group moved off, Dana then came up beside her. "My, Nora, everyone was stunned when they saw you, even me, for that matter."

"I was nervous walking down. Could you tell?"

"Not really, no."

As Dana said this, Tennent came by. "Nora, look at you! So pretty! You look very different to the girl I know."

Eleanora gave a laugh. "Thank you, Tennent. And I do feel different."

He smiled and took another good look at her. He then turned to his wife. "Dana, honey, the others need you in the kitchen."

She nodded her head and was about to leave when Eleanora asked, "Do you need any help?"

"Of course not, Nora. You've helped enough already. You go and enjoy the party."

They both left her.

Eleanora walked over to the next open room, where the dancing was being held. She watched three dances take place, all with different types of music being played, from slow to fast tempos. The orchestra was wonderful, and each musician played according to their talent. The best part, Eleanora thought, was the piano man and the way he ran his fingers smoothly along the keys, sounding each tune that played from underneath.

Throughout the party, Eleanora tasted some of the appetisers that were served by Marie and Jill. Their faces beamed with smiles upon seeing her in a changed state. They complimented her and bid her well for the rest of the night. Even Dashier, whom she stumbled upon, praised her appearance.

Later on, Eleanora made her way through the crowd watching the dancing couples. She headed over to the side porch, which led outside, slightly away from the party. She stood against the marbled railing, placing her fingers firmly around it. She was standing underneath what appeared to be the most mystical night sky she had ever looked upon, where the moon shone its clear silver radiance amongst the multitude of stars. These twinkled heavenly like they were dancing amongst each other, side by side, all together.

She then looked down to her hands and was in deep thought for a while. Not long after, she was interrupted by someone who came forth and made their presence known.

"What are you doing out here all alone, not joining the party?"

A shiver ran over her body that had nothing to do with the cool, misty night.

It was Sir Kingston who came her way. Eleanora turned around and saw him stepping closer towards her with his hands behind his back. Then, he was right by her side.

She responded, "I do not fit in with the crowd. I am but a plain pebble amongst all the shiny gems." She had the courage to face him.

He looked at her; his eyes never shifted away from her own.

His voice was deep but utterly soothing as he replied, "Why fit in when you can stand out?" She looked at him in a questioning way when he spoke this. He continued, "You have definitely stood out amongst all the guests here. Eleanora, you look beautiful."

This warmed her heart and caused her to smile. Her lips parted, wanting to speak what was in her heart, but instead, she muttered as she looked away, "It is not me that is beautiful but the dress. It is nothing but a façade, one that will end after tonight."

This left Sir Kingston silent for a few moments. He then turned his body the other way, leaning his back against the marble railing. "You know," he began, "I have never seen Pearl wear that sort of dress before. I don't believe it could be hers."

"Dana and I altered the original dress. It wasn't to our liking, so we had the idea to change it. Pearl did say she never wanted the dress back, especially if I was to wear it."

He gave a laugh. "Really?" He looked down at her dress once more. "Well, I do believe I prefer this."

Eleanora was surprised, not expecting he would favour her choice and style over Pearl's.

It was silent again between them. However, the sound of music that was played and hands clapping to the beat filled this silence. Eleanora listened and then heard Sir Kingston clear his throat as if he wished to speak. When he did, he asked in his sumptuously rich, lavish tone, "Would you care to dance, Eleanora?"

She was speechless when he asked this of her and didn't know what to say at first.

"But I have never danced before," she replied, lowering her head.

"Never in your life? Not even a simple one?" he questioned.

"Never," she affirmed.

"Well, then, I will have to teach you. Shall we dance?"

He reached out his hand for her to take. She smiled at him and placed her hand neatly on top of his. He led her to the centre of the porch as they still held each other's hands firmly together. He entwined his fingers with hers. Eleanora watched carefully as he did so. He brought her other hand and placed it onto his right shoulder. He then stepped forward, coming closer to her but still leaving a small gap between them. He placed his other hand down to rest on her lower back. Eleanora felt her body freeze as he held his hand there so tenderly. She started to become nervous, never having been in this sort of position with Sir Kingston before.

He began to teach her a simple dance step to the traditional Estleton waltz. "Follow me now," he instructed. "Side together, side together," he began.

Eleanora looked down to her feet, watching her steps as she followed his lead.

"Now we both turn around and repeat the other way." He glided with her until they completed this the second time. "Let go of this hand and pull away still holding my other one." They did this simultaneously. "Now turn around, coming back to me." Eleanora twirled until he reached back for her hand. He then continued on with the simple side-together step. "There we go. You must be wearing good shoes," he said with a chuckle.

She pulled her dress up a little and showed off her boots. They were the ones she normally wore. "These are the only ones I have. But don't tell anyone," she said with a giggle.

He chuckled again before replying, "You have my word."

She dropped the bottom of her dress back down again.

"Another musical piece is about to begin," he remarked.

They got into position, and this time, a much slower piece of music was played. He held her by the hand again as he looked down at her. He started to lead the way as she followed him, repeating the steps like they had practised, only now, dancing to the melody of the music.

Sir Kingston took Eleanora around the porch. Each step was well-executed, and each twirl flowed perfectly. Eleanora was delighted as she waltzed about with a gentleman for the very first time. She had forgotten all about the crowd that was inside, and it seemed that she and her master were the only ones on earth as they danced about. She felt as if she were in the meadow, which was a calming setting to dream of while they danced lightly on their feet. Sir Kingston turned Eleanora around as she spun a few times here and there, always falling back into place with him. She felt this was right, that this was what she had dreamed of, a magical night such as this, where she could be carefree and do the things she'd never experienced before. She felt completely safe within her master's arms, and the way he swiftly moved about in tune showed how much effort he was putting in to please her.

The music continued, but Sir Kingston made his way to the middle of the floor. He began to sway very slowly with Eleanora. He gazed down at her, and his emerald-green eyes glowed with a different light all so suddenly. Eleanora was aware of the way he turned his eyes down at her, but she could not describe what was different about the way he did it. She bit down on her bottom lip, feeling the nervousness come upon her once again, this time, causing her body to heat up rapidly. She noticed the way he continued to look down at her mouth and how his own seemed to want to linger close by hers. There was some sort of temptation she could feel rousing within him, but she knew that couldn't be a possibility. Eleanora suddenly felt overwhelmed. The way her body reacted to every single move he made caused her to tremble inside. She thought she was going to start to shake if she stayed in this position any longer.

She slipped her hand from his and took a step back from him, still gazing into his eyes. She recognised the way they struggled to return to reality, the way they flickered and looked back at her. It seemed as if he were in some sort of trance.

Then, a voice was heard, one that ruined the intense yet satisfying moment.

"There you are, James!"

"Pearl!" Sir Kingston exclaimed. He spoke quickly as if to explain his actions. "I was just showing Eleanora how to do the waltz." He glanced at Eleanora and then back to Pearl as his eyes widened.

"Really?" She stretched out the word and seemed irritated to see them together once again. "James, you promised to dance with me tonight. Did you forget?" she demanded and fluttered her eyelashes.

"Of course I haven't," he replied.

Eleanora was uncomfortable just standing there in between them while they had a conversation. She said softly, "I should go now." She took one last look at Sir Kingston before she took her leave from his side.

From a distance, Eleanora watched the way Sir Kingston and Pearl danced together. It looked almost unnatural, unbalanced and not smooth at all. It was as if Pearl was trying too hard to show off her dance style. Eleanora couldn't claim that she was any better, but something about her first dance tonight accompanied by her master made her feel something special that seemed to connect her to the dance. It made her feel things she never imagined she would feel with anyone. She couldn't describe it, but she knew she felt unexpected emotions whenever she was around him.

The dance had finished, and all the gentlemen bowed to their partners while the ladies curtseyed. Eleanora headed straight to the drawing room and closed the door behind her. She was alone there, and that was how she wanted it, so she could think quietly without any interruptions.

Not long after, however, the door opened and shut again. Eleanora turned around in fright and saw Pearl quickly walking towards her. "What do you think you are doing?" Pearl started.

Eleanora kept silent as she took note of Pearl's expression. Her bright eyes fiercely stared at her, and her cheeks were bright red as they burned with jealousy. Pearl stood as if ready to attack, but it was her mouth that would be doing all the shaming. "How dare you waltz down the stairs in my gown, which you purposely ruined! I bet you did it just to get back at me!" she accused immediately.

"You allowed me to keep the dress, for you wouldn't wear it after me," returned Eleanora, defending herself from the sudden accusation. "So, yes, I altered it to suit me," she added.

"Do you know how much that dress cost?" Pearl looked furious. She then narrowed her eyes and said, "But what bothers me the most is…*how dare you dance with Sir Kingston*! Do you not understand that you are just a servant, and he is someone much greater? You cannot be associated with him in that way. What would people think?" She paused, trying to regain her breath that seemed constricted by the tightness of her gown. "Don't you see that Sir Kingston just feels sorry for you? He has no intention to become any closer to you. I see the way you stare at him with those wicked eyes of yours. I am telling you now…" Pearl stepped forward menacingly. "Do not think for a moment that he could like you; you are out of your mind if you believe so." She paused and then changed her tone. "I want you to leave the party by telling him that you are not feeling well. And tomorrow, when you are working, as you are a servant, you keep to yourself, for that is what you are."

During this, Eleanora was both perplexed and shocked by the things that came out of Pearl's mouth. How could she possibly believe that Eleanora had intentions towards Sir Kingston in that way?

Eleanora felt that her lips were tightly shut. She was afraid that if she were to part them just a little bit, she might start to cry. However, although she tried to stop it, a tear escaped from her eye and rolled down her cheek. She knew Pearl cared not for what she was feeling nor how she hurt her. Eleanora also understood that it was Pearl's jealously and her dislike that caused her to lash out at her this way.

"Do you understand?" Pearl insisted.

Eleanora nodded her head and wiped her tear away, trying to put on a brave face. She hastily left the room before another cruel word could be said.

She was now on her way to find Sir Kingston, but when she did, he was caught up in conversation with the many guests surrounding him. She tried to squeeze through and get his attention, but it was impossible. Instead, she went looking for Dana and notified her that she was feeling too tired and unwell to stay any longer at the party.

"Are you sure you must retire to your chamber now, Nora? The party is still going."

"Please tell the master when you have the chance. I am truly unwell at the moment."

"If that is what you wish. I shall tell him when I have the chance. I guess it is best you get to sleep early as you have to work as usual tomorrow. Get better soon, my dear."

Eleanora retired to her room for the rest of that night, obeying Pearl's demanding orders.

# Chapter 17

That night was a restless one. Eleanora was awake till two the next morning. She could not possibly go to sleep when all she could think about was what had happened earlier. She took the time to think about it all, but it only left her feeling more confused. She second-guessed herself countless times, and many questions with endless possible answers to them went in circles around her mind. But she could not figure out the right answers. That only left her contemplating even more so. She was not only confused by it all but upset at the way she had been treated. She didn't expect any better from Pearl, for that was her way with those under her. But when it came to Sir Kingston, he never treated her as an inferior. Instead, he allowed her to voice her opinion and do what she believed was right. He was always good to her, even in the most unexpected times.

She began to cry while lying on her bed, facing the high ceiling above her, for there was nothing else to do but push her misery away. Her eyes stung with the saltiness of her tears, and she constantly wiped her face and sniffed while she wished this terrible night, which had started as a dream, could end within the blink of an eye. Eventually, her eyes grew heavy, and she drifted off to sleep. That night, her sleep was fitful, and she dreamed of many things, some good and some bad.

\*

It was a bright early morning. The sun shined intensely through the white curtains of Eleanora's room. As she awoke, she checked the clock and saw it was already fifteen minutes past seven. She had not gotten that much sleep, but she knew there was no way she could stay in bed any longer; she was already late, and for the second time now. She arose and walked barefooted to the window and drew aside the curtains. She squinted in the sunlight that came straight towards her and fell in a ray onto the floor. She managed to slip into her uniform and walk down the stairs fairly slowly. She felt dizzy a couple of times while doing so, not knowing what was wrong with her.

When she was walking down the main stairs, she saw Sir Kingston resting against the bannister. She saw him look at her quizzically. Eleanora thought also to herself that he must find her different now compared to last night as she had returned to her servant outfit, the one she was always supposed to be seen in and nothing else. Eleanora made one last step towards him. Not a word was said just yet, but his gaze remained fixed. He then spoke to her.

"You didn't stay at the party the entire time?"

She replied, "I did tell Dana to tell you of my reason."

"Yes, and she delivered it to me," he confirmed. "But why didn't you come to me instead?"

She breathed a short, soft sigh. "I tried. But you were too preoccupied with all the guests. I couldn't just interrupt you, now, could I?"

Those same eyes continued to scan hers after the response she gave. He nodded his head slightly and looked down at his knee. "So, were you feeling unwell?"

"Yes," she replied simply. "I'm sorry again for being late this second time. I had a huge headache when I woke up, and I have one even now as I speak."

"You have a headache?" He took a step towards her.

"Yes, and I am feeling quite…quite…quite diz…zzy." She slurred her words and fell forward towards Sir Kingston. He immediately reacted and caught her before she fell.

*

Eleanora was slowly becoming conscious again, yet her eyes remained shut and heavy. All she could hear were muffled voices in the background. Her mind ached, and she began to feel the heat rising in her body, causing her temperature to strike up and sweat beads to form on her forehead. She heard the door close and then reopen some moments later before footsteps approached her bed. Soon, Eleanora made out who the voices belonged to. The person who just entered muttered, "How is she doing, Dr Marton?" Eleanora could distinguish the deep yet soothing voice of Sir Kingston, the voice she knew so well. Eleanora then recognised the name Dr Marton and remembered it was the physician who had come over to examine the master.

"Not very well at the moment, I must say," Dr Marton said with a sigh. "But take ease; it's nothing serious."

Eleanora forced herself to gradually open her eyelids despite the pain she was in. Her vision was blurry at first as her watery eyes tried to focus. But when she blinked a few times, her vision cleared. She observed the way both Sir Kingston and Dr Marton looked down at her as they stood by her bedside.

The doctor brought a calming smile to his face. "Eleanora, you are awake, my dear!"

"What's wrong with me?" She tried getting up.

"Do not move. It's best you lie down and rest," the doctor advised. "You have a slight fever, Eleanora. But it should go away in a few days' time. There's nothing to worry about, I can assure you."

"How did I get the fever all so suddenly?" she asked further.

"You must have stressed yourself from all the excitement of the party. I think you also overworked yourself. Perhaps you are worried about something. Is there anything you need to tell us?" He looked at her expectantly, but she just shook her head. "Very well then. Make sure you stay in bed."

Dr Marton looked over to Sir Kingston and directed, "She will not be able to work for a few days; otherwise, she will just get worse. She must stay inside and eat normally. That way, she will recover faster." He took out a small bottle of medicine from his briefcase and handed it over to Sir Kingston. "Make sure she consumes this twice a day, morning and night. It will also help her recover sooner and help with that headache of hers."

He turned to Eleanora again. "I must be on my way. I will check on you in two days' time to see if you have made progress." He smiled. "Get well soon, Eleanora."

"Thank you, Dr Marton," she replied.

He stroked her cheek with his finger once before taking his leave.

"How long was I unconscious for?" Eleanora asked as Sir Kingston looked her way.

"You were out for about an hour," he indicated to her. "Do you remember anything at all?"

"Only when I was speaking to you. Then I felt dizzy, and everything went black from then till now," she explained. She then asked, "How did I get here?"

Sir Kingston let out a cough to clear his throat before he answered, "I...uh...carried you to your room."

"Oh, you did?"

"That wouldn't be the first time I have carried you," he teased.

"Yes, you're right," she agreed and smiled softly. She looked away, towards the window.

He then asked, "Do you want me to open it, for some fresh air?"

"That would be lovely. Thank you, master," she said with a smile.

He quickly moved to the window before unlocking it and opening it wide. He stood there for a short moment before he turned back to her. He then remarked, "The party was grandeur! All the guests favoured it over any other party I have hosted before. Thank you, Nora."

"I'm pleased to hear that."

"And you enjoyed yourself, with it being your first?"

"Yes, I did." And she had, except for Pearl's confrontation, which she wouldn't dare tell him about, or anyone else for that matter. She wanted to change the subject, so she said instead, "I will try to get back to work as soon as I can, master."

"There is no rush, Nora. You must rest properly. I don't want your health to deteriorate any further."

"I remember someone once told me that walking it off is the best medicine," she reminded him.

Sir Kingston chuckled. "You have a good memory, don't you?"

Eleanora giggled, and he went on, "Well, in your case, it's different. You are always working too much. I can't risk having anything happen to you."

Eleanora nodded. "Has Dana been informed about this?"

"You do worry too much, Nora," he said with a laugh.

Eleanora blushed.

"Listen, Dana already knows of the situation. She only hopes you get better. She will be up here to take care of you soon." He took a breath and sighed. "Now, rest easy. I will check on you later."

"Okay. Thank you again." Eleanora relaxed back onto the bed.

Sir Kingston left her, leaving the door open.

*

It was not long after when a knock was heard at the door, and Dana arrived with a tray of breakfast, which she placed on the table. She stepped towards the bed and looked down, asking, "How are you feeling, Nora? I heard you have a fever and a headache."

"My head is still sore, and I do feel quite warm," Eleanora explained.

"Well, I am here to look after you if you need anything." Dana went over to the small table and brought over her meal. "Here, you haven't had your breakfast yet, and the doctor said you must eat."

Eleanora sat up, her back resting on the pillow against the bedframe. "I do not feel like eating too much, though."

"Very well. Just eat as much as you can. And then you can rest." Dana poured some milk and honey into her tea. She then spread the butter and freshly made strawberry jam onto some toast. She handed it to Eleanora, who nibbled on the bread at first and then took a bite. However, the fever didn't allow her tongue to enjoy the sweetness the jam provided. She could only take two bites before she placed it back down onto the plate. She took a small sip of her tea to soothe her throat.

"Is that all?" Dana remarked.

"I really cannot take another bite. I can't even taste the sweetness of the jam the way I always like to."

"That's a shame. At least try to drink your tea before it gets cold."

Eleanora took another couple of sips to please her.

"Do you need anything else before I leave you be?"

"No, thank you, Dana." Eleanora tried to put on her usual smile.

"I will check on you every now and then. Don't forget to take your medicine." She paused. "Rest well, Nora."

*

That day, every couple of hours, Eleanora was visited by Dana, who checked on her and made sure she was getting better. Dashier, Tennent, Jill, and Marie also visited her once or twice. Eleanora only slept for a couple of hours, and after that, she remained resting in her bed. Sir Kingston also checked on her, as promised, by the late afternoon.

The doctor arrived again a couple of days later, just as he had proposed. Eleanora felt better than the last time he was there. Her headache had gone the day before, her eyes no longer felt heavy and tired, and the fever was gradually abating. She had tried to get out of bed, but on Dana's orders, she wasn't allowed until the doctor had inspected her condition.

"Your health is improving, Eleanora, which is a splendid sign. You may go outside in the sun and breathe in some fresh air, for I believe that will do you some good."

As soon as the doctor left, Eleanora did exactly that. She strolled in the garden around the manor and in the fields for almost an hour to regain her strength and energy. That night, she had some tea with Dana, Marie, and Jill and went back to bed early, ready to start work the next day.

# Chapter 18

Eleanora was to complete the simpler jobs around the manor and not the overly physical tasks that would put her at risk of feeling unwell again. She worked inside the manor alongside Marie. After Marie had finished sweeping, Eleanora took over and polished the marble floor. She kneeled down on the floor, the bucket filled with hot water and the soap beside her. She dipped the sponge into the bucket and then squeezed out all the excess liquid. She then wiped the floor, removing all the dirt and stains. As she did so, she continuously hummed very softly to herself a musical tune she remembered from the party. "Hmm…hmmm…mm…hmmmmm…"

After some time, she neared the main stairs as she continued to hum, allowing her mind to escape reality for a short time. She was startled when she heard the bucket tip to its side and all the hot, soapy water spill out onto the floor. It created a puddle that soaked the bottom of her dress right up to her knees. She looked up and saw it was Pearl who had committed the cruel act.

"Oopsies!" Pearl faked a surprised expression. She continued on her way while glancing behind her with a sly, sneering smile at Eleanora, who looked shaken. Pearl finished off her act with a cruel laugh on her way out.

Eleanora tried to quickly wipe up the water from the floor. Suddenly, Sir Kingston was there; he bent down low in front of her and used a dry cloth he must have found to soak up the pool of water. His head was down, focusing on clearing up the water. Eleanora couldn't help but admire the way some of the strands of his hair fell to the side of his forehead. She smiled a little at this, but then she wondered why he came and helped her the way he did. She was a servant, she thought, and yet, he came from his own will.

She couldn't help but ask, "Why do you help me, master?"

She watched as he stopped moving his hand. He lifted his face to her, his eyebrows furrowed slightly. He let go of the soaking-wet cloth and took her hand. He brought her up to a standing position with him, and they faced each other. Eleanora looked up to him, wondering what he was thinking inside of that peculiar mind of his.

He now said in his deep tone, "I saw what Pearl did to you, Nora." He paused, shaking his head. "She had no right to do what she did. It was childish indeed. And now, she has demeaned herself in my eyes." He looked ashamed of Pearl's actions.

Eleanora sighed, looking down. Sir Kingston bent his head down a little and brought her chin up slowly until her eyes met his. His thumb gently stroked the bottom of her chin. Eleanora thought she would tremble if he continued to do this, but her nerves soon started to settle as she felt the warm and soothing sensation of his thumb brushing against her skin.

"I know you are upset by this," he stated, removing his thumb from her skin.

"I'm fine, really," she said.

"You are not bothered by this at all?" he questioned with eyes glaring.

"How can I be when I am used to it?" she then stated.

She observed the way the pupils of his eyes dilated sympathetically with pity; his lips were tightly shut as they pressed down forcefully onto each other. After a moment's silence, he switched his focus to upstairs as someone came their way.

"Marie," he called. "Would you come and help Eleanora finish cleaning down here?"

She nodded. "Yes, master."

"I must go," he muttered to Eleanora.

She nodded her head once and stepped to the side so he could be on his way.

*

189

Later during the day, an incident occurred that caused Dr Marton to be called instantly once again – this time, to examine another patient within the household. Tennent was lying flat on his stomach as the doctor inspected his spine. The doctor brought his hand down to his lower back and worked his way up.

"Ahh!" Tennent cried as the doctor squeezed the left side of his back.

"Pain seems to be there," Dr Marton muttered to himself.

Sir Kingston looked over to Dr Marton as he continued to move his hand upwards.

Tennent reacted again as he moved closer towards his spine.

"And there." The doctor removed his hand and declared, "Well, Tennent, it looks like you are in great need of healing time. You have strained your back while working, and age has played a part in this too."

"I'm old before I even feel old," Tennent remarked.

Dana stood on the side looking down upon him.

"It happens to many people before they even reach old age," Dr Marton mentioned.

"What do you suggest is to be done, Dr Marton?" Sir Kingston asked firmly.

The doctor looked to him and stated, "Well, for starters, Tennent shouldn't be doing any more physical work for a while."

"I will be able to continue working normally, won't I?"

Dr Marton turned to Tennent, stating, "Yes, you will…eventually, but you must take it easy and reduce the amount of heavy work you do and split it up throughout the week so you are not doing everything all in the one day. I suggest for now you stay in bed. And rub some of this oil on. It will help with the pain and soothe you." The doctor handed the bottle of oil to Dana.

"For how long?"

"It could take up to three days. But I suggest you take the week to fully recover." He paused. "You badly strained your back while cutting the logs of wood, Tennent. You need to be more careful next time."

"Well, it isn't my fault that I'm stuck in bed for the next few days. It's all in my back." Tennent now turned around slowly with the aid of Dana. He put his shirt back on, covering his bare chest.

"Get better soon, Tennent. I will return, and hopefully, your back will be all healed again and ready to start moving." Dr Marton left the room, farewelling Sir Kingston before he did so.

"Oh, master, I'm sorry for all this inconvenience," Tennent began.

"Oh, don't worry, Tennent. I'm just glad you didn't stub your toe or cut your thumb off," Sir Kingston teased him.

"But, master," Tennent continued, "I have so much work that must be done around here. All the wood still needs to be cut, especially with winter approaching. And the animals…"

Before he could continue with the list, Sir Kingston stopped him and said, "Forget all that."

"But, master, these tasks must be done."

"I will take over your jobs," Sir Kingston reassured him.

"You, master?" Tennent's eyes widened. "Why don't you just hire someone temporarily?" he suggested.

"Because I want to do it. Besides, I will only take on the physically demanding work around here. The rest will be suitable for the others to do, I'm sure." He took a breath while looking down at him. "Take care of yourself. Dana will obviously be looking after you from here until you get yourself back up again." He was heading towards the door when he turned back around and said with a smirk on his face, "Now, don't move from this room."

Tennent responded, "You bet I won't."

Sir Kingston chuckled at his annoyed tone.

*

It was early afternoon the next day. The sun was high, shining its incredible light and heat upon the land.

"I cannot believe Tennent strained his back yesterday," Eleanora spoke in a sympathetic tone.

"I cannot believe it either," Dana responded. "He will be in bed for a few days."

"But the doctor did say he can resume his regular duties when he is well again?"

Dana nodded. "Yes, but he needs to be more careful next time and not overdo it," she explained. She lowered her head, continuing with her usual work in the kitchen.

Eleanora exhaled and spoke again, trying to comfort her, "Don't worry, Dana. I'm sure he will be fine. He will get better, and his back will be stronger than ever."

She laughed. "Oh, Nora, you are so optimistic. But you're right, and I shouldn't worry. I'm just glad he didn't harm himself any worse than this."

It was quiet for a moment. Eleanora then brought up another subject. "So, I heard Sir Kingston is taking care of the hard jobs around here."

"Yes, he is." Dana then looked over at her and said, "I see you're done there." She nodded her head at the peeled apples.

Eleanora looked down to her bowl. "Oh, yes, I have," she said with a laugh. She handed Dana the bowl while asking, "What are you going to be making with these apples? Apple pie?"

"Of course! And with the leftovers, I'm going to make an apple caramel sauce," Dana said more brightly.

Eleanora smiled. "I can't wait to try the sauce!"

"You will be the first to taste test and see if I have perfected it."

"Aren't I always?"

After Eleanora had finished up in the kitchen, she decided to stroll to the back of the manor. She stopped herself when her eyes suddenly caught sight of the one she admired. She jumped a step back in nervousness and tried to take a steady breath before she stepped forward again while holding onto the side of the wall. Eleanora fixed her eyes on Sir Kingston, who worked not far from where she stood underneath the roof of the back porch. His back was facing her, and she could not see his face. His upper body was exposed, and the sun shone on him while he was working. He took the axe that was placed against a large stone and swung it up behind him. With one great show of strength, he cut the log of wood, precisely splitting it in half. He placed the axe back down again, grabbed the logs of wood, and threw them in the pile along with the rest.

Eleanora went on watching him as he continued working with a smooth rhythm. During this, she also observed the way his back was reddening in the sun and dripped with fierce sweat. His veins stood out against his well-muscled arms as they flexed in motion. Eleanora felt her heart skip a beat every time he lifted that axe up. She couldn't stop her curious eyes as they wandered all over him. Her lips parted, and for some reason, she felt a yearning desire to see more of him. And because of this, she thought she would tremble, so she held onto the side wall even tighter to balance herself in case she was to fall.

A short moment later, she heard a voice echo from behind her.

"Nora!" Dana called, startling her and causing her to hastily step away before she was caught staring at the master.

Dana walked towards the open door.

"There you are, Nora," she said.

Eleanora felt embarrassed and hoped Dana hadn't seen what she was doing.

"Yes, Dana. What is it?" she quickly spoke.

Dana eyed her for a moment and then asked, "Would you mind helping me a little in the kitchen? There are some things I forgot we still need to do."

"Yes, of course." Eleanora then noticed Dana was holding something. "Is that for the master?"

"Yes, it is. He has been out in the sun for too long now, and I'm sure he is in great need of water."

"Oh, I can do that for you, Dana!" Eleanora insisted eagerly.

"Why, thank you, Eleanora."

Eleanora hoped Dana wouldn't realise that she wanted to see and be near the master. She then took the jug and cup from her. Dana smiled and started to head off. Eleanora watched, making sure she had gone back inside. She then turned and went down to meet with the master. As she walked towards him, her heart began to feel heavy with exhilarating nerves, and even though the weather was quite warm, her body shivered. Her mind was racing with many different sentences to start their conversation with.

When she was just a few steps behind him, she managed to say, "You have been working very hard this afternoon."

His emerald-green eyes met with hers as he turned and smiled. "As you can see."

Eleanora shifted her gaze to the pile of wood and then looked back at him again. She watched as he wiped the sweat from his forehead with his hand and then ran his fingers through his hair.

"Here, this will quench your thirst." She poured the ice-cold water right to the top of the glass. She handed it to him, and he took it from her slowly, never losing eye contact with her. She watched as he brought the glass to his dried lips and finished the water in one go, not taking any breaths. She examined the way his throat moved every time he swallowed. Her eyes now lowered to his collarbone and then down to his chest area. It was stained with sweat, and his fine hairs shone in the sun. The sight of his sculptured body reminded her of when she saw him naked while she saved him from drowning within his own bathtub. But, of course, it wasn't until he was soundly lying on his bed that she had properly examined him, just in the way she did now. However, this time was different, for she wasn't so nervous seeing a man's flesh as she had been the first time. She was, instead, rather fascinated and curious to see how his sturdy body worked.

Sir Kingston finished drinking within a few seconds. He asked for another glass, and she quickly filled it to the top again. This time, she observed the way some of the water dripped down from the rim of the glass and trickled down to his chest. Eleanora looked away for a moment, overcome with the many indescribable feelings rushing through her very being. They were feelings Eleanora had never experienced before.

Sir Kingston handed the glass back to her. She poured the rest of the water into his hands, and he splashed it onto his face, cleaning it and wiping his hair back.

"The sun is really intense," she remarked as she took a seat on the stone.

"You can say that again," he said with a chuckle. He looked away for a moment and then resumed gazing at her. "You seem brighter than usual," he commented.

She blushed instantly; her shyness was now exposed in front of him.

"I wonder what it could be?" He smirked and then chuckled again. Then he said, "I should resume my work." He reached for the axe that was leaning beside her. He held onto it firmly with both hands and swung it behind him once again.

This time, Eleanora had a different view of him. She saw the way his muscles bulged on his side as he held the axe. And when he threw it over his head to strike the piece of wood, his chest rose, exposing his ribs. Once he brought the axe straight down onto the wood, his back and shoulders rose and fell. He exhaled deeply and tried to suck in more air.

"You cut with precision," she complimented him.

He faced her with a small smile.

She hopped up from where she sat. "I will leave you to it," she said and gave him one last smile before she left.

# Chapter 19

It was a challenging week for Eleanora. It was a time filled with confusion and mixed emotions that stirred her heart in so many ways. It began to beat ferociously, though in a pleasant way, whenever Sir Kingston was in the room, or whenever his name was mentioned or even spoken about. She just couldn't control the way her heart would leap every time. She tried to stop this reaction of hers, but every time she managed to calm her nerves down, the blood running through her veins would resume its quickened pace through her entire body. She felt desperate as she knew she could do nothing about it, the thing that caused this, whatever it was. She didn't understand why she felt this way, or why her body would tremble when his presence was near, or why when their eyes met, she would feel her face turn into a red shade of shyness. She couldn't speak of any of these feelings to anyone else, not a single soul, for she wouldn't be able to describe them. And if she could, they would think her mad for the inexplicable emotions she was feeling. So she kept trying to get past them on her own.

*

The following Wednesday, just before noon, Sir Kingston was informed that an unexpected visitor had arrived at Kingston Manor. He came bolting down the stairs to the Grand Hall to see to this. He found Tennent, whose back had now recovered, and he made it known that a young lady was waiting out in the front courtyard and demanding to speak with Sir Kingston without delay regarding a rather important matter. At first, Sir Kingston refused and scolded Tennent for allowing her past the gate. He ordered for her to be sent back by his command, for he had no interest in a strange lady who had shown up uninvited. But once Tennent mentioned that Eleanora seemed to be the subject she wished to discuss, his eyes narrowed in speculation.

"And how long was she lurking about by the entrance gate?" Sir Kingston asked.

"I'm not sure, sir," Tennent said while holding onto the rim of his hat with both hands. He then added, "While I was doing my duties, I spotted the strange lady dressed in a cloak with her head covered by the hood. I called out, demanding to know what she was doing there by the manor." He paused. "She sounded desperate, sir," he ended.

Sir Kingston exhaled a heavy breath before instructing, "Bring her to the drawing room."

He then rushed to the drawing room, swung the door open, and made haste to the centre of the room. There he stood, wondering what he was about to get himself into and what this all had to do with Eleanora.

The young lady finally arrived.

"Shut the door," commanded Sir Kingston without any hint of welcome to his tone.

The lady obeyed, then turned around; she was holding her cloak over her arm. When she stepped forward, Sir Kingston's eyes widened with a glare. "I recognise you," he stated to the lady, who was dressed in a silver gown.

He was a few spaces before her; his stance was as still as that of a guarding soldier. His mouth parted as if he wished to speak, yet no words broke the silence.

He finally said, "You are Miss Mandy Dusilla, Eleanora's cousin." His eyebrows furrowed, creasing his forehead as he suddenly remembered all the things Eleanora had told him about how cruel life was with her relatives.

His faltering tone changed to a demanding one. "What are you doing here, showing up like this unexpectedly in my manor without consulting me first?"

She took a step forward as she hastily replied, "I have something very urgent to tell you that is of great importance." She then added, "You were the only one I knew I could turn to."

"Is this about Eleanora?" As Sir Kingston mentioned her name, it left him feeling frightened about what this urgent matter could be.

"Yes, it is." She lowered her eyes to the floor.

Sir Kingston thought she looked disappointed with herself...guilty even. He waited for her to start explaining, but she remained mute. He exclaimed, "You better not have come here to take her back! Because I will not allow it!"

"I am not here for that," she replied softly.

"Speak then! What have you come here to say?" His eyes widened once again, and his fierce temper was almost about to get the better of him.

She warned him, "You must not tell any of this to anyone, especially Eleanora for now; that is, until you can make things right for her."

"Make things right?" he questioned, desperate for a clearer answer.

"I will tell you what I have heard accidentally." She began to explain, "It was two days ago, on Monday morning, when I was going about my usual business. We had a visitor at that time, a man of quite old age whom I later learned was a lawyer. They were speaking in the drawing room, just the two of them. I was very curious to know what the matter was because Mr Miles – that was his name – only came for serious matters, and this one, I was kept in the dark about. I stood by the open door and eavesdropped on their secretive conversation. As I looked through the gap, Mr Miles was seated by the desk, writing and taking notes on some paper whilst my mother was talking to him. I managed to hear some of the conversation."

Mandy paused before continuing. "My mother spoke first. 'When will I claim the rest of the wealth, Mr Miles?' And he answered, 'Very soon, I can assure you, Madam Dusilla.' He then reiterated, 'I must have you sign a few of these documents first, and then the transaction will take place as soon as I finalise these.' My mother answered eagerly, 'And I will now own the rest of my brother-in-law's wealth? All the lands he owned, everything that he left for his only daughter?' And Mr Miles nodded his head, affirming this. 'Yes, to the very last cent, all will be yours.' Then my mother uttered in a wretched tone, 'I cannot believe it took this long,' and Mr Miles responded, 'Well, as long as it is being done now...thanks to me.' I saw the look on my mother's face."

Mandy paused the story as she described the image. "It was one filled with determination and greed. I have never seen her look like that before in my entire life. It frightened me as I knew nothing of whom they were referring to...until they spoke of her."

Sir Kingston remained listening; not a single word escaped his lips as he was too intrigued by this revelation. He started to propose in his mind where this was heading and how Eleanora fit into this puzzle of secrecy.

Mandy continued with her account. "I heard Eleanora's name being mentioned as well as mine. My mother spoke again, saying, 'I have gotten rid of that stupid, worthless niece of mine. She is nothing...a nobody. She will never know her true origins or what she is worth, now that I have taken all of her father's possessions and great wealth. I am the woman I've always dreamed of being; I will be the richest one in all of Estleton!' She exclaimed this with more happiness than she had ever shown before. 'And what about your daughter?' Mr Miles now referred to me, and my mother answered, 'My daughter will marry a rich man who will look after her. I will make sure of that. She won't need any of my wealth.' And Mr Miles said, 'If that is what you wish.' Mr Miles handed over the documents, and my mother instantly signed them without hesitation or any sort of reluctance."

Mandy ended the story but continued speaking her mind. "I had now learned that my mother was stealing all the money, wealth, properties, and possessions of her late brother-in-law. This was all to be passed down to his only daughter, Eleanora. She was to take the inheritance. And yet not a cent will be given to her name. I didn't believe this at first because Eleanora is a servant and was born to parents of a low status, so this did not make sense to me at all. At least, that was what I was told. I thought this cruel and morally wrong. I have always disliked my cousin because of the things my mother has always made me believe of her ever since I was a little girl. I know the way I treated her all those years was appalling. I regret it greatly now." She lowered her head, looking ashamed of herself.

"Please, continue," Sir Kingston urged.

She took a breath before she did. "I waited until my mother headed out as she needed to do something. This was my opportunity to have a look at the paperwork to learn the details and to confirm that I was hearing correctly. I went inside the room and notified Mr Miles that his coachman urgently needed him, which, of course, was a lie, but it was the only way to get rid of him. He groaned and went out of the drawing room, leaving his satchel behind, as hoped. I hastily made my way to the desk and opened his bag. I flicked through all the paperwork that there was. I read, my eyes scanning all the small print on each page. After some time, I discovered that Eleanora was no servant at all. She was, in fact, the daughter of Sir Portina, who is my uncle by marriage. All my life, due to my mother's words, I had thought him to be a poor man. But now I held his will. It clearly stated that the guardian of Eleanora would be her aunt, whom she was to live with and be in the care of until she was twenty-one years of age. His daughter would receive full ownership of the inheritance when she turned eighteen. But until that time, his wife's sister, my mother, would keep it safe for her."

Mandy paused and looked down. "That is when I realised my mother had not kept her part of the deal for her sister's child. She had disowned Eleanora and stolen everything from her. I found another will, which is a fake one, rewritten to state that my mother had full ownership of her brother-in-law's inheritance. Other documents, including Eleanora's birth certificate, were placed in that bag. Mr Miles, the lawyer, was in on the whole thing as his signatures were all over each page. I knew I had to do something, for it was not right for my cousin to be treated this poorly and unjustly. I couldn't and I wouldn't allow it to happen to her. So, I quickly seized all the important papers that I needed as hard evidence of the truth. These, I will give to you, Sir Kingston. I have no connections with lawyers, or anyone for that matter, to take this up. I need you, for you are a well-known businessman who is also the master of Eleanora. I knew I could come to you to fix this problem. Though I do not know you that well, I trust you will do this for Eleanora. My mother deserves to lose everything after all the suffering Eleanora went through all those years, with my mother making her believe she was someone she was not."

Mandy paused and sighed. "The next day, Mr Miles came by and said that the papers were missing. My mother became frantic and demanded to know if there were copies. But he said there were no copies, only the originals. She was furious. I knew that I had the most important treasure in my hands that could save Eleanora and allow her to live a life in luxury and to be the well-known woman she is meant to be. I pondered for half a day as to exactly what I should do. I knew you were my only and best option. So the next day, today, I set out to come to you alone, with no one to know of my presence here except for the servants of the estate. I have come to bring you this terrible news, which will eventually end the pain and suffering Eleanora has had to endure all these years of her early life. I trust you will end this and allow her to live in happiness, the way she is meant to live."

"I still do not quite understand something about this matter." Sir Kingston went on, "How has no one heard of this? Since Eleanora's father is as you claim Sir Portina, and since he was well-known, wouldn't they have known about his daughter?"

"That is the terrible thing you see; it was told that Eleanora also died that day her father did. My mother fabricated a lie that was so sickening I myself cannot believe she could ever do. She told everyone that the young daughter and her father were riding together when he suffered from a heart attack which was the only truth in it all. When Eleanora's father fell from his horse, it was startled and galloped away at a rapid speed. Eleanora, who was riding behind him, was thrown off and died from her injuries. When it came to the funeral and burial, my mother…" The lady looked away with her eyes shut. She took a breath as she tried to steady herself. She then returned her gaze to Sir Kingston before she continued. "My mother used the body of another dead girl to pose as Eleanora for everyone to believe that she too had died that day. And the few servants at our estate who knew this not to be true were silenced by her. She blackmailed them all, threatening to ship their family off to a far-off place where they would become lower than servants…slaves, and never to see them again. The servants obeyed, also keeping this outrageous secret, afraid of losing their loved ones. It was the servants who told me this bit of information when I approached them about what I had found out about Eleanora to see what I should do. I know now that they are very ashamed of themselves and truly remorseful about keeping the matter to a hush all these years. That is why Eleanora was never allowed into society and was always locked away inside the gates of Mallow Hall. And that is why my mother changed her name so no one would suspect anything. I am ashamed to even call her my mother after all she did."

"I cannot believe it. I cannot believe it!" Sir Kingston repeated the words in greater fury. "How could your mother have hidden such a secret so well? How could she even possibly think to do such a cruel and wicked thing?" Sir Kingston tried to take a breath. "It is evil…to the core!"

"My mother must have had great connections in order to have pulled this off. I had no part in any of it for I am Eleanora's age and had no sense of what was happening at the time. But now that I do, I have come to you for this must be exposed."

Sir Kingston was both astonished and confounded by Miss Mandy's great tale. His eyes concentrated heavily on her during the duration of the long story she had revealed. He could not believe the words she was saying nor the things she had discovered about Eleanora. He was mystified...baffled by the situation at hand. His mind ran wild as he tried to put all that was said together correctly in his mind again. When he soon realised that Eleanora had been cheated all her life by the one woman, who ruined her even till now, it brought a heavy and agonising feeling to his very heart and soul. He was strongly resolute to avenge Eleanora in this situation and take back what was rightfully hers. He knew how much she had been through, and this brought determination and the will to see justice done. He would help her and restore her to who she really was, for she was not supposed to be a servant living a miserable life of constant labour. No, she was much more than that, Sir Kingston thought to himself. She was the heiress of a great fortune. And with that, he knew he would do everything in his power and control to see it bestowed to her, for he didn't want anything but for her to simply be happy with the riches and treasures she was always meant to have.

*

During all this, the scheming eyes of Pearl Nables had been looking through the slightly opened door as she eavesdropped. She had heard all that was said and even prolonged her stay to listen to the plans both Sir Kingston and the lady were discussing about how to approach this illegal act. Pearl was completely shocked by what this lady, whom she did not know personally, was acknowledging regarding Eleanora. She was instantly envious of Eleanora. Pearl's eyes widened throughout the tale, and her mouth fell open in silent exclamation when the true identity of Eleanora and her origins were revealed.

When Pearl realised that the conversation had ended and that Sir Kingston was approaching the door, she vanished before she could be seen to be listening to the secret conversation.

Pearl immediately ran to find her father to reveal her findings. She spotted him walking down the main stairs, perhaps coming from his chamber. She rushed up to him and told him to follow her back into his room. She could suddenly feel her face was flushed from the exciting news she was so desperate to tell. She quickly shut the door behind her and repeated all she had heard.

"Pearl, are you sure this is true?"

"Father, I know what I heard," she said.

He didn't say a word after that. He looked to the floor as his eyes seemed to be searching for some answers to this. He then muttered loudly, as he raised his gleaming eyes, "How did a stupid girl such as her all of a sudden become a rich woman of Estleton?"

"I don't know what to do anymore." Pearl sighed in defeat. She then exclaimed while walking around the room, "This whole time she was a servant, and then all of a sudden, her cousin shows up from god knows where and has hard evidence that she is in fact not a servant! I just do not believe this."

"Me neither. She is higher up than the both of us put together. She could outdo you."

"What do you mean by that?" Pearl was puzzled.

Her father walked up to her and explained, "Well, James seems to have a certain fondness for that servant girl. I do not understand what he sees in her, but he is always taking her side. What if he ended up liking her more than he already does? She will be rich, as you said she would be. This will destroy our plan if he decides to be with her and not you, for she is wealthier and has a better fortune to her name."

"Are you saying he will take more interest in her than me?"

"That's how it looks to be!" He raised his voice. "We do not know exactly what he will do, but I know for a fact that James is not fool enough to allow her to just walk away when she has prosperity written all over her name."

"I will not allow that to happen!" Pearl screeched out.

"Then I suggest you do everything in your power to make James yours. But for now, we must return home to settle some affairs. But we will be back soon, before anything can happen between those two."

Pearl nodded her head, determined to do all she could to make Sir Kingston hers.

*

Eleanora was outside drawing water from the well. Once she had completed the task, she started to carry the bucket back to the manor. While walking towards the front porch entrance, she saw someone she did not recognise at first come out by the front door. When Eleanora was able to properly see the face, she gasped, dropping the bucket of water onto the ground. She couldn't believe her cousin was present in front of her after so many months of not seeing her or wanting to think of her ever again. She tried taking a breath as her cousin approached her. Eleanora decided to pick up the bucket and place it upright on the ground. She rose slowly and tried to remain calm upon seeing her cousin stand in front of her.

"Hello, Eleanora," Mandy said softly.

Eleanora had almost forgotten how her cousin sounded, but this time was different as, for some reason, her voice was gentle rather than provocative. However, Eleanora couldn't reply. She couldn't forget the way she had been treated all those years.

But there was something Eleanora was dying to know. So she decided to ask, her tone harsh, "What do you think you are doing here?" She expressed no smile, no friendly demeanour; instead, her face was expressionless.

Mandy exhaled a breath. She said, "I have come here to sincerely apologise for all that I have done to you."

"Why would you come all the way here just to apologise in a way that should have been done years before? Why have you come now?" She was curious to know but not eager, for she had no care of her apology.

Mandy sighed. "Listen, Eleanora, I have done much thinking over these past few months. I truly am sorry for all you have been through. The other servants back at Mallow Hall have missed you too." She sighed again. "But I am not asking you to forgive what I have done, simply to accept my apology knowing that I really do care about you and wish only the best for you."

"All right then. You have apologised, but I do not think I can ever forgive or forget what both you and your mother have put me through. So, if you please, I want you to leave me and never come here again. This is my life now, and I am very happy here," Eleanora said firmly, never removing her eyes from her cousin.

"Very well, cousin. I will go now."

Eleanora couldn't believe Mandy still had the audacity to call her "cousin" after all this time. She thought it cruel to do so.

Mandy concluded, "Good luck with everything, and I only hope all will be well in the end." She left, passing her side. As she did, Eleanora spotted Sir Kingston standing at the front door and gazing back at her. Her eyes instantly met his. She pressed her lips hard together and walked straight up to him.

"Did you know she was coming over?" As she said this, her voice almost broke.

Sir Kingston shook his head with his arms crossed as he leaned against the doorframe. "It was as much a surprise to me as it was to you."

She looked down and thought for a moment. "I cannot believe she came all this way to apologise. I do not believe her."

"You shouldn't be too harsh on your cousin, Nora."

Her eyes looked into his as she wondered whose side he was on. "After all she has done to me?" she questioned.

He unfolded his arms and stood tall, taking a step towards her. "I'm just saying, you should trust her and believe she is being sincere. People can change, you know."

Eleanora could not respond to this.

He then instructed, "Would you gather everyone to the Grand Hall? I have an announcement to make to you all."

Eleanora nodded her head and went along to do so.

# Chapter 20

Everyone gathered in the centre of the Grand Hall, including Mr Nables and Miss Pearl. Sir Kingston arrived shortly after and stood straight as he made the announcement.

"First of all, I will begin by telling you all that our guests this past month, Mr Nables and Miss Pearl, will be returning home this afternoon." He paused before continuing, "And, secondly, I must tell you all that I will be leaving on a business trip early tomorrow morning, just for a couple of days. I will be back here before you know it. So, as always, Dashier is in charge of the manor until my return."

"You will be back in two days, master?" Dana asked.

Sir Kingston nodded his head, clasping his hands together in front of him. "Yes, I will, unless I have a change of plans, in which case, I will notify you immediately." He paused again. "Everything must run the same while I am away. I trust the manor will be safe and sound, as it has been in the past." He waited for a moment before he dismissed them. "You may all resume your duties."

"I'm so glad Pearl is leaving us," whispered Marie as she turned to Eleanora. "Right, Nora?"

"Hmm? Oh yes," Eleanora answered. She then lowered her eyes to the floor, for though she was glad to hear that she wouldn't have to see Pearl anymore, she still couldn't help but feel her heart weigh her down.

She remained standing there, holding onto her fingers. Only one other person didn't leave the room, and as she raised her eyes, she saw her master, who approached and stood in front of her.

"Nora," he half whispered. He brought his hand over to her and leisurely stroked the strands of her hair with his fingers.

Eleanora could sense that tears were about to build up in her eyes. She took a breath as she forced them back.

"Master," she breathed out. "Please, master, do be careful when you are gone. Return to the manor safely."

He never took his fingers away from her. "I am always careful. When am I ever not?" It was only now that he stopped stroking her hair and removed his hand. He sighed, looking down. "Nora, I…I won't be gone long, you know. I will be back before you know it."

"I know," she replied, her voice becoming a whisper. She cleared her throat and said, "Then go quickly so you may return quickly."

He chuckled as he took her by the hand and held it for a few long seconds. How he lifted it and took it into his own made Eleanora feel incredible things inside her. She wanted this to last forever, just this moment. He smiled at her and let go of her hand, letting it drop back in front of her. He turned and headed his way up the stairs.

Eleanora exhaled a deep breath. What continued to play in her mind was the fact that the master would be leaving the manor for two days. Eleanora knew it wasn't long, but she couldn't help but feel in despair at the idea. She didn't want Sir Kingston to be out of her sight. She had the constant urge to wake up in the morning and see his face while serving breakfast to him, the way he smiled to her every time, and the way his eyes illuminated with their bright emerald-green shade. She knew she would miss those small things, which, to her, were magnificent in so many ways indeed.

*

It was not until much later that afternoon that Sir Kingston farewelled Mr Nables and his daughter, Miss Pearl, before they were to set off in their carriage. Dashier packed all their luggage in preparation while they said their goodbyes. All the other servants were also there standing in a line, watching as they made their departure.

"Thank you for allowing us to be ensconced here this past month. It was nice seeing you and the manor once again, James."

"Always, Rupert." Sir Kingston smiled while shaking his hand before Mr Nables hopped into the carriage.

Now it was Pearl's turn as Eleanora watched attentively. "Thank you, James. It was a pleasurable time with you." Pearl smiled, fluttering her eyelashes at him.

"Anytime, Pearl." Sir Kingston spoke quickly, seeming to ignore the flirtatiousness of her tone.

"I hope to see you again very soon," she remarked with a smile that Eleanora thought was a little too eager.

"Not too soon, I hope," Tennent whispered, and they all giggled at his comment.

"I have enjoyed every shared moment together, just like when we were little children. I hope we can move forward from here-on." She embraced Sir Kingston, her arms wrapping around his shoulders. He returned this embrace, with his own arms wrapping around her.

Eleanora was frozen in silence, her eyes remaining fixed ahead. Suddenly, she saw the way Pearl moved her lips and kissed Sir Kingston on the cheek, opposite to where his scar stained his face. And when she moved her lips away from his side, a cunning smile appeared on her face as she directed a smile at Eleanora. But Eleanora tried not to be bothered by this. She was just glad and thankful that Pearl was leaving and hopefully would never return again. But that was unlikely as Eleanora had heard that the two were likely to get married, and this made Eleanora feel afraid of the future to come.

She watched the way Sir Kingston released Pearl from him even though it looked like she wouldn't have minded prolonging their embrace. Pearl beamed one last joyous smile before stepping into the carriage. She took one last look from the open window at the manor and then Sir Kingston. He waved his hand as the carriage took off. They all watched until the carriage made its way out of the gate. Sir Kingston turned around and glanced at everyone before he quickly made his way back inside again.

*

It was early morning, and Eleanora dreaded the day that was to come as she knew the master was to leave no later than five o'clock. She rushed out of bed as there were only fifteen minutes before the clock would strike. She opened up the window, quickly breathing in the fresh air and the early morning dew. During this, she contemplated whether or not she should speak to the master about what had been weighing heavily on her mind since the night before. When she decided she would, she hastily dressed into her uniform and went down the stairs till she reached the Grand Hall. No one seemed to be about as yet, and she went into the kitchen, where Dana was already preparing breakfast for the rest of them.

"Good morning, Nora!"

"Oh yes. Good morning, Dana," Eleanora replied hurriedly, even though she was focused on finding Sir Kingston before his departure. She hovered by the window and saw that just by the fountain was Sir Kingston, with Tennent preparing his horse and Dashier by his side. She watched as he wrapped himself in a black cape that matched his black hat.

"He is about to leave now," Eleanora muttered out loud. She turned around to face Dana. "How long has he ever been away from the manor?"

"I'd say a month was the longest."

"A month!" Eleanora exclaimed.

"Don't worry, Nora. He will be back soon. It's only for a couple of days, don't forget," Dana reminded her.

"Oh!" She chuckled nervously, hoping Dana didn't suspect anything from her sudden outburst. She looked back out the window and watched as he climbed onto his horse in one swift movement. Dashier was now nowhere to be seen, and Tennent had

210

already left to open the gates for the master. All of a sudden, Eleanora had a change of mind and quickly left the kitchen. She rushed to the front door, which had been left open, and ran quickly down the three steps.

His horse was already cantering off before she could reach him and tell him what had been playing on her mind. She watched him ride away; he was gone.

# Chapter 21

That day, everything went by as normal. Much work had to be done around the manor in order to keep up its appearance. While Eleanora was cleaning downstairs in the Grand Hall, she felt the atmosphere was carefree, yet she couldn't help feeling melancholy.

The next day, she made sure she didn't think much of the master's departure and, instead, focused entirely on her daily work. She worked hard, knowing it would be the only way to calm her spirits and hinder her mind's constant thoughts. She used this opportunity to preoccupy herself with her duties; otherwise, she thought, she may crumble silently.

\*

It was now the morning of the third day, the day Sir Kingston was to arrive back from business as he had stated. Eleanora, along with the rest, prepared breakfast and waited for his arrival. Once all had been prepared and set, Eleanora rushed to the garden and pulled out some lovely burgundy roses and pure-white tulips. She placed them in a vase, as she always did, and put them as the centrepiece on the dining table to welcome him back to the manor.

"When is he arriving, Dana?" Eleanora exclaimed in desperate eagerness.

"Hold your horses, Nora!"

She couldn't help but shiver with agitation.

"He should be here soon, no doubt. He said that he would be back on the third morning. We just have to wait." Dana then went along to prepare the plates. "For now, let us all eat our breakfast." She served each plate of food as they all took their share and sat around the table. "Nora, you keep looking out the window. I assure you he will come."

"Don't worry yourself, Nora. Come on. Your meal is getting cold," Tennent then added.

Eleanora started to take a couple of bites of her toasted bread that was spread with butter and jam.

"What did the master say about why he was going out for business?" Jill asked.

Dana looked to her and answered, "I'm not entirely sure. He didn't fill me in on all the details. He just said he had business to deal with in regards to one of the hotels he owns." Dana turned to her husband and asked, "Did he tell you exactly what it was for, Tennent?"

"No. All he mentioned to me was just that. It was something of great importance, and he needed to go out urgently." Tennent took a bite of his toasted bread with eggs. He spoke with his mouth half full. "The master doesn't really like to let us in on all the details of his work and businesses and whatnot."

Marie stood from her chair and went to fetch a cup of water. When she returned, she brought up the subject of Pearl Nables. "Aren't we all feeling much more at ease these last couple of days without Pearl being around?" she said with a laugh.

"I agree," Jill said. "It feels much more relaxing. Sometimes she would order one of us to do something she could have easily done herself."

"Like what?" Tennent asked.

Jill began to describe one instance. "Like that one time I was bringing tea up to her room, and she asked me to pour it for her, and when I did, she then ordered me to light a candle, which was sitting right beside her. Honestly, she is so spoilt. I might as well have done everything for her."

"What about the time," Marie now began, "when she wanted her bedsheets changed. I changed them the first time, and she didn't like them. The second change, she complained about the feel of them, for they were making her itch. I changed them once more, and she despised the colour, stating that it was revolting. So, in the end, she decided she preferred the first ones, though they were not to her absolute liking. She couldn't even make up her damn mind, I'm telling you. She is a walking frustration."

"God help us if Sir Kingston is to marry her, which he is by the sound of things," Tennent remarked.

"Do you think he will?" Jill questioned, almost coming off her seat.

"Of course, silly!" Marie rolled her eyes. "Haven't you known they are meant to be together? Her father was closely acquainted with his father."

During all of this conversation about Pearl and Sir Kingston, Eleanora began to feel her stomach stir and her heart beat madly inside of her. She could not eat as she placed her half-bitten bread down onto her plate. Hearing all this talk about the two and a marriage between them in the near future made Eleanora feel like she was already defeated. She couldn't help the way she felt about Sir Kingston, and she didn't know why she felt this way, but she just did. She knew Pearl was not a good woman, and for them to be as one would bring forth a horrid reputation and stain to Sir Kingston's name. It would be like an unsoiled piece of paper where the ink had suddenly spilt and blotted stains onto that paper, tarnishing it so it could be of no good use. Eleanora couldn't possibly think or believe that he could truly love her, that he would spend the rest of his days with a spoilt and unpleasant character. Eleanora began questioning his character and whether he didn't mind that sort. Or whether he preferred another kind of character, one like hers perhaps?

A gloomy feeling prevailed over her while the others continued to gossip. She stared down at her hands, which clutched each other, trying to calm herself down and rid herself of this unwanted feeling that never ceased.

Dana's voice interrupted her thoughts.

"Nora, you don't look too good. Is everything all right?"

Eleanora raised her head and saw the worried looks on all their faces. She tried to smile and then muttered softly, "Yes, of course. I am just not that hungry."

"Do finish your breakfast," Dana insisted. "You need it for energy, especially when you have been working non-stop these past couple of days."

To not allow anyone to become suspicious of her feelings on the matter, she nodded her head and brought the piece of bread to her lips. She took a small, uneasy bite and forced it down her throat as she tried to contain her emotions.

*

A few hours later, there was still no word or sign of Sir Kingston's arrival. Dana said not to worry, for he may have stopped somewhere or was just running late. She mentioned that this had happened once before.

It wasn't until the next day – late afternoon it was – that it was decided something had to be done.

"Where could he be?" Eleanora was worried sick for her master.

Dana responded, "He might still be staying at his hotel. But if he were, he would usually have sent out word. I would have thought a letter of some kind should have come by now, but it has not."

"Then what are we to do?"

"I will go and see him," Dashier said, coming forward. "Perhaps when I go, I can then ask why he hasn't returned. It will just be a check-up, for this is rather odd."

"Yes, it is best that you go, Dashier. Hopefully, you will have good news to tell us," Dana agreed.

Dashier put his coat and top hat on and took one of the horses. "I will be back by late tonight, I'm sure," he farewelled and was off.

*

It was about to strike nine o'clock. Dashier hadn't arrived back to the manor yet. The place was feeling eerie and almost empty. It was awfully quiet with nothing but soft slurping sounds echoing within the drawing room. Eleanora was having tea with Dana as they sat quietly, just waiting for something to happen. Eleanora noticed the way Dana looked at her a few times now and then, almost in a curious way, as if wondering something to herself. Dana then placed her teacup down on the small table in front of her. She paused for a moment and then spoke, breaking Eleanora's eye contact with the fire that was settling in the fireplace. "You seem to be the most anxious about the master out of all of us, Nora." She seemed to wait for a response, and when she was given none, she continued, "I wonder why that might be?"

Eleanora exhaled a breath and replied, "Well, I do care for the master and his safety. Is it wrong of me to do so?"

"No, of course not. We all care for the master." Dana paused. "You know, I am glad that you have come to like him. In the beginning, I remember how afraid you were." She waited again. "Nora?" she called.

"Sorry, Dana. I was just thinking of something. But, yes, I do like him and am not afraid the way I used to be. He has changed my judgement of him, and now it is a good one, you see."

"Well, I'm glad," Dana replied with a quick smile as she picked up her tea and nodded her head.

\*

It was just past ten when the halls echoed with the sound of the front door opening. Eleanora jumped in her seat and glanced over to Dana. They both quickly made their way out and saw it was Dashier. The others, too, came down the stairs and joined them.

Dashier hastily made known at once, "The master is not there. I have looked in the hotel, but the proprietor said he hasn't checked in at all or seen him since the last time he did."

"Oh my!" Dana exclaimed.

"Have you received or heard of anything?" he then asked her.

"No, unfortunately, we haven't. Not even a letter."

"Maybe he is on his way now," Tennent suggested.

"I don't think so. I made sure to travel the way he would to get here. No sign of him anywhere."

"What are we going to do?" both Marie and Jill asked in turn.

"We have to wait till morning perhaps," Tennent answered.

"Yes, Tennent is right," Dashier agreed. "There is nothing much we can do for now. We should all go off to bed and see what to do tomorrow morning. He may still arrive without warning."

"Maybe he has been caught up in something very important and has not had the time to contact us for whatever reason," Dana suggested.

"Well, we won't know for sure until we hear from him again," Dashier concluded.

Everyone headed upstairs and into their chambers as it was already late. Eleanora rushed quietly to Dana and asked, "Dana, the master will be back, right?"

"You have nothing to worry about, Nora. None of us do. Trust me, he will return. Even though this is unlike him, the master can take care of himself. I bet tomorrow he will come. Don't you worry, all right?"

Eleanora nodded her head once and looked into Dana's eyes, knowing deep down she, too, was worried for the master but had to put up a brave and hopeful façade in order to help Eleanora overcome the worries that clouded her mind.

# Chapter 22

That night was an agonising one for Eleanora. She had to endure constant tossing and turning the entire restless night. She couldn't sleep, and just resting her eyes pained her. She was afraid for Sir Kingston and couldn't stop wondering why he had not returned to the manor and why he had not sent word. What if something had happened to him? What if he was hurt? Would she be able to survive this night without knowing that he was safe and sound? It was the unknowns that weighed her down so greatly. Not knowing was the hardest part of all because it kept her questioning, and then thinking, and then feeling, and then back through the same process once again until she could bear it no more. But Eleanora knew she shouldn't think this way. She wanted to have hope and to use that hope to regain her strength. She needed to be strong even though she missed him with every heartbeat that pounded beneath her chest and every single breath she took. It was long after midnight when Eleanora finally made her rest and shut her eyes hoping to dream at ease.

*

The sun shone brightly through the white, transparent curtains. Eleanora squinted her eyes open, realising that the next morning had come. She hurried to the window and drew the curtains back, allowing more sunlight into the room. She had slept in a little more than usual due to her bad night's sleep. After she dressed herself, she scurried down each stair until she got to the main floor. She spotted Dana and the rest in the Grand Hall. They greeted her, but Eleanora didn't care for that right now. All she wanted to know was if they knew the whereabouts of the master.

"Any luck?" she asked breathlessly.

"None," Dana told her frankly. Eleanora bit her bottom lip hard when she heard this. She then noticed that Dana looked as if she didn't get much sleep as bags had formed under her droopy eyes. "I am going to go into town and see if I can find anything on his location. Besides, there are some things that need to be bought. I shall be back before noon."

Eleanora and the others farewelled Dana and Jill, who went along too. The rest of them continued the day as normal with work around the manor.

*

When Dana and Jill arrived back from town with some bags in their hands, their faces were serious. It was a sign that there was no word or sight of the master himself. But for some reason, Dana seemed more troubled, more disturbed than usual.

"What is it, Dana?" Eleanora asked, alarmed at Dana's expression.

Jill looked miserably at the floor, and Dashier, Tennent, and Marie came rushing in.

"Dana?" Eleanora repeated urgently.

Dana released a breath. Then she put down the bags on the floor beside her feet and explained, "Whilst in town, we heard some rumours going about."

"Rumours?" Tennent questioned as his eyes widened. "Were they about the master?"

Dana nodded her head in response. "Well, I'm not completely sure, but they might be."

"Oh, do tell, Dana! We haven't the time nor the patience," Marie exclaimed harshly.

"Please, Marie," Jill cried.

"I'm sorry," Marie muttered, looking down at her hands.

Dana continued, "The rumours were that someone was travelling on horseback on the same road that leads past the manor. That person had some sort of accident."

"Accident? What kind of accident?" Dashier now questioned.

"I'm not sure. I couldn't get the whole story, but that man was nowhere to be found, just his horse."

"Well, what does that have to do with the master?" Marie asked.

"Because it happened on that very morning when the master was supposed to arrive back at the manor. And it occurred at that very path that leads up here."

Eleanora placed her hand over her mouth.

"There's still no evidence that it was the master. Who did the horse belong to?" Dashier asked.

Dana replied, "There was nothing on the horse to say who the owner was. But the horse was brown, the same colour as the one the master took."

"Maybe it's just a coincidence?" Tennent remarked. "It has to be."

"Why don't we go down to see the horse, then we will know if it is one of our own?" Dashier pointed out.

Dana shook her head. "No, we can't. The horse apparently got away while they were trying to catch it, and they don't know where it is." She then added, "The people Jill and I were speaking to didn't know the identity of this person. There still requires an investigation on the disappearance of that man. And that man might well be Sir Kingston," she concluded.

"It can't be!" Eleanora cried. Her hands began to shake, and her mouth trembled.

"The master hasn't contacted us in days now," Dana reminded them. "It is most likely he is the man that disappeared. What other person ever takes that same route to the manor? Only the master would take that path."

It was silent for what felt like an eternity to Eleanora. She still couldn't comprehend everything that had been said. She felt as if all hope was gone and that she would never see Sir Kingston again. It pained her because she missed him incredibly, and nothing, *nothing*, could ever fill the hole that opened within her aching heart. She thought now that she had missed an opportunity she would never get back. An opportunity to tell him how much she cared for him and could not go a day without seeing him or even speaking the most simple words to him. She began to breathe heavily and couldn't seem to think straight. She thought this was the end of her master, the end of her.

"He cannot be gone!" she cried out as everyone turned to her. She looked back at them, and her eyes quickly filled with tears that burned with salty, bitter despair. "He can't!" she cried out again. Placing her hand over her mouth to try to contain herself from breaking down into any more tears, she ran hastily up the stairs as fast as she could. The others tried to call her, but Eleanora only continued to stumble her way up the stairs, almost falling a few times while rushing up.

There was only one place she could go. She ended up at the top of the manor, at the rooftop where all was free and serene as it was supposed to be. She held onto the railing and cried out her heart's misery and anguish. She pressed the palm of her hand to her forehead, trying to soothe the pain that kept thumping away at her. She tried many ways to calm herself down, but nothing could keep her from feeling despair, for she not only cared for her master but she also felt something within her heart that she'd had no explanation for...until now. When she realised how she felt and why, it opened her heart to what could be and might have been. But knowing it was impossible brought more misery to her heart and soul. She felt her little world fall apart. He was the significant aspect of it, her master, Sir Kingston, who had brought her consolation and tenderness all of her time here. At first, her world was insignificant, but as she gradually got to know him, this gave her life meaning and made her feel anew. He also treated her as an equal and didn't care for what society made her out to be. He treated her right. Indeed, he did.

While Eleanora allowed the breeze to cool her distressed face, she was suddenly interrupted by a voice.

"I knew I would find you up here." Dana sounded relieved. She walked up to her and questioned, "What has become of you, Nora?"

Eleanora turned around swiftly and wiped away the tears that stained her face.

Dana grabbed her hands. "I know you are worried, Eleanora, for the master. We all are. And for some reason, you more than any of us. I wonder why?"

Eleanora shook her head slowly. "I'm just scared…afraid…fearful that he is the one that just vanished and will never return." She looked down to where Dana held onto her hands, caressing her comfortingly with her fingers.

"Nora, we will do everything we can to find the master. Don't you worry about that." She paused, sighing. "If there is ever anything you need to talk to me about, anything at all, then I would appreciate it if you would just tell me. Tell me the way you feel and think about things. I may be able to help guide you to the right path."

"Thank you, Dana," Eleanora whispered, not realising the true meaning of her words.

"Do not weep any more, my dear." Dana embraced Eleanora reassuringly.

During this, Tennent came up and exclaimed joyously, "Quickly, the both of you. I have spotted the master on his way here right now!"

Dana looked at Eleanora and smiled at her. Eleanora was still in shock; she didn't know if this was real but desperately hoped that it was.

*

Tennent and Dana left at once while Eleanora stayed behind as she wanted to take this moment for herself and calm all the agony and discomfort she had been feeling. Then she rushed to the edge of the roof to see if she could spot someone riding down below. But it was hard to observe any clear movement with all the trees obstructing her view. She decided to head down and dashed her way to the first floor and then out the front door, being the last to appear. Sir Kingston came riding on his horse towards them, and in one swift movement, he jumped off his horse and paced himself until he stopped a small distance from everyone else.

Eleanora, her heart still fragile, noticed the way his face was full of smiles, his eyes glimmering as if nothing had happened. He stood tall and proud as usual and greeted everyone at the same time. Eleanora didn't understand this at all, the way he was acting after all this time. He hadn't said a word about his late arrival. She felt as if this were all a nightmare and that the ground would shake, waking her up from slumber. But when she realised this was real, she suddenly felt something unexpected erupt from inside of her.

She made her way hastily to Sir Kingston, shouting out in frustration and despair, "How could you do this?" She was now in front of him. Her eyes melted with new tears that she didn't seem able to stop. She cried out, louder this time, "How could you do this to me?" She had repeated the heartbroken words while hitting his chest with hands formed into fists. Eleanora then felt his grip as he took hold of her. She looked up to his eyes, which were wide with confusion and bewilderment at her unexplained behaviour.

"How could you show up like this?! Do you know what you put me through?" Her voice broke midway as she could hardly cry out from all the exhaustion she suffered. She continued to cry and wail to him as she struck each ball of her hands onto his chest, pounding him harder each time. She didn't care what she looked like or what the others thought of her insane reaction. All she thought about was how he dared to waltz up here and pretend that everything was the way it always was supposed to be.

"Eleanora!" he finally called after being silent. But she only continued. He then grabbed each of her hands with his own and forced her to stop. "Eleanora!" he said more firmly with a raised voice. His eyes met with hers again. Eleanora saw how he gazed at her in bewilderment. Her own eyes were wet with tears that she could not contain.

He still looked too perplexed to understand anything at that moment. "What is wrong?"

She struggled as she tried to remove her hands from his tight and forceful grip. She finally yelled one last time, "I don't believe you!" She forced her hands away from his with as much strength as she had left in her. She took a step back, and after taking one final glance at him, she ran away.

Eleanora ran down the hill and into the small forest with added tears blurring her vision, though she knew where she was going. She couldn't stand being there any longer or seeing him at that moment. She needed to be away from everyone. She needed to be alone before things began to crumble even more. She was out of breath and almost fell, when she caught a tree, swinging her arms around it to stop her legs from continuously running. She took this moment to breathe even though it was rather difficult with her heart beating wildly with every second that went by. She inhaled deeply one last time and ran onwards until she reached the narrow river, where she threw herself down to the comfort of the grass. She knelt down, her head forward while cradling her churning stomach.

*

Sir Kingston gazed at everyone who had witnessed this unexpected act. He was desperate to know what had become of Eleanora and why she had been crying and striking him. So he asked, "What is the matter with Eleanora?" He looked around to see who would respond. "Answer me, now!" he ordered in his loud, commanding voice.

Dana stepped forward and filled him in on everything about how they thought something tragic had happened to him and why there was no reason given to them for his late arrival.

Sir Kingston stared at the ground, reflecting on all that had been said; his mind was focused on the one person he knew had suffered the most. He raised his eyes back up and said, "But I did inform you that I would be arriving late. I sent a note; did you not receive one?" They all shook their heads. "How could this be?" he muttered loudly. He then concluded, "I finally understand everything perfectly." And without any more delay, he rushed over to his horse and jumped back on it, throwing one leg over to the other side. "I must find her! YAH!" he sounded as the horse galloped away in the direction Eleanora had run.

*

Sir Kingston found Eleanora by the river. He came down from his horse and removed his black cloak and hat and dropped them onto the grass. He started to walk over to her. As he grew nearer, he heard her weep to herself. It made him pause, halting him from going any further. He stared at her, seeing how much he had caused her to suffer. His heart filled with remorse.

He continued making his way to her until he was right there by her side. He, too, fell to the ground, and within an instant, he placed his arm around her. "Nora?" he said gently. But she continued to weep and hide her face with the shaking palms of her hands. "Nora!" He pulled her towards him. They were now both kneeling, facing each other. "Oh, Nora, I am so sorry," he muttered. He took her hands away from her face, desperately wanting to see the beauty that always reigned in her. "Please, do not weep more than you already have," he said, trying his best to comfort her. He moved her closer to him. He then brought his other hand forward and began wiping her tears away from her eyes.

As he did this, Eleanora finally managed to speak, although her voice was not strong.

"I thought you were gone. I thought you were never coming back…"

"Shh," he hushed her. "I was filled in on the whole story."

225

"Why didn't you reach out to us instead of making us worry…making *me* worry?" Eleanora asked; her eyes glistened the same way water does when the sunlight hits the surface.

Sir Kingston grabbed her hand and held it just underneath his chin. "I did, Nora. I wrote a note stating that I would be staying away for another two days. I sent the note out to the post." He began cursing under his breath, "Damn post! Damn that dreaded post for not doing their job correctly! I will find out who is behind this. Damn them all!" He now looked to Eleanora, his eyes gazing down to hers.

"But Dashier came one day to your hotel where you were staying, and you weren't there?"

Sir Kingston sighed. "That's because I had to travel to some other place for a business reason. Let's not talk about this anymore. The important thing now is that I am back and that you do not need to worry anymore."

Eleanora looked down after this. Another tear trickled down her rosy cheek. Sir Kingston lifted her chin up and saw this. He caught that tear with his fingertip while saying, "Why do you continue to cry? I am here now, aren't I?" He wiped the trail mark that the tear had made.

"Because I missed you," she finally said, struggling to speak these words. Sir Kingston paused and stared at her. Eleanora continued, "I couldn't sleep during the night. I could hardly eat. I was caught up in work as it was the only way to take my mind off you even though it was hard to do so, every second of the day, not knowing where you were and when you would come back. I just wanted you to be here, safe and sound." She began crying some more. Sir Kingston took Eleanora and embraced her tightly. Eleanora rested her head on his chest, crying her tears that fell onto his clean white shirt. She gripped tightly onto it and pulled him in as close to her as she could.

Sir Kingston had his eyes lightly shut, resting his chin on top of her head while he caressed her hair. He wanted to feel every part of this comforting moment. When he reopened his eyes again, a tear slithered down his cheek and ran alongside the imprint of his scar. Suddenly, his mouth parted as if he couldn't breathe and was trying to exhale all the suffocating pain that caused his heart to ache. He finally released Eleanora from his embrace and was relieved when he saw she looked less upset. Her hair, though, was all messed up. He brushed away the strands covering her eyes and wiped the bottom of her eyes with his thumb.

"You know, that wasn't the kind of welcome I was expecting," he said, wanting to bring cheer to her face. She chuckled, and a smile grew that brightened the colour on her cheeks even more. "There's that smile." He stroked her cheek. "I missed that smile," he then said.

She looked up to him with the same glad smile. "Master?"

"Yes, Nora?" He never looked away from her.

"I'm sorry for the way I acted earlier. The way I struck your chest with my hands. I apologise. It was not right of me to do so. But I only did it because I was in great shock and relief at the same time. I couldn't control myself…my sudden outburst."

"Yes, you really did leave a bruise on my chest. You are quite strong, I must say," he said and laughed. She looked a little anxious. "I'm teasing, Nora. You have nothing to apologise for. I understand why you did it – because I worried you by making you think I was in danger."

"But it was wrong of me to strike my master that way. It was shameful, and I did it in front of everyone."

"Do not berate yourself for the way you felt."

She didn't speak another word on the subject.

Sir Kingston continued to gaze at her for a moment. He was contemplating how he should speak of another subject, one that was close to the heart. He commenced, "Nora, there is something I've been meaning to tell you for quite some time now." She looked up at him with wondering eyes. "But I never understood it or knew exactly what it was, until now."

"What is it, sir?" Her eyes appeared curious to know but also frightened at the same time.

227

"Nora, I only speak from the heart." He paused. But before he could resume, he was caught up by her innocent gaze. The beauty that radiated from their azure blue washed over him, hypnotising him. He hadn't forgotten what he was meaning to say but instead muttered, "Your eyes."

"What about my eyes?" she questioned softly.

He looked at them and saw they were a deeper colour than usual. "They are magnificent. The way you gaze up at me in such an innocent way shows the beauty that lies within them…within you." He watched as Eleanora blushed after these words were said. When he kept gazing at her, she looked down and bit her bottom lip. She lifted her head up when she heard him then say, "Do you know how many times you have tortured me with that nervous habit of yours?"

"What habit are you referring to?" she asked with a smile.

"You know what habit," he replied, a playful grin forming on his thin lips.

"Do you mean when I do this?" She bit her bottom lip again in front of him.

Sir Kingston's hungry eyes were wide open, and his mouth slightly parted. "So, you do know what I am referring to," he groaned deeply. He brought his thumb to her bottom lip and gently caressed it. "Eleanora…" He spoke her full name this time. "I must tell you what I am feeling inside of me."

She was still while he now stroked her cheek very slowly.

After he had prepared himself, he moved his thumb away and began, "You know, the first time I met you, I thought you were just an ordinary servant girl. I didn't really think to spend much time getting to know the real you. Well, I guess that is what is expected between a master and his servants."

He inhaled a breath and slowly let the air escape out. "But after a while, I started to see the innocent, lovely, and wonderful person you are." He paused, thinking, before starting up again.

"My whole life has been empty, with nothing but darkness that fills it. But everything I have been through in the course of my life, every bit of sadness I have ever gone through, has been taken away by you." He paused, smiling. "You, Eleanora, have brought me back to life. You have given me a reason to keep living. You have a ransom on my captive heart."

He had made such striking statements that Eleanora's eyes sparkled with fresh tears.

"Without you, I would not be here today. You saved me that time I almost drowned myself; that is something I shall never forget. And you have made me see things differently from the way I used to; my eyes were clouded by darkness from my past, whereas yours sought a beaming light that you believed would strike past the clouds anew. I see things more clearly now and in a lighter shade, especially when I'm around you."

He now covered the side of her face with his hand. He slowly moved his face and pressed his forehead onto hers as they were now linked, in mind and body. Sir Kingston didn't say anything for a short while, wanting to breathe in her scent that seemed to possess him. He looked tenderly into her eyes and then whispered to her, declaring, "I love you, Eleanora. I love you with everything that I am. Every beat my heart makes, it makes only for you."

"Oh, master!" she responded with eyes alight and lips curling into a joyous smile.

He gave her a kiss on her forehead, pressing his lips down onto her soft skin. He then looked back down at her and whispered, "Tell me you love me, Eleanora. Tell me you love me," he repeated to her again. He began travelling his lips down the side of her face, kissing her. He then mumbled, "I know that you do. I just know it!"

A tear dropped from her eye and then another. As much as she wanted this, something was holding her back, and it was the fact that they were from two completely different worlds.

"Sir Kingston…"

He removed his lips from her and looked at her.

"We cannot be together," she put it plainly, though the words burned inside her.

His eyes filled with confusion. "Of course we can. Who says we can't?"

"Society," she stated bluntly, looking away.

"Since when do you care about what society thinks?"

She faced him again and argued, "Look at me, and look at you! I am nothing but a servant, and you are a wealthy man who is respected by all. We are complete opposites and can never be together. It's not the way life is," she concluded as her voice broke.

"But don't you see, Eleanora? You are my life."

These heartfelt words made Eleanora's heart flutter.

He continued, "And you are the one who taught me that you shouldn't care what society thinks. You always said that being yourself is to be your true self. Are you telling me now that you are afraid of what other people will think of us?"

"Of course not!" she cried, her face wet with fresh tears. "It's just that…it is not how the world works. No matter how much I want to be with you, I just can't."

Sir Kingston expressed a smile once Eleanora confessed this.

She then added, "And what about Pearl?"

"Pearl?" he questioned in surprise. "What about her?"

"Aren't you two supposed to be married?"

"Married?" He gave a loud chuckle after hearing this. "Where did you hear that absurd idea from?"

"Everyone has been talking about how the two of you are meant to be together because your fathers were closely acquainted."

"I will tell you right now, Pearl and I will never be," he said firmly.

"But I saw the way you acted with her, the way you two laughed and spent most of your time together."

"You observed all this?"

"I couldn't help but to," Eleanora said, feeling embarrassed.

"You were not jealous of her, were you, Nora?"

"I was not jealous of Pearl!" she assured him hastily.

"But you were jealous?" he continued with a smug look on his face.

"I was a little jealous, yes. Not of her, but because of the way I felt for you. She was always near you."

Sir Kingston sighed as he reached for her hand. He then said, "That has nothing to do with me wanting to marry her. Yes, I have known Pearl for a long time, and I know she would wish to be with me. But I cannot give that to her."

Eleanora was glad when he confirmed this.

He held both of her hands now as he said, "Nora, even though we may be opposites, our hearts are a perfect match. I am a perfect match for you because I love you, and I shall never stop loving you. Please, Eleanora, don't shut me out because of society's expectations. Expectations are an illusion. But what I feel for you is true and real. I love you, Eleanora, unconditionally! My love is not conditional on who you are or where you come from."

Eleanora watched the way his chest rose up and down after expressing his total and complete love to her.

She finally declared, "I love you too, master. I love you more than my own self." She gazed deeply and passionately into his eyes, which lit up in their emerald-green colour.

He then brought her close to him, filling up the space between them. His voice was deep and resonant as he exclaimed, "Oh, how I love you, Eleanora!" He brought his face down to her, and before he made any other movement, he whispered, "How I wanted my lips to linger on yours." He moved forward and placed his mouth close to hers. He then held his bottom lip over her top lip. Finally, he pressed his lips onto hers and kissed her with much passion.

Instantly, she felt the connection between them, a sensational feeling that was igniting and stimulating her entire body.

Eleanora had never felt this way before with anybody, had never felt the kind of love she felt for Sir Kingston. She knew she would always want this, to have a taste of him, to touch him. She had never felt more alive than she did today as her body trembled with passion, desiring to feel more of his touch. She held onto the back of his raven-black hair while curling her fingers in between the strands. This kiss meant everything to her; it was the start of a new her, a new beginning, a new life she would have with the one she loved.

Sir Kingston continued kissing Eleanora deeply with an exhilarating passion that only grew. He had waited this long to finally touch her, to connect and to unite with her as their hearts and souls became one. He had never known love and had always been sceptical about finding true love, thinking it didn't exist in this cruel world. But meeting Eleanora had changed his ways. He thought he would never be loved because of his past, and that frightened him to the pits of his soul. But not anymore...not when he was holding onto the one who had changed him into a better man with a different outlook on life.

Eleanora parted her lips a little and half whispered, "Do you, master, really take me, a servant? Is this really happening or is it all just a dream?"

His eyes flickered open, and a smile formed on his lips. He kissed her once and replied, "I take all of you for who you are, not for what." He then chuckled. "And, no, this is not some fairy tale or dream. It is real," he whispered to her.

This placed a loving smile on her face as she gave him a kiss.

He then asked, "And do you, Eleanora, take me, even though I carry a dark, secretive past?"

"Whatever your past was, it doesn't change anything. What matters is right here, right now, for I love you truly with all my heart."

She gave him another smile, a different one this time, which made Sir Kingston kiss her with everything that he had. He slowly and gently brought her down to the grass.

Sir Kingston lay on top of Eleanora. He trailed his lips down to her chin and started moving down to her neck, which she stretched out. She shut her eyes while his lips planted sweet kisses onto every spot of her skin as he continued his way down. Her arms were wrapped around him, holding onto his broad shoulders, pulling him in closer to her body. He began to unbutton her collar that wrapped tightly around her neck. Once he did, the neckline was opened up, exposing her collarbone. He kissed her softly and tenderly while his lips made their way across.

"Oh, master!" she exclaimed in a loud whisper.

He brought his mouth back up to her ear and whispered back, "Say my name."

He looked at her, and she then whispered, "James."

He smiled as he heard her speak his name for the very first time. He then placed his mouth back to the side of her neck and kissed her pure, soft skin. He placed a final kiss on her lips before he moved his lips away.

Sir Kingston lay on the grass beside Eleanora. He held her close to him. She started to slowly trace the scar as her finger followed it from the side of his eye, down to the corner of his mouth. When she left her finger there, he pecked her fingertip lovingly with his lips. A smile gleamed from her face as she looked at his happy face. She rested her head on his chest, wrapping one arm around to his side as he continued to hold onto her.

"You know, Nora, you don't have to work for me anymore," Sir Kingston started.

She lifted herself up. "Why not?"

"Because we're together now, and there is no need to."

"But you are my master, and I must serve you."

"I don't want you to work for me anymore. I want you to be with me and be my friend, to keep me company every second of every day."

"Then what would the others think?"

"Why? Do you want to keep this a secret?" he questioned.

"I want nothing more than for people to know about us. So, we will expose this?"

"Maybe it's best we don't tell people right away. I think we should wait for now. But not for long. I want everyone to know that you are mine."

She smiled at him. "All right then. It means I will resume my position as your servant."

"Very well then. But only for a short while, Nora."

"Even if I was not your servant anymore, I would always serve you for the rest of my life. You are the master of my heart. And I shall serve yours."

He brought her hand to his mouth and placed a kiss on top of it. He smiled as she rested her head back down again.

After a moment of resting, Eleanora mentioned, "I can hear your heartbeat. It is very soothing to the ear."

"Would you also like to feel it?" he offered.

She rose up from him and placed her hand where his heart was. "I can't feel it much."

He unfastened the first four buttons of his white shirt and opened it up. He took Eleanora's hand and placed it firmly onto his chest, keeping his hand on top of hers.

"Do you feel it?" he asked.

She nodded her head. "It feels wonderful."

She brought herself closer to him. She placed her mouth delicately onto where she felt his heartbeat and placed a kiss on the very spot.

Sir Kingston felt her lips attach themselves to the surface of his skin where his heart beat tenderly inside of him. He felt the affectionate way she slowly lifted her lips from him. He looked into her eyes, locking them with his. She had now rested both hands onto his chest as he came in closer to give her another devoted kiss.

# Chapter 23

They interlocked hands as they strolled back to where the horse was resting. Sir Kingston helped Eleanora as she swung herself up and onto the horse. He then did the same in one quick, easy movement and took his place behind her. He signalled his horse forward, and it trotted at an easy pace back in the direction of the manor. When they arrived at the front, Sir Kingston hopped off his horse and led it to the farmhouse. There, he held onto Eleanora as she dropped off, her feet landing safely on the ground.

"May I have one more kiss before we head back inside?"

She nodded her head and gave him a quick peck on the lips.

"Is that all?" he questioned with a chuckle.

"I think we have shown enough affection for one day."

"Don't forget, Nora, we won't be showing any more affection for quite a while, not with everyone roaming about the manor."

She started to walk off, leaving him behind. She stopped suddenly and then turned around, running back to him. He caught her in his arms, and they shared a passionate kiss. Eleanora stroked his hair back, and it fell quickly to his side. "Of course I want to kiss you. I was only teasing." She started to giggle, and he smiled too.

He then looked over to the manor and said, "Let us go before the others grow in worry, for we have already been gone a long time."

Eleanora nodded and they began to walk side by side, heading towards the front entrance.

When they entered together, everyone came to meet them in the Grand Hall. Eleanora noticed all their faces expressed concern, perhaps due to wondering what had prolonged them.

Though it was Dana who had a questioning look in her fine eye as it appeared she could tell something had happened between the master and Eleanora.

"Eleanora, are you all right?" Dana hurried to her, embracing her in her arms.

"All is well now." Eleanora smiled in return, appreciating her concern.

"But why did you run away like that?" Marie then asked.

"I was just upset and surprised all at the same time. I wasn't thinking straight," she answered, feeling a little embarrassed by the awkward situation that had occurred earlier.

"Thank you, everyone!" Sir Kingston exclaimed. "There is no more to say here. Can you all get back to your duties."

They obeyed his command and scattered, resuming their previous positions. Eleanora faced her master and gave him a hopeful smile. He returned this with a quick wink that caused her to feel heat radiate in her cheeks. She followed the others as Sir Kingston returned to his usual business around the manor.

*

Later in the evening, while the servants were preparing dinner, the topic was raised once more.

"You really did hit the master's chest real hard, Nora. I could even feel it from where I was standing," Jill mentioned.

"Didn't you get into trouble with the master for the way you acted? It was kind of disrespectful if you ask me," Marie butted in on the subject, speaking her mind.

"Now, now, Marie. Nora only did it because she thought he was never coming back. She was surprised when she saw him arrive all relaxed and was probably confused by this," Dana said soothingly.

"Thank you, Dana." Eleanora appreciated her intervention once again. "What Dana said is true. I didn't mean to strike him as so. I was just feeling many things and had the urge to do so because I really did think he was dead or missing, as you all made it out to be."

"That was my fault. I am sorry, Nora," said Dana, taking the blame.

"So he just let you off the hook?" Marie went on.

"The master understands me," Eleanora told her straight while preparing the vegetables.

"Well, I guess," Marie replied.

Dinner was now to be served. As usual, Eleanora was serving the dishes to the master. She and Jill took the trays of plates and headed to the dining room. When they entered, Sir Kingston was sitting quietly, waiting patiently to be fed. Eleanora knew that he didn't dare lift his eyes to her, not wanting Jill to notice the smile that always appeared when his eyes met with hers.

They placed the plates down in front of him. Jill finished up first and left the room. Eleanora went around, close by the master, and placed the final plate down in front of him. Before she left his side, Sir Kingston touched her hand and quickly placed a small piece of notepaper inside her grasp. She glanced back to him as she made her way out of the dining room. Before entering the kitchen, she glanced at the note he had given to her. It read: *"Meet me in the library after dinner."* A nervous smile curled her lips as her stomach grew butterflies that never stopped fluttering. She placed the small piece of paper into the pocket of her dress and made her way into the kitchen.

\*

After dinner, Eleanora headed upstairs to the library. She had given an excuse to Dana that she was feeling rather fatigued and would retreat to her chamber earlier than usual. She was glad Dana agreed instantly and without question that she should get her rest. As Eleanora was just before the door of the library, she took a breath, calming the nerves she felt whenever she was about to see her master. She couldn't help feeling them rise within her as she always had a sense of urgency to see him.

When she opened the door, she spotted Sir Kingston. He turned and ordered, "Shut the door behind you, Nora."

She did as she was told and went forth to him. "I thought we weren't going to meet each other, for it is too risky?"

He came towards her as he said, "Yes, but I can't help myself, you see. I needed to see you…Well, I wanted to see you." A small smile appeared as she looked down at her hands. "You cannot still be this nervous in front of me, I'm sure?"

"You always make me feel this way," she replied with a small, sweet smile.

He was close to her now. He took her by the hand and led her to one of the vintage sofa chairs by the fireplace. "I was wondering if we should read something together. I don't get to spend much leisure time with you, and I think it would bring us closer. Don't you agree?"

She nodded her head firmly.

"Most of the time, you are obeying my orders and doing things that I want you to do," he said with a chuckle. "But that is going to change." He paused for a second. "So, does reading sound good to you?"

"Yes, I would love to read together."

"And what would you like to read?" he asked with a smile.

"I didn't get to finish one of the books, the one with all the poems you recommended to me that one time. Do you remember?"

"How could I possibly forget?" He made his way straight to the bookshelf and climbed the ladder to retrieve the very one. He returned to sit by Eleanora on the extended seat.

*

The fire in the fireplace crackled, creating a relaxed and soothing mood for this simple yet fascinating activity. All was well and comfortable. Sir Kingston and Eleanora took turns reading aloud each poem and discussing it afterwards with one another. Sir Kingston enjoyed listening to every word Eleanora breathed out in such a natural and eloquent way, which he knew she was not used to doing, having only ever read to herself. He gazed at her as her mouth expressed each word with great enthusiasm. His smile never disappeared, only taking joy from this special and precious moment in time.

He adored Eleanora. He adored the way she spoke, the way she looked, the way she thought about things. He adored her whole self. Looking at her made him realise how lucky he was, how powerful fate and destiny had been to bring them together after all they had been through in their lives. He felt at peace whenever he was with her. And now, hearing these words from the poem sing out from her angelic voice made him feel as if he were in a place that was greater than heaven above.

"You read that so beautifully," Sir Kingston complimented her. A smile sparked on her face. He took her hand and brought it up slowly to his mouth. He pressed his lips down and kissed it multiple times. During the last kiss, he parted his lips and allowed them to brush against her skin.

"James," she murmured.

"Hmm?" he groaned under his breath.

"What did you think of this poem?"

He detached his lips from her hand. He lowered her hand but continued to hold it, playing with her fingers. "What do I think about the poem, you ask?" He thought for a moment. "Hmm…It was a lovely poem. Only a minor criticism I would say is that I think it was a little exaggerated." He noticed the way Eleanora's face took on an expression of surprise. "Well, don't you think?"

"I guess a little, but it was necessary to enforce the idea of love and what a beautiful gift it is." She paused to allow him to speak.

"It is good sometimes to use exaggeration, but some of the words and phrases made the poem feel a little melodramatic. Don't get me wrong, Nora. The poem was not unpleasant, but I feel love and romance should be portrayed with more simple yet unexpected turns of phrase while using a natural style of writing. I mean, look at us. Our love for each other was unexpected. It came, and it conquered our hearts. Don't you agree?"

"I do see your point about this poem. But even though this isn't my favourite, it still sounds beautiful because of its meaning."

"The poem was pleasurable, but I think I took more pleasure in hearing your voice." Eleanora's smile was brought instantly to her face. Sir Kingston then looked up to the clock and saw it was almost eleven o'clock. "Eleanora, we should probably head to bed. I've got a number of things to do tomorrow."

She, too, turned to see the time and nodded her head.

He took her by the hand, helping her up. He then placed the book of poems back neatly in its rightful spot on the bookshelf. He hopped off the ladder, returning to Eleanora. He took her hand as they exited the library.

He whispered to her, "I will walk you to your room." He led her, still holding onto her as they made their way. When they reached the door, Sir Kingston spun Eleanora around and looked down at her. He waited a moment and then said, "It was nice being able to spend time together like this." He brushed her hair back behind her ear. "You are so beautiful," he whispered as he continued to gaze down at her lovingly. He bent his head down and placed a soft kiss on her forehead. A smile lit up his face. "Sleep with pleasant dreams!"

"Pleasant dreams, James," she whispered back. He let her go, and she opened the door as quietly as she could. She looked back and expressed a goodnight smile to him before she shut the door softly.

# Chapter 24

I t felt different waking up early the next morning for Eleanora. It was different because she was waking up to a world where she finally felt loved. She opened her eyes eager to begin her day. She went over to the window and opened it up for the fresh, cool air to breeze over her. As much as she wanted to enjoy this serenity, she still had work to do this early morning.

Eleanora skipped her way down until she reached the kitchen, finding Dana already preparing breakfast for everyone.

"Good morning, Dana! Slept well?" Eleanora asked cheerfully.

"Yes, I did. You seem to have too."

"It was a marvellous sleep. I haven't had one like that ever in my entire life."

"Really?" Dana eyed her with a questioning expression. "Well, I'm glad, Nora. Now you don't have to feel tired while working," she said, which awoke Eleanora from her daydream.

"Oh yes," she agreed and chuckled a little.

"Nora, are you sure you're feeling all right?" Dana asked with a concerned look.

"Never better! I'm over the moon!" Her eyes lit up as she smiled.

"Hmm..." Dana murmured.

Jill and Marie entered with a bucket of milk and a basket full of eggs. "Jill almost wasted an egg. It nearly fell from her hand while she was trying to juggle three of them," Marie said.

"Thanks for blabbing, Marie." Jill then argued, "You only provoked me to do so since you're the one who said I wasn't good at juggling. So, I wanted to prove you wrong."

They began quarrelling like little children.

Dana had to say twice "That's enough, you two!" before they paid any attention. Dana then firmly told them, "We cannot afford to waste any eggs. Jill, do not juggle again. And, Marie, if the girl can't juggle, then don't make her."

Marie laughed at Dana's remark.

"Now, I will help Eleanora serve breakfast to the master while you two clean up this mess."

Jill and Marie groaned as Dana handed Eleanora a tray and directed her to go off.

*

They entered the dining room, where Sir Kingston was seated at his place as usual. They said their good mornings, and he did the same. Dana inspected the way the master's eyes instantly followed Eleanora as she went around to serve him his meal. Eleanora poured the milk from the jug into a glass and put it down in front of him alongside the bread and butter, and Dana followed with his main meal. He gave a small smile to them both, but Dana could see the way the master's eyes were completely fixed on Eleanora. The way she smiled at him made her very suspicious about the two of them. She had never in her entire life ever seen the master look at somebody the way he did her. He seemed more content this morning and was looking unusually cheerful. Something was different, she thought. The two of them were different, especially in the way they acted towards each other. And she had witnessed this first-hand.

*

Something else occurred that sparked Dana's interest and made her determined to watch their every move. It wasn't until later that morning, when Eleanora was by the well collecting two buckets of the fresh spring water. As she drew the first one, Sir Kingston came by. Dana was a fair distance away, observing this from the inside of the kitchen window. She had seen the master and the way he leaned his body against the stone well, his arms crossed while a smile formed. As Eleanora was drawing the second bucket of water, Sir Kingston took hold of the rope and helped her pull the bucket up. He stood rather close behind her; his chest was right up against her back. His face was side by side with hers as he leaned forward. They managed to grab the buckets, with Sir Kingston holding one and Eleanora the other. The two were laughing as they started making their way back inside. Dana quickly resumed her work, kneading the dough to make fresh bread for later that day. When Eleanora came into the kitchen, she brought the two buckets and placed them on the side bench. "I made sure I filled the water right to the top, Dana," she said.

"Thank you, dear." Dana came over to use some of the water for her cooking. She then mentioned, "You know, Nora, you shouldn't take all the credit. I saw the master helping you out there just now."

"Oh?" She sounded surprised that she'd been caught by the eyes of another. Dana observed the way her face shifted from being ebullient to now seeming mortifyingly guilty. Eleanora then quickly explained, "The master was just helping me out as he could see how heavy the buckets looked. He was being a true gentleman."

"Yes, I see," Dana muttered softly. She continued her cooking while Eleanora went to do some other work outside.

*

Sir Kingston was walking down the main stairs when Dana approached him. She called to him and said she had something important to ask him.

"Then ask away."

"Not here, though."

"Very well. Let us go into the drawing room," he advised.

She followed him as he paced into the room and asked her to shut the door behind her. He stood by the window, seeming to enjoy the view.

"Sir Kingston, may I ask you something that might come as unexpected?"

"And what might you need to ask of me?" He turned around with his hands interlocked behind his back. Dana cleared her throat. She knew she was about to accuse him of something in a way that was completely out of line. But she knew what she'd seen, and she couldn't help but think something dangerous was going on. She looked directly into his eyes and managed to ask, "Are you and Eleanora keeping something from us all?"

She noticed the way his eyes narrowed a little and his mouth tightly closed. This change of expression instantly told Dana that her suspicions were true indeed.

"What are you talking about, Dana?" he finally said.

"What I mean is, is there something going on between the two of you? I have seen the way you suddenly act towards her and how she behaves around you. I can't help but notice these small details. As you know, master, I am a very observant woman. I have a sharp eye, so I know what I see is true."

Sir Kingston looked down for a moment, and Dana could tell that he was completely shocked that she had already figured something out. All Dana was now waiting for was the confession.

He raised his eyes back up to her and stated, "Dana, I love her."

She saw the way his eyes expressed complete earnestness when he finally made this statement. She had never seen him this sincere and vulnerable before, especially when speaking about love. Of course, Dana couldn't believe what she had just heard. She was bewildered when the master didn't deny anything and unexpectedly told her the straight truth from his very tongue.

"Oh, master!" She sighed. "How long has this been going on?"

"I have loved her for a while now. It was only yesterday after she had caused that scene that we confessed our love for each other." He turned back around to face the window.

Dana went on, "I knew there was something strange going on by the way Eleanora was acting. Not just today, but for the past weeks, she hasn't been herself. She always seemed to be upset about something. Now I finally know it was her heart that caused her trouble." Dana fell silent for a while. She then managed to continue speaking her mind. "But, sir, you know quite well a servant cannot be with a man such as yourself. Do you know the risks you are taking? Are you sure you love her that way because, I am telling you, Nora is a sensitive girl. And what about Pearl? We all thought the reason for her coming here was for the two of you to get closer."

He turned around again. "I know all too well that this cannot happen. It is society that shames itself. I will confess that I love her because I do; with every heartbeat in my chest, I do; with every single breath I take, I do; and with every cell in my body that makes up who I am, I do. I love her as if she were my very own. I love her so much I would die for her. I love her so much I could not live if she were to go away. She is everything that I am, and I am everything that she is!"

Dana was now speechless at hearing his feelings put into words.

He went on, saying, "As for Pearl, I have never loved her."

"I believe you, Sir Kingston. I have known you since you were a baby, when I first cradled you in my arms. I believe everything that you say and feel is true." She paused, and then her tone changed. "However, it is society that would shame you. Everyone will be gossiping and your reputation will be ruined because you fell in love with a servant girl. Now, I'm not saying Eleanora is not good. Oh, how I cherish her presence! But I just don't want to see the both of you get hurt by the cruel words people will say behind your backs if this were to go forward."

"There won't be any words," he muttered loudly.

"What do you mean?" she asked.

Sir Kingston walked up to her and said, "It is because I found out about a week ago that Eleanora is, in fact, not a servant."

"What are you talking about?"

Sir Kingston began to explain how Eleanora's cousin had visited him to inform him of the news. He had not gone on a business trip as told but had gone to contact his lawyer and bring Eleanora's evil aunt and her lawyer to justice for the immoral and unjust deception they had committed. Dana couldn't believe what she was hearing for the second time that day. She was both mortified and outraged by the cruel acts perpetrated against poor, sweet Eleanora. But Dana was glad that Eleanora now had someone like Sir Kingston to look after her and bring back what was rightfully hers.

"You cannot tell Eleanora about this!" he stressed.

"Nora should have been the first to know, master. It is only right. She doesn't even know who she really is. We must tell her!"

"Not now, Dana. I want to finish up with my lawyer first and make sure I fix this before telling her. The process is underway, and it was beneficial to have hard evidence of this thanks to her cousin. If it weren't for her, I would never have known this…Eleanora would never have known her true origins. And that is a cruel thing in itself!"

"You loved her even before you knew about this, I can tell," Dana stated.

"Yes, I did. And even if she was a servant, I would fight for her. I would still have proclaimed my love to her, for nothing is more worth living for than the one you love."

Dana was touched by the way Sir Kingston spoke about his love, Eleanora. She knew exactly what a kind and honest man he had always been and that Eleanora was in good hands. She knew how lucky she was.

"Dana," he said in a commanding tone. "You cannot tell anyone of this, about Eleanora and me, and especially about her true identity. Do you hear?"

"Of course, master," she agreed without question. "But I am allowed to speak to Eleanora about the two of you?"

"If you wish," he breathed at last.

*

Dana found Eleanora watering the garden alongside Jill. They looked to be engaged in conversation, so Dana waited. When they went their separate ways, Dana seized the opportunity and went straight down to Eleanora. She was watering alone as Dana went up to her and asked, "How are you, Nora?" She didn't want to startle her and instead wanted to approach the topic gently.

Eleanora held her watering can upright and turned around to face her. "I'm doing well." She then mentioned, "These flowers need a good drink."

"Nora, Sir Kingston told me something earlier today."

"Oh?"

"Yes, he confirmed it once I mentioned it."

"And what might that be?"

"Something I definitely was not expecting, I must admit, Nora. Especially from the master."

"What do you mean?" Eleanora continued watering while she slowly moved along the flowerbed.

"Sir Kingston is not like other gentlemen, I'm sure you have realised. He is different. And I never thought he would fall in love with someone like you."

Dana attentively watched the way Eleanora froze. After a sudden pause, she turned around and put her watering can on the ground.

"How do you know of this?"

"I figured something was going on between you two, and I just had to ask."

"So you asked the master?"

"Yes, and I'm glad I did. I never thought he would be fond of you and in such a way."

"Do you mean that you find it odd for him to have a certain fondness towards me?"

Dana could tell by her tone that she was beginning to be upset by the words she used.

Eleanora continued, "It's because I am a servant, isn't it? That he shouldn't have genuine feelings for me? It would ruin his entire reputation. Is that what you are saying?"

"No, dear child, I am not," Dana began. "You misunderstand me, Nora. What I mean is that I never thought he would marry someone like you, honest and kind, innocent and beautiful in a completely modest way. We all thought he would marry some snobbish woman who had wealth and connections to her name. But, instead, he has surprised me, and I am satisfied and thankful that he has chosen the right one for him and that those temporary vanities do not mean anything to him. No matter who you are, Nora, you are one of a kind. And that is why the master loves you. I am truly glad for the both of you."

Eleanora expressed a smile that warmed Dana. "Thank you, Dana, for your kind words. I'm sorry. I didn't mean to accuse you."

"Oh, don't worry about it, Nora, really," Dana replied with a chuckle. "Well, I best be going now. I just wanted to let you know that I am happy." She embraced Eleanora and whispered, "Your secret is safe with me; you have no worries on that count." She gave Eleanora one last smile and walked off down the path.

Moments after this, Sir Kingston was walking down the hallway of the second floor when he glanced into the entertainment room as he was going past. He halted and stood by the doorway. He saw her standing there quietly by the balcony and looking at the view of the front courtyard. He crept up to her; silently, his feet made quick movements towards her. When he got to her, he stretched out his arms and wrapped them around her waist, bringing her up against his body. Eleanora turned her head with a gasp and touched her chest, calming herself down.

Sir Kingston smiled at how frightened she was in that split second. He travelled his hands up to where her hand was placed upon her breast. He placed his hand on top of hers and calmly massaged it with his thumb. "I do apologise. I didn't mean to scare you like that," he said playfully.

"You make fun of me because of my startled reaction? You could have given me a heart attack!"

"Quite the opposite actually," he remarked. He then whispered gently into her ear, "I can make your heart come alive again."

She looked into his eyes. Her mouth then parted slowly as if she were dying to feel his lips on hers once again. He granted her wish and kissed her gently, which only ignited a desire for more.

Sir Kingston released his lips from hers and continued his kisses down the side of her neck. He knew Eleanora was enjoying this intimate moment by the way she held the back of his head, pulling him against her. She closed her eyes as he continued with the endless kisses he placed on every inch of her soft skin.

"James...we should stop now before someone passes by and sees us," she moaned.

"I guess you're right." He was frustrated that they had to hide these moments of affection, but he knew it would only be for a short while and that it was for the best. He removed his lips reluctantly from her neck. He licked his lips, wanting to still taste her. She turned around and faced him with a small smile. "What were you doing all alone here anyway?" he then asked.

"I just came from watering the garden. I thought it would be best to get a view of it from up here. Don't the flowers look so sweet from up here?"

His lips raised to a small grin. "They do, but so do you." He watched the way a smile appeared on her face and then said, "You shouldn't be working this hard, Nora. I see the way you work. You will exhaust yourself."

"I have enough energy to last me the entire day. It's easier when you're young."

"Yes, when you're young," he muttered softly, remembering for a short while the days when he was young. He looked at her for a moment, just analysing her face. "Do you know how beautiful you are? I have always thought you to be. And your name, Eleanora, suits you completely. I remember that night at the party I hosted here in the manor, the first time I saw you, and in that dress...I'm telling you, I was stunned. And when we danced...it took every fibre in my body to resist kissing you. You don't know how strongly I wanted to feel my lips on yours. I'm just lucky that I finally got the chance to show my love to you."

Eleanora stepped forward and placed a single kiss on his lips.

"By the way, Eleanora, there is something I must tell you."

"That Dana is in on the secret about us?"

"My, that woman is fast," he murmured.

"She told me while I was watering the flowers."

"Yes, well, she was suspicious, and she called me aside to tell me she had figured it out. I couldn't lie to her face because I trust her, and I know she will keep the secret for now."

"Well, I am glad. And that she approves."

"Yes..." He nodded once. "I have some business work to take care of. I will see you later, Nora."

"I should go down and resume my work too."

They left the room separately.

# Chapter 25

It was the next day, and a splendid morning it was until it was ruined by some visitors. It was around ten o'clock when Eleanora and the others heard Dashier notify the master that a carriage was on its way, and Sir Kingston paced his way outside to see to it.

"Don't tell me it is them again," Marie muttered under her breath to Eleanora and Jill.

The servants went along and waited by the outside corridor. Eleanora was desperate to see who had decided to arrive unannounced, hoping it wasn't Pearl and her father.

But unfortunately for Eleanora, out of the carriage stepped Mr Nables and his daughter, Miss Pearl.

Mr Nables had an expression of determination plastered onto his old wrinkled face. Pearl had a cunning smile that seemed to not have left her face since the last time she was there. Eleanora felt the tension and heat rush through her veins. She couldn't believe they had returned after just a week. She knew trouble would occur and things would come to a head.

"Why have they come?" Eleanora asked, her eyes fixed on Pearl.

"I do not know," Dana replied while also watching.

"Let's try to hear what they are saying," Jill suggested.

"Rupert? Pearl? This is quite a surprise!" Sir Kingston declared.

"We knew it would be," Mr Nables said with a chuckle. "We have come only for a short time, perhaps a couple of days or so if that is all right with you, James?"

"Of course, Rupert. You are both always welcome to come and stay."

"Excellent! James, may we be served tea right away?" Mr Nables seemed to be in a hurry. "We have much to talk about, you see," he added.

Sir Kingston nodded his head and called out, "Dana!"

"That's my cue," Dana remarked and rushed towards him. "Yes, master?"

He then ordered, "Prepare tea and biscuits. We will be in the guest entertainment room."

"Of course, master," she replied before turning to the others. "Come along, ladies. We must prepare quickly."

Eleanora, Marie, and Jill followed after her at once, heading straight for the kitchen.

"Can you believe it? That woman and her father have returned!" Marie sounded frustrated by their sudden arrival.

Jill agreed. "I know! She has probably come back to persuade the master to marry her with the help of her father."

Dana glanced over at Eleanora, who was starting to feel uncomfortable at the idea, for she knew the kind of woman Pearl was and the extremes she would go to just to get what she wanted.

*

Eleanora and Marie came up the stairs with a tray each in their hands. They entered and placed the trays onto the tall table that was on the side of the room upon entering. Eleanora turned to see where the guests were seated. Mr Nables sat on the single vintage sofa that faced the balcony. Nearby was his daughter, who sat alone on the extended sofa. They both faced Sir Kingston, who sat on a single sofa facing the doorway.

"The usual tea, Rupert?" Sir Kingston asked.

"Yes, please."

"And, Pearl?"

"Yes, James, thank you. But no sugar for me. I'm trying to maintain my figure," she said with a boastful smile.

"Marie, Nora, tea with milk, and no sugar for Miss Pearl, another with milk and three sugars for Mr Nables, and tea with milk and honey for me. Gently stirred for all."

"Yes, master," they sang in unison.

"Nora, you make the master's and Mr Nables' tea. I want to make Pearl's," Marie whispered hurriedly.

"What are you going to do?" Eleanora asked as she saw her face brighten with ambition.

"I'm going to put three sugars in her tea; she's trying to remain thin. Well, a little sugar won't hurt anybody," Marie whispered her plan while the grin only grew on her face.

"But wouldn't she notice?"

"Who cares?" Marie put one last spoon of sugar in and stirred it ferociously.

"I guess you're right," Eleanora said and laughed quietly.

Marie went over to give the teacup to Pearl. Eleanora served tea to Mr Nables and then to Sir Kingston. As she approached the master, a small smile appeared on her face. When she handed him the tea, his fingers lightly brushed over hers. Eleanora felt his soothing touch, which ignited her heart, but she knew she was being watched by all and had to keep a straight face and continue with her duties. She returned with the plate full of various biscuits and placed it on the low table before them. Eleanora and Marie took the trays and returned downstairs.

*

The company were blowing and sipping on their tea while Sir Kingston watched in silence.

"How have you been, James? It's been a while, hasn't it?" Pearl asked happily.

"Didn't feel like long to me," he replied to her plainly.

"Well, I have missed you, very much," she went on.

Sir Kingston had his hands clasped together in front of him, with his elbows resting on the armchair. He pursed his lips together and nodded his head.

Mr Nables then spoke up. "James, we have come to see how things are around here."

"Oh well, the manor is running just fine, thanks to all my servants. It is still tranquil around here. And business is doing much better now."

Mr Nables then said, "Don't you feel it is a little too tranquil around here? I feel your life is missing something, something that would turn it around and make it more pleasant."

"What do you mean?" Sir Kingston separated his hands and relaxed them over the edge of the chair's arms.

Mr Nables shuffled forward from his seat a little and went on, "Well, it seems you are always alone around here. You need to have someone to keep you company."

Mr Nables then said directly, "You should be thinking about having a wife."

"A wife?" Sir Kingston chuckled as if in shock at the idea, though he already knew exactly what Mr Nables was getting at.

"Now, James, I know you haven't always considered marriage or prioritised it. You are always putting work first, but this is something you should be considering before anything else."

"You are absolutely right, Rupert! I shall have a wife, and very soon, I should say!"

"Splendid!" Mr Nables shuffled back into his seat comfortably. He continued, "Your father and I spoke about bringing the two families together. My daughter and you shall be finally united as one."

"You mean Pearl and me?"

"Yes, you and Pearl!"

Mr Nables' smile was a little forced, thought Sir Kingston.

Pearl then interrupted, "James, my tea is very sweet. One of your servants has added sugar to mine. Do they not understand the language or are they just plain stupid?"

He replied sternly, "I can assure you, Pearl, none of my servants is stupid."

"Rest assured, James, Pearl was only joking," Mr Nables said quickly.

"Dashier!" Sir Kingston called at once.

Dashier came in quickly with the brown case. "I'm sorry, sir. I forgot to offer you your pipe and cigars to the guests."

"That won't be needed as I do not smoke anymore," Sir Kingston advised him. "If Mr Nables and his daughter are inclined, then offer the cigars to them."

Dashier turned to give Mr Nables a cigar, and he took one, as did his daughter.

"I'm surprised, James. You are not smoking anymore?" Mr Nables then asked.

"Yes, well, I realised it's not good for me to keep it a habit," he answered with a smile, reminiscing Eleanora's persuasion on the matter.

"Yes, but once in a while never hurt anyone," Mr Nables said persuasively. "But if that's what you wish."

Sir Kingston noticed the strange look he gave him.

Pearl then commented, "I have never imagined James to give up his pipe. It was like your treasure."

It was quiet now. Sir Kingston then said, "Could you please return Miss Pearl's teacup and bring one of the servants back up here to serve her a fresh cup with no sugar added."

Dashier nodded his head. "Yes, Sir Kingston," he said and went away to deliver the message.

"I'm terribly sorry, Pearl. They must have made a mistake."

*

Dashier entered the kitchen, where Dana and Eleanora had been cleaning up. Before he delivered the message, asking for a new tea to be brewed, he said, "The master just refused his pipe."

255

"What do you mean?" Dana asked.

Dashier further explained, "Well, I was offering him one like I normally would, and he, all of a sudden, stated that he no longer smokes. I wonder why." Dashier paused as he seemed to be thinking. He then stated, "I have always known him to be a smoker, and now the sudden change. I don't get it." He shook his head.

Dana then said, "I'm not sure either, but it is best for him. Do you know how many times I have tried telling him that I do not like the idea of him smoking? I mean once in a blue moon is fine by me, but not all the time."

"Yes, I guess so. You know, as a matter of fact, I don't remember the last time I even gave him his pipe. I always thought he would take it for himself," Dashier then mentioned.

Eleanora remembered when she first spoke to the master about his habit. She smiled to herself when she realised that he had listened to her and only her.

Dashier then ordered, "I need a fresh tea to be poured for Miss Pearl."

Eleanora laughed and said, "I was right that she would notice. I bet she's steaming mad right now."

"Why? What happened?" Dana asked.

"Marie put three whole spoons of sugar into her tea when she clearly stated she wanted no sugar to maintain her figure."

"Oh, that Marie!" Dana scoffed.

Dashier then commented, "I bet she is watching over her figure just to impress the master. I heard Mr Nables speaking about wanting to marry Pearl off to Sir Kingston."

"And what did he say?" Dana quickly asked.

"Well, I was ordered to come down here, so I'm not sure. I better get back up there. And, Nora, hurry with that tea, or better yet, don't hurry. Maybe it will make her madder than she already is," he said, and they all laughed.

"I wonder how the master is going to respond to Mr Nables' wishes about him and Pearl?"

"Don't worry about that, Nora. I'm sure the master will come up with something to say."

"Yes, but it is not him I am worried about; it is them and what they will do if they were to ever find out." She looked down at the tea sadly.

"Nora, Sir Kingston will never let them do anything to you. You have my word on that."

"I know, Dana. I know." She paused for a moment. "I should get back up there before she really gets angry and starts giving me death stares. I'm telling you, Dana, if looks could kill, I would be just a pile of dust within an instant."

Dana chuckled at her comment while Eleanora took the teacup and was off.

She eyed Dashier before entering and smiled at him. He nodded at her and returned her smile. When Eleanora entered the room, the first thing she saw was the open door of the balcony and felt the breeze rush over her, refreshing her body as well as her mind. She glanced up at everyone, and they fell silent. She took a quick glance at Sir Kingston, whose eyes never left hers. She then looked towards Pearl, who had an emotionless expression on her face; her eyes narrowed as she continued to stare at Eleanora. She began walking past Mr Nables to get to Pearl. She kept an eye on the teacup in her hand and tried not to spill it. But as Eleanora was not paying attention to anything but that teacup, she tripped over the foot of Mr Nables. She lurched forward and splashed the hot tea onto the top part of Pearl's dress.

Immediately, Pearl rose from her seat and screamed, "Look what you did, you foolish servant girl!" Both Sir Kingston and Mr Nables stood up from their seats, and Dashier came shooting in from behind.

"You ruined my gown! Oh, it's burning my chest! I can feel it seeping through to my skin!" Pearl continued to screech from the burning pain.

Eleanora froze for a short moment when she saw what trouble she had accidentally caused Pearl. This was not what she needed at all. "I'm so sorry. I tripped and almost fell. I didn't mean to..."

But before she could apologise any further, Pearl screamed, "My skin is burning me!"

Eleanora hastily made her way to the table where there was a small vase of flowers. She followed her instincts by taking the bunch of flowers out and throwing the cold water quickly onto Pearl's chest.

"What have you done?" Pearl cried in irritation.

"You were burning. I splashed cold water on you to relieve the pain," Eleanora tried to explain.

Sir Kingston now stepped in and said, "I will bring you some ice. Then you will be all right."

"Does it look like I will be all right?" Pearl's voice was harsh. "That servant girl ruined my new gown that I only just bought, and she caused me to be in this much pain! I'm telling you, my skin will be all red! And then she throws some water on me! How dare she!" Pearl's eyes were glowing with a fierce intensity.

Sir Kingston tried to reason with her by saying, "Pearl, it was an accident. She tripped."

"It was no accident! She wanted to splash the hot tea on me and mock me on purpose!"

"Your servant girl is very foolish, James. And this is not the first time we have said this about her," Mr Nables interjected. "She should be punished!" he declared, raising his voice.

"I will not punish her, for she did not do anything wrong!" Sir Kingston snapped in frustration.

"Then I will! She deserves to be taught a lesson!" Mr Nables stepped forward to Eleanora and exclaimed, "This should teach you to never treat my daughter this way again!" He put his hand out, ready to strike Eleanora.

Her heart was beating hard, as if it were about to leap out of her chest. She saw the way his eyes were determined, and his hand looked hard as a stone. As he swung his hand, about to strike her across the face, Sir Kingston rushed in front of him and took hold of his arm before he could commit the act.

"Don't you dare hurt her!" his voice roared in a tone of great anger. Sir Kingston stood tall as he protected Eleanora, who stood innocently behind him like a little lamb that was about to be ensnared by a ferocious wolf. She felt as if she couldn't breathe. All she could do was watch in horror as her love continued to hold onto Mr Nables' arm in his strong grip. Sir Kingston then threw Mr Nables' arm down.

"She's just a servant!" Mr Nables exclaimed.

Sir Kingston then exclaimed, "She is a woman, and you never touch a woman, ever!"

Eleanora still couldn't believe what was happening. She felt her stomach tighten and her heart beat madly. Her fright caused a tear to escape from her eye.

Sir Kingston then took a steady step towards Mr Nables and muttered angrily, "I want you to get out of here. Leave this instant! You are never welcome here again. Do you hear me?"

"Are you serious, James?" Mr Nables stepped back a little.

"Dead serious! Now, get out!"

Mr Nables almost fell back from the terrifying gaze that never left Sir Kingston's face. As he was making his way out, he yelled in return, "Your father would be very disappointed with you right now, James! You will never be a loyal son to him!" Before he left, he stood by the doorway and turned around, saying, "You would choose her over me and Pearl! That is pathetic, James! Utterly pathetic!"

"I said *get out!*" Sir Kingston ordered one last time.

Then Mr Nables was gone, cursing as he made his way out, and Pearl hastily followed after him.

"Dashier, make sure he has left the manor," Sir Kingston ordered quickly, and Dashier left at once.

Eleanora felt she needed to get out of the room. She was finally able to move her stiff feet that had been glued to the floor, and she hurried out. She stood helplessly with her back leaning against the wall of the corridor as she was unable to move any further. She had never heard Sir Kingston use that kind of tone before; it seemed to have shaken the entire manor. She began to cry just thinking of all this, and tears streamed down her face. Eleanora knew she was a sensitive girl and to be accused of doing something wrong caused her dread.

Not long after, she heard Sir Kingston come bolting down the hall. Eleanora felt his body press lightly against hers as his thumb caught every tear that was shed, tears that carried heavy thoughts and emotions. "Hush now. Don't cry, my dear," he uttered in a deeply soothing tone in stark contrast to how it sounded before.

Eleanora whimpered and sniffed, unable to calm herself. The tears kept spilling out, one after the other, as she tried to hide her face with her hands. Sir Kingston began stroking her hair back behind her ear, while his other hand held hers, giving it a comforting squeeze.

She started to speak while her mouth quivered. "I didn't mean for this to happen. I tripped and spilt that tea on her by accident. And I threw that water thinking I was only doing the right thing." Her voice broke at the end of her sentence as she started to cry once again.

"And you were," Sir Kingston tried to tell her. "I know it was an accident." He paused as he looked at her face, which was stained with tears. "I know how frightened you must have felt."

"He was about to strike me," Eleanora managed to say.

"I know, and I was never going to let that happen, not for one moment." He paused, taking a deep breath. "You must also be frightened by the way I yelled in such an angry manner. Forgive me if you were afraid. I am not usually like that, really."

She shook her head. "No, don't apologise. You were only defending me."

A small smile appeared on his face. He then chuckled. "I must have seemed scary, however? Like a monster perhaps?"

Eleanora managed a small smile also. "You are nothing like one," she said, feeling buoyed by his humour.

"There's that smile that always brightens your face and lights those sweet eyes of yours." She looked at him peacefully now. "Now, let's clear those tears from your eyes." He began wiping her face; her eyelashes were still wet from her tears, and Sir Kingston wiped them also. He then pressed his lips onto her forehead and kept them there. He kissed her a few times and slowly moved his face back down, close to hers. His nose lightly touched the tip of hers. Her eyes had now fallen down, looking away from his gaze.

"Eleanora?" he whispered. But she couldn't seem to raise her eyes back to his. He then brought his finger to her mouth and drew the outline of her bottom lip. She managed to lift her eyes, feeling the delicate touch of his fingertips run over her lips as if he were creating some sort of artwork.

"Master." She gazed into his eyes, which looked down at her with sincere affection. "Thank you for defending me back there. It must have been hard for you to do."

He shook his head a little. "It was not hard at all. I will always choose to defend and protect you over anyone else. Understand?"

Eleanora nodded her head a little, feeling her eyes glimmer with great satisfaction.

"Always," he said, breathing out the word. He brought her in and wrapped his arms around her. She rested her head on his shoulder.

He kissed the side of her head and said, "I love you, dear Eleanora."

# Chapter 26

The next day arrived, and everything went back to normal around the manor. However, Pearl was still present, which caused a tension in the atmosphere. Sir Kingston hardly shared any words with her, which annoyed her greatly. She still couldn't get over the fact that he had chosen someone like Eleanora over her and her father. But she started to wonder if it could be due to her secret identity.

Pearl knew that everyone in the manor had heard about what happened as it was written all over their faces. It irritated her that she was alone in the manor with no one on her side.

While everyone was busy doing their duties, Pearl took the opportunity to meet with her father, who explained he would sneak in around the back but only for a short while. When she headed outside and met with her father near the bushes, he had a plan devised.

"Pearl, the only way you will ever have a chance with James is if you do what I tell you."

"What is the point?" she complained. "My chances with James are ruined, all because of that Eleanora girl. He cares for her more than he does me. Besides, he does not love me the way I love him."

"Are you giving up now?"

"I will never give up on James. I just don't know what else I can do." Pearl looked to the ground in defeat.

"I know exactly what you can do to eliminate that girl," he said firmly.

Pearl's sharp eyes raised up to his devious-looking ones. She had a questioning look on her face, waiting to hear this plan her father seemed excited about.

"You found out that Eleanora is really not meant to be a servant. And I think that can work to our advantage here. You must find the evidence from James in secret. Get it and show Eleanora who she really is. Once you have done that, you explain how James has kept this from her for a long time now, making her unable to trust him. Tell her that he used her so he could steal all her wealth for himself because he is selfish. If you do this, I have no doubt she will run away and never return, leaving you to be the one who gets James in the end."

Pearl listened, and her mouth grew into a cunning smile that imitated her father's. She automatically agreed to the plan, wanting to do just about anything to ruin the relationship they had. "I will get it done right away. I heard James has a meeting with a couple of his employees coming up very soon. He will be too busy to notice me snooping around," she said and snickered.

Her father did the same and nodded his head. "Get to it then, and I will be back, perhaps tomorrow or the next day, so you can report on the matter."

"Father, I only wish you didn't quarrel with James. What if he never speaks to you again? How will that end up for me?"

"Don't you worry about that, Pearl. James will have to allow me back into his life sometime. I assure you he will."

They exchanged one last look, and Mr Nables made his way off before anyone could spot him on the premises. Pearl went back to the manor, determined to complete the deed that would banish Eleanora, hopefully forever.

Pearl made her way quickly up the stairs, where she ran into one of the servants.

"You!" she called in an abrupt tone.

Jill looked up and replied, "Yes, Miss Pearl?"

"I want to know the whereabouts of James. Where is he?"

"He is in a meeting as we speak," she said plainly.

Pearl was becoming impatient and completely frustrated. "Yes, but where is that meeting being held?"

"Down in the drawing room, miss."

"That's all I needed to know," Pearl replied haughtily.

She quickly made her way into Sir Kingston's room, making sure no one saw her enter. She shut the door quietly behind her and began searching all the places she thought he would keep the documents. After checking each possible place, she made sure to return everything to the way it was, not wanting him to suspect a thief. She had checked almost everywhere and was becoming annoyed. She hoped the documents were in his room, for she didn't have the time to continue her search across the entire manor.

"Where could they be?" Pearl muttered impatiently to herself. She then went over to one of the drawers by his bedside and looked inside again, moving her hand further in. She then realised that some were papers sticking out from the corner. As she put her hands in deeper, she found the papers and grabbed them at once. She quickly skimmed through them in delight. She had found the hard evidence; it was finally in her possession. She returned everything to how it was and closed the door quietly before hastily making her way to her room, which was just a few doors down.

*

After examining the legal documents properly, Pearl went searching for Eleanora, prepared to reveal the secret that had been kept from her. Pearl saw her walking up the stairs and going to the fourth floor. She followed her quietly and spotted her enter a room that she had never been in before. The door was kept open, and Pearl flew right in. She realised this must be some sort of common room where the servants prepared themselves for the day.

"There you are!" Pearl's high-pitched voice made Eleanora jump. She enjoyed watching the way she turned around and took a step back, her eyes widening in fright.

"Listen, Pearl. I really do apologise for what happened yesterday. I didn't mean to…" Eleanora began, but Pearl quickly cut her off.

"I am not here for your apology, Eleanora."

Eleanora's face looked puzzled, and Pearl thought it was perhaps because she acknowledged her by her first name.

"What are you doing here then?" Eleanora asked cautiously.

Pearl was determined to win her trust. She stepped slightly closer, which caused Eleanora to back away a little. Pearl began saying, "I have come to bring you something very important. I know we want nothing to do with each other, but when I found out something, I knew it would be morally wrong if I was to not disclose it or do anything about it."

"There is nothing you can say that will make me trust you," Eleanora told her honestly.

"Oh, but trust me, Eleanora. This will," Pearl remarked with a smirk.

Eleanora looked a little shaken, and her hands quivered, which made Pearl's confidence grow.

"Go on then," Eleanora said.

Pearl got straight to the point, not wanting to waste any more precious time.

"Last time I was staying here at the manor, I overheard a conversation between Sir Kingston and your cousin, whom I believe is Miss Mandy Dusilla."

"How do you know about that?" Eleanora narrowed her eyes.

"Let me finish, Eleanora," Pearl huffed. "I didn't mean to eavesdrop on their conversation, but looking back now, I'm glad I did." She gave a bright smile. "What they were discussing is something that will change your life forever." She paused, seeing the puzzled look on Eleanora's face.

"Eleanora, I found out that you were never meant to be a servant. Your whole entire life your aunt has been lying to you, causing your life to be miserable. Your cousin explained to Sir Kingston that she found proof that you are, in fact, the daughter of the wealthiest man in the land of Estleton. Well, your father is not alive anymore, but you would be considered the wealthiest person now due to your father's inheritance."

Pearl watched the confusion grow on Eleanora's face, the way her eyes shifted with disbelief and her mouth parted as though she was breathless. She continued to observe her silent reaction as she used this opportunity to stab her with a knife. She made known, "Sir Kingston has known about this for a while now. Did he not tell you anything at all?"

Eleanora didn't respond at first. "No, he didn't because there is nothing to tell, for I don't believe a word you are saying."

"How can you not believe me? You must!" Pearl raised her voice, only to provoke her. She walked a little closer. "Do you not understand that you were never meant to be a servant? You are meant to be an upper-class woman. You have been deceived your entire life, and now you have been deceived by Sir Kingston himself. You say he cares about you and does good for you. Do you think he is doing good for you now by keeping this secret from you?"

"Leave him out of it. He would never betray me like that!"

"Oh, but he has! You are so naïve and blind! How can you not see it?"

"Then prove it!" Eleanora raised her voice in irritation.

Pearl smiled and pulled out the documents from behind her back.

"Here is the evidence I found stashed in one of his drawers in his chamber."

"Were you snooping?" Eleanora came forward now.

"I had to in order for you to believe me. You wouldn't otherwise."

Pearl handed the papers to Eleanora, who skimmed through them, her eyes scanning them in a flustered way. She heaved as she tried to gasp for air. Her eyes widened as she seemed to find something that caught her attention. "This can't be," she muttered in bitter, grave awe. Her eyes rose to Pearl, who had a conceited look on her face.

Pearl wanted to further place doubts into her mind about Sir Kingston's loyalty to her as a master. "I am ashamed that Sir Kingston has not said anything about this to you. He doesn't care about you, and the only reason he is keeping you around is for your wealth since he knows the truth about you. But, eventually, he will take that wealth and cast you aside like you are nothing! Is that what you really want or do you want to take back what is rightfully yours?" Pearl waited for her response.

Eleanora then said, "Why didn't you inform me about this when you knew at the same time as him?" Her voice trembled in frustration, and Pearl could tell that her mind was all over the place.

Pearl stated, "Because I couldn't find where he put those papers, and I knew I needed evidence for you to believe me. Besides, I left not long after that, and I couldn't go searching or confronting him right away. I needed to make sure what I heard was correct and that I didn't misunderstand."

Eleanora was mute again while looking down at what was in her hands. She held onto the papers firmly and began making her way out of the room.

"Where are you going?" Pearl yelled from across the room. Eleanora ignored her and swiftly made her way out. A grin came upon Pearl's face as she remained standing there, laughing very strangely to herself.

Eleanora rushed down the stairs not knowing what to think or how to feel. All that was on her mind was to find Sir Kingston and confront him about the documents that could change her life forever. She hastily made her way into the drawing room. She went inside and found it empty. She continued her way to another door that led to a smaller room. She opened that door without knocking and made her presence known in an abrupt way.

She saw that she had interrupted a meeting that was going on between Sir Kingston, who was seated behind his desk, and two other gentlemen dressed in suits. The two men turned around when they heard the door being swung wide open. They looked at Eleanora while Sir Kingston wore an expression of great concern.

"Sir Kingston, I must speak to you this instant!" she demanded.

One of the men, who was his employee, turned back around and said, "How rude of your servant to show up like this in such an unmannered way, Sir Kingston."

Sir Kingston looked at his employee and then returned his gaze to Eleanora.

She stepped forward and said, "It is very urgent, sir!"

Her adamant tone made Sir Kingston do what he did next. "We were just finishing up, Nora." He then said, rising from his seat, "Gentlemen, we are finished here. Please take your leave."

The other employee then remarked in disgust, "Do you allow your servant to rule over you, Sir Kingston? Who is she to end this important meeting?"

Sir Kingston looked frustrated with their remarks and told them in a firm tone, "One more word from either of you and you will not be allowed to go back to work again!"

The two men walked past Eleanora in defeat as they were sent out. Sir Kingston stood behind his chair and rested his hands on its back.

Eleanora faced him, her hands shaking, as she hoped this was all just a misunderstanding. But how could it be, really, when the evidence was right in her hands?

"Now, Nora, what seems to be the matter? You said it was urgent?"

"It has to do with these," she stated, holding up the papers for him to see.

His eyes narrowed, and his face looked puzzled. "What are those?" he asked; his expression was blank.

"Perhaps if you take a closer look," she said and tossed them onto the desk in front of him.

He took the papers, and after a brief moment, he looked up and asked, "How did you come into possession of these?"

"So you do know what they are. It doesn't matter how I got them; I just did." She took a breath and asked, "Is this all true? Was I never to be a servant? Was I never meant to live this kind of life?"

Sir Kingston looked away for a moment. He then returned his gaze to her and nodded, stating, "You were never supposed to be a servant. You are Lady Eleanora Portina, heiress to the wealthiest and most respectable man of the land, Sir Winfred Portina. May his soul rest in peace."

Eleanora took a minute to fully take in what he pronounced her to be. The name was proclaimed by Sir Kingston with such reverence that Eleanora wondered about this distinguished title that seemed to be hers. After all this time, thinking and living as a real servant, she had finally discovered that this was not who she really was, that she had lived a life in constant pain and agony when she could have been living a life of great fortune and prosperity. A life where she was respected by all. Her eyes instantly filled with tears as she looked up to Sir Kingston.

"How long have you known about my true identity?"

"Nora," he cried.

"How long?!" she demanded in a raised voice. Her eyes were fixed on him, hoping his eyes wouldn't be what deceived her.

He sighed and returned an answer. "For almost a fortnight now."

His words turned Eleanora ice-cold. All her thoughts seemed to freeze, and a tear trickled down her cheek. She couldn't believe that the one she loved had deceived her all this time, that the one she loved had lied to her and never told her the truth of who she was and where she came from. After finding the love of her life, she now felt broken and betrayed and knew that she was nothing to him, that he had no care for her feelings or what she would go through when she discovered the truth.

"How could you not tell me this?" she asked, her voice breaking.

"Nora, you don't understand." He started to try to explain his reasons when she cut him off in anger and disappointment.

"No, you don't understand! Do you know what it feels like to be lied to and deceived your entire life? I have just found out that my aunt had been keeping the truth away from me ever since my father died. She made me believe that he was a poor man and that my mother was poor too. I was too young to know any better." She took a moment to control her breathing and steady herself. "All my life, I have been treated in the most miserable way I could've possibly known. I have been spat on like I was dirt because of what I was. I still don't even know the full story, but I know now that I have been taken advantage of, kept in the dark about my true identity. When was I ever supposed to learn of this?" She spoke with repulsion and distress.

"I am nothing but alone," she concluded.

"You are not alone." He stepped to the side of his desk, but she only took a step back.

"I cannot trust you anymore, sir," she then stated to him.

"Please, Nora. I know you do not mean this. I have never done anything for you to doubt me."

She then took another step back while shaking her head. "Was the only reason you confessed your love to me that you already knew who I was and what fortune I had to my name? You did admit that you knew almost a fortnight ago. And you only told me you loved me this week."

"I would never do that to you," Sir Kingston cried and shook his head.

"Admit it!" Her eyes were ablaze. "You never loved me when I was a servant. But as soon as you found out that I was the exact opposite, you told me you loved me." She paused, her heart stammering within her. "It is not me you love but the idea of me!"

The room was filled with a tension that made it seem harder for Eleanora to breathe as she felt all was caving in on her.

"Eleanora, I didn't deceive you!" Sir Kingston also raised his voice.

"How can you make me believe you? Because at the moment, I don't." Her words turned into a cry as she reiterated, "I am alone in this world."

"You are not alone!" he, too, restated.

Eleanora noticed how he was about to move forward when she quickly reacted. "Do not come near me!" She appeared frightened of the man who used to be able to go to her with passionate kisses and touch her in the most tender and loving ways possible. But right now, she couldn't allow herself to forget what he had done to her; she just couldn't. All her life Eleanora had been vulnerable, and trust was something she could not find easily with people. Many times, people had betrayed her, left her alone in the world without a helping hand; there was never a real sense of security for Eleanora. And now, once she believed she had found that secured haven, everything suddenly turned against her, and what she thought would be forever crumbled. She could not go through that again, and because now she was feeling the exact same way, helpless and destitute, she knew the only way to move forward was to be on her own, for no one else cared to look after her the way she needed to be looked after.

When Sir Kingston heard her warn him to stay away, he felt true despair. He could not ever stay away from her and being told this caused him the utmost agony.

"Eleanora?"

"No!" she finally yelled. She took a deep breath and said, "I don't ever want you to find me or go after me. I just want you to leave me alone!"

"I will not let you do that! You belong to me! You love me, and I love you! You are not in the right state of mind. Please let us talk about the matter calmly and allow me to explain the truth."

"There is nothing to explain! You made me fall in love with you! Something that I thought was never possible with the two of us! I will never call you my master again! I will never call you my love again! I…I detest you!" she concluded, crying those words out.

Sir Kingston never thought such sharp, bitter words could escape her lips; they were words he never dreamed she would ever say to the one who stole her heart away and cherished and loved it. Sir Kingston felt as if a dagger had been plunged straight through his heart without warning. When he looked into her eyes, it didn't feel the same. His heart had shattered and fallen into a deep and dark abyss where he felt himself destroyed and in ruins. There was no returning, not without her love for him. He watched as tears streamed down her face.

She took one last look at him and left, quickly running out, determined never to see him again.

Sir Kingston clenched his teeth. He wrapped his hand into a fist and turned to the wall swiftly. He plunged at it, punching hard with no regret, creating a hole in the wall. Consumed by the pain he felt building up inside of him, he hit his forehead on the wall, drowning himself in tears. He tilted his head up to the ceiling and screamed with all his might, "ELEANORAAA!" And with one last bang, he struck his head on the wall as he threw himself at it, feeling the most gut-wrenching agony he had ever felt.

# Chapter 27

It isn't life that is cruel; it is people who are cruel, for the people of society are the ones who create such norms to be conformed to and pursued without any real thought or feeling to the dignity of a human. Life itself should be beautiful, Eleanora believed. Alas, that wasn't the case, for society demanded that it should be predictable and restrained.

Eleanora had never felt as betrayed as she did by Sir Kingston. After all they had been through together, this was how it ended. Eleanora felt this was the end for her, the end of love, and the end of her freedom. There was nothing more she could look forward to, the life she thought she would live, with the one she loved with her whole heart, had been shattered completely before her.

Eleanora panted up the stairs. Her tears blurred her vision, and her breathing was unsteady. She caught the railing as she almost fell and then stumbled to the top of the steps. She hurried down the corridor of the fourth floor, her feet trembling all the way, until she reached her chamber. She grabbed her old satchel from underneath her bed and began packing the few small things she had that were hers.

"Nora? What is going on? What happened?" Dana voiced from behind in a concerned tone.

"I can't do this anymore!" New tears began pouring down her face as she tried to speak.

Dana went up to her and took hold of her arms. "What do you mean? Tell me, Nora. What has happened?"

Eleanora stopped packing and looked to the floor. She tried to be stronger than her emotions, but it was rather difficult when all she could think about was him and what he had done.

"Is it Sir Kingston?"

"He betrayed me, Dana. He betrayed my trust and my heart."

"He would never do such a thing," Dana asserted adamantly.

"But he did! He knew about my true identity. I found out before that I was not born to be a servant, and when I confronted him about it, he told me it was true. He had lied to me all this time, and worse yet, he confessed his love for me after he found out who I am. He never really truly loved me the way I believed he did. He only said he did because he wanted me for my inheritance." She turned her face away, walking towards the window. "Oh, my heart!" Eleanora clutched onto her beating chest. "I feel it wanting to escape me and leave this useless, helpless flesh of mine and be away with it." She held firmly onto the windowsill to hold herself up, for she thought her legs would give in.

Dana then confessed after a moment's silence, "The master informed me about the secret about you." Eleanora turned around slowly after hearing this. Dana stepped forward and quickly began, "Eleanora, listen, Sir Kingston didn't tell me at first, but when he did, my reaction was surprise and confusion at the same time. I instantly thought that you, of all people, should be the first to find out. He told me not to tell you or anyone else for the time being. He explained his reasons and what happened."

She took a breath, pausing. "Eleanora, Sir Kingston was the one who went straight to his personal lawyer with the evidence about you. He went during those days he said he was away for business, when we all thought he had disappeared. The reason he went was to expose the theft and falsehood your aunt and her lawyer committed. They are the ones who are in the wrong here, not the master. They prepared a fake will from your father in order to get all his money, all his properties, and everything else, without you knowing about any of it. Your aunt never told you who you were because she wanted that inheritance that was supposed to be yours and took it for her own good and pleasure. She despised you because you would be a rich heiress, the richest out of all the ladies of the land. That is why she did this."

Dana sighed before continuing. "Sir Kingston knew all that your aunt and her lawyer were doing because of your cousin who came to visit him that day. She told him everything, knowing he could do something about it, for he was your master, after all. Your cousin chose your side, and she chose the good and moral side, the just side; she chose you over her own mother. Sir Kingston promised that he would expose their evil scheme and take back all that was rightfully yours. But he couldn't tell you any of this because it was too dangerous in case the secret leaked to the wrong people. Who knows what your evil aunt and the corrupt lawyer would have done to hurt you, or anyone else for that matter! They could have done anything just to keep what doesn't belong to them to begin with. Sir Kingston didn't want you to have to go through the pain and worry. He wanted to take it all upon himself. And he managed to do just that. He and his lawyer have almost sorted matters and will soon put your aunt and her lawyer in prison for the evil deeds they have committed. He wanted to keep you safe until it was all resolved and cleared before he told you."

"Oh my!" were the words that fell from Eleanora's tongue.

Dana nodded. "Sir Kingston couldn't believe this himself. He knew the kind of life you lived and wanted to make sure you had everything back in your name, all that was lawfully yours." Dana now approached her. "You see, Eleanora, Sir Kingston didn't betray you, or deceive you. He didn't confess his love for you to take your inheritance. He confessed his love because he loves you dearly. And I promise you he does. I have nursed him since he was just a baby, and I know he would do anything for the ones he loves. And ever since he found you, you have brought light to his dark and terrible past. You have given him a life, one with love that he could never cease to cherish. He loves you with all his heart and would do anything for you. I know this because he tells me these things."

Eleanora placed her hand to her mouth and looked ahead in shock. She felt as if she couldn't breathe. She had turned him away from her, spurned his love and crushed it with her words. She had destroyed all that could have been, all because of what she was made to believe.

"How did you find out about your true identity?"

"Pearl came to me and told me. She told me how the master was only using me. I cannot believe I was so naïve once again to listen to her. But she had the evidence and said she found it in his chamber and eavesdropped one day when my cousin came to tell him about me."

"Eleanora, you know what Pearl is like. She will manipulate the truth to get her way. And that is exactly what she has done to you. You should have trusted the master and asked him for his side of the story."

"I'm a fool, Dana," Eleanora blurted with a cry. Her legs collapsed, and she fell to the floor. She tightly held her stomach as she felt her whole being moan in despair. "I am a stupid and naïve fool!" she cried out, tears leaking down from her aching eyes.

"No, you are not." Dana joined her on the floor and cradled her. "You were just confused and shocked. You are an honest and innocent girl who only has good intentions."

Eleanora panted alongside her cries, "I must find him, Dana, before he does something he might regret!" Her body quivered and trembled.

"Eleanora, contain yourself!" Dana exclaimed.

"But the things I've said to him – they hurt him, Dana. I could even see the pain in his eyes." Eleanora crawled over to her bed and cried some more as the events replayed before her eyes.

Dana came and sat by her.

"How will he ever forgive me? How will I be able to mend his broken heart, which I crushed before his very eyes?" Eleanora felt her hair being gently brushed back. She was then pulled up and saw Dana's hopeful gaze.

Dana then uttered words of wisdom. "If he truly loves you the way I know he does, he will forgive you, and only needs your love to bring him back."

After a moment, Eleanora managed to pull herself together. She sniffed and wiped her tears away. She stood up and stated, "I must find him!" She was determined to fix this tragedy before it was too late.

Eleanora dashed all the way to the bottom of the stairs in the hope of finding Sir Kingston. Unfortunately, he was nowhere in sight. She then spotted Dashier, who was entering by the front door just as she was exiting. She came to an immediate stop and puffed out breathlessly to him, "Dashier, do you know where Sir Kingston is?"

The butler stared down at her; his small eyes widened at her distressed state. He replied, "I saw him pacing down towards the forest about twenty minutes ago. I do not know why he would go down there or when he will be back. Is something the matter, Nora? He did look quite troubled if you ask me."

"All will be well, I hope," she quickly muttered and then rushed out the door. She wondered where he went. Could he be by the river? The place they first expressed their love for each other? But as Eleanora made it to the destination, he was still nowhere to be found. She looked at the river, and the water helped to calm her. She gazed at her reflection as it looked up to her from the water, which was like a glass mirror. A tear fell from her eye and merged with the rest of the water down below. She regretted her behaviour, and if only she could turn back time, she would take everything she said back and replace it with appreciation and gratitude instead. She despised herself at that very moment and only wished he would forgive her even though she didn't deserve it. She was mad at herself for not placing her trust in him after all the good he had done for her. But as much as she despised herself right at this moment, she had to go and search for him before it was too late.

She hopped over each stepping stone and made her way across. Once on the other side, she walked along the path towards the meadow. She knew that was the only other place he could be.

Eleanora looked ahead and saw that he was there. He was sitting on a piece of stone block and looking out at the serenity of the open meadow, where the afternoon sky splashed pastel colours on the horizon. Eleanora took a breath of the fresh air to allow it to calm her nerves and settle the emotions that burned in her heart. She was relieved that she had finally found him and that he was safe. But she knew that, within him, he was aching, even though he was trying to find solace in the peace of the meadow.

She continued her path toward him, and when she was just a few paces away, she called out, "Master?"

Eleanora could tell that he was startled by the sound of her voice by the way he hesitantly turned his head to the side. However, he resumed his forward position and dropped his head to his chest. Eleanora thought that he either believed it was just the wind playing tricks on his mind or that he wanted nothing to do with her. Whatever the reason for him dismissing her call, she knew she could not give up...she would not! She continued walking slowly towards him and stood not far behind him. Another breath was exhaled before she tried again.

"Master?"

Eleanora noticed his head rise. She waited a moment before she asked, "May I sit beside you?"

He turned his face to the side again and muttered, "No one else is sitting there."

Eleanora moved her feet over the grass and quietly took her seat on a stone block next to his. She looked down, smoothing the folds of her dress. She then saw him curl back into his previous position. Her stomach began to churn, upset with the way she had caused his suffering. She pressed her lips together and then slowly and gently spoke, hoping to get through to him.

"Master, I...I should not have confronted you that way, the way I did. It was completely wrong of me to disrespect you in such a manner. I had no idea why you did the things that you did, which is what caused my behaviour towards you. I didn't trust you when I should have after all you have done for me. I failed you." When she got no response from Sir Kingston, she looked down to her lap. Her heart felt like a stone; she knew that his pain was her pain and that she, too, had to try to endure.

Suddenly, she felt the warm touch of his hand on hers. Her eyes instantly looked up to his, and their eyes met. The pain in his eyes still lingered beneath the emerald green, which only caused Eleanora more heartache. Sir Kingston said quietly, "You have not failed me."

"But I have," she cried, slipping her hand away from his. "I accused you of deceiving me, using me for my inheritance. I accused you of not loving me when you did with all your heart. I caused you unnecessary pain because I believed that you wronged me. I am a stupid fool for ever believing that you could do any of those things to me." She then mentioned, "Dana explained everything to me, and I realised my mistake." She paused as she shook her head. She then continued saying, "I was lied to about my entire life; my entire existence felt as though it had no meaning. And just because others have deceived me in the past doesn't mean you would have ever done so to me. I was hurt when I found out about who I was. I could not believe it myself. Suddenly, my whole life changed."

He then asked, "Who told you about your true identity?"

Eleanora released a great sigh. "It was Pearl. Once again, I was naïve enough to believe the things she said. She's the one who provided me with the evidence and told me that she overheard you speaking about this matter with my cousin. She's the one who told me that you were only using me to steal my fortune and would then cast me away. And I believed her, every word of it!"

Eleanora was frustrated with herself. She returned her gaze to him again and said, "I am sorry for the way I treated you before. I hope you can at least accept my apology, for I know that forgiveness is impossible. I do not deserve you. I don't." A few tears began to trickle down her cheeks. She turned her face away and wiped her face. Eleanora felt as if the air was thickening, making it hard to breathe.

Then Sir Kingston moved from his spot and kneeled before her. But she still could not look at him, not after what she did. He took hold of both her hands, wrapping them with his. "Eleanora, I accept your apology and forgive you." She now looked at him as he continued to speak.

"I understand why you confronted me the way you did. I know that all your life you have suffered, and suddenly this secret was exposed without you even thinking it could be real. You were scared, frightened of the truth, so afraid that your mind was not in its right state. It would have been difficult for you to comprehend it all after it was revealed to you in such a devious way by Pearl. I understand that the way you reacted was out of confusion. So, yes, I do accept your apology and forgive you. Your actions were understandable. Do not feel guilty or ashamed."

Eleanora was shocked that Sir Kingston was still able to accept her folly. She could see how understanding he was, which only made Eleanora realise how wonderful he truly was. The way she treated him, accusing him of something terrible while he was only trying to protect and save her, made her believe that forgiveness was out of the question. But on the contrary, he accepted her apology fully and forgave her as he understood her earnest reasons for acting the way she did.

"You are too good to me," she said.

"I can never be good," he breathed out. "But I am a man of my word when I say that I will never let anything bad happen to you, ever."

Eleanora looked into his eyes, but after a short moment, they turned away from hers as if something was still bothering him. "Is something the matter?" She was almost afraid to ask. She suddenly felt cold as he slowly took his hands away from hers. He turned his body around, looking out into the distance where the sky soared above the forest. Eleanora felt a lump form in her throat, for she had never seen his expression this way, ever. A saddened expression it was indeed, one that shunned her completely. His eyes had lost their glimmer, and she knew he was thinking of something, something he could not get out of his mind, something that pained him.

Eleanora thought back to the situation that occurred earlier. She tried to remember if she had said or done anything to him that would cause him to still feel this unbearable pain he carried upon his shoulders. Suddenly, she froze as the words that had slipped out of her mouth came back to her. She felt horrible again at that moment as the words played furiously in her mind and she understood why he was still distant with her.

She shifted herself closer to him while saying, "I know why you are feeling the way you are." She paused a moment, observing that his face did not move. "It is because I told you that I detest you." The very words felt like poison on her tongue as she revealed the answer.

His head bowed down, confirming to her that it was exactly that. "You know I did not mean it. I only said it in the heat of the moment," she tried to explain. "I know I acted childishly with such words. I was afraid because I thought you betrayed me, and I was confused. But I tell you this now. I could never have meant those words."

She touched his hair, which was cool from the chill of the gentle breeze. She began to brush her fingers in between his wavy locks, looking at him with remorse as her eyes glistened with the deepest regret. She watched as Sir Kingston clutched onto his chest as he tried to steady his breathing when he turned to face her. She then continued speaking from the bottom of her heart. "In fact, it is quite the opposite. I love you, more than ever before, James."

Sir Kingston looked to her as warmth returned to his gaze.

She stopped stroking his hair and smiled softly.

"You called me James?" he uttered.

"I love you more than my own self, Sir James Christian Kingston," she finally said.

He shut his eyes and gently smiled.

She moved towards him and gave him a kiss on his cheek, on his scar. Slowly, she removed her lips, and when she did, he took hold of the side of her face and kissed those lips as they melted harmoniously into his. He whispered to her in between their kisses, "I love you, Eleanora. I love you, unconditionally." He kissed her again, and Eleanora wrapped her hands around his neck. As they kissed, they fell slowly to the grass, with Eleanora lying on top of Sir Kingston. His hands travelled up and down her sides and to her hips.

"I never want to lose you," she said as her voice broke.

"And you never will," he responded in his deep tone. He brought her back up again while she continued to hang onto him. His hands moved up to her back as he steadied her.

"Eleanora?"

He seemed eager to ask her something as a twinkle sparked the colour in his eyes.

"Yes, James?" she said, using his name again.

His eyes looked brighter than ever before. "Be my wife!"

Eleanora looked at him with an extravagant certainty about what her answer would be. She felt incredible when she heard him ask this. Her heart rejoiced, feeling overjoyed that they would seal their devotion. She nodded her head while smiling.

"I will!"

Sir Kingston beamed at her response as he carried her up to the top of that hill. He carried her by her side, holding her underneath her legs, and soon he strolled down the hill and into the meadow while they laughed with sincere joy and happiness. He took Eleanora as far as he could to the centre of the meadow, where the flowers seemed to dance and cheer, waving their petals in joy. He spun himself around, still holding her as he cried out, as glad as could be, "Lady Eleanora Kingston!"

Eleanora giggled all the more while he twirled around. He slowed down as their foreheads touched, and then he stopped dancing about and placed her back down, lightly to her feet, where they touched the grass that grew baby flower buds. She brought her hands from around his neck to his shoulders and laid them on his chest. She enjoyed the mesmerising way he looked down at her as she could see that he was the happiest man he could ever be, not only for himself but for the one he loved.

"Is this all just a magical dream?" she uttered, knowing how wonderful this moment was for her and him.

Sir Kingston placed his hand to the side of her face and spoke with a kind of wonderment.

"It is magical, but it is more than just a dream. It is real."

She smiled at him, knowing that he had accepted her for who she was and not for what she was. He returned the same smile, and Eleanora knew it was because she had accepted him despite the dark secret that would no longer haunt him, as the light shining through to end his misery was cast by her and only her. She believed their love for each other was unconditional, as nothing, not a single thing, could turn them away from each other.

They had both finally learnt to love and to feel love from one another. Their hearts were inseparable. Their hearts became one and would forever remain one because it was their love that was unconditional. They stared at one another, seeing their reflections in each other's eyes.

Sir Kingston bent his head down and brought Eleanora's hands into his hands. He pressed his lips down onto hers, feeling the endless desire he always felt for her. Their kiss was filled with passion and a commitment to one another. It was a kiss filled with both innocence and tenderness.

# Chapter 28

They returned to the top of the hill. There, they rested underneath the single large tree that stood grandly with its exposed roots that flowed until their ends were buried into the ground. Sir Kingston had himself against the smooth bark. He then pulled Eleanora towards his chest, and she lay against him. His arms were wrapped around her waist, and their fingers were entwined. She rested the back of her head onto his shoulder as she gazed at the sky; the sun was now setting, allowing the moon to emerge. It was a glorious view as the sky created a masterpiece of pastel colours that blended into each other as one. A gush of wind blew their way as the cool night air was beginning to set in. It was refreshing, but it left Eleanora shivering. Sir Kingston removed his black cloak and gently placed it on top of her body.

"Is that better?" he asked.

"Much!" she said, smiling at him. She returned her gaze to the sky, where the sun was now kissing the horizon from afar. It gradually sunk down until it was no longer visible except for the rays of its calming colours.

"How beautiful is the sunset!" Sir Kingston remarked. "I'm glad we watched it together."

"Me too." She turned to face him now. "I cannot believe that soon I will be Eleanora Kingston!"

"Lady Eleanora Kingston," he said, adding the significant title.

"Yes, Lady," she corrected herself.

"Thank you for accepting my proposal. You have made me the happiest I could ever be."

"And you have given me everything I could have ever asked for. So, I thank you and appreciate all you have done for me."

They gazed at each other for a moment. Eleanora then asked a question that had been on her mind.

"James, did you ever know my father?"

He answered, "I'm not entirely sure if a man that visited my father's manor went by the name of Sir Portina. Many other highly respected gentlemen often visited him for business or other affairs." He paused and looked to be thinking. He suddenly exclaimed, "Yes, now I remember exactly! Your father came over once – I recall my father telling me that he was the wealthiest man living in Estleton and that he was the only one who was truly modest about himself. So, I would say that your father was a good man. I'm sure he was well-liked and respected by all."

Eleanora smiled.

Sir Kingston now asked a question. "What do you remember of your father, Nora?"

"Well, not much. As you know, I was only a young child when he died. But I remember he used to tell me stories, as I've mentioned before, and we would play outside together whenever he had the time. I could tell it was hard for him when my mother died. I knew my father was always busy, but he always tried to make time every day for us to spend time together. But when he died, everything became a blur to me, and I never understood enough to know that he was not a poor man. As a child, you don't know these things." There was silence for a moment. "At least I had the chance to spend part of my life with my father. I never knew my mother. I wish I could see her. She died because of me, because I was born," she ended sadly.

Sir Kingston shifted himself up a little. "I hope you are not blaming yourself for your mother's death, Nora?"

She looked up to him with uncertainty.

"Your mother's death was something that was out of your control. Do not blame yourself for it. You were meant to be born and live a life of happiness. And I will always make sure of that."

"I know you will," she replied. She placed her arm across his chest and rested her hand on his shoulder. "James? Did my father die from a heart attack? Or was that a lie my aunt made me believe?"

"That was the only thing that she told you that was true. What shocked me most was when she pretended that you had also died that day."

"Died! What do you mean?"

Sir Kingston sighed. He then told Eleanora what her aunt did the way her cousin had told him. He concluded with his own statement, "Your aunt did all this in order to get what she wanted. She devised this plan making people believe it to be true, and it worked. How she had gotten away with it all these years concerns me. But not anymore, for she will soon pay for what she has put you through all this time."

"She shut me from the world all my life! All so her lie could be executed!" Eleanora tried to take a breath. She continued, "I wasn't even there when he died, you know. He had the fall not far from the estate. He told me he would return, but he never did. My aunt told me that it was because of old age and that it was because he worked too hard around the estate. Of course, as a child, I believed her. That's when she made out to me that I was to be a servant and work for her. How could Molly and the others keep this hidden from me? Did they never feel any sympathy with the way I was treated? I was never meant to be one of them!"

"As your cousin has put it, they are truly remorseful for keeping this from you. I am not saying what they did was excusable, however, it must have been hard for them because they were thinking about their families and what would happen if they were to expose this. But no matter, it should have been exposed for your life had been tortured away."

Eleanora thought to herself for a moment. She then mentioned, "I recall the gentleman at the party who spoke to me brought up the name of Sir Portina and his daughter Eleanora. I can't believe that I finally realised he was referring to me without any of us even knowing the true story."

"She has fooled the whole of Estleton, that woman," Sir Kingston muttered.

It was silent for a brief moment. Sir Kingston then said, "I still cannot believe she told you that she owned Mallow Hall Estate and that she married a rich man. Your uncle was never rich, nothing but a simple middle-class man. It was her brother-in-law, your father, who was rich. He built his prosperity and success all on his own over the years even though he had a sizable inheritance from his parents long ago. And that's when he met your mother, who unfortunately was brought up in a poorer family of eight with your aunt. But your father took her in and loved her and started a family with her, which is how they had you."

"You know more about my origins than myself." Eleanora was surprised by how much he knew but was glad of it.

Sir Kingston chuckled and held onto her tighter.

"I am just glad that it will be over and the truth will be set free, thanks to you," she said.

"If it weren't for your cousin, I would never have known," he told her. "She made a choice, and that choice was the right one."

"I perhaps should go to visit her and thank her."

"That is a good idea," Sir Kingston agreed. "You always lived at the Mallow Hall Estate, didn't you?"

"All my life. I used to enjoy living there until it became a place where I suffered the most."

"You know, Eleanora, the estate belongs to you now."

"It does?" She sat up from him in shock.

He nodded, smiling at her reaction to this. "Your father owned it, not your aunt. She only lived there and took it from you when he died. She wanted it for herself. It really belongs to you, just like everything else that is stated in your father's will."

Eleanora lay down again. She was flabbergasted. "I never even dreamed the estate would ever belong to me. I always thought it belonged to my aunt and her late husband."

"Your aunt does not own anything. As I said before, your father became even wealthier through his hard work in his business. He flourished. Your aunt was jealous that one of her sisters could marry a gentleman such as him. She was cursed with jealousy of your mother and resented that she now was far better off than she was. And it was worse when her husband died only a few months before your father."

"So, all her hate for me was because of jealousy? That my mother married into a rich, well-known family? Just because she was now gaining all the pleasures and luxuries in life, she had become jealous?"

"Unfortunately, yes. And I'm sorry you had to suffer because of it."

"What has become of my aunt now?"

"She is still living at the estate, but my lawyer is almost finished with charging her with theft and all the wrongdoings she has committed against you and your deceased father. She will go to prison as will Mr Miles, her lawyer. She doesn't know it yet, but the police will most likely be visiting the estate in a couple of days. We have already arranged for the estate to be kept under your name. You can do whatever you like with it."

"Such a huge responsibility! I do not even know where to begin."

"You have nothing to worry about. I will help you with all your father's properties and everything else. I will make sure everything is still running and all the fortunes go into your possession."

"You mean *our* possession," she corrected him.

He gave her a puzzled look.

"We are to be married," she stated. "Everything I own is yours. I will share with you all that I have."

"And everything I own is to be yours, including Kingston Manor. But is that where you would like to live for the rest of our lives?"

"I do cherish the manor. It is what brought us together. So, yes, I would like to if you do too?"

"Of course!" he said happily and smiled at her.

A few moments later, Sir Kingston chuckled as he reminisced. "Do you remember the time when you bumped into me after you had finished picking some vegetables?"

Eleanora chuckled also and nodded. "Yes, I do. I thought you were going to punish me."

"I probably should have since you were so clumsy," he said, laughing. "It just proved to me how childish you were at the time. But it was that childlike innocence that I became fond of." He paused as he remembered another moment. "And that wasn't the only time you were clumsy. When you were balancing over that bridge, I really thought you to be silly for doing so."

"Pearl put me up to it," Eleanora revealed.

"Pearl?" he questioned. "Why didn't you tell me so on that day?"

"I was angry with myself for ever listening to her. She dared me to do it because she said she had climbed over that bridge once and you were there to witness it."

"Well, I can tell you right now that is not true. You shouldn't have listened to her lies."

"But that wasn't the main reason why I balanced over that bridge," Eleanora said slowly, just beginning to understand the reason herself.

"Then what was?" Sir Kingston lifted himself up a little.

"I wanted to impress you," she confessed.

"Impress me? My, Eleanora, you are a silly girl with silly ideas!" he teased. "But that is exactly what I love about you." He chuckled and kissed the top of her head.

After another moment, he asked, "What did you first think of me when we met?"

"Are you referring to the day when you visited the estate or at the manor?"

"Hmm…both," he decided. "I remember seeing you for the first time and wondering who this servant girl was serving me tea. Never did I imagine that you would be the one to serve me at my manor."

Eleanora gave a small smile. "When I first met you while serving you tea, you looked at me in the strangest way possible. Those eyes of yours never left my mind, to tell you the truth. I became afraid of you."

"Afraid?" he exclaimed. "Was I really that scary?"

"Not scary…" She shook her head "But different…mysterious in a way that I could never comprehend nor fully explain. And when I saw you again in the drawing room where we first spoke, I felt that same mysterious aura come from you. You were definitely someone I thought would be hard to please and satisfy. You always had that look on your face."

"What look?" He was both puzzled and intrigued.

"I'm not sure, but it was a questioning one. You always seemed secretive, like you never wanted to show the real you. But that all changed when we became closer to each other."

"Hmm…interesting," was all he could say at that moment.

"But there were times when you were charming in your own way. At the dance party you hosted, I could feel myself become more vulnerable around you."

"You had always sparked my interest, Nora. At first, I didn't think much of it, but eventually, I grew weary of the fact that my feelings became stronger towards you. I was weary because I was afraid to allow myself to fall for you. But, eventually, I just couldn't contain myself any longer."

Eleanora rested on her side after this was spoken. She then asked, "You know, I always wondered, why did you end up changing your mind about accepting me when you clearly were after a male servant? What made you, a gentleman so wealthy, with many connections and a great reputation, end up choosing me after you were played by my aunt?"

It took a long moment for Sir Kingston to answer this sudden yet profound question. After some contemplation, he lowered his eyes down to her. He didn't say anything at first as he still couldn't figure out the real answer. He then began to say, "You know, Nora, deep down, I don't know why I changed my decision; however, I do know that it was fate that led me to it. And that is what I believe, that I was meant to take you into my life and experience love with you." He exhaled slowly. "I guess when it comes to fate, there are never really any real answers to questions such as these. For it is fate that opens up pathways and makes possible what once seemed impossible."

Sir Kingston noticed the way Eleanora stared at him while he spoke these words; she looked captivated by them. He continued, "I never enjoyed the idea of buying a servant, let alone any human being that was up for sale; however, that's how society is, and I never really thought about the damage it does to one's mind…being sold. I despise it completely now. Really, I do. Though I hate the idea, I'm glad it happened. I don't know any other way we could have met otherwise…unless fate would have made a way for us, somehow."

They sat for a moment in silence, contemplating his words. Sir Kingston then watched as Eleanora brought her hand to the left side of his face. She drew her fingertip along his scar like she did once before. She then proclaimed, "I wish that as I trace my finger over your scar, it would make it disappear. If only I had the power to do that, I would." She then brought her lips to the scar and kissed him there. Sir Kingston couldn't move as he felt the soft placement of her lips and she tenderly stroked his skin. A groan escaped his mouth as he could no longer contain himself whenever she touched him like this. She moved her mouth down to the side of his neck and began slowly kissing him. "How do you like that?" she whispered into his ears as she now started to kiss them.

"Why do you do this to me?" he groaned again. "Don't you know I am weak and powerless when it comes to you?"

"All the more reason to do it," she replied mischievously.

Sir Kingston pressed his lips onto hers. Every touch, every scent, he savoured; just being around her made him feel more alive.

They parted their lips, trying to breathe. They smiled at each other once more before Eleanora returned to resting her head on his chest. They examined the sky, which was now a dark navy blue filled with the sparkling lights of the stars.

The night sky was becoming darker by the minute. Sir Kingston advised Eleanora that it was time to return to the manor before anyone grew anxious about their whereabouts.

They now exited the forest and were about to continue forth when Sir Kingston stopped Eleanora and grabbed her by the arm. "Wait, Nora."

"What is it?" she said, startled.

"Everyone will be wondering where we were this entire time. I want to announce to everyone that you are my fiancée. I want them to hear the good news."

"You do?" A smile grew on her face.

He gently stroked the tip of her nose with the tip of his finger before moving it back down to her chin. "Yes, I do." He bent his head down and gave her a joyous kiss.

*

From a distance, high up behind one of the side windows of the manor, were envious eyes that had seen the couple kiss. Her teeth gritted as she seethed, and the blood in her veins started to boil. Her sharp nails, which were long enough to be claws, screeched over the glass window, causing an irritating sharp sound that not even she seemed able to bear. Her chest was pounding within her in great anger and defeat as she continued to observe the way they expressed their affection towards each other. It made her sick to her stomach, and she let out an awful screech, like a witch that had been drenched in water and was slowly fading away. She could not believe what the one she was desperate and determined to make her husband was doing. She could not believe that he would choose a servant girl, who was not, in fact, one but would always remain one in her eyes. A treacherous little elf, that girl; it seemed she had bewitched Sir Kingston into falling under her spell.

Yes, it was the eyes of Pearl that had seen the act. It was her heart that was filled with the curse of wicked jealousy as she continued to stare at the two expressing their love for one another. If that was even what it was? Pearl knew this had to be some sort of mistake. Perhaps he was using her, as she thought, to steal her fortune before abandoning her. Soon, a sneaky grin grew on Pearl's face as she hoped and believed that her theory was true. She vanished back into the shadow of her room.

*

Sir Kingston held Eleanora's hand as they entered the Grand Hall. It was Dana who stumbled upon them first, seeing their first true sign of affection together as a couple. She smiled as she walked a little closer to them. "How very much you are suited. I am glad that the man I nursed and have known has finally found the love that not even he was ever expecting to come forth and fill his heart with the purest of joys and wonders of love." She placed her hands together on her breast and smiled even more widely. "I am most glad to see you two together!" she exclaimed. Dana then asked, "Are you going to tell the others, master?"

Sir Kingston smiled while looking at Eleanora. "Yes, I will. Bring them all down here, will you, Dana?"

She nodded her head and dashed upstairs.

Not long after, they arrived. Once they stepped into line, their eyes focused on the way the master held onto Eleanora's hand.

Eleanora saw the surprised looks on all their faces as their mouths widened and their eyes were filled with great curiosity.

"I would like you all to meet my fiancée, Lady Eleanora Portina, who will soon be called Lady Eleanora Portina Kingston!"

Silence descended on the room after the news was told. They all seemed to have millions of questions that rushed all at once through their minds in this moment of pause.

"When did this all happen?" Tennent asked first.

"Why is she referred to as 'Lady'?" Marie followed straight after.

"How did we not know of this?" Jill added.

"Please, master, tell us what the meaning of this is," Dashier summed up for all of them.

"Hold all your horses for a moment. I will explain to you all." He let go of Eleanora and began pacing slowly in front of them.

"Dana, can you believe this?" Tennent then asked his wife.

"Oh, Dana can believe this. She was the first to know," Sir Kingston said and smiled at them while his hands were clasped behind his back.

"And you could not even tell me, your husband?" Tennent's eyes bulged as he spoke.

"Tennent, leave your wife alone. I made sure she would not speak a word to anyone upon the matter for safety reasons." Sir Kingston took a breath. He then began to explain, answering all their questions, even the ones that were unsaid.

Their eyes brightened with astonishment as they were told that Eleanora was the wealthiest lady in the land because of her father's inheritance.

"It was fate that brought them together!" Dana made known to the others.

"It truly is!" they all agreed.

"Well, I have a few things to take care of," Sir Kingston then mentioned. "Dashier, Tennent, I need to speak to you. Could you meet me in the drawing room?" They gave a nod as Sir Kingston turned to Eleanora and whispered, "I will see you later before you go off to sleep." He kissed her on the head and stroked her arm before slipping his hand away from hers.

Immediately, both Marie and Jill ran up to Eleanora, holding her hands with enormous smiles plastered on their faces.

"I can't believe it about you and the master!" Jill exclaimed first to her.

"Me neither," Marie agreed. She then added, "I never expected you, Nora, to fall in love with Sir Kingston of all gentlemen. I mean, we never even noticed anything. When exactly did this all happen?"

"I'm not entirely sure, to be frank with you. But I know that my feelings began to develop over time, once I saw a side to him I never thought he could possess."

"You are very lucky, Nora," Jill said. "The master is such a good man once you get to know him. And now, after all these months being here, you fell in love with him, and he with you. I'm sure you surprised yourself even."

"Yes, I did. I never knew me coming here would make my life this happy."

Jill continued, "And you discovered who you truly are. I am very glad you are now able to live a life finally knowing the truth about yourself. How cruel your aunt is! I remember all the things you told us she used to do to you. But now you are free!" She embraced her in her arms. She then took a step back and looked awkward. "How silly and improper of me! I shouldn't be in such close proximity to you now that you are much higher than I am."

"Please, Jill, I am not like the others. I do not follow the expectations of society. I am my own self with my own mind. You shall hug me. And now, I shall embrace you all." Eleanora joyfully wrapped her arms around Marie and Dana, with Jill caught in the middle. A group hug was formed, a sign of friendship despite their social status, of which Eleanora was glad.

# Chapter 29

It was after lunch the next day that Mr Nables was due to return. Pearl secretly met with him at the same place they did last time. However, this time, she had much to tell as she explained that Sir Kingston had made Eleanora his fiancée. This was something Pearl had not been expecting from him. She knew it was too late and that nothing could change his mind. She felt as if she was already banished from his life, cast aside because of Eleanora.

Mr Nables grumbled furiously upon hearing all that his daughter had to say. His eyes narrowed, and the colour of his eyes intensified with immense rage; his mouth twisted with curses he muttered under his breath. "I cannot believe that after all I have done for James, he betrays me and you by marrying a lowlife who does not deserve to be titled an heiress with great status and inheritance to her name!" He waited for a moment. "There is something I must tell you, my daughter. It is about James."

"What about him?" Pearl was starting to feel concerned, especially by the serious expression of her father.

"Pearl, my darling daughter, I have kept this secret for many years now, and I feel that I should tell you, for no one knows but my own treacherous soul."

"What do you mean, Father?" Pearl tried to steady her apprehensive self.

"You know about the death of the late Sir Kingston, my late friend, James' father?"

Pearl nodded her head slowly and asked, "Yes, but what does this have to do with taking down Eleanora?"

"You will soon find out. They say it was James who killed his father."

"What? That can't be!" Pearl was puzzled by her father's accusations.

Mr Nables briefly went on with the tale of how it occurred.

Pearl was in absolute shock, only hearing this for the first time. She thought she would tremble from the revelations made.

Mr Nables went on, "However, it was not by the hands of James that his father died. It was I, Rupert Nables, who took the life of James' father! I was the one who shot him to his death as he died right in front of his son's eyes! I was the one who made James believe it was him, and all this time, I punished him for it! I left him a scar on his left cheek as a reminder of his father's death and who was to blame for it!"

Pearl watched the way her father's eyes glittered as he made his confession.

A sudden snapping sound was heard. "What was that noise?" her father asked, moving his head around like an owl.

Pearl then exclaimed, "How could you?! How could you do this, Father, to James, and to his father?!" She could not comprehend this all at once as her mind was in a complete state of shock.

He replied, "Because James' father was a very rich businessman. Everyone looked up to him with great respect. I was his jealous friend who wanted everything that belonged to him. In order to get what I wanted, I had to first kill him."

Pearl still couldn't believe that her father could announce this so proudly and with no remorse about his evil actions from the past. "How can I ever call you my father again?" Pearl cried, her chest heaving with emotion. She then exclaimed, "James is my friend! You brought both of us up together, and now I only hear about this today, after how long? James doesn't even know the truth!"

"And you shall tell no one about this. Do you understand!" her father demanded harshly.

"James must know!" she cried.

"No, he will not! And if I find out you snitched to him, or anyone else for that matter, I will make sure James will never be yours!"

"But James doesn't even want me!" she argued.

"Oh, he will. Trust me." A cunning grin appeared on Mr Nables' face.

*

Eleanora took a step back, placing her hand over her mouth as her eyes widened with tremendous fear. She had heard everything that had been said.

Eleanora hastily made her way towards the manor without being seen. She could not believe that it was Mr Nables who had murdered Sir Kingston's father. And all this time, her love had been living with a lie. A lie that completely ruined him; she knew that Sir Kingston believed his whole life that he was the one who brought blood to his father, that he was the one who ended his life. She thought about how Sir Kingston lived his life believing this, just the way she herself had been living with the lie that she was just a servant. Eleanora felt thankful that the truth was finally out and that she was able to discover that it was not Sir Kingston to blame for his father's murder after all. She was thankful that he could now live without feeling constant guilt. However, she steamed with fury that someone who was thought to be a close friend to the late Sir Kingston could betray him and kill him just for money. Eleanora felt she had just enough details to inform Sir Kingston of what she had heard. She had to tell him right away, to free him from the sins he thought he had committed, and before they could get to him first as something unknown was being planned.

Eleanora sprinted to the Grand Hall. She twirled around as she tried to see if anyone was around. She was about to go up the stairs when Tennent came from the drawing room.

"Tennent!" She rushed to him at once. "Oh, Tennent! Please tell me where Sir Kingston is?" The words jumbled out of her mouth from the fright she still felt after learning the truth about Sir Kingston's father.

"The master is in the library. I will send him down here for you."

"No, don't bother. I will go to him." Eleanora left with no other words of explanation and hurried up those stairs to the third floor.

She barged into the library. Sir Kingston turned around, and she ran to him without hesitation. He caught her within his arms as she almost fell. "Eleanora, my dear, why do you look so distressed all of a sudden?"

Eleanora was panting from running up the stairs. She clutched onto both his arms as if her legs would collapse beneath her. "James," she said and then took a deep breath. "There is something you must know." She tried to calm herself down before she went any further.

"What is it?" he asked with concern.

"I was outside when I witnessed Pearl meeting up with her father. Her father is here, and I went close to them to overhear what they were saying because they spoke both our names."

"That devil has returned?" Sir Kingston's eyes almost jumped out of their sockets.

"Yes, but I found out something," she continued, trying to get all her words out. "James, I found out that you were not the one who killed your father."

"What are you talking about, Nora?" He let go of her and took a step back.

She realised she had to slow her words down and let him know exactly what she heard. "Mr Nables was revealing to his daughter a deep and dark secret. From this, I learnt that you shooting your father was all a hoax. The person who murdered your father was Mr Nables himself. I heard him confess it to Pearl with his very tongue."

Eleanora then saw the way Sir Kingston's eyes shifted in puzzlement. She explained further, "He admitted that he shot your father and only made you believe it was you because you were just a little boy and didn't know any better. He used that opportunity and did what he had to do. He never cared about your father or you. He betrayed him for his money. He knew your father was highly respected and an important man when it came to business. He envied him and wanted it all for himself. He doesn't care about you, James. He never did. And that's why he gave you that scar, to make you believe, to make you feel guilty, to feel that it was you when really it was him."

Eleanora took another breath. She then muttered softly. "I'm sorry, James, that you had to hear it like this, after so many years."

She could see the pain in his eyes; they glistened with tears as he recollected his dark past. She understood what he was feeling inside his heart…inside his soul. She knew how it felt to find out that something you had believed your whole life was false and how it completely changed and turned your entire world upside down…it was a terrible kind of agony. Eleanora felt the same way about her own situation, though that was nothing compared to Sir Kingston's torment. But she had also felt a different kind of agony, and she knew Sir Kingston must be feeling it too – the agony of betrayal but also the sense of relief when everything at last made sense. It was hard to comprehend it entirely, however.

Eleanora watched with worry as Sir Kingston brushed his hair back, with his fingers running through each strand. He kept his hands holding the back of his head as the pupil of his eyes constricted with fear. His heart began to pound.

Eleanora stepped towards him and caught hold of his hands. "I knew it wasn't you. I had this feeling inside of me that you couldn't have been the one to kill your father. I know what you must be feeling right now, but you have nothing to be guilty about, because it was not done by your hands but by the man who you thought cared about you."

Sir Kingston lowered his eyes to her. "You always told me how you believed that it wasn't me. But I always believed that it was. You have unravelled the truth behind this awful secret." He clenched his jaw tight, growling, "How could I have been so naïve…so oblivious to not know that it was him all along? That he had betrayed his friend and his son…me."

"Because you were only a child," Eleanora whispered sadly.

He paused before asking, "Did anyone else know who committed the sinful act?"

"Not that I know of. Pearl has only learnt about this too. I saw her expression; she was just as shocked as I was. She had no part in it."

A growl escaped from Sir Kingston's mouth. His facial expression changed instantly; his eyes grew dark with fury yet his face became paler. He let go of Eleanora's hands and bolted towards the door.

She rushed after him, all the way back downstairs to the first floor.

"What are you going to do, James?" She was frightened because he looked to not be in the right state of mind.

"I will not let this go, not for one second!" He spat the words out as he strode towards the front door. Just at that moment, Mr Nables arrived, without Pearl, however.

Sir Kingston didn't even have to think twice before he paced towards the man he thought could be trusted. "How could you! You…you traitor!"

"What are you talking about?" Mr Nables had a sly smirk on his guilty-looking face that revealed the whole story.

"I know what you did! You murdered my father!"

"And where did you hear that lie from?" Mr Nables asked as his eyes narrowed with deceit.

At that point, Sir Kingston noticed the way Mr Nables switched his focus to behind him, his mouth curling into a grin and his eyes staring wickedly. He then heard his name being called out by the sweet voice of his love. He turned and looked at her.

Without warning, Mr Nables flew to where she stood, and like a vulture, he swooped in and snatched her.

"Nora!" Sir Kingston yelled as he watched the dangerous beast capture her in his arms.

"James!" she yelled back as Mr Nables took hold of her and dragged her outside and past the fountain.

Sir Kingston followed hastily to where he dragged her.

"Don't come any closer!" Mr Nables ordered him. He had one arm tightly fixed around Eleanora's chest.

Sir Kingston watched the way Eleanora struggled as she placed both hands on his arm, trying to free herself. And even though he was much older than her, she was powerless against his fierce determination. Sir Kingston didn't listen to his words as he continued towards them to free Eleanora. Just then, Mr Nables pulled out a sharp knife from his back pocket and placed it right to Eleanora's neck.

"Come any closer and I will kill her!" Mr Nables roared ruthlessly.

This caused Sir Kingston to come to an immediate halt; his feet didn't dare take another step. "Don't you dare touch her, Rupert! So help me god!" Sir Kingston yelled.

"Then I suggest you obey me, James," Mr Nables sneered.

Pearl had now stepped into the scene and stood not far from her father.

"Pearl, please reason with your father. Please get through to him." Sir Kingston's voice cracked in fear.

She stood there with her nose pointed high and her hands clasped in front of her calmly.

"I'm sorry, James, but you deserve much better than someone like her."

Sir Kingston fumed, his heart wildly beating and his blood racing inside his veins. He felt the betrayal overshadow him; he did not know which way to turn.

"How could you!" He then turned back to Mr Nables. "Let her go, Rupert!"

"Sorry, but I cannot do that. You see, James, life isn't always how it is meant to be."

Sir Kingston cut him short. "Don't begin telling me what life is supposed to be! Don't do anything stupid! Release her, now!"

"You know I would; however, I have given you so many chances. I have tried to persuade you to marry my only daughter like you were meant to do. But instead, you ignore such a brilliant gem and choose to be with someone like her...a piece of hay." As Mr Nables spoke the last few words, he placed the tip of his knife closer to Eleanora's skin.

Sir Kingston never took his eyes off them, watching every movement Mr Nables made.

"Of all people, you chose to be with her, a servant girl with no hope or family."

"She is not just a servant girl," Sir Kingston responded. "She brought joy into my meaningless life, and hope. She saved me from a sin I thought I had committed long ago. When, in fact, that sin came from your very own hands. And now you want to do the same to her. I won't allow it!"

"How touching," Mr Nables said sarcastically.

"You have made me lose all respect for you," Sir Kingston continued. "My servants will hear all this and will come down here soon to see what is happening. And then you will be finished."

"The one who will be finished is both you and your proclaimed love. Besides, no one will come. I had Pearl go and trick them, making them all believe that you wanted to speak to them. She locked them all up upstairs in one of the rooms. How naïve your servants are."

Sir Kingston's eyes widened as he realised that there was no chance that someone would help them and that it was up to him to save Eleanora before anything could happen to her. He knew that he would risk his own life for her. He would do anything to save her and make sure that she was safe. He could not bear it if something was to happen to her. He already hated seeing Mr Nables place his dirty hands over her and taint her skin the way he did, frightening the poor girl and making her think this was the end of her. But, no, he would make sure that it wasn't and that she knew that.

"How could you, Pearl? How could you follow in the footsteps of your father and help him with this? It is cruel, and after all I've done for you and him." He tried to appeal to her conscience in any way possible.

"I wouldn't have been this way if it weren't for you choosing a servant over me. I tried desperately to get your attention, but all you wanted was her. I dreamed every day that you would be my husband and that we would live a happy life together, and we still can, if you just let her go and take me instead." It was as if she was using Eleanora's life as a bargaining chip. Her jealousy had gotten the better of her and caused her to do these cruel things to hurt both him and Eleanora. He knew there was no chance of getting through to her, not when she was so possessed by sinful jealousy.

Mr Nables then drew attention back to him. "Since you won't obey what we say, I will just have to make you suffer and watch her die little by little through torture. And don't worry about the pain you will feel living a life without her, for you won't get to live once I'm finished with her."

Sir Kingston squinted his eyes when Mr Nables moved the knife against the side of Eleanora's head. He could feel Eleanora's panic as she flinched under the touch of the knife.

Mr Nables began to speak again, torturing not only Eleanora but Sir Kingston himself.

"Would you like me to draw my knife all the way down her face and create a scar to match yours?" he said and chuckled.

"Don't do it!" Sir Kingston cried, raising his hands in front of him, pleading for him to stop.

"But it would be hilarious to watch her suffer, and you."

"Just like when you gave me this scar as a little boy!" Sir Kingston turned his face a little and showed him the very one. "This scar you wrought upon me as a reminder of something that never happened. It was meant for you and worse. But I want to

304

hear it from your own deceitful mouth, that you are the one who shot my father that day! That you are the one who murdered him right in front of my eyes! That you are the one who made me, an innocent boy, believe that it was me my entire life! You pretended to care for me and bring me up as your own, when really you just wanted my father's fortune and to take it all away from me. Am I wrong? Please tell me if I am!"

Sir Kingston's voice only grew louder and firmer as he challenged him about all the things he knew to be true. He did this to buy time while he thought of a plan to save Eleanora.

Mr Nables began to laugh wildly, like he had no control of his own body and mind; he seemed possessed by the devil himself. Sir Kingston could see the way the laugh rang through Eleanora's ears as she shut her eyes and squeezed up her face. Sir Kingston could feel her disgust as Mr Nables held onto her, placing his large, filthy hands onto her body to restrain her.

"I have no need to deceive you anymore," Mr Nables said with a sneer. "So, yes, I am the one who shot your father to his grave! And, no, I do not regret that day for one second!" he declared proudly. "I shot him from the back between the gap of the slightly ajar door to the drawing room. And when I knew it was the right moment, I pulled that trigger and knew there was no turning back."

Scenes from that day flashed in Sir Kingston's mind. A tear slithered down his face as he finally learnt the truth. He stood before the man who killed his father, and now, he threatened to do the same to the one he loved, the only one he would ever love. And he could not possibly allow that to happen. "How could you do it? You betrayed my father! You were his best friend!"

"I was his best friend; that is the truth. However, I envied your father. I wanted everything he had. Everything was given to him so easily, and I had to do everything I could to try to be better than him."

"My father worked hard for what he earned!" Sir Kingston corrected him.

"I wanted it all! I was hungry for money! I wanted to be respected and highly appreciated by all. But I couldn't do that when your father was in the way…my way."

"And do you see where it has gotten you?"

"Yes, I do. The only reason I ever looked after you as your guardian was to claim your inheritance when I found out he left nothing for me and all for you. Except for part ownership of one of his hotels, but you were the main owner. That would do nothing for me. I needed more. I needed everything you were to have. And the only way to get that was for you to marry my daughter, an idea I broached with your father. He, of course, didn't agree because he didn't believe in arranged marriages. He wasn't completely against the idea, though, since we were close, but ultimately, it was your future, and he didn't want to force anything upon you. Once you married my daughter, it would've been easier to claim your inheritance and take it for my own since you would've shared all your fortune with her. But since you will not yield to it, I will now take things into my own hands and kill you off instead while taking everything for myself. It is the only way; I have waited too long."

Sir Kingston could not believe what Mr Nables was saying. After everything, Mr Nables had no care for him, not even the slightest bit. And now, he could die from the man's selfish schemes.

Within an instant, Sir Kingston observed Eleanora grab the opportunity to slip from Mr Nables' arm while he was distracted. She was about to make a run for it when he quickly grabbed her dress from the back and pulled her in towards him. He held onto her much tighter and harder this time.

"So, you took this opportunity to escape from me, did you?" He sounded more furious than ever now. "What did you think was about to happen?" he asked, sneering at her. "I will punish you for that!" He brought the knife to the side of her head again and made a little cut.

"Ahh!" Eleanora whimpered as he nipped her skin.

Sir Kingston stepped forward and cried, "Don't hurt her! Rupert, leave her alone!"

"I don't think I can. I will hurt her even more, slowly and painfully. And I will eventually kill her. And you will see the entire thing. But don't worry. You will be next, I assure you."

"Father, please don't hurt James," Pearl cried out unexpectedly. "Do what you want with her, but do not touch James."

"Yes, darling, but it is the only way if he will not listen or obey my commands."

"Do what you will to me, but do not hurt Eleanora. Take me instead," Sir Kingston pleaded. It was agonising and torturous seeing Eleanora suffer at the hands of Mr Nables. Sir Kingston had to be careful here, not to give a single chance for him to strike. He could feel his heart leap every time his eyes met with those of his loved one. He could see that she was afraid of what might happen to her. But he could also see how brave she was, the way she tried to breathe calmly and relax herself. Sir Kingston decided to take another step forward, determined to get Eleanora and keep her safe in his arms. He continued to walk towards them. This only made Mr Nables walk back, dragging Eleanora along with him.

"Don't come any closer!" Mr Nables warned him.

But this only increased the determination in Sir Kingston's heart. "Not until you let her go!" he responded sternly.

"I will not do that!"

Mr Nables continued making his way around the fountain, seeming uncertain about where he should go. "I'm warning you, James! Do not come any closer!"

"You have no authority over me," Sir Kingston replied with his arms straight by his sides. He looked at Eleanora and gave her a signal with a shift of his eyes. And then when he nodded once, she took the final chance to escape from the vulture behind her.

With one swift movement, Eleanora stomped on Mr Nables' foot, causing him to release her unwillingly. "Ahh! You stupid girl!" he yelled like a dangerous beast as he held onto his foot.

"Eleanora!" Sir Kingston called.

She ran instantly to him, and he wrapped his arms around her in sweet relief. He kissed the top of her head and cried, "Thank god! Oh, my dear Eleanora! You are safe!" He touched the side of her head, pressing his thumb down to her small cut. There was a line of blood that had drizzled down the side of her face. "You are so brave!" He kissed her again, this time on her forehead.

"Oh, James!" she cried, touching both sides of his face.

He looked behind her as something caught his eye. Mr Nables came pacing back towards them, limping a little on his foot. "Get behind me," Sir Kingston quickly warned Eleanora. She obeyed without question. He held onto her hand as she held onto the side of his shoulder.

"You will regret this, James!" Mr Nables began firing his words. "You and your precious little servant girl!" he mocked as he headed closer towards them. He took out his knife once again and held it up high, and as he was about to strike, Sir Kingston took hold of his arm and pushed it back away from them. Mr Nables almost fell back.

Sir Kingston charged at him now. He balled his hand into a fist and punched his face. Mr Nables fell instantly to the ground and lay there on his back. Not long after, though, he rose back up and leapt onto Sir Kingston, pushing them both to the ground.

"James!" Eleanora screamed in fright. The expression on Mr Nables' face was devilish; his silver-grey hair was wild, and his eyes filled with hatred. He tried to grip his hands onto Sir Kingston, but he wouldn't let him. But with one big blow, Mr Nables punched his opponent straight in the face. Instinctively, Sir Kingston tried to dodge the blow, and Mr Nables' fist hit the side of his mouth. He then heard Eleanora scream out his name again in fear. He turned to see that Pearl had Eleanora by the arm and was screeching, "You will never see James again!"

"Get off me!" Eleanora cried as she tried to fight back. But Eleanora was smaller and had not the strength to get away. Pearl continued to grab her violently and push her away from Sir Kingston.

This only enraged Sir Kingston further. Suddenly, Mr Nables held tightly onto Sir Kingston's half-open shirt and pulled him up as he got up from the ground. But Sir Kingston took this chance and began throwing fists at him, one after the other. "You ruined my life!" Sir Kingston roared. "You took my father's life!" He threw another punch. "And you hurt the one I love!" His chest was pounding heavily as he continued with his punches.

Mr Nables' face now looked battered. His nose was crooked and bleeding, and a purple bruise shadowed his swollen eye. And yet, his mouth remained grinning.

Sir Kingston finally stopped punching him and took one last look down at his disgusting face. He was breathing heavily as his shoulders rose up and down quickly. "You still have the audacity to smile the way you do!" He shook his head. "No…This will be the last time you ever smile!"

"Go ahead. Kill me!" Mr Nables said in glad defiance. "Kill me, the way I killed your old man!"

Sir Kingston then brought his face close to him and growled, "I am nothing like you!" And with one last punch, he caused Mr Nables to fall flat onto the ground, where he lay still and unconscious.

Sir Kingston waited a moment, looking down at his defeated enemy while Pearl came running to her father's side and shook both his arms. Sir Kingston then turned to face Eleanora, who sighed with relief. In this moment, she felt complete joy, and she knew that her love finally felt at peace. Eleanora observed the way Sir Kingston stood tall and strong like a warrior who had won victory over his opponent in a battle. Of course, it was not an easy battle, for his white shirt was torn and stained with blood; he was also covered in sweat.

She could hardly wait another second before she ran to him, jumping into his arms as he caught her and twirled her around. Eleanora had her arms wrapped around his neck. Sir Kingston continued to hold her up with a smile of relief and happiness.

"You saved my life! You saved me, James!" Eleanora was truly grateful as she said this to him. She ran her fingers up the back of his head, brushing her fingers against the strands of his messy hair.

"I don't know what I would ever do if I were to lose you, Nora." He paused and lowered his eyes. "I was afraid."

She raised his chin up a little and held it there for him. "I was afraid too," Eleanora began to say. "But I had hope and trust that you would save us. And you did, James." She smiled at him and touched the side of his face, seeing the emerald green of his eyes sparkling with love, the way they always did when he looked at her. He returned an affectionate smile to her.

"Come, let us go and clean up," she suggested.

He nodded his head and gently put her back down to her feet.

As they were about to leave, Pearl called out, "Do not walk any further!" Her voice sounded unsteady and hysterical. They both turned around and feared for what she might recklessly do in her frantic state of mind. "You took away everything from me!" she began to say to Eleanora as her eyes were fixed only on her. "You, Eleanora, took the only man I ever dreamed to be with!"

She walked a couple of steps towards them. "I do not care whether you are a servant or a rich woman. You took the only thing that could ever make me happy. You took my James away from me!"

"I was never yours to begin with, Pearl" Sir Kingston responded.

She ignored him and continued to stare at Eleanora.

"Please, Pearl. Go and live your life. You will find the right man for you. But that man is not me."

She shook her head in disbelief, and tears streamed down her face.

"I don't want another man!" She raised her voice as she wiped her tears away. "I want you!" she yelled. "And the only way to do that is…is to banish her from this life!"

Pearl grabbed the knife her father used that was lying on the ground. Its tip was already stained with Eleanora's blood. With this knife, Pearl stood back up. It all happened too quickly as she threw the knife with force at Eleanora.

As it came flying, cutting through the air towards her, Sir Kingston pushed her away to the side.

"James!" Eleanora cried.

He held the side of his left arm and examined the wound. "Lucky it's just a scratch," he informed her.

"Yes, but it's bleeding!"

He held onto Eleanora's hand and looked over to Pearl. She stood there with frozen wide eyes.

"Leave, Pearl, and take your father with you!" he yelled at her. "Now! Begone!" he roared as she scurried back to her father.

Sir Kingston took Eleanora and headed inside the manor. She looked back at Pearl one last time as she struggled to rouse her father.

# Chapter 30

Sir Kingston took Eleanora to the kitchen. She sat down on a chair while he went to get a damp cloth. He returned and brought his chair close to her. He turned her face slightly and began tenderly wiping the trail of blood that had dried down the side of her face. He inspected the cut closely, and his heart hurt as he remembered the day's events and the way his loved one had been cruelly treated. He let out a soft sigh once he finished and placed a small bandage to cover up the cut. "There, all better now," he said, putting a brave smile on.

Eleanora rose from her chair and went to rinse out the cloth. She brought it back, stating, "Let me fix you up now." She stood before him and lifted his chin gently. She inspected his battered face, but she thought that the face of the man she loved was more handsome than ever. She touched the purplish-green bruise that coloured his skin on the edge of his mouth. She recollected the way Mr Nables punched him, how she felt despair and agony with each blow. She gently pressed the damp cloth on the open cut of his bottom lip. She then wiped the blood that had drizzled a line down to his chin. She then went over to the sink again to wash the cloth with fresh, cold water.

When she returned, Sir Kingston had removed his shirt that was stained with blood from the fight. She examined the scratch where the knife had split the skin on his arm. Trails of crimson-red blood had already oozed down his arm and were slowly beginning to dry up. She took a deep breath and started wiping his arm clean. While doing this, she remarked, "That knife wound was meant for me. But instead, you pushed me aside and took it yourself."

"I would do anything for you," he responded. "I would rather suffer a thousand times than for you to get hurt one single bit."

Eleanora presented him with a small smile, knowing this to be true, and continued tending to his arm. She grabbed a linen bandage and wrapped it around the wound.

"You suffered for me," she began. "I...I can hardly bear the thought of ever losing you. My heart ached every time I saw the way you were in pain, and now, my heart still aches to see you like this. Oh, how I love you, James." She wrapped her arms around him and began to cry on his shoulder. He pulled her in to sit on his lap and comforted her while her tears fell and melted into his skin.

"Shh, Nora. Please don't cry for me. I cannot handle the way you suffered either. The way he put his hands on you. I wanted to get those filthy hands of his and make him wish he was never born."

Eleanora stopped her crying and moved her head away from his shoulder. She looked down to his chest, which glistened with sweat, and she slowly ran her fingers across it.

"Eleanora?"

She looked up, leaving her fingers against his sticky skin. He began to wipe her tears away from her cheek the way he always did, with tender care and love. He then whispered to her, "I love you, with every beat of my heart." He moved his face towards her and placed his mouth to hers. She kissed him back, their lips moving passionately in perfect harmony.

She lifted her head away a little and whispered back, "I love you too, so much." She went in and kissed him one last time, feeling every remnant of pain turn into a wonderous emotion of ecstasy.

"You always know how to make me feel better," she then said with a smile on her face. She ran her hands back up to his shoulders, and then after a moment, she gasped.

"James, we forgot the others! They're still locked in one of the rooms upstairs!"

"I had completely forgotten. Come on. Let us go and release them. They must be very worried." He gave her a quick kiss on the forehead before they stood up.

They made their way to the third floor and tried each door to see which one was locked. They eventually found that the hostages were in the library. Eleanora heard murmuring voices from inside.

"Master, is that you?" came Dana's voice.

"Yes, and Nora is here too," he made known.

"We were trapped in here by Pearl. There was no way of escaping and no key," Dana explained.

Tennent's frustrated voice was then heard in the background. "We've been locked in here for almost an hour now."

"I will get the key for this door. Don't you worry," Sir Kingston reassured them all.

He hurried his way back down the stairs to retrieve the key while Eleanora waited by the door.

"Nora, what happened? Why did Pearl do this to us?" Dana asked.

"It is better if I explain everything when we are face-to-face," she answered.

Then Marie's voice rang out. "When I get out of here, I'm going to tell her off. That is what I am going to do!"

"You have been saved the trouble. Even though I would find amusement in that," Eleanora admitted.

"What do you mean?" Marie asked.

"Because she is gone, along with her father. Don't worry. I will explain all when you come out of there."

Not long after, Sir Kingston arrived back with the rounded steel hoop that chained all the keys together. He picked out a large key and turned it in the lock, finally opening the door.

They all rushed out one after the other in a panic. They all immediately started asking questions upon seeing the injuries of both the master and Eleanora.

Dana was the first to react. "Oh my! What has happened to you both?"

Dashier then asked, "Master, what has become of you and Nora?"

"We will explain soon. For now, inform me how you all became trapped in this room like birds?" Sir Kingston requested.

Dashier explained, "Pearl told each and every one of us, one after the other, that you needed to meet us in the library, for it was extremely urgent. She seemed rather desperate and looked upset, implying to us that it was a matter of importance. But once we were all in the room and waiting, she tricked us and went out with a wicked laugh that echoed through the halls."

Jill continued, "We have been stuck here for almost an hour now because of her."

"Please tell us, sir. What has happened for Pearl to be so cruel? Why did she do this?" Dana asked for them all.

Sir Kingston glanced over at Eleanora and sighed. "Come, we shall speak about this down in the Grand Hall. You all deserve an explanation of today's frightening events."

He led them downstairs, and they followed behind.

When they were all gathered in the hall, Sir Kingston began describing the course of events. They all reacted in shock when they heard all that he described. But the part that brought their mouths to fall below their chins was the confession Mr Nables had made about him being the one to murder Sir Kingston's father. Of course, Jill and Marie were unaware of this as they were never informed that it was believed to be Sir Kingston. They seemed dazed as they listened to all the tales they were told. The others, including Dashier, Dana, and Tennent, looked more than relieved to hear the good news, the news that the master himself was not the one who brought death to his own father.

They all crowded him, their eyes stunned by the truth. Their mouths smiled as they realised this day was a new beginning, the beginning of a new chapter in their lives to come.

"You are free, master, from your own guilt, which was never meant to be yours to endure!" Dashier spoke at once.

"What a cruel and heartless man that Mr Nables turned out to be! I am deeply saddened by what he did to the poor late Sir

Kingston," Dana mentioned in a sorrowful tone with her eyes lowered in remembrance.

"We all are," Tennent added.

"After hearing all of this, we are just glad that you and Nora are safe and together," Marie commented.

"Yes, we are truly glad," Jill said and nodded her head in agreement.

They all turned to Eleanora once Sir Kingston gazed her way. His eyes were fixed on her, making her the centre of attention. "She is the light that dispelled the darkness that once filled my life of ruin and torment. She is like no other. A rare one she is indeed, one I will cherish within my heart for as long as I shall live." He spoke as if he were hypnotised, yet his words were clearly straight from the heart.

He stretched out his hand, and she placed hers on top. He claimed her as he took her in by his side. He bent his head down to her and uttered for all to hear, "I will forever be grateful to you, for entering my life when my soul had been suffering from bondage. You have lifted that suffering and taken it away, Eleanora."

He gave her a kiss, a kiss that sealed their connection forever, and for all to see.

# Chapter 31

It had been three months since that day. The days gradually turned ice-cold, and the nights were misty and long. The trees were bare, and the petals of flowers were covered with frost. The bitterly cold weather had penetrated its way across the land, but it would soon turn to spring.

Eleanora stood on top of the hill before the meadow and watched as the sun went down, illuminating the half-melted snow that still lingered over the flowers and all the land with a soft glow. She took a deep breath, inhaling the coolness of the air. She held onto the hand that touched her womb, the hand of her husband, Sir James Christian Kingston. His arms were wrapped around her waist as he pulled her into his chest and draped his cloak around her body to shield her from the rustling wind. His warm breath was against her ear as he tried to warm her skin from the cold. He whispered gently, "Isn't this marvellous?"

They both continued to look out into the distance where the sun almost kissed the horizon of the field. "It is indeed," Eleanora softly replied. "I cannot wait to begin picking the flowers once again," she said wistfully.

"I'm sure you can't," Sir Kingston said and laughed joyfully.

They were both at peace, knowing that just being together was enough to satisfy them both.

\*

Yet, it had been three months, and many events had taken place since that day. Sir Kingston and Eleanora were married in a church nearby the week after all the commotion with Mr Nables had taken place. There as witnesses to the marriage were Mr Dashier Smite, the butler, Mr Tennent and Mrs Dana Pester, Jill and Marie, as well as two close friends of Sir Kingston who he knew from his business dealings. A small, simple, and modest wedding party was held in the manor with just these few guests as was the wish of Eleanora herself. Sir Kingston didn't mind this at all as he wanted to please her in any way he could.

Not long after, two weeks to be exact, when Sir Kingston and Eleanora had returned from their honeymoon, Dana and Tennent were gifted with a baby. Dr Marton, the physician, said that the baby had been growing in Dana's womb for almost a month without them realising. They were thrilled and overjoyed with this miracle child they had been waiting for. It truly was a blessing to see their faces lit up with joy and laughter. Sir Kingston decided to throw a small party for the couple when he learned of their joyous news. Straight after this, Dr Marton returned to the manor, recognising that Eleanora, too, was pregnant with a child. Everyone rejoiced, especially Sir Kingston, of course, as he was the happiest man he could ever be after hearing he was going to be a father. His eyes filled with tears, and he knew that he would do everything in his power to protect this child of theirs.

Soon after, Eleanora and her new husband visited Mallow Hall Estate. Many memories were brought up instantly, some good but most heartbreaking. But Eleanora was ready to forget the bad ones and create some new ones with her husband. The estate was kept under both their names as advised. Most of the furniture was replaced with the new pieces from Sir Kingston's business factory as Eleanora wanted to start afresh and provide a new look that would diminish the unwanted memories of her time there as a servant girl. The servants she had worked with most of her life were all surprised to see what had become of Eleanora. She forgave them for not informing her that she would be sold and for the terrible secret they had kept from her all these years. She would not hold that grudge against them any longer, knowing that even to this day, they suffered with the guilt. She allowed them to remain within the estate and maintain it while she wasn't living there, for they were trusted servants. The estate was another home for her and Sir

Kingston, and they would go and stay there whenever they felt they wanted a change of scenery, even though the wonderful scenery of the manor was always the most favoured.

What happened to Aunt Dusilla and Mr Miles, her lawyer, was something that had been a long time coming. Mr Miles was stricken from his position and put into prison alongside Madam Dusilla. They were to be punished for thirty years for the damage they caused and the money they stole. However, Mr Miles had to serve an extra five years, thirty-five in total, due to the high position of his legal occupation. They were both shamed and spoken about no more.

Her daughter, Eleanora's cousin, Mandy Dusilla, had found a man of her own and was soon to be married. Eleanora gave her five thousand sums of her fortune to show her gratitude and appreciation for revealing the secret and to also help her with the wedding arrangements. At first, Miss Mandy could not accept this great amount, but Eleanora insisted, claiming her as her cousin and feeling grateful to at last have a known living relation be kind and thoughtful towards her. They were good friends now and visited each other regularly. Mandy was also pleased to hear about her cousin's marriage as well as the child that she was expecting.

Mr Rupert Nables was charged and convicted for the murder of the late Sir Kingston. He was arrested the day after the confession of his treacherous act to Sir Kingston and Eleanora. He was also sentenced for the attempted murder of both Eleanora and Sir Kingston. According to the high courts, he was to be hanged for his crimes. However, Sir Kingston, being a respectable and well-known gentleman, didn't allow death to be his punishment. It was not because he felt sympathy for him. No, it was because he instead wanted Mr Nables to suffer the rest of his life knowing what a cruel and horrible man he was and the horrific actions he had caused. He wanted him to live in suffering knowing that he could not get what he wanted and to always know that he and his wife were to live in triumphant joy for the rest of their lives.

Mr Nables was sent to prison and was exiled from society. He was without a home, wealth, or status to his name, and without his dignity as a person, he lost everything, including his daughter. Pearl Nables changed her last name due to the shame of her father's imprisonment. She was no longer a high-class woman as others looked down on her when they heard the tales. She became a lonely woman living simply in a small home with no company. But she had gotten what she deserved. After all, she had caused the pain and suffering of Sir Kingston and Eleanora. They never saw her again, and it was as if she had vanished, having no place in society at all.

*

The sun soon disappeared, yet its rays of light continued to cast a glow in the sky. This was one of Eleanora's happiest days. She was finally content after all she and Sir Kingston had been through together. It was a struggle, but in the end, their love for each other stood firm, and they would never, never doubt each other again. Eleanora's love for him was humble and innocent. Sir Kingston's love for her was kind and sincere. But the thing that they both shared was the passionate love they felt for one another, the endless love they felt every second of the day and with every breath they took. Every beat of their hearts was only for each other, for they were each other's beacon of hope.

"If our baby is a boy, what should we name it?" Sir Kingston asked, his arms still wrapped around her waist.

Eleanora thought for a moment and suggested, "We should name him after your father."

"You would do that?" He looked down at her.

She turned her face up to him and smiled. "Of course. He was a great man, your father. You loved him and looked up to him."

"We should also add your father's name, for he, too, was respected by all." He then suggested, "And if it is a girl, she should take the names of both our mothers."

"Yes, that would be nice, whichever way it goes," Eleanora agreed happily.

"Well, eventually, it could go both ways if we were to have another baby."

Eleanora chuckled. "Let's focus on this one first." She then turned to him again and said after another moment, "But another baby with you would make me happy, truly."

He looked into her azure-blue eyes, which sparkled with life. This view was more beautiful, in his eyes, than the sky itself. Nothing could ever be as beautiful as her. She looked back down to the meadow. Sir Kingston then brought his lips to her and kissed her cheek lovingly.

"I love you, Eleanora, my dear," he declared before he, too, returned his gaze to the meadow.